I0575862

Conquistadors of the Mesa Verde

A Novel by

KILION RAY CLARK

Index

INTRODUCTION

The story of *Conquistadors* began to form in my mind when I awoke from an abnormally vivid dream one wet April morning. It rains a great deal in the springtime in Tennessee, and I worked nights at the Post Office at the time, so I woke up around 4 o'clock in the afternoon feeling struck by what I'd seen. *Moved* by its clarity and realness, it was as if I were a cameraman, shooting a scene in a movie from a life I felt I once lived. This dream became a waking memory; I remembered everything, I need not write it down. Feeling what could only be described as synaptic flashing, I understood immediately that this dream was a "divine light bulb," if there could be such a neologism. A sign from God is what I'd called it. I'd been waiting for it.

In sudden real time, I made numerous prophetically grand connections to a past which I'd been confidently on the trail of for years. I fastidiously cross-examined the meaning of this dream's deeper messaging, and by following the signs I thought God was sending me in my life, I felt I finally found my missing piece: *Purpose*. The purpose I lost when I left the Service. I was opened up to a new source of it, and this dream was the catalyst; *I needed to write!* Someone else needed to hear this madness. Surely an intelligent person would appreciate the extreme lengths I went to in its creation. I was *called* to write this book. From the very beginning, I've felt that this story was charged with an ancient and powerful energy, and that's no exaggeration-the writing of this book opened up long-dormant spiritual channels within me. Still though, I had only one scene to go off of: the dream. A key sequence, for which the mystery of was yet to be deciphered. Eventually though, it all fell into place. Everything else mandalically sprang forth from that one central vision. And for my readers: yes, the dream is in there, written sure as I lived it.

A quote I read in the best-selling book by Dr. Jordan Peterson titled "*12 Rules for Life*," went something like this: "A drop of inspiration can lead to a river of dreams." That one line has echoed in my mind ever since. I realized that these drops of inspiration I'd received came from a literal dream, and that, I felt, was a sign, connecting the quote to the dream. Now keep in mind: I'm just a postal worker. Dr. Peterson's book was just one of many books I've read on my fifteen-minute breaks. I registered it as an important quotation then, but who was *I* to think I could write a captivating novel? Did I seek to become the 'Postal-Working Genius?' No, not really. Yet, I will tell you, and you will see, how simple words when used effectively, can move people to do huge and impactful things; as Dr. Peterson's words moved me to do so.

That *one* book I read on my break had the one line that stood out to me.

The one line that gave me the courage to pursue this project with passion.

Thus, from the outset, my goal for the book was to create a complicated map of sorts. A map of my mind, for my distant grandchildren to piece together their whole lives. A riddle, for them to ponder over, and wonder, what in the world was going through my mind when I wrote this? It's my fear of being forgotten, I'm afraid. This book was just going to be for the generational entertainment of my family. It was a simple therapy at first, unburdening myself of the thoughts that ran wild in my head all day.

But that was before it became what it became.

It became a fast behemoth.

I brought with me a new take on words, which my editor had a great deal to say about, but then again, he had the grisly task of editing 130,000 words typed in size ten Courier Prime. I whittled it down for the sake of clarity and conciseness. Infusing the words with my own spins of undiluted logic, I took it up on myself to create, with intention, a uniquely complex and richly haunting story that muddies one's own perceptions of time, life, and death. A novel so one-of-a-kind that it would either wildly succeed, or wildly fail, neither of which really mattered because it was never about money anyways. I just wanted to challenge myself, and to leave something behind that said I was here. The vanity in that very statement being something central to all of this, in this story about glory, and the search for it. A story as old as time.

Writing a novel is hard work. It's an enlightening, and humbling journey. For me, it was a journey of the soul; to create a fiercely original story that doubled as a gigantic mind-addling puzzle. A straightforward story, with an underground labyrinth of hidden riddles, clues, and synchronicities, buried underneath the very surface of the text. When you write a story about past lives, the gap between them creates the opportunity for never ending layers of "What If?" Things are complicated because you must multiply (Time x Choices x Karma), which invariably creates a never ending amount of possibilities and in-betweens, but worry not; it's all in there. I've made the many connections. The answers are there, and for you to see the bigger picture, you must think *across* time. You cannot think of regarding this story in the linear mode you normally attribute to timekeeping. You must regard time here with circular passage, going around and around again. You'll know when you break through the surface, it'll feel like somebody turned on the lights, and the deeper you go, the more connections you make, the more tangled up in the darkness you'll become. Like falling into a wormhole.

All this for my readers to enjoy for long after I am dead. Words are forever, are they not?

I always believed in the mighty power of dreams, viewing them as glimpses into the veil of the unknown. Hell, I'm sure we all do. At the time of this unique dream, I was stuck in the trap of monotony, every day the same, and *seeking* a change. Life had become a repetitive cycle and I needed to break it up. I needed to reclaim something for myself, because I, like so many people, was caught up searching for the fabled *American Dream*. It is indeed a beautiful thing, but not without its woes. When I left the Army, my purpose was hung up in the closet with my uniform. My American Dream took an unexpected turn towards something else. I wasn't fulfilled, and was living miserably because of it. I left because I thought it was the best thing to do for the future of my family, but I would be lying too if I didn't say that it broke me. When my time was up, I took my honorable discharge and walked away from the only place I felt I ever belonged. It was a very hard thing to do, and something I still hurt over.

As a civilian (veteran), never forgetting I only had to work thirty more years, I sought to make my life more reflective of the time I spent *away* from work. I started the road of self-enlightenment. I escaped this cultural nightmare by unplugging myself from social media, reading more, and turning off the news. With my reinvigorated artistic spirit rising up, and these various coincidental inspirations happening all around me, I once again reexamined this special dream with fervor: I could see it. The purpose was out there. The signs confirmed to me I was on the right path. I only needed to reach out and seize the opportunity while it was there, and not be afraid of the risk of failure.

That being said, when I joined the Army, I wanted to be an Infantryman, or *Grunt*, as we are called. The "Bottom of the Barrel," as some have also called us. I know what they meant. They didn't mean it offensively, but rather to say, why would anybody volunteer to be in the muck? I'll tell you why. You must first understand that we are products of our environment. In World War II, my grandfather George Glen Clark marched all over Europe with the 79th Infantry Division. He fought in the Battle of the Bulge and was captured, becoming a POW (prisoner-of-war) in a Nazi Prison Camp for four months, which is a terrible story for another time. We kept his shadow box on the wall in my childhood home, and I always saw his Bronze Star and Purple Hearts gleaming behind the glass. He came home a hero, though he rarely talked about it from what I understand. Most of them didn't. In today's world we praise the soldier, which is why I always thought of him as a hero. But oddly enough, his nightmare fueled my distorted vision of honor and glory, seeing his medals and awards on the wall, always nudging me, reminding me I'll never do what he did. That was his life, and this one was mine.

Conversely, my father graduated high school in 1976. He'd missed Vietnam, but saw how badly the men were treated when they came home. He was brought up on the peace and love side of the fence, and naturally, he was my personal steward into a lifelong fascination with the 1960s and 70s. So when the Universe sent me to Fort Campbell, Kentucky, home of the 101st Airborne Division *Screaming Eagles*, and I was assigned to the 3rd Battalion 187th Infantry Regiment *Iron Rakkasans*, a unit with massive accolades in the Vietnam war, the fire of pride and egoism burned even greater within me.

3-187 was famous for fighting the battle of Hamburger Hill or *Dong Ap Bia*, a battle in which the Battalion sustained 70% casualties fighting uphill in Hell for ten days. During my long strange trip with those guys, it was not uncommon to memorize pages and pages of unit history, and if you were asked a question you couldn't answer, you did push-ups, or ran, or worse. Physical punishment, or as we called it, getting *smoked*. During those crucial formative years of my early adulthood, I was completely immersed in this special environment, frozen in time, stuck in those Vietnam days, holding shoes too big to fill, and knowing I could never do a damn thing about it. It was a matter of timing, and I wasn't on mine, or even the Army's time: I was on God's time from the very beginning.

Micromovements.

While I was there, we celebrated the Hamburger Hill Veterans every year from May 10th through May 20th. "*Hamburger Hill Week*" as it was called, was a boisterous annual reunion event where we celebrated the selfless sacrifice of those courageous men. One day, we'd listen to their stories in a packed auditorium, gripped by their words, reliving it with them. Another day, we'd take them to the ranges to unload ropes of belt-fed ammunition on M60 machine guns like they used during the war. At the end of the week was a big party on *Kemple-Yates Field*, which took place after we'd finished doing a grueling endurance event, like rucking 31.87 miles around the base, or climbing 3,187 stairs at Nissan Stadium, which we did in Nashville one year. There was typically a live country-music act, several kegs of locally sponsored brew, and the food was taken care of by the Family Readiness Group. Nothing else compared to it. We had a blast celebrating those men, and I felt very honored to be a part of such a storied legacy.

All that we did because the unit was "3-187," so we did physical fitness events to the tune of those specific numbers. It was called *Iron Warrior*, and it was meant to build *Esprit De Corps* by putting us through a crushing physical challenge, which it did. Watching not only myself, but these other men do it too, made me proud of being part of a unit so dangerously fit. I was one of them. On one occasion, I rucked 18.7 miles with a 240b machine gun, 50lb rucksack, and a full kit of body armor. It was a delirious hike, and a long night of immense suffering that put half the company in the back of an *FLA*. Of course, it's all to prove beyond a shadow of a doubt the strength of our name.

Rakkasan translates into "Falling down Umbrella Men." It was a name given to us by the enemy. Our symbol; the enemy's own, the famous Japanese *Torii*, the traditionally red, sacred Gateway to Honor, which is now too, a personal symbol of my own identity. The evening would be capped with speeches, awards, creeds, and songs. It was such a time and place to be. A completely different world right here on planet Earth. Raised into a cult of lethality, who the hell was I doing these crazy things? Maybe it's something only a soldier can understand. The following day would be the Ball, and we had a hotel room just for the booze...

I earned my Air Assault Wings at *The* Sabalauski Air Assault School. We'd ride around in the same thunderously loud Chinooks which dropped Clyde LeBouef deep into the jungles of Vietnam. I trained similarly, on foot, and in the worst terrain we could find, but it was nothing like what those guys endured. Those men were, and always will be, monuments of a changing America; an America that was tired of losing her sons.

It was a *calling* that beckoned me to serve, a theme which greatly influenced the writings of this book. This book *is* that beckoning call. The deeper lessons from my time there I only began to understand once I'd broken free of the institutionalization that chained me.

"The Vietnam Connection," as I unoriginally dubbed it, describes the quagmire of psychology I found myself in. In a way, it's my own way of explaining how being surrounded by that profound history of the Vietnam war during my own military service deeply affected me. And not only that, but also the literal reflections of that rippling history, which I've noticed at various points in my own life before, during, and after my military service. Since leaving, I've made further connections to signs that were unclear while I was serving, but now that I can recognize them, I see which direction I was being pointed in all along. In light of all of this, it was after that famous dream I wove in my "Vietnam Connection," and the inspirations for Clyde's birthplace, background, and beginnings became clear, and the rest fell into place shortly thereafter.

I'd begun to read more for leisure, spending my work breaks devouring not only masterwork novels like *Don Quixote* and *One Hundred Years of Solitude*, (which are chapters of my life all to their own) but many books covering many different subjects. I didn't do much of that in the Army. My standard-issued service literature were machine gun manuals, *The Ranger Handbook*, and other "necessary" doctrine. Separately, we carried a stack of about ten pages which were stapled together and folded up inside of a plastic resealable bag. We called it a "Joe's Cheat Sheet." It was nothing but pure Infantry knowledge. We would study and reference it every day until the information was burned into our heads, and if someone with more rank on their chest walked by and asked us a question over something from that stapled mess of degraded paper, and we didn't know the answer, we'd get smoked. So I kept my head down and studied my cheat sheet hard. I kept mine in my shoulder pocket.

Reading *normal* literature brought back to me the endless imagination of my youth. I was teaching myself and having fun, college be damned; I'd just be a well-read Postal Clerk!

I even learned how to do Rubik's cubes, and would do them in my car as I was waiting to head inside to the timeclock.

The year leading up to writing this book was a period of my life I call a "personal renaissance" period. I adopted the philosophy that growth was necessary for me to find my elusive purpose, and that in the name of progress, I needed to be more than *just* a veteran; more than *just* a postal worker. I knew that before I put on the uniform, I was on my way to becoming somebody, a unique person, with something to give to this world, and the Army put that on pause. Now, I don't want to misconstrue my feelings for the service, I am beyond grateful for getting the chance to wear the uniform and serve my country. It was an experience that molded me into the man that I am today, and I am forever thankful for it. But I'm a *reformed* veteran. Like one of those guys who came back to the states and found himself in San Francisco, digging the scene on Haight-Ashbury, turned on and tuned in. That is to say, I was always a hippie at heart. And I felt it, too, I always felt like an old soul. Us Generation Z (1997-2012) born from Baby Boomers are odd ones. We are the last messengers of that groovy generation, as they're all getting older, and so are we.

I've only recently been able to pick up where that eighteen year old boy left off, and even though I never went to college, I understood that just because I wasn't in school, didn't mean I stopped learning. My education had kept on whether I knew it or not; Life was educating me, and my college years were spent in the greatest fraternity on Earth. But as a civilian, I needed a new challenge. Something to push me the way I'd been pushed by Uncle Sam for years. That's why I set out to write this novel. I was the only person who could bring this story to life, and it would've been a shame to let that vision disintegrate back into the ether, having never realized its full potential. It was a level of daunting I felt comfortable with. I found it to be a ton of problem solving, puzzling myself on purpose like I did with my Rubik's cubes. It was like putting the brain through a marathon race; at mile eighteen, you start to see the Wizard. By the end of it, you've descended completely into madness, lost in it absolutely.

Writing and publishing this book at the age of twenty-seven also played on the superstitious nature in me, as I've been dodging that mythical "Twenty-Seven Club" all year, fearful of some terrible tragedy befalling me before I'm able to publish the work which I've poured my soul into, but the irony is such in life that I would not be surprised if all my effort to avoid it was in vain.

My mission was to leave behind a piece of literature for the world to remember me by; if it never sold more than a few copies, I was okay with that. This was the unburdening of years of caged thought. I wanted to give my own family, now and down the line, a glimpse into my bare soul, and the world a chance to share in the wonders of the imagination with me. I needed to contribute my piece to that fading period of time. *This is only the beginning.* Life is too short to stifle your true self for anyone, including yourself. You must follow the signs that point you toward your calling, there's no time to waste.

So long as I'm living, I can dream, and that means I can dream up more books to write for some time yet. So long as the good Lords' willin' and the creek don't rise!

And now I wish you, my friends, *Happy Reading,* and may you long enjoy the story of *Clyde LeBouef* and the *Conquistadors of the Mesa Verde.* May you see the deeper lessons within these words and follow them closely, or else you'll be hung out to dry on some hill somewhere.

In my search for purpose, I created a story that'll twist my mind for the rest of my days. And hopefully, yours too.

And to think, it all started with a dream.

I guess that's what dreaming does; it takes you places.

-KRC

ACKNOWLEDGEMENTS

There are many people I have to thank for making this dream possible. First and foremost, I thank God, for giving me my purpose again. He knew how badly I needed something more in my life, and he has blessed me abundantly. For this I give him *all* the glory. Furthermore, I need to express my deepest gratitude and thanks to my wife of seven beautiful years, Jasmine, who let me work unbothered for eight months at the kitchen table while I wore headphones 24/7 and zoned out everything around me, including her. I know I wasn't the best husband during this time, and I'm sorry. She understood how important it was for me to bring this dream to life. Thank you Sweetheart, for your tremendous patience, support, and faith in me, I love you.

Next I must thank my parents. To Mom and Dad, for always believing in me, for giving me the freedom to be myself, and for being tremendous people with the biggest hearts. You were okay with me breaking out of the box of conformity, which most of my peers were being confined to. You let me know that it was okay to be different, to be uniquely *you*.

Dad, you let me experience vicariously through you the trip in time that was the 1960s and 70s. The gift of musicianship which you gave me has profoundly influenced the course of my life, and the music of that time, which became the soundtrack of my life, has greatly enhanced my Earthly experience. I was blessed to have the greatest Dad anyone could have wished for, and I hope to one day be that man for my own children, but you will always be the *Superdad* in my book.

Mom, I am a broken record of you. Thank you for leading me to the light of the Lord. Thank you for putting in me those qualities of love and compassion, because the love you have for your kids has been, and always was, the force that moved you in life, always unashamedly saying how your world revolved around your kids. I love you, I hope I've made you proud, and I hope to one day find the strength to get through your memoir, but I still can't get through the first chapter without crying.

I cannot fail to thank David Vanwinkle, and Creston Jonesvines, two former leaders of mine whose mentorship over me in those crucial formative years taught me more about being a man than I would've guessed possible. Rakkasans, my brothers, the impact of serving with you is worthy of a book to itself. To my good friend Eric Sorrelhorse, after we lost contact, I came to feel like you were one of those passing spirits in my life who was put there by God to keep me on my course. I greatly miss our conversations and hope Uncle Sam is treating you well. My phone is always on.

Thank you Robert Marinelli, who's single book recommendation changed my life and opened my eyes. An ancient soul, his encouragement held me accountable. Your words were not wasted on me, and I am thankful, my friend.

To my editor Joe Pierson, I sincerely appreciate all your hard work on this book. You did a fantastic job. I called you "Big-Shot Chicago Joe" to all my friends at work, and I hope we get to work together again.

Lastly, but no less important, I give tremendous thanks to you, my Postal family. You, who I call my friends, entertained my endless hours of talking about my book. You all supported that vision without judgement, and I'm sure I sounded like a madman, but you never made me feel that way. It's like I always say to you guys: "I'm living the dream." Because I really am.

I often say that working the mail is my passion, and indeed it is. I treat every piece of mail as if it were my own.

And with *that*, I am grateful.

-Kilion Ray Clark

Chapter 1

THE LURCHED SILENCE

The name Sergeant was like a drug that got him high every time he heard it. The power that came with it, the weight of its responsibility; for him, there was no denying it was hard earned and came at a heavy cost. Clyde had spent the last three years of his relatively short life fighting on the front lines in murderous Vietnamese jungles. Risking his hide daily in a war that, as far as he could tell, nobody was winning, but rather, everyone who played was a loser, losing something far greater than territory and ideologies: losing their humanity, their sanity. The jungle providing the menacing backdrop for the shockingly ugly campaign, the worst that twentieth-century America had yet seen.

The United States of America had triumphed in not just one, but two World Wars, setting an unprecedented standard of wartime achievement. America created an impressive arsenal during the country's mobilization efforts, and we were prepared to fight next in Korea. The Red Scare of communism stirred in free men a great patriotism. To safeguard the peace of the New World, we went to war with them, with many brave young souls answering their country's call to put a halt to the spread of Korean totalitarianism.

Unable to contain it, bitterly strife engagements and guerilla skirmishes sprang up all across Southeast Asia, with genocidal regimes willfully endangering or murdering their own people. In the wake of all of that, the United States of

America had been pulled into a full-scale military operation in the mysterious subtropics, where a resilient people put up an incredibly hard resistance. Where Clyde LeBouef found himself in a place called the A Shau Valley, crawling on bare hands and knees through the cold, wet jungle floor, slowly moving through dead, waterlogged foliage that littered the ground. In a constant state of paranoia, cold tears fell from dead eyes as he clutched his lost friends one more time. There were no winners in war, only losers, each man understanding his own safety was not guaranteed. To shake the hand of Death before the game was the gentlemanly thing to do. Only after Clyde did that could he battle the fear, which drove men mad. They lost themselves out there and were never found. Their eyes were hollow vessels, their souls missing in action after confronting the grave realities of combat. The aftermath of the psychological destruction was beyond the means of normal, rational explanation, as there could be no assythment for the many tragedies of war.

Clyde LeBouef was born in Bossier City, Louisiana, but most people just called it Bossier. Growing up the youngest of five in a Creole family, Clyde observed with his little eyes his father Lawrence to be a tremendously hardworking man, an old-fashioned type of father, who believed a man should always be the pillar of strength in his own family. Seldom he forgot the duty of his charge, a proud blue-collar laborer and Frenchman who had once helped translate for the French civilians when his unit pushed through Normandy, liberating the oppressed peoples. Lawrence had inadvertently answered a call to defend the homeland of his kin from the terror of the Third Reich. He'd served with distinction and was Clyde's hero in youth.

Clyde's mother, Annette, was a proper woman, always taking care to paint her face for her husband with her favorite palette of assorted crimsons and cinnamon shades, which complement the dark-brown eyes of her people. She cooked for her children their favorite meals whenever they asked, and taking her time to diligently dress them, she never sent them out of the house looking shrewd or unkempt. She carefully, and with the love that only a mother has for her children, wiped their wet cheeks when their father's shouts drove them to the point of tears.

Pa could be harsh, but he had marched all over Europe fighting the Krauts, so nobody could blame him for being that way. The two of them brought up their family with a unique blend of French and Spanish traditions, militaristic discipline, and strong values. She raised her five children all to be polite, well mannered, and proper. But she was helpless at keeping them contained, for they all possessed adventurous spirits, and loved to play outdoors, get dirty, and get into trouble; what kids always did in those days.

They were a close family,

Raised in a modest Louisiana home, with three rooms to share among the seven of them, it was a cozy home, set beside a heavy marsh, the classic prairies and rolling hills, pine forests and slow-moving lagoons. It was the type of landscape conjured up in one's imagination when one thinks of swampy Louisiana bayous. A noble land, which was once owned by the Spanish and later by the French, until Thomas Jefferson crafted a historic deal with Napoleon called the Louisiana Purchase, which was signed April 30, 1803, soon making the relatively new waterfront city a great carnival melting pot, blending together different cultures, languages, and people. The ignorant clashed with their neighbors for speaking a different tongue than they did, and at the turn of the century, there were many different dialects being spoken. People from widely diverse cultures converged in the coastal city of New Orleans, people who had journeyed across the oceans to come to this place in search of opportunity. To craft for themselves a new life, with the promise of a good future in a land where the streets were paved with gold.

Clyde loved many things about his home. Mardi Gras and the parties in the streets. The beautiful mixed women dressed themselves in purple, green, and gold costumes, flamboyantly adorned with sequins and rhinestones, exposing their cleavage, with beads tucked into the crease of their breasts. Masks, wigs, music, it was a fun time when mixed with the public booze and cheap drugs that flowed equally freely through the dark alleyways and untraveled city side streets.

He loved to fish as well, stomping around in the mud when he could. Often he'd be wearing his waders in waist-deep water, waiting to catch something for supper, a practice given to him by his father, and his father before him. Bossier was a special place to be raised; it was his home, and he thought of home often.

At night in the bush, when Clyde was most consumed by his perpetual states of paranoia and fear, he'd clench his eyes shut and picture his wife, Santina, waiting eagerly for him on safer shores. It was when the times were hardest, and his will to continue was very low, when he would pull his lost morale from unknown reserves, finding a forgotten strength that her visage alone must have restored. Her portrait was either in his helmet or his pocket, never far away, for when his soul needed a quick reprieve.

Santina had married him before he left for the war. They wouldn't dare let each other get lost in the sea of strangers. The couple vowed to take on life together, the two of them, after the war was over and life resumed.

The simple memories of life back home were often enough for Clyde to muster his hope. There were many times at night when he spoke to her picture, talking to her, even if only in his imagination. He needed something to hold on to out there, and holding on to her gave him hope. His men held on to him too, since they counted on his expertise to get them through the messy bits.

Clyde was hardened by the years of fierce combat and the trauma of surviving the inhumanity of war. Boys left their homes in droves to get to the front, coming from every corner of the mainland. They might have looked ordinary, with boyish faces, foul-mouthed and rowdy. And if you passed him on the street on an ordinary day, you'd think nothing strange of him, but for the people who knew him, if they really knew him, that is, they'd have known where he'd been and what he'd done.

For Clyde, 1968 and 1969 were years of confusing torment. He had long dreamed of being the hero, fighting in the great wars like his forefathers had done in decades past, but many nights he cursed that naivete, the folly of getting what you wished for echoing in his mind, for now, he was constantly switched on, in a state of constant adrenaline-soaked fear. Others had it worse, shell shocked, seeing shadows in the trees. They had to become creatures of the jungle, hyper-aware and wired. Ready to run, ready to kill, ready to do whatever it took to get out of that awful place alive. He possessed the mindset of the patient hunter, using the enemy's own guerilla tactics against them; Clyde served as a scout in a Long-Range Recon Patrol team. His business was primarily stalking, and silent death, but they couldn't help but get called back to the front to assist in the search and destroy operations, or to offer support for units in contact.

The green jungle canopy provided little relief from the blistering heat, where temperatures spiked into the triple digits during the daytime and the heat evaporated the rivers, causing a constant residue to stick to the skin. Muggy, uncomfortable, it was the perfect conditions for bacteria and sickness to thrive and spread, breeding grounds for it, really. The conditions were awful, and leading patrols through that dense brush was equally scary. They needed to remain absolutely quiet, so far behind the enemy lines.

The vengeance of the monsoon season was upon them, and they'd been walking blindly at night through sopping wet fronds in a delirium induced by dehydration, lightning furies, and fear. The fear that Charlie—the Viet Cong soldiers—were lying in wait, as they were. The gripping paranoia, getting stuck weaving in and out of the braided vines, getting tangled up in the natural cordage, which came in a variety of different textures and sizes, made him angry. All carried water, salt, cigarettes, and ammo.

They were eaten alive daily by intrepid soldier ants and monstrous mosquitoes, which left welts the size of quarters. Snake and spider bites were potential death sentences, and one always kept an eye out for the venomous creatures, after learning from the ones who'd been in the country longer the various hazards of daily life in the jungle. It was sometimes so densely vegetated that Clyde could only see a few meters in front of him, so he'd get real close to the guy in front of him, who was doing the same thing himself. The blind were leading the blind, potentially walking themselves into certain death at any given moment. One had to disconnect from reality for the sake of one's own mental well-being.

Fear would grip the men before the violence started, and with their sixth sense, they could tell when they were about to make contact. Their desire to live rose up over their benign and sarcastic requests for the ends of their own miserable sufferings. They made dark jokes to ease the cruel reality of their calamity, but when it suddenly became real, as it did randomly and sporadically throughout the day, the time for jokes would be over. The serious men emerged from the shadows, leading the forward assault.

Then there were the sickos, the ones who derived pleasure from it. For them, death was just a doorway we all must pass through. They bore no grudge over the taking of a human life, for the lives of communists meant little to them. Most of the men felt that way, feeling sorrier for the civilians caught-up in the crossfire.

There are no words fit to describe it, nor would you want to know what it feels like yourself, but it can be said that Clyde's spirit moved somberly, believing himself that only God could wash his hands clean of the blood that had stained them.

Rising through the ranks was less a choice and more a necessity. It was a post that weighed on him heavily. With the grave only one misplaced footstep away, he used the great burden of responsibility to give himself restored motivation and purpose. If he had purpose, he had reason to push on, and push on they did. Clyde had little time to reflect on the achievement of his promotions, because all vanity and ego aside, what mattered above all else was that his men made it home. He cared little for decoration, more concerned with not getting caught with his pants down in No Man's Land after dark.

Clyde had taken point on many of their long-distance recon patrols, steering them carefully past the planned chaos of a strategically placed ambush. Instantly, the adrenaline would propel him into a hyperconscious state of mind, where everything slowed down and the minutes seemed to drag. This was not just a job; this was life or death. The repetitiveness made it *seem* like a job, and eventually, calling it "a job" helped them desensitize themselves to it, in their numbness, haunted at night and in their dreams for their wrongdoings during the day. The cursed thoughts came to them mostly when they were alone; that was when they crept up on Clyde. The pain he kept sealed behind pursed lips, never a word, and too prideful for weakness.

They would count down their time as if they were serving a jail sentence, while the constant battery of skirmishes continued, day after day and night after night. Some days it relented a bit, but they had learned to be wary of those periods of stillness. The jungle was a scary place when it was quiet, and they had to be equally still to remain undetected by the enemy. Clyde's team moved mostly at night. Operatives of stealth, they were ghosts when they were lost in the bush. But they had to be, the enemy was everywhere, looking for them, placing booby traps and tripwires to blow up the unsuspecting American GI, waiting in the shadows. They had to be quiet to stay alive.

Quiet days weren't really a break in combat either, but rather a strategic pause. It was the enemy taking their leisure, plotting quietly, planning diligently, finding a way to inflict more critical casualties. Maybe they'd be looking through a sniper's scope hundreds of meters off in the distance, spying their every move, lying patiently, waiting for the split-second chance to squeeze the trigger and send the round. Clyde did not trust the quiet, and he was the wariest of them all, forever emphasizing the importance of maintaining noise discipline by restricting their speech to hushed, low whispers.

Nonverbal communication was also especially important; the soldiers' unique form of sign was how they communicated over the gunfire, explosions, and general madness of jungle combat. Their quiet discipline was paramount to getting through the night undetected, unwilling to risk giving away their position. Through gritted teeth, they silently screamed when the brush started to break and too much noise was made. Clenching their fists tightly and squeezing their eyes shut, the potential repercussions for such a simple mistake could mean one's life. One unsecured canteen falling to the ground, ringing out once it hit the rocks, to the horror of everybody else, could be all it took to trigger a deadly disaster.

Clyde still had much courage in his young, good heart, and the selfless disregard he had towards his own life earned him the respect of his comrades, who knew that even though he was a young man, he was as good a man as they had known. He had learned by paying great attention to those who had come before him, recognizing it was no coincidence when incompetence led to mission failure. He carefully cherry-picked the good and bad qualities from all his leaders, past and present. Learning from his fallen predecessors, he'd take notes, being careful not to repeat their same fatal mistakes. He had to learn for himself his own formula, and he did that through careful repetition and experimentation on the field of battle.

There may too have been a twisted feather in Clyde's cap. Maybe it was the constant, crushing stress and danger they lived with, but Clyde, at such a young age, had developed a complex relationship with Death. One and the same, they were; where Clyde went, Death followed, watching, waiting for his turn to seize hold the soul that'd been dodging him for too long. On the contrary, where Death was, Clyde was headed, and that was the simple nature of their acquaintance. A yin/yang duality, life and death were. The two swirling around each other, dancing amid the rice paddies, napalm, and straw shelter villages gone up in flames.

For him, playing God in that unforgiving arena among the fields wherein lay many a dead man was no place he wished to remain. He certainly would never wish war on anyone, not after seeing the thousands of young lives cut far too short, the countless thousands of sons and brothers, killed in a land thousands of miles away from the only kin they ever knew. Calling out in their last moments to those loved ones they had cherished in life, yearning to again feel the warmth of the homes that had kept them.

Yet here they found themselves, in a land of exotic people, who worshipped exotic deities and carried with them an Oriental magic that seemed to curse the feet of trespassers.

Clyde, however, possessed something other people his age did not: a license to kill.

That was a power so vast that it became a detriment to his health, riddling his mind over it. A power that lessened those good qualities he was raised with, compassion, empathy, and love. It diminished the value with which life was examined. The flame of life was too easily extinguished. Out there, it was a gamble: You were here today and gone tomorrow, and he never knew which it would be on any given day of the week. He'd seen his friends perish. He'd listened to their dreams once too, and watched with mortified eyes as they were struck down, slain, or horribly maimed.

Those who weren't physically hurt suffered too, for the rational psyche they once possessed, the mental matter which once held together their very fabric of normalcy in the world, had been ripped asunder, replaced with the pervasive evilness of the times. The American infantry needed to match or surpass the wickedness of their foes just to balance the scales.

Paranoia had crept her long, slippery fingers into the cracks of Clyde's brain; he now lived with it, carrying with him a great suspicion of anyone he did not personally know. He vowed one night, in his hooch in the rain, that Vietnam would not be the place of his ending. He resolved to himself that he had a greater mission, a higher purpose. Alone in his thoughts, he tried to relax but found it impossible. Rarely had he written home, save for the handful of times he wrote just to let Santina and his parents know he was alive. Clyde figured if anything were to happen to him out there, they would be the first ones to know, when those two soldiers in dress uniforms rang the doorbell, bearing that solemn look and carrying that dreadful news, which all mothers of soldiers quiver in fear of to receive. News that they avoided like the plague, the fear of it keeping them too, awake, late into the night.

Clyde had reached the end of his service thrice combat wounded with thirteen notches on his belt, six that were never confirmed, a modest number compared to some. He kept it to himself. He learned to cope by dissociating from that twisted reality entirely, choosing only to stay temporarily in this horrible chapter of his life. Sergeant Clyde LeBouef was still wounded from a gunfight when his CO ordered him to get on the first chopper out of there the next day. His time was up. Exhausted and psychologically checked out, Clyde grabbed his bags and his M-16 and hopped on the first Huey he saw the following morning. The bird took off, hovering over the tall grass laid flat by the rotor wash. Looking out over the edge of the bird and down at his brothers, who were going under the wire later that very night, he said a quiet prayer of gratitude and thanks to God for seeing him through the worst of it.

He spent several weeks getting checked out and cleaned up in one of the army field hospitals. While he didn't have it nearly as bad as many others did, he was still the worse for wear. Those three years in the service were undoubtedly the most physically strenuous, sickness-stricken, mentally debilitating years of his life. The squalorous living conditions were atomically subhuman, but the POWs would tell them of horror stories much more nightmarish.

Constantly fighting the insects and critters of the jungle, they were surrounded by darkness, and poisonous plants. Through thick spider webs they saw the poor flies trapped, living in the lice-infested cages, dodging the prodding bamboo shoots of their captors. They ate slop, slept in their own waste, and were made to endure the worst torments earthly people were capable of committing. Many would never escape, succumbing to the hopeless disparity they'd found themselves in, abandoning all hope of living.

Proud as he was, it was hard to feel proud about some of it, but instead of dealing with it, Clyde preferred to shove that skeleton deep into his closet. The men were harder in those days, but they had to be. His parents were part of the Greatest Generation; he had no right to complain. He was *eager* for it, he enthusiastically signed his name on that dotted line, not knowing what he had really gotten himself into. Now he was preparing to go back home, and he was having crippling anxiety over it.

On the flight to Germany was when Clyde knew the worst was behind him and that his real life could start. He worried he wouldn't be able to adjust, or that he'd be looked at differently, but he daydreamed of patriotic parades and festivals full of fanfare. The "welcome home" celebrations that would accompany their return from war would see the women line the streets for the weary men in uniform. To savor those glories like the veterans of the great wars had received was a just reward for fighting such a hard fight. *We're next*, he thought. *It's our turn.*

Unfortunately, though, Clyde had shut out the western world while overseas. Had he not, he would have already known about the vastly differing court of public opinion back home, pertaining to the war. America was changing; the sweeping counter-culture movement of the late 1960s was in full effect. It was a different America than the one he left. The men were growing their hair long, the women were no longer wearing brassieres, and they were all wearing "bell bottoms." He blamed the acid.

First he was flying into Chicago, then he'd make his way to New Orleans. Last stop, Bossier City. His arrival home would not be what he expected, but rather, an intense culture shock. Clyde sank down in his all-too-small plane seat when he realized that those rumors he heard were true. The war was not perceived in a good light, and the people were madly against it. Against sending their boys to be used as simple pawns and expendable government drones.

Well, he had survived the wringer, when so many others had not, and that alone said more than he needed to say himself.

Chapter 2

CASTAWAYS

The place of their isolation was not an island, far out to sea. Nor was it a mountain of cold and ice. Indeed, as far removed from society as they had now become, it was more as if the latter was true. The jet rolled along the tarmac, the burning summer sun illuminating the bright-blue backdrop from which they looked out at the myriad shapes of clouds blowing gently in Chicago's midwestern breeze. Seeing the sky over the red, white, and blue in a new way, more special now it was to them, to savor a blue sky in a free country again.

All the civil unrest in the world at home meant very little to Clyde. He didn't care; he was just happy to be on friendly soil, far away from that terrible place. He had seen the unreal, and it was locked lips he'd have on it.

Clyde strained his coffee-colored eyes to see out the small window of the aircraft. Indeed, he saw a small crowd of anti-war protestors gathered there on the tarmac. Hippie trash, and nothing more. He felt bad for that generation, really, but their own conviction in their beliefs jostled him enough. He felt a wrench in his gut, a deep twisting feeling that started in his dry throat and made its way slowly down to his disappointed heart. For him, it was unfathomable. Surely if they'd throw curses at *them*, then he could presume too that they spoke to their mothers with the same flagrancy.

That was unacceptable. Had they no shame?

Coming to a halt, the plane slowly shut down its engines. The seatbelt signs clicked off, and everyone started to stand up in their seats, quickly crowding the small aisle in the much-too-small cabin. Outside, the stairs were brought over. It was getting really hot in there, and Clyde felt a little better when the door was finally opened. Cramped and all too eager to get out of that plane and into Uncle Sam Land, they filed out of the plane, and the hippie chants grew louder and louder. He could hear them from inside the plane as he slowly shuffled toward the nose. Shaking the pilot's hand as he turned to exit, for the first time in years he tasted clean American air, and it tasted good.

The smells came back to him; the sight, foreign as it was to him, was very welcome, but short lived. They shuffled down the steps, clinging to the thin railing for support, moving headfirst into the crowd that had gathered around their plane, waving their signs and crudely hand-painted banners, sounding off with their silly mantras. These people were the cowards, hurling their lame insults, spitting in the face of all that America stood for. America had honored her troops in the past, but not this time. This time, they were denied even the humblest glory which was to be their simple reward. A welcome home was all they asked.

As Clyde made his way through the crowd and into the airport, he took the public display of ignorance for what it was and tried to shrug it off. Granted, it wasn't the homecoming he expected, there was no one throwing any flowers at their feet, no flags waving gallantly, but so what? Those might have just been childhood delusions, but he swore he remembered it differently. The WWII guys had gotten the royal treatment, and rightfully so.

There was security on the tarmac, trying to get a handle on things before they escalated past the point of no return, but even they were acting like a bunch of sorry bastards. Clyde felt hot, irritated, and mad. His neck and chest began to itch, sweating underneath his dress uniform, in a terrible discomfort. He felt a bit claustrophobic, he felt a bit small, and for a fleeting second, ashamed, but only for a second, for he would not deny the past. Then they saw the worst of it.

The most capitally offensive behavior of them all; they were spit on too.

Clyde kept his composure and kept walking straight. Some of the other GIs broke ranks to give it right back, escalating the situation toward violence with every push, shove, or slur that was uttered. Aside from the protestors, the stares of the people inside of the airport didn't make him feel very *at home* either. He was on friendly soil, but he still felt out of place, a stranger, even among his own people. There was simply no common ground to be shared any longer between himself and ordinary folk.

Clyde was a well-mannered, polite, and respectful young man, largely in part due his southern nature and upbringing, in conjunction with the discipline and work ethic that he'd learned from years in the service. Not an impolite bone in his body, and that greatly reflected his admirable character, a calm professionalism, a coolness he radiated on the outside as he moved through Chicago O'Hare International Airport. Inside, he burned, feeling the eyes on him, almost wishing he wasn't wearing his dress uniform. He hated the eyes on him.

But Clyde was always a dapper one. His uniform, like many others, was adorned with the many medals and badges he had earned, his marks of *honor*. To him, the uniform symbolized the great sacrifice that many of his comrades made, and he'd be damned if anybody made him feel bad about that. While he was polite, he was no pushover, and heaven forbid anybody pushed him, because he'd show them what it was to cross an unsettled old sergeant. He was so serious now in these times, the effect of having to face life's most bitter realities, so early in one's time.

His next flight was direct from Chicago to New Orleans, and the trip went by rather fast as his mind wandered to a different place. He sat there, in the little airline seat, looking out the window of the plane as the thick cumulus clouds drifted by, their marble splendor, countless, innumerable shapes. It was easy to pass the time that way, drifting off into his comfortable stare. He didn't need to be engaged in distraction to be contented, simply *being* was enough. His eyes fixed off in the distance on some unseen, unknown point.

What he was looking at was a mystery to others; for him, it was a brief and quiet respite from the chaos of the world, his way of regaining a sense of spatial awareness in the tight world around him. Here he reflected on his existence. He thought of people he missed, of things that haunted him, of confronting those malignant memories—but finding the fortitude to confront such things was hard to do alone. And alone was how he preferred it. In the comfortable stare, his mind was a playground, and simultaneously it was a place of tranquility, removing himself from the present and quieting the many great dilemmas of life, which we must face alone. No one ever knows about the lonely battles and quiet victories.

Arriving uneventfully in New Orleans, Clyde had to raise his hands to the sky and give thanks to God for getting him through it. Clyde stood at the baggage claim while the flexuous carousels wound around with a variety of multicolored suitcases, carry-ons, makeup bags, and the like. The American servicemen and the other passengers were all eager to find their bags and their rides.

For Clyde, the latter consisted of two olive-drab standard-issue army duffel bags, tagged and painted with his name and unit on the canvas bottom. Their contents accounted for everything he needed to survive. All he had to his name after giving his gear and equipment back to Uncle Sam was crammed inside the two incredibly durable bags. Clyde was leaning towards minimalism now anyways. In his own observations, he'd watched how little it took for Vietnamese children to find simple amusement in the world around them, how few possessions they had, which was something that didn't seem to bother them in the slightest. Even though many had nothing for themselves, they didn't miss the things they did not know they were supposed to miss.

Clyde still managed to sneak a couple of war trophies inside his bags: Gook knives, lighters, money, jewelry, little mementos really, expended rounds, maps.

He made his way home via the taxi he'd procured shortly after walking out of the airport double doors. The last leg of a long trip home. Bossier City was on the bend, and Clyde would soon find himself facing a different challenge entirely, the challenge of living a life of domestication and comfort. The challenge of having to match the slowed down pace of everyday living, that would be his pain. For the bright young man, who had yet to see a miracle, needed to see some good in the world before he could forgo his adventurous spirit. It was not right, but he felt for the men still over there, and felt guilty that he was free, and they were not.

The only remedy to feeling so lost is to revive the spirit again in the life that is beautiful around you, which Clyde was determined to do, busying himself with piecing back together something resembling a dignified life for him and Santina.

The middle-aged, slightly graying Hungarian man, with a fat neck that tucked away in its folds a glimmering golden rope chain, pulled his checkered green cab into the beaten gravel drive of Clyde's family home. Clyde was desperately looking forward to getting out into the air, having been suffocated by the man's cologne the whole way home. They shared little conversation, keeping the radio on low to ease the silence, driving down what one could consider an exhibit of classic bayou imagery. A place filled with so many cherished and wonderful memories, yet after so long, it felt strange to come back to it. He was still in shock that his epic was over. Clyde watched as the beads of rain raced each other down the windows. He'd been anticipating this reunion for years. His wife, his parents, his siblings, all of whom were waiting for his return, were there, beyond the closed doors.

We often cling to the only thing we can in times of great peril, the blessing that is family. The great foundational grounding force.

His story, however, was not one he wished to reveal to them. Not for fear of their judgement, or lack of understanding, for they were his own flesh and blood, but because he did not wish to relive those pained memories himself. In the story of his life, he wished to put Vietnam further back behind even those chapters of his life that were the furthest away, further delegating the skeletons back into his haunted past. Incisive of the choices he'd made, it was now a battle with the reverberating consequences of his actions he faced, what comes around goes around, and inside, Clyde knew it was the karma he feared.

Back home for everyone else, their lives were, for the most part, unaffected by the war, unless of course it was their own son or husband out there on the front lines. But for the rest of working America, the war was just another news story next to the crooked politicians, civil unrest, and the overall societal changes happening in every other corner of backwater America. Days of American prosperity were on the loom, even though the war waged on steadily without the slightest degree of let-up. There were still swaths of troops actively engaged in heavy combat operations, men out there suffering through dysentery and fever in the murderous tropical rainforests, paranoid. Clyde had been there, and narrowly dodged death many times. Now it was time to face the music of the world. Now he could rekindle the flame of love with his wife, Santina, who he would go and see tomorrow, after first light peeked over the delta.

Clyde hopped out of the taxi, grabbing his own bags from the back seat, and shuffled over to the driver's side window to leave the sweaty Hungarian his lousy fifty-cent tip.

Walking up the rest of the drive, he heard the familiar crunch of gravel under his jump boots as he approached the porch. He stood under what once was a tight, red, canvas-covered porch roof, now a dirty, faded shade of crimson, with holes big enough for the rain to seep through, pouring a steady stream down onto the porch below. On the front door he gave three raps and waited. The locks behind the door began to rattle, and he heard the excitement on the other side as his parents messed around with the locking mechanisms. They rarely got visitors, so they knew something was up. People don't just knock on people's doors at midnight; at least there they usually don't.

He was afraid he wouldn't recognize them anymore, his parents, that they would be like strangers to him, and that worried him, because he loved them, but he knew he wasn't the same. He didn't know what they would make of him, having endured such an ordeal. The door opened, and standing before him was the towering giant of a man he remembered from his youth, although now they were about the same height.

"Oh my God!" said Lawrence LeBouef. "Oh my God!" he repeated louder, his voice beginning to break. "I don't believe my eyes ... Annette! Annette! Get out here, honey! It's Clyde!"

Chapter 3

THE PARISH

Clyde drew in a homestyle grin from ear to ear. "Now, Daddy, I sure am happy to see you!" Clyde exclaimed as he set his bags to the floor, reaching up and grabbing the old man tight. "How you doing, Pa?" he said, his heart full at seeing his dad again. Stepping from the porch and over the threshold, the two walked inside, and Clyde exhaled a breath of relief, seeing the very heartbeat of the home alive and pumping with hot life and blood. Such a warm welcome it was to be seen by both Mom and Dad.

"Good to see that this place ain't changed," he said. "Wow, I missed you guys. You guys look good," said Clyde, looking them both up, down, left, and right. He then went on to cheerfully exchange hugs with his mother, a short little lady who was patiently waiting for her turn next to her husband, with her warm motherly expression and clasped hands. Her gold jewelry popped against her olive skin and red nail polish. Her name was Annette, and she was the source of the Spanish blood that flowed through Clyde's veins.

"You know we couldn't change it while you were away. Your room is the same as you left it." Her Creole accent forced her to say *jus'*. Mom looked good, a real elegant lady, she always kept the heath going, all year long. Birthdays, holidays, graduations, bridal showers, funerals, she was always on the phone with the relatives, keeping a constant wire of information flowing with the relative and nonrelative information regarding the family affairs. In the old days, the conversation was filtered down at the dinner table, and she spoke to them about their days at school instead.

Clyde shuffled through, taking his shoes off at the rug. "Where is everybody?"

Clyde's mother took his jacket from him and hung it on the coatrack nestled in the corner by the front door. "Well, everybody's older now, honey. They've all got their own lives going on," she said, tidying the shoes by the door.

"The only one that we hear from is your brother Les. The girls are running around doing their own thing, and we haven't heard from Dean since he moved out to California."

Leslie was Clyde's oldest brother, senior to him by six years. Leslie hadn't gone to war, he'd missed it, and was fully involved in the world of academia, studying biology on his own dime, hoping to take his science degrees with him on the road, but even while he was furthering his education, he always made time to call Ma and Pa at least every other day, if not every day.

Clyde's mother Annette's fastidious and people-pleasing nature, was a direct result of her descending from a long line of obsessive homemakers. Being the mother of the home ran in her family, and she did what she could to make her own husband and children happy, whether it was cooking for them, cleaning their sheets once a week, or folding the kids' laundry nicely. Even if they just wanted someone to talk to growing up, Annette was never out of earshot. They all loved the food she made, which they shared together, as frequently as they could in those days. At the old family table, the whole nest sat at once, but now it was just the three of them, and it was a lot quieter than before.

Clyde's father, Lawrence, had determined he was through biting his tongue any longer. "I know it must have been hell, son. I haven't been able to read the papers since you left. It was always on the front page. Your mother and I were worried out of our skulls for you the whole time," he said, getting himself worked up, before quickly feeling the relief when he looked at Clyde again. "Son, we're happy to have you home is what I'm *trying* to say," he said, patting Clyde on the shoulder as he passed through the kitchen on his way to the recliner.

Clyde gave his reply. "Yeah, Daddy." He paused, one corner of his mouth pulled up toward his ear as he gave a halfhearted smile, as he looked off into space blankly. "It was really something."

Annette looked at him from the sink, watching the young man at her table who she knew looked to be an older version of the baby she had raised. Her eyes welled with quiet tears that'd never fall as she busied her hands with the chores of the house, to distract herself from the hidden troubles of life as a housewife and mother.

Without speaking more than was necessary, Clyde pardoned himself and went upstairs to take a hot shower in the privacy of his own bathroom. The silky torrents poured down on him like cleansing, hot rain. Such a simple pleasure he had taken for granted. The soap he used to scrub away years of blood, grime, and death. Washing his body with the fragrantly lathered washcloth, he'd smother over the scars with the soapy suds, covering with remorse the past reminders of nightmarish engagements, where he'd given his own youthful flesh.

Drying himself off, he stepped in front of the mirror, taking a good long look. He'd gotten himself a haircut a couple of weeks ago, his last haircut for a while, he thought. He'd lost a good amount of weight, the skin was looser, but more tanned. Only twenty-two years old, but he felt older than that. He looked a bit older, that was visible through the eyes, reflecting back into the world the bad things he'd seen with them.

With just a towel on, he walked into his room and over to his bed, where he grabbed his dress uniform, taking one last good look at it before hanging it up for good. Getting changed into pajamas and throwing on a pair of slippers felt silly at first, but he had to admit the soft fabric was quite refreshing, and had a refreshing fragrance too, due to Ma's laundry magic.

He shut off the light and walked out into the hall. His mom and dad were still awake downstairs, watching TV.

"You guys got some new pictures done!" Clyde said from the top of the stairs, observing the framed portraits of Lawrence and Annette.

"Yeah, your mother wanted new ones," Lawrence said from his recliner, "so we went and took a couple." he smiled. He was usually a man of few words, but often in days gone by, he'd kept parties greatly entertained, and being this way, he was always playing host right alongside Clyde's mother.

He continued to shout down the stairs. "Tomorrow I'm gonna head into town to see Santina!" Clyde said. "I can't keep my wife waiting much longer."

Lawrence looked disturbed at that, and he had to inform Clyde that Santina, in fact, had moved out of Bossier and into New Orleans with her family. Clyde didn't know that she moved because he didn't fancy news from home while he was gone. That brought outside distractions, which was no good. He fished around for a response.

"Well, I'll make the drive in the afternoon, then."

He hadn't seen or touched his wife in three years, and the anxiousness he felt at their first meeting was now starting to build. The suspense, exciting and nerve-wracking at the same time. He thought of her every day while he was gone. What she was doing, where she was, who she was with where she was, if anybody at all, and where. Paranoia, dreading the worst, how could she have stayed true to him after so many years? To have a love so strong that no other option was viable *but* to wait, that was the best-case scenario, and the one that Clyde had placed his hopes in, even though he knew it was asking a lot, of anybody.

He sat in the living room, catching up with his parents. Clyde was told about all the goings-on in the family, learning about what his siblings were up to, when the dog passed away, why they hadn't got a new one, how was work going, all these normal questions that usually come up during familial visits.

About his plans, Clyde knew he needed a job. He had to work. Sure, he could've used his G.I. Bill and gone to school, but working was what paid the bills. Honest, blue-collar work is what built this country, it was only right to be a hardworking man, a provider, and as he didn't know what he'd be good at in school anyways, he decided that for his family, he'd work as hard as it took. The concept of being back with his wife had reminded him how much he wanted a family.

He'd always wanted to be a dad, in part because of the great relationship he had with his own father. Clyde had grown to appreciate his parents more after he left home, missing the home-cooked food especially.

To a degree, it was homesickness. He felt sorry for being gone so long and for not keeping better in touch. He just didn't want to worry anybody needlessly; if something was wrong, they'd find out. The age-old adage "No news is good news" was Clyde's traditional standpoint.

Clyde had gotten many things from his dad; great taste in music, earfuls of sound advice, many life lessons he was taught as he was growing up with Lawrence. He inherited his dad's zest for language, always willing to debate or argue on a firm opinion with strong opposition, which not everybody always agreed with, but his charisma and charm disarmed people, in a way that despite his blockheadedness, he was still looked at with great admiration. Clyde had these things as well, but being a young man, he was often not given a second look while standing in a room with the older folk, as they were having grownup talk, which was in their heads, outside the scope of his understanding, or so they falsely assumed. Now especially, Clyde could speak on a great many matters, things that a lot of people probably would rather not even talk about.

Clyde had pondered his mortality for a long time. Seeing what he'd seen, he understood now the grim nature of life, how all of us are to pass beyond the doorway through which we all must walk. He thought of his aging parents. He got to know his parents later on in their lives, so Clyde had unfortunately not gotten a chance to know his grandparents, only through stories, brief recounts his parents had made. This gave him a deeper appreciation for his parents, because he knew that life really was so short, tomorrow was not promised, and he didn't understand where the time kept going. Some people's time could be short, while others could be given a great long time to do a great many things, experiencing much in life, but to be given that honor, you must first sow in life the seeds of good.

These concepts were something more akin to philosophies in the East. People in Bossier weren't busy thinking about life after death, in the Bible belt, you only had two choices, heaven or hell. It was very cut and dry, and it was simply put that when God called you home, you went. If you were a good person in life and did good unto others, you'd enter the kingdom of God, blessed to walk beside the Lord for all eternity, assuming you've accepted him. If you'd done evil, or sinned grievously, then damned your soul would be, and off to the flames you'd go. Clyde grappled with that. Thou shall not kill. Clyde had broken that one. He'd killed when he had to, but it wasn't that he was worried about it, because God would understand that they were at war. He was worried that the way he'd felt when he took those lives would call for stricter judgment. Partly the thrill, partly too the mountain of guilt. He felt bad, and wished he did not have to suffer those confused emotions. It was something that he *had* to do. Again, the flame of life is easily extinguished. Clyde had seen this up close. He had watched before, the flicker slowly blow out.

He had seen the final moments of life, watched as the spirit had passed on to whatever was next. That was what brought him revelation and hope. Hope that there was something more after all of this. There had to be, because he had seen hell, and been part of the tortured damned living in its thrall. He couldn't help but feel he was paying for something.

The good souls would get rewarded, and the bad would endure one hundredfold worse hells than the one he had been through in the Vietnam. These things normal people his age didn't really wonder or discuss.

It wasn't that these thoughts crippled him with anxiety or made him live in fear; he was not frightened of dying. Rather, such complex questions gave him many things to think about, and for much of the day, he would ruminate on these deep questions of life. While other folks were busy catching up on the sports or the news, living in distraction, going through the motions, He, was determined to *live* and not take these things for granted. He would live a good, proper life, with his wife, and they'd have kids, and he would work, retire, and pass away, surrounded by his family. *That was the plan.*

Climbing into bed later than usual, Clyde let himself drift into a deep, cumbersome sleep, no longer able to keep his eyes open.

Sleep wrapped him in its shroud, its veil of recoup, and for the first time in a long time, Clyde could dream. The worries of the past were gone; He was surrounded by those he knew, those he loved, and so he slept peacefully.

Though he had spent some time visiting his parents, he just couldn't shake a weird feeling. He'd known his parents his whole life, yet it had almost felt like they were strangers. People he recognized but just didn't quite know anymore. It had been too long, with too much trauma in between. He hadn't much to say because there wasn't a whole lot that needed to be said. He didn't know if it was because he was a bad person or just a bad son. He felt a slight twinge of isolation at that thought, and in those moments, chose a higher road.

He knew he was different, but coming to grips with the challenges of his life and the vast personal changes he'd undertaken would have to wait. His mind had settled down, and he drifted away, into the sleep of dead men. The feathered pillows stuffed under his heavy head, blankets keeping him cozily nestled in their fresh aroma. It was rejuvenating, and restored some life to him.

He woke up when he felt like it.

Skies over Bossier City that morning were clear, as blinds were drawn, windows opened, and the southern heat wafted into homes all around. Morning kitchens everywhere lit pilot lights for starting their stovetops in preparation for breakfast. Birds took to the skies with gentle cheeps heard for morning amusement and delight. Clyde propped himself up on the headboard as he leaned forward and stretched his arms out, arching his back to twist himself into great release. The sun was out, promising to the people today would be a good day.

Shuffling himself to stand, and rubbing the sleep out of his eyes, he wandered over to the bathroom, which was attached to his bedroom, and started to get himself ready. His hair was only slightly disheveled, considering how hard he had slept. He actually felt well-rested for the first time in a long time and used this newfound energy to put some time into his appearance this morning before heading out for the day.

He wanted to make himself sharp for Santina; she deserved a put-together man, and he was lucky to have her.

She had married Clyde right after high school, and everyone always called them a good-looking couple, saying they looked like they belonged together. Clyde was madly in love with her and had been restlessly thinking of their meeting for weeks, months, years.

He had grown up with parents who had not only raised several kids together, but had stayed married and in love, which could be quite hard to manage, as marriage is hard work. But Clyde was a natural romantic, and she felt that way too, believing in *old love*. When she had seen Clyde off to war, many tears were shed at the uncertainty. The fright gripped the whole family, and everyone slept a little less easy because of Clyde's decision to volunteer for it. With these thoughts in his head, he finished his morning routine by brushing his teeth and giving himself a shave. Shaving felt good; it felt clean and professional. He had been a sergeant, after all. There were certain standards he was expected to uphold, personal hygiene and precise adherence to the grooming regulations to name a few. He was scrupulous in his dress and appearance, bordering on the line of obsessive-compulsivity.

"Morning, Ma, morning, Pa," Clyde said as he came whizzing down the stairs, all ready to go. It was a Thursday morning, so Clyde's father would have to head to work before too long. They were finishing up breakfast, which was still hot on the table; eggs, bacon, potatoes, some leftover sausage, and biscuits and gravy. It was a smorgasbord, more food than could be consumed by the three of them, but Clyde's mother was used to cooking for a big family, so she always made too much.

"Morning, son! Leavin' so soon? Ain't you gon' have some breakfast first?" Lawrence said to Clyde from the kitchen table, sipping his coffee behind the daily paper.

"I know I should, but I really need to get going, Pa," Clyde said. Food wasn't important.

"Can I borrow the car?"

At this, Lawrence let out a laugh. "Borrow my car?" he said dramatically over the hilarity of the request. It was all in good jest though, because of course Clyde could borrow the car, but his young age had clearly not bore him yet any instruction in subtlety or finesse.

His parents understood that he needed to get out of the house. So, whatever he needed they would be happy to provide. Lawrence responded, first looking for Annette. "Uh, yeah, I guess I don't have any quarrel with that, assuming your mama doesn't need it, of course?" more of a question than a statement.

"No, sweetie, I don't have any problem with that at all, but you need to eat. You're nothing but skin! No fat!" she said as she waved the spatula in Clyde's direction, to which a simple 'yes, ma'am' on his part sufficed. She fixed his plate, and though he really wasn't hungry, his mama cooked, so he needed to make an effort. It would make the cigarette he hadn't stopped thinking about all the sweeter.

Scarfing his food down in seconds, Clyde thanked his mother for the wonderful meal, and he said goodbye to his parents as he made his way out. Pulling out the pack of smokes from his pocket, giving one a light and taking a good long pull, he exhaled the vapor from his lungs. *These*, he thought, would be the death of him. Taking in the scenery around him, he was reminded of his childhood spent in this home, and how many days he had walked out that same screen door and onto the porch, the creaks and groans of the rotting wood all too familiar to him, sounds from a different time.

Every day he went out that door and onto the porch then down the steps, either off to catch the school bus or to take that short walk into town. Or just to go around the side of the house to play with his brothers and sisters, as they spent much of their time outside growing up. Now they were all busy adults living their own lives. He hadn't heard from any of them in a long time, but the phone worked both ways, and so did the pen for that matter.

But what mattered more at that moment was seeing if he could still drive. He had not been behind the wheel of an American-made car in years. It was exactly the kind of exhilaration he'd hoped for, too, getting behind the wheel. It came with a freedom of its own, adult independence, going off on his own, down the great road unknown. Despite it not being his own car, he was driving, or his own place where he was staying, he wanted to go enjoy some of that hard-fought freedom. He also was ready to hear some music, and wanted to see if that had changed at all either.

Clyde put on his sunglasses, rolled down the windows, and pulled out of the driveway, slowly at first, to get a feel for the strange vehicle. Then it all came back to him, just like riding a bike. He was off down the street to go and see the missus.

Bossier had hardly changed. The schools were still in session at that time of year, with kids humming around outside, going to and from their classes. The morning people doing their ritual morning routines, the same daily commutes, running petty errands or heading to work. Everybody had a different reason for being on the road that day. He was no different, except he didn't have a job to get to, nor was he in a rush. It was his first day back; he could take his time.

The people were the same, and they could still be seen sitting on their porches or out in their yards. The same people you'd see on the street in one town you'd see in another. The smells were familiar, and the air was hot and sticky, which was a feeling he couldn't seem to shake, but there was a breeze that hit him as he hopped out of the little family car his parents had loaned him. He felt deep nostalgia, the water towers and old buildings were like monuments.

On the natural side of things, the old marsh was a cryptid terrain, which sent shivers down the spines of skeptics when they stepped across the betting line after midnight, when one might hear the devil's jazz trumpet coming from within the foggy swamps.

He now had to make his way to New Orleans, and it was only eight in the morning, still early. He'd gotten Santina's new address from ma, and she'd told him all about the job she'd taken, cleaning rooms at the historic Hotel Monteleone.

On his way down to the Old Capitol, Clyde thought of his wife and how this was the part he was most nervous about. Their meeting had been a long time coming. He tapped his thumb on the steering wheel along to the music, but the radio wasn't playing loud enough for the tones to properly distract him. Not yet ready to fully confront his feelings, the feeling like something wasn't right. Clyde was on the mainland, but his head was still overseas. The best thing for him to do was to take it one day at a time, but he didn't know how to do that, he was accustomed to thinking several moves ahead.

Clyde hopped on the highway, and the car picked up speed. The speed limit seemed to be a little too fast for Clyde, who was white-knuckling the wheel amid traffic that had increased in volume *and* speed. It had been quite a while since he'd been this way, so the route was unfamiliar, but that was just because there had been no real reason to go to New Orleans before the war.

He had been there a few times, and had a few wild Mardi Gras down on Bourbon Street, most of which ended with him blackout drunk and waking up not knowing where he was. His parents were unaware of this, as he'd fed them a pack of lies. Getting out of the house was important to him. He didn't like to be cooped up; cabin fever was common for him in youth, and this wanderlust was but one pillar which led him to join the war effort. He wanted to experience life and get out and do it on his own terms, as young men do.

The wind slapping his face, blowing through the windows into his hair, that tasty cigarette, the loud music, it was liberating. There was nothing like having a full tank of gas. He could go wherever opportunity took him. He'd seen hiring signs outside of plenty of different places. He didn't really want to work just yet, but he knew he had to. He could not be without a plan, he needed a way of earning income. He didn't want to deal with the public; being demeaned and berated by rude and unruly people was out of the question. He'd never exploded on anyone before, but now, who knew?

His mind never shut off once it started going; he'd follow one thought to the next, a never-ending stream of thinking, planning, and paying attention. He was hyper-alert to everything and once fixated on a particular thing, he would ruminate on it for some time. He was certainly wiser than someone in their early twenties should have been.

It was a five-hour drive to New Orleans. He'd procure a room for them at her place of employment. He hadn't told his folks he'd be spending the night, but he'd call when he got the chance. Approaching the city now, the traffic had begun to pick up even more, and this was nerve-wracking for Clyde, but his mantra, which he kept repeating, was if he followed the rules of the road, then everyone else would too. Nobody starts their day planning to get into an automobile accident.

Now, he wasn't sure exactly where the Monteleone was, but he'd figure that out too. No problem. Pulling into a gas station, he stopped to ask the gas monkey for some directions.

Clyde committed the instructions to memory, as memorization was part of his game. He had a great memory and always paid great attention to detail. No fact was so small, no matter so insignificant that it escaped him; he saw everything. Clyde was trained in picking out those strange anomalies, relying on that sixth sense and instinct to guide him.

Clyde bought a pack of smokes, a case of beer, and two ham and cheese sandwiches. Just something to get him through the day. He was staying downtown for the night, but he still needed to phone home to his mother to let her know he'd have the car longer than he'd initially planned. He'd ring her once he got their room. Paying for his goods and the fill-up, Clyde made his way back into traffic, repeating the instructions the boy had just given him. He began to weave his way through the different side streets and back ways, eyes wandering, looking for a big sign or some big hotel or something, something pointing him in the direction of the French Quarter. He hadn't exactly gotten a description of the place, either, which he now realized in hindsight. But following those instructions as best he could recall, he found it eventually.

People were everywhere, blocking the streets, walking in the road, jammed into the sidewalks, all up and down Bourbon Street. Clyde hated crowds. He felt like people couldn't be trusted, and when there were a lot of people, it meant there were a lot of unsavory characters floating around, waiting to pick somebody's pockets, or stick them up, or worse. It equaled trouble in Clyde's mind, and something he'd make a mental note of. He pulled up to the Hotel Monteleone, after a long trip, and stepped out of the little car to stretch his legs. He cranked the windows back up, took a few deep breaths as the nerves were beginning to hit him now. He felt like his stomach was turning, but he tried to ignore it. He regretted not stopping for some flowers or something he could give to her. Unfortunately, all he was bringing was himself, and he hoped that'd be enough.

Clyde took one last look at himself in the side mirror on the door and fixed his hair with a cheap comb, looking into his own unfamiliar eyes, which gazed back at him and through themselves. Those coffee-colored eyes were the way to his soul, which had seen more ugliness than he cared to remember. He was home now, he reminded himself. On the move once again, but he had realized that while time had seemed to stop for him, his life on pause while he was at war, everyone else had kept moving forward. Everyone else was now working their easy nine-to-fives, having their families, making new memories, and enjoying their peaceful lives. He was now looking to have that slowed-down life for himself. He adjusted his trousers and his shirt, which was tucked in, and made his way toward the front doors.

The towering metropolis stood before Clyde, its French Colonial architecture something truly to marvel at. The white marble, so intricately carved at the entrance, people were coming to and fro, it was business as usual, a typical day. Clyde was astonished at the size of this remarkable hotel. Sure, he had been to New Orleans, but he had never really given a second thought as to appreciating something so mundane as a hotel.

It seemed almost like a blessing for his wife to have gotten a decent-paying job here. Heading inside, Clyde was astonished; the lobby was even more ornate than the brilliance of the building's exterior design. The floor, still shimmering from its nightly shine, reflected the intricate flickers of the imported chandeliers, the cream pillars supporting the mosaic ceiling, the wonderful assortments of various flowers strewn about. The place was very classy, very rich. There in the lobby stood an old relic, a wonderfully stained grandfather clock, towering over everybody's heads, Father Time watching over the guests.

Clyde made his way deeper inside. People of all kinds were walking about, suit-and-tie gentlemen with their fancy wives, younger folks, families with kids of all ages and pet-carrier cages, everybody had business there that morning. Bellhops followed close behind with luggage in tote. The lobby smelled like cigarettes, perfume, and alcohol—a good time, that is to say. Seeing the place was worth the drive alone.

Making his way through the people, Clyde went and stood in line behind an older couple waiting to book their room. Clyde needed to first inquire about his wife. It had been too long since he'd seen her. His heart beat a little bit faster. The people around him were loud, everyone humming their own nothings to each other. A few more people came up and got behind Clyde as he stood in line. He couldn't help but feel as though they were standing right on top of him, and this made him uneasy. They were close enough he could hear everything they were saying, nothing important, basic small talk about the city and their visit, but too close for comfort. Clyde was amused when one of the people behind him complained about the muggy weather. It wasn't even the worst of it yet; it was only March. Growing up here, he was used to it, and being in the jungles of Vietnam, he was now at home in it. Tourists will always find something to say.

All walks of life, he thought.

He looked around, curiously drawn to the interesting bar, which resembled some sort of circus big top tent. A very interesting place this was, and a beautiful hotel.

Finally, it was his turn to go up and speak to the desk lady.

"Next," the woman said, in a monotone voice, which was easygoing and semi-friendly.

"Yes, ma'am, good afternoon. I'm here to see about a woman who works here, Santina's her name, I'm her husband you see, and I'm just back from Vietnam. She's my wife, you see, and she's got a job here, last I heard, so I was hoping to see her if she's working today."

At the word *Vietnam*, the desk lady, whose name was Margaret, which Clyde found out after looking at her name badge, slowly looked up from what she was doing, and her eyes fixed on him. She gave a giddy laugh from behind the glass. "Oh, I'm sorry for staring! It's just for a long time we were wondering if you were as handsome in person. Turns out you are! Mr. LeBouef, welcome home!"

Clyde felt a little uncomfortable and hot at the odd scene this lady was creating. She was drawing a lot of eyes. It was nice of her to welcome him home, even though she was just a stranger. He realized a lot of the noise had died down around them. Margaret pulled herself together. "Yes, Santina is great, we all just absolutely adore her. She *is* here today, on the fifth floor if I'm not mistaken. Head on up. She'll be inside one of the rooms with the open doors, okay? All right, sweetheart, welcome home, take care now, okay, buh-bye, mhm," Margaret's enthusiasm and gusto gave Clyde relief and optimism.

It was all worth it. His trip was not in vain; things were coming together.

"I greatly appreciate it, Ma'am, really I do!" said Clyde, equally enthusiastically, moving with haste in concerto with the music that had been playing in the lobby the whole time.

Margaret smiled wide as Clyde LeBouef took flight, clasping her hands in front of her chest, as if her own heart had been touched by finally getting to meet the man they'd heard so much about, and for their own sweet Santina to be joined again with her nearly estranged husband. He'd been a ghost in her life for years, and he suffered inexpressible guilt over it.

Chapter 4

THE MONTELEONE

O pting to take the stairs instead of the elevator, Clyde was delaying the inevitable. He had to face her, and had to explain why he hadn't communicated for so long, why he hadn't written more. He had to answer the hard questions, had to talk with her about their love, which had once burned so brightly, seeming there could never be a force which would sever them, that young love that had carried his heart through the turbulent storms of war. There was much that needed to be said, but there was a great deal Clyde didn't feel like talking about. He didn't want to recall his time over there; he was still processing that for himself. He didn't want their time to be sullied by argument, either. He simply wanted to give her the love he pictured giving her while he was away, and now that the time was here, he was quite nervous, but ready to rise to the daunting occasion.

With heavy steps, he climbed the first floor, then the second, holding on to the handrail, the chips of dry black paint flaking off as he used it to propel himself forward. Why was he nervous? He began to wonder, why should he be nervous? His pace quickened, taking double steps, until at last he had found himself at the fifth and final floor, high on adrenaline again.

Heart pounding and eager, he drew a quick, deep breath, and pushed the door open, stepping past the threshold and into the great hallway. Glancing left, then right, then left again, and right once more, Clyde turned to the right, making his way down the corridor, reading the numbered signs on the doors as he passed them, looking for an open one. But one after the other, each door was closed, with nobody inside doing any sort of cleaning that he could see. He kept going down the hallway, waiting for the moment of truth, but it was the voice that called out from behind him that made his very heart stand still.

In that gentle, serene voice that he instinctively recognized, he heard his name come from behind him. "Clyde?" she said, as if she were asking a question. As if she doubted the very apparition that she had seen with her own two eyes, wondering if her mind was playing tricks on her.

He stopped and turned to look. In her full work attire, with a feather duster in one hand and a cleaning rag in the other, she stood, in all her beauty at the other end of the hall.

"Clyde!" she exclaimed.

They rushed to meet one another, running at a quick trot. Santina tossed the duster and rag to the floor and jumped into his arms, wrapping her legs around his waist as he grabbed her up and squeezed her as tightly as she had squeezed him. She buried her head into his neck and started to sob tears of joy. Clyde would have been remiss not to notice his sweetheart genuinely missed him.

A great big kiss, followed by another, and another, and then nuzzling, all while she clung to him like salvation. "I missed you, Clyde, I really missed you," she said, in between deepening sobs, crying with great exclamation.

"I know, sweetheart, I know," he said, stroking the back of her hair, "I'm home now, for good, and I ain't ever going to leave you like that again, I promise."

Santina hopped down and stood there, looking up at him, into his brown orbs, deep into the crevasses that swallowed the many horrors, heroics, and secrets he wished to hide. "I waited and waited for you! I waited for letters! I wanted to hear something, Clyde, anything! Not knowing is what hurt me the most," she said through sad, red, wet eyes. Her worry had consumed her.

Clyde knew that was coming; it was the elephant in the room, and better they addressed it straight away than argue about it later. In that hallway, tears streaming down her beautifully high cheekbones, drops of rain on that soft sand surface, how it hurt for him to see the pain in her expression, but he had accepted this long ago when he stopped writing. He simply couldn't let himself long for home, or long for love, because he didn't want to be let down if he stepped on a landmine.

He had fought hard for this moment; it was years in the making. Simply carrying her picture on all those patrols, having a piece of her to get him through the long, rainy nights, and dragging paranoia was pivotal in keeping him grounded in reality. She could not deny that he had made good on his promise to return.

"I know I need to explain myself, and I will, but what matters is that I'm here with you now, okay?" he said, reassuring her as he pulled her into one more hug, an embrace which said sorry better than his words could, and brought healing for the two of them.

Her voice was different than he remembered, and she had lost weight, now just a dainty thing. But even though her hair was a mess, and her skin was dirty from the work she'd done today, to Clyde she was the most resplendent creature he'd ever laid eyes on. The love was still there, even after all this time. "I'm sorry," he said one last time, with husk in his voice, and she knew that he meant it.

It's been said that absence makes the heart grow fonder, and this rang true. What had their parting words been? Simple goodbyes? Never, for it was never just a simple goodbye, it was an "I'll see you when I see you." That was safer and spared more of their feelings. Goodbye is final and determinate and had no place in their dialogue; it never did. It is better to rip off the bandage quickly, than to pull it off slowly.

"What time do you get off? I'm thinking I might run down to the desk and get us a room here tonight. I've gotta get the car back tomorrow, but I need to bring my stuff down here from Bossier. Where've you been staying?" Clyde asked, trying to figure out if he was homeless or if indeed they had a place to stay. They slowly walked hand in hand back the way she came, to a room on the left side of the stairway entrance.

She swung his hand in hers, "Well, I don't get off until five thirty, so I have to stay busy until then, but Margaret can get us a room for the night, and I'll come as soon as I get off the clock," she said, removing the question of his temporary lodging.

"I've been staying with Mom and Dad; they're not far from here. We'll go see them tomorrow before work and see if they can let you stay there awhile until we can afford our own place. What do you think about that?"

Clyde thought it was a great plan. In the meantime, he could get those beers in the fridge to chill for later that evening. More importantly, his tour of service had invariably caused Clyde to involuntarily partake in a long period of abstinence, which would hopefully soon be over.

"Sounds good to me! I'll let you get back to it! I'm going to go see the desk lady," he said, looking down on her from above. "Sounds good, baby, I love you," she said, kissing him sweetly. She had to stand on tiptoes.

"I love you too, baby, I'll see you in a bit." said the husband to the wife.

At this, Clyde turned away toward the stairway door, getting one last look at her as he pulled it open. She hadn't taken her eyes off of him, and as he gave her a wave, Clyde felt much relief; he felt as if this burden he had been carrying had been lifted. His very soul was rejuvenated by having laid his eyes on her. Back down the five flights of stairs he went, and back to the front desk of the lobby, where Miss Margaret was in her beat-up rolling chair, helping the hotel patrons. To the back of the line he went, waiting patiently once more.

"Next guest."

Stepping forward to make his request, Clyde leaned on his elbow against the edge of the counter, casual and cool. "Yes, ma'am, it's me again. I was wondering, how much for one room for one night?"

"For you, Mr. LeBouef, it's on the house. Don't you bother about it. You'll be in 318; it's got a double bed," she said. She took on a Mona Lisa–like presence, giving Clyde the spontaneous smile she gave to everybody. This arrangement Clyde found most suitable, as he didn't have much cash on him, just a couple of ten-dollar bills.

"Ma'am, I greatly appreciate it, I really do," Clyde said, putting his wallet back in his pocket.

She reached from the ring board behind her and pulled the key for 318. Handing it over, she proceeded to continue her script. "There's a telephone in the room, fresh towels and soaps, room service, everything you might need, and if you need something else, don't hesitate to ring us. There is also a continental breakfast served in the morning, starting at 7 a.m."

"Thank you again, ma'am, I really do appreciate it," Clyde said as he reached under the glass to grab the little silver key. He made note of the goodness of people, the hints of kindness still lingering in the world. Room key in hand, he went out the front doors, out to his car, which was parked out on the street. Fishing around in the back seat, Clyde grabbed his alcohol. The precious drink cradled under his arm, he locked up the car with his one free hand and walked back toward the front entrance. Heading inside, this time he took the elevator, not the stairs, to the third floor. He stepped over the threshold and turned left, watching the numbers on the doors shrink until he found himself at room 318.

He unlocked the door and stepped inside. It was a nice room, much nicer than what he was used to. It would be most suitable for one night, and better still, it was free of charge. Setting down his armful of things onto the bed, he went back into the hall and back up to the fifth floor, where Santina was still working away inside one of the rooms, getting the creases out of the sheets, minding her folds, and cleaning the mirrors. She was like Annette, fastidious, raised in those very same strict Spanish households, which were immaculately kept by the women who ran them.

"Baby, I'm in 318," he said as he knocked on the door, giving her a quick startle.

She turned. "Okay, baby, I'll be there as soon as I can," she said, patting down the comforter.

Clyde went back to room 318 and threw himself spread-eagle onto the bed, furthest from the door. Kicking off his shoes, he sat up to take off his socks and unbuttoned the shirt he'd been wearing. He went over to the radio and turned on some music. Rock or Jazz or country music, anything was fine at this point. Lighting a cigarette, Clyde went over to the fridge for another beer, but it was still room temperature. That didn't stop him, they drank warm beer in Germany. Number three, down the hatch. He sat at the foot of the bed, chain smoking. Why was vice such a strong power? Why was he so defenseless against it? He remembered he had to call home and let his mama know he'd have the car until the afternoon. Reaching for the telephone, he rang home, and waited until somebody answered, and Annette was who answered.

"Hey, Ma it's me. Hey, I met Santina here at the hotel. Is it cool if I keep the car until tomorrow and bring it back late afternoon?"

The darling voice of Annette came through. "Yeah, baby, that's fine, just have it back before supper. I've gotta run into town to grab a few things. Do you need anything?"

Clyde thought for a few seconds. "You think you could pick up some bourbon?"

Annette laughed. "You are something else. I'm sure your daddy could go for a couple drinks. He'll have one with you. He's been talking about you all morning."

Clyde assured her he'd have the car back by tomorrow afternoon, and he'd be sure to give Pa a *proper* visit.

Cracking open his fourth one, Clyde walked about the room, the clock showing him he still had a few hours to kill until Santina was off of work. He sat down in a chair in the corner of the room and gingerly sipped this one, chain smoking Marlboro Reds, bare feet propped up on an old ottoman. He had briefly drifted off to sleep when he heard a knock on the door, which jolted him wide awake. Looking at the clock and realizing it was six o'clock sharp, he made himself ready and went over to open the door.

Santina was still wearing her work clothes but had her purse with her and her hair down. She was striking.

"Finally, that's over with. Long day for me!" She set down her things and looked at Clyde, who'd stood to greet her.

This man, she knew him, she recognized his face, she remembered his voice, which had been so soft on her once. The sweet things he used to say, the way he had loved her, which had her hooked on him from the start. They were quick to get married, young love, which had burned deep within the two of them. Those butterfly feelings they had felt when they were young, she couldn't help but still long for those things now, but deep down too, she feared things had changed with Clyde, she feared he would not let her love him. She knew him too well, and she knew just by looking at him, that he had been through a nightmare.

She followed the news, read the headlines, and she was filled with worry, just like Clyde's parents. She was grieving for him, unsure of his situation, and often fearing the worst. The pain of not hearing from him was a slap in the face of their marriage; she deserved to know he was alive at least. Heading to the shower, Santina undressed from her work clothes and stepped under the hot water, steam clouding around her. She washed her long, black locks, massaging the soap deep into her roots. She grabbed a wash towel and lathered up the suds, gently caressing along the curves of her slender frame. She enjoyed a relaxing steamer, but not wanting to keep him waiting too long, she turned off the water and grabbed a plush bath towel. She was drying her sopping wet hair off when the bathroom door began to creak, and Clyde poked his nose in.

"Clyde!" she exclaimed, and as quickly as he had poked his head in, he pulled it back out, both of them laughing with one another.

All their vulnerable feelings were still fresh. While they had known each other for a long time, coming back home after so many years, things couldn't help but feel new again. It was a strange anxiousness, mixed in with self-consciousness, wondering if things would be the same as they once were, but knowing that they could not be. For how could they?

Coming out with her towel draped over her breasts, exposing just her legs, she went to join Clyde where he lay on the bed. "You know, you don't have to talk about it with me if you don't want to," she said, tracing a finger on his chest. "I understand, ya know? I prayed for you all the time—" She flattened her hand. "—and waited for you, oh how I waited for you." Running her fingers along his muscular shoulders, he wrapped an arm around her to bring her in closer.

"I just don't have too much to say about it," Clyde said, looking down past her feet at the wall. "It was probably everything you'd heard anyways." He paused. "It was war." Bringing his eyes back to hers, he began to recount the horrid conditions.

"It was hot for one thing, every day, and if it wasn't hot, it was raining, and if it wasn't raining, well, we were getting eaten alive out there by all sorts of different things, mosquitoes and ants like you'd never seen, real messed up, real messed up," Clyde reiterated the last part, just to hit it home. "Then there were the people who lived there. They didn't want any of it either; they were just caught up in the middle of it like us."

The truth was, Clyde wasn't sure anybody would comprehend his pain. The tragedy of death. The confusion, mixed with guilt. To kill someone in war was a protected sin, by God, under one ultimate condition: It happened at his time and place of choosing. No bullet ever hit its mark without first being stamped with the Creator's approval. Though they fought not to get wrapped up in the ethics of it, they had to acknowledge the dilemma of their conscience. Out there was where personal morals were tested, but there could be no mercy for a merciless enemy. The laws of war were easily cast aside to make way for vengeance. They killed a few of the ones that surrendered and collectively agreed to never speak of it again.

Clyde focused on the woman lying beside him, knowing all his old woes were behind him. He played to her meek nature, taking the time to reassure her once more that he was here to stay.

"All that matters now, baby, is that I'm home and I'm yours," he said, looking down at her as he stroked her hair. She rested her head on his chest, the safest place she could have been. He faintly caught the scent of her vanilla perfume, remembering it was his favorite. Her soft chorus put him at ease, her heartbeat slowing down with his. Listening to her speak in those breathy whispers, like they did when they were kids, drove him crazy, back when they were trying not to get caught.

Pervasively high-strung as he was, he could *almost* relax when he was with her. Clyde sat with her and drank his cheap beer, and they caught up on a great many things. She told him about school, which she was paying for all by herself. She let him know how her parents were doing. Her dad had taken work in the city and had moved the whole family out there, and since she was staying with them while Clyde was gone, it only made sense that she followed her family. Clyde couldn't fault her for that. Fighting with the loneliness that Clyde's absence caused her, she admitted, was the hardest part. They talked about their future together and the beautiful things they believed it held.

Clyde went off to shower, cleaning himself up rather quickly. He hopped out of the steam that had just started to condense on the mirrors and went straight to bed, surprised to see the lights were already off and the ceiling fan was turned on.

He climbed into bed, sufficiently lacking any sort of nighttime attire, and he met his woman's own bare flesh. Her skin was cold, but that quickly changed, coiling themselves up into one another, him taking her, and her surrendering herself to him, longing for that feeling. They enjoyed the reward of their patience for some time into the night, indulging in the blissful ecstasy of one another, as if it were the very first time all over again.

Chapter 5

THE HOME WE BUILT

The first several months at home were pleasant, and with the help of his wife, who supported him through all the different changes and loved him through the fits of anger or depression, Clyde was able to find decent, steady work nearby that paid well. It was factory work, nothing fancy.

Joining the civilian workforce was a culture shock. It blew him away to see the line workers step off the line, cursing their managers out for not getting them their breaks on time. They called the bosses every name in the book, and they'd still get to keep their jobs. Gotta love union work! The work ethic was different as well. Clyde's attitude was optimistic, as he was making money and the people weren't too bad, and the work wasn't too bad either. It kept him sore the first couple of weeks, but his feet eventually callused over as he got used to walking on the concrete floor. Anytime it came around, he was signing up for overtime, thinking the more money they had, the better life would be.

After several months of saving and bouncing between his parents in Bossier and hers in NOLA, the two of them were able to afford themselves a small home outside of the city, with just enough land to have some privacy and seclusion from the relentless city beat. Louisiana was, and always would be, home for them, and at the end of a hard day on the job, Clyde would come home, have a six pack, and relax. Maybe something stronger if the day was hard. Santina would have something ready for supper, and the two of them would enjoy their evening meal, then go for an easy walk in the shadow of the weeping willow trees, or in the large garden that was Santina's laborious undertaking, where she carefully nursed heirloom tomatoes, cucumbers, jalapenos, onions, and leeks.

Sitting on the porch in their rockers, they would unwind together and finish out their day together in bed, side by side. Clyde and Santina held on to their honeymoon type of love for as long as they could.

But as time went on, a few beers turned into a few more, and the stronger drinks weren't just reserved for those hard days anymore. Clyde was no longer feeling that spark that life had once given him. The spark had died, and he found himself remembering the bad things from the war all over again. He'd get sentimental and feel dreadful nostalgia, lamenting over his bottle about the friends he made and lost. He missed the hardships, because even though they were trying and difficult times, they had made him the man that he was now. It had given him a sense of purpose, and now he felt ordinary, just a number in a long line of numbers, going to work day after day just to provide a modest life. Nothing Special. It was highly aggravating, but it was the American dream, and he couldn't give that up.

He was so young when all of his life fell into place, he wondered if this was all there was to it. All he needed to do was work for just thirty more years, and then what? Watch himself get older in the mirror with each passing birthday? He was like everybody else, everybody else who had dreams. Everybody else who ever wanted to be a movie star, or a musician, and like everybody else, watched as those dreams slowly died because they had to go to work, until eventually, work became the dream, and the old dream was gone.

He packed a lunch and went to work dutifully, always on time, always working hard and doing the right thing. But it nagged at him still, because Clyde couldn't help but feel like he was watching his potential disappear. The precious years of his youth would come and go all too fast, he thought, and the war in Vietnam was still going on! At the end of the day, when he made it back home from work, he'd be reminded of the family who loved him, the wife who supported him, the wholesome woman who nursed him along his road to recovery. Many nights he'd awake from terrible nightmares, and poor Santina was left trying her best to coax him back to safety.

Closing himself off was a self-preservation tactic, a defense mechanism he relied on his whole life. Shutting his emotions down, never revealing what it was he was really thinking or feeling. At work he was happy because the job was so repetitive, he could occupy his hands with his work and let his mind wander every which way. He'd lean into his work to keep himself distracted, working off his ghosts day by day. The same work, the same thing, *every single day*, for eight hours a day. He knew he was watching his youth and his dreams escape.

Clyde looked to booze to lift his moods, but it was only a temporary solution, for once he had more than he should have, he was right back to being the same asshole he always was. He wasn't a great husband when he was drinking. It made him lethargic, irritable, and only seemed to make him remember all the more what he was trying to forget. The pains and aches he lived with gave constant reminder of the years he spent pushing his body to the limit. He was still a young man; just aged sagaciously.

The months went by slowly at first, but then the year was over. Clyde and Santina spent Thanksgiving and Christmas at both sides, with both families hosting very festive parties with long tables of food and drink for family and friends. Indeed, spending holidays with family is what the holidays are all about. Keeping up the appearances of having it all together was important too. The two of them kept their problems at home behind closed doors, and instead of resolving their grievances with proper communication, Clyde shut down, when all Santina wanted to do was communicate. He, in his foolishness, couldn't see that she was trying to understand him better.

On the weekends, when she was home studying or taking care of things around the house, Clyde would go out with his friends, whom he'd recently reconnected with. Griping to them seemed to make the marital problems not exclusively his own. They went on fishing trips to Lake Pontchartrain, where they caught the best speckled trout. He'd let his hair grow out; disheveled and sporting a shorter black beard, he was a contrast image from the clean-cut, straight-edge soldier he used to be. He didn't care to maintain that stringent self-discipline he had practiced in his former life. There was no need for it; all he did was go to work with all the other nobodies. There was nobody for him to dress up for. After rolling out of bed, a T-shirt and jeans and he was out the door as is, keys in hand, still hungover from last night's drinking.

He held down his job, which at least helped him justify his case of functional alcoholism. The disgruntled young man didn't seem to care much about labeling his problem, as he only saw it as a way of settling his mind. The addiction cast darker clouds over an already darkened sky. When he looked in the mirror, he couldn't find himself, and he looked hard at the face, unused to seeing himself look like such a man.

After getting home from work and getting a couple of shots of whiskey in his system, Clyde would be all fun at first, active from the moment he stepped in the door, helping with the dishes or helping her beat the linens. Before supper, she had him, but once he ate his food—which he did very quickly, as a soldier does—and had his supper cocktail, then he'd be stuck on the sofa until he eventually passed out, sleeping the evening away on the loveseat until Santina came from her nightly reading and got under the dead weight of her drunk husband, dragging him physically to bed.

The weeks all looked the same, and it was this repetitive mode of living that had driven a wedge between them. It was the normal, humdrum existence that everyone was seemingly living and loving. Monotony is the great destroyer of young men, for when his sense of purpose is lost, he spends the rest of his life searching for that Holy Grail. For all his personal faults, all of his shortcomings, Clyde still tried. He heard her when she spoke, and her words cut him, because he knew she was right, because her words were the truth. He *did* have a problem, and rather than sweep things under the rug or shove another skeleton in the closet, she knew that dealing with their issues head-on would be the best thing for them. That being honest and open would save them. He did try, but he took one step forward and two steps back. He'd forget she needed affection. She was just a girl, she'd say; he could be sweet to her, and it would be okay. It was only love that she needed, but the poor thing had found herself married to somebody completely different now.

One day, Santina finally reached her breaking point. She had enough of him not being himself. Tired of his drinking, tired of his lack of effort, his inability to love her the way she needed to, and tired of carrying the weight of their relationship alone, in an act of love, Santina hatched an idea.

Chapter 6

A HARD TALK

"I'm over it, Clyde!" she yelled with frustration from across the kitchen.

Clyde, taken aback, had just walked in the front door after getting home from work.

Angrily she continued, arms crossed over her nightgown. "You want to come in here drunk again after we've already talked about the drinking," she fumed, her Latin blood hot with rage. "We've talked about this, Clyde!" The poor thing was heading towards a cry. "I don't even know you anymore. You need help, and I can't do it. I don't know how."

The levee that was holding back the full force of her tears finally broke. He made her grind her teeth. He made her want to pull her hair out.

Clyde paused at the front door, motionless, with a stupid drunken grin appearing on his face. She launched a slipper in his direction, the flimsy footwear causing him no real pain.

"Baby, please, don't be mad, okay? Please, don't be mad. Really, it's Friday night. I do this every Friday night," he pleaded, starting to slur his speech. "I just wanted to hang out with the fellas was all. It's all good, baby, it's all good." He held his hands up in defense. "I'm not even that drunk." As if on cue, some unknown force tangled his feet, and he drunkenly stumbled over them trying to take off his muck boots.

Santina was angry, and fearlessly stood directly in front of him, looking up at him while she raged, forcing him to hold himself together in fear of making matters worse. "You drink after work, you drink when it's the weekend, you don't communicate with me, you don't care about me or how I feel, you're selfish, and you only want to do what you want to do, and if it's something you're not interested in, then you can't be bothered to do it or even think about doing it!"

Shuffling in his socks over to the fridge, he pulled out a cold glass bottle of Coca-Cola and tuned her out.

"I have tried to get you to straighten up. Now it's a problem, and your friends are a problem too," she said, pointing her finger in his face. "I don't know why you push me away so much. I just want to help you. You're sick! You're sick, and you need help!"

Drinking his cola as he lounged in the recliner chair, her words went in one ear and out the other, the old crone nagging away again. Finally, wishing for it to relent, he mustered the courage to step inside the ring. "Yeah? And what kind of help do you think is going to help me? Huh?" he said, the aggravation rising up, though he fought to suppress it. "You think some head shrink somewhere sitting me down on a couch and talking to me about my feelings is going to fix me?" he said, unempathetic and cold. "I'm tired of it too," he said, looking over at her from the recliner. "Tired of you giving me this bullshit all the time."

He didn't mean to be such a jerk. Once upon a time, he was sweeter on her than anybody else had ever been, sweeping her off her feet after graduation, despite her abundant admirers, unwilling to let his soulmate go anywhere else in life without him. He couldn't bring himself to tell her of his deepest wounds. He walked around the world with hollow eyes, a far-off, lusterless look. In dormant anger over the betrayal of his countrymen, remembering how when he returned, they cast him aside, not wanting to look at the monsters they had made.

Only God would hear him on those long commutes to work, and at night as he lay there in bed. That was when he confronted those tragedies. Staring at the ceiling, eyes open to the darkness, praying for forgiveness, begging for mercy when it came to Judgment Day, sinking into the depths of his hauntings, and thinking lament-filled monologues to the Lord during the day, hoping that God could still hear his thoughts, for they were thoughts he could not speak aloud.

Tears fell from his eyes, because the little boy inside was crying for help too, but he didn't know who else to turn to. If even his prayers had gone unanswered, he knew help was beyond him.

She knew he was hurt; she could see it spread on him. How could he not be, having gone through all the herculean labors of his life in just a few short years?

"No, you aren't going to see a 'head shrink,' Clyde," she said, making air quotations with and squinting her eyes in jest. She stood there, arms crossed, looking at him with disappointed brown eyes like his ma used to give him any time he wandered in too late or too high.

"You're going to go see Ms. Claudia," she said, eyes ablaze, her cheeks rouge, she wore the cute floral nightgown Clyde bought her for Valentine's Day.

Across the family room, he turned his head. "Ms. Claudia?" he said, iterating it again slowly, questioning the name, raising his brow.

"Yes, dear, Ms. Claudia LeBlanc, she's the one you're going to go see, and *you* are going this weekend."

Clyde was confused. The ball had been thrown into left field, and he sat diagonally bewildered.

"She's going to help you, and help me. She's going to fix us," Santina said.

Turning toward the mantle, where she kept several saints, she spoke wildly her Spanish Caribbean tongue, saying prayers quickly, and in succession, making the sign of the cross over her chest and closing her eyes, pacing short steps back and forth inside the living room.

Clyde sat perplexed, finding himself wondering more about the identity of the mystery woman who would help him break his curse.

"Whoa, whoa, what're you doing all that for? What's all this?" Clyde said, laughing off the strange antics of his wife, whispering to the sepulcher. Standing up from the recliner, Clyde finished his non-alcoholic beverage, now feeling relieved, for the argument was ending. Granted, there was a catch to his being let off the hook. The air in the room was now slightly less stifled, and in his drunken, wobbly blur, he wandered over to the kitchen to toss the empty can and run some cool water over his face.

Santina, collecting herself, made her way over to his recliner, making herself comfortable in his well-worn seat. Sweeping her black hair behind her ears, the rage within her came to a simmer. "Ms. Claudia comes highly recommended to the women around here. She's a powerful *bruja*, who fixes husbands for their wives. The ladies at work were talking about her. Women send their husbands to Ms. Claudia for a session or two, and she helps them figure out their issues. She gets them to see the changes they need to make, and shows them the path they are meant to be on. She has great power to sway even the most wicked of men back to being sweethearts. The ladies at work think she could help you, with your drinking and with all the stuff from the war. I want you to go see her, Clyde." She grabbed his hands. "Let's give magic a try."

The ball went past left field and out into space. This was completely unexpected, out of the blue. Never in a million years would Clyde have guessed *his wife* would recommend he go see a witch doctor, but he felt pulled by the idea, drawn to the unique arrangement for some reason.

"You mean she does Voodoo or something?" Clyde asked. Being as he was from Louisiana, his simple upbringing taught him that spell work, rituals, potion brewing, and curses was the work of Voodoo, which was taboo for him growing up in the church.

"No, baby, it's not Voodoo; it's something else," Santina said, further elaborating, "She just sits you down and brings it all out, all the bad, all the evil energy. I really don't know how to explain it; she just shows you the bigger picture, I guess. She's a very powerful woman."

Clyde was listening now. Using the kitchen island to help himself stand upright, he rested his elbows on its flat surface. Oddly, the idea strongly appealed to him. He was not familiar with Voodoo, but he also knew that all the praying he'd been doing hadn't been doing him any good as far as he could tell. He was stuck in his job, his wife wasn't happy, their home felt like a cage, and he felt like a burden to her and to his family. He knew he needed to quit drinking, but for Clyde, it was so easy to just come home and drink away the problems, drowning the skeletons so he could forever wipe clean his knowledge of their existence.

He could better handle the drudgery of the American dream, he could better tolerate the monotony, the repetitive motion of putting one foot in front of the other. When he drank, his body ached less, and he felt like he was more light of heart, but he was the only one who saw it that way.

"Okay, let's say I do go and give this lady a shot. What if nothing happens? Are you going to leave me if I don't stop drinking?" Clyde asked, the serious question making her think, while he stood fearing he'd been faced with an ultimatum. Santina looked sorry, with her sad brown eyes. The truth would just add insult to injury. But she couldn't keep going; she had to stand firm with her resolutions. Santina knew in her heart that anything was worth a shot at this point, religious dogma or not. The other ladies swore by it, so why not? Why should she have to continue suffering? She didn't see him having a problem agreeing to her terms, as he was the one in the doghouse. And besides, what harm could come from a therapy appointment with a witch? She'd be lucky if he took it remotely seriously.

In subtle tones she spoke callously,- "I *will* leave you if you don't change, Clyde. Somebody else will treat me the way I want to be treated." She slid down into a defeatist slump, hands clasped in front of her as she sat opposite him. Maybe it was the ultimatum he needed, one that would stir his former fight, when in days not so far in the past, his life depended on it. It was likewise here; their marriage depended on his effort, and he strongly felt the pull of change, as if the very seasons of his life were changing in front of him.

He listened, not looking at anything in particular, just falling once more into that comfortable stare, where his thoughts were private and quieted. No anger within him; he couldn't begrudge her for wearing her heart on her sleeve. She had been honest and truthful and even proposed a solution. It was his fault, and he knew that he'd been downward spiraling for months. It was only right for him to make the change, once and for all, and for good this time. All the circumstances of his life were laid bare in these moments of desolate awareness as he seemingly looked at nothing. He yielded to her reasonable demands, the room spinning as his forehead started to get hot.

"All right, baby, sure. I'll play along." was all Clyde said.

She sighed a sigh of relief. "Great."

What it would entail, he did not know. What good could come of it, who knew? For his Santina, who'd been put through so much these last couple of years, he would put his pride to the side and give change a try.

"Ms. Claudia works at a boutique on the corner of Saint Anne, off of Bourbon Street; it's not flashy or anything. It's unassuming. It's a brick building with black shutters and big red canopy out front. You can't miss it. You have to go there and ask the person behind the counter if Ms. Claudia is seeing any patients." She paused her instruction, making sure it registered. "That's the code phrase," she continued, Clyde nodded along, actively listening.

"She'll schedule an appointment with you, and you guys can go from there. Sound good?"

It was a lot to take in, given his current state of inebriation, but Clyde made good on his keen memory and took a mental note of all she had said, giving all the necessary attention to detail. He too was feeling good about it and was determined to make a change happen, though he still wasn't quite sure what she was getting him into. Talk of Voodoo was a big deal; he couldn't tell anyone about it, for fear of ostracization. It was witchcraft, and the fact that Santina had been the one to bring it up threw him for the wildest loop of them all, since she was a devout Catholic. Such was her frustration that she turned her back to the light and turned toward the darkness.

It was spells and curses and potions and all sorts of other made-up, superstitious garbage that he really didn't take very seriously. Nor had he given any real thought to the spiritual retributions that might be provoked by the employment of such things as the dark arts. He should have paid more attention growing up; he'd have known Voodoo was everything but his own ignorant misconceptions. Clyde wasn't afraid of anything anymore. He had made his peace with dying a long time ago, and with it, he lost much of his faith in God. It was a travesty, given how much time and effort his parents put into instilling into their family the lordly light. Religion was the cornerstone of any strong family foundation, especially in the South, especially in Bossier.

"Yes, ma'am, copy all, thank you," he said, coming over to her and placing his hands on her delicate shoulders, lifting her chin so he could look her directly in the eyes.

"Hey, I'm sorry, I am, I mean it. I can change, really."

Clyde searched for gentle mercy in her puffy red eyes, which she just rolled as she bid him good night.

He took a seat at the dinner table to be left alone with his thoughts; the room had been spinning for quite some time, and he knew it was his bedtime as well. He went to the bedroom, put on his long johns, and crawled into bed with his wife, unshowered, unshaved, and needing to be up for work in a few hours. He lay down with his next moves in mind, and Clyde LeBouef was determined he would make good on his promises this time.

Falling into a deep slumber, tucked tightly in the plush white comforter and quilted throw blankets, Clyde rested, alive and warm. A vivid dreamer, his subconscious mind went awry as his imagination played for him starkly lucid pictures of green valleys and foreign-looking cliffs. Deserts with flowered cactus and vultures swooping down from above to feast on the carcasses of decaying animals. The poor doe, who once in the prime of her life had been a stark reminder of the goodness and purity in nature, carrying the gentle heart of soft things in this world, now lost to time, predators, disease; there could be no saying which.

All must go to a place where one knows not where one goes, yet knows go, we all must.

Even the deer, who on light feet, saw the world as her Easter basket, fearing only what nature told her to. They would eat the leaves and enjoy the verdant wilderness, but nature had not prepared them for the arrival of the hunter. The hot sun beat down on exotic jungle, the canopy an emerald kaleidoscope, with every element of nature accounted for, earth and wind, fire and water, a dream so lucid, in a place he swore he must've been before. The towering crags, and long, open valleys, where all natural life could thrive without the pestilence of man to spoil her. The heavy rains brought gushing water into the canyons by great rivers, whose many tributaries carried the current toward crystal flowing rapids, scorched in an unrelenting heat, to be cooled again under lunar light. In the daytime, the sun dried the land, and at night, the moon filled up the empty reservoirs with her magical tides, pulling from every corner of the globe to fill the sunken streams and bring water back to the world. Stretching herself thin, she had all day to prepare for her nightly charge. Coyotes arrive, and the birds scurry away, the clutches of canine teeth make off with what's left. He wakes up then suddenly, in a jolt, as he'd done since '68. Dreams he rarely could recall most of the time, despite putting a dreamcatcher next to his bedside.

Clyde woke up and went to work like any other normal morning. Now no one wants to work, but work is good for the spirit, and he leaned into his work to take out the frustrations of life. If they all had to suffer, then his suffering would at least be in prideful silence, with the ironic chagrin of one who knows there's no escaping the machine. The only thing that made work better were the ladies. They made the air smell better, the atmosphere lighter, and made him work harder. He always worked harder when they were around.

He took his breaks alone, though, sitting in the corner, reading his books, getting away from his thoughts and diving into his imagination. Those brief indulgences of solitary entertainment let Clyde dream he was someone else. He could be on a whaling ship, deep in the Arctic, or a Hindu pilgrim, moving through the vast Himalayan tundra. Reading was good for him; it exercised his mind and kept him sharply versed. His father, a self-taught man, taught his children that reading was fundamental and an essential practice. Always pulling from his French folk wisdom, and his backwater bayou roots, Lawrence had many words of practical wisdom for his children or the misfortunate passerby.

At the end of the day, driving home was his decompression, leaving the hard day's work behind. Doing his best to switch his mindset to that of the attentive, affectionate husband, who upon returning from his daily obligation, longed for the company of his dearly beloved. Every day was the same, and the lack of surprises was good, because he didn't care for change, but he'd try it for Santina. Generally, once Clyde figured out the best way to do something, he'd do it the same way every time, and his way became the only way to do it. Breaking routine unnerved him to no end, as Clyde could be a control freak, which was more to blame on his obvious but undiagnosed and untreated obsessive-compulsive disorder. He expected the house orderly and clean, and if it wasn't, then Clyde had something smart to say, and she'd be disappointed all over again, losing confidence that he was making progress, and in herself. She wasn't smiling as much. All they could do to get through weeks like this was just make it to Friday.

Make it to the weekend.

Chapter 7

VOODOO WOMAN

Rain pattered the sidewalk as Clyde made his way up Bourbon Street. The air was musty, and the humidity thick, carrying the smell of roasting coffee and Cajun herbs, the salty Gulf air, the smell of food, the senses relished, bringing alive his salivary glands. Shuffling along with his hands in his pockets, Clyde scanned up and down the sidewalk, taking in all the different characters as he passed them by. People were still out and about despite the rain, families carrying umbrellas around to protect their hair and their kids. Clyde never really understood family trips to the French Quarter, as it could be and usually was a highly debaucherous place. It was a touristy party city, and despite the inclement weather, the tourists refused to flush their dollars down the toilet of a hotel by letting a little rain ruin their highly anticipated trips. Parading around in their costumes, with their makeup running down their carnival-painted bodies, they carried home their cheap plastic souvenir cups.

This was his home, and these people were here on holiday. While they welcomed all to come see the highly sophisticated exhibitions of French Colonial design, the visitors oohed and aahed, but generally showed little appreciation for, or desire to understand the roots of their culture, the history associated with the world-famous architecture. Passing the strangers and the bums still drunk in the gutters, Clyde carried on towards his destination.

Through the slow drizzle falling from the gray skies above, he made it to the corner of Saint Anne's and Bourbon Street, where off to the side he saw the red brick building with the black shutters and red canopy. A flickering red neon sign said *open*, and the poster in the window read "Ms. Claudia's Magnifique Boutique." Yep, this was the place.

Squaring himself away and flicking the cigarette from his hand, he walked in through the stained-glass door, which rang with windchimes from the other side as he pushed it open. The bell on the counter rang in unison as he walked in through the front door. He saw racks of colorful and stylish clothes, mostly a combination of vintage and modern fashions, gowns and dresses, slacks and skirts, beauty goods, bonnets, creams, handmade soaps, and sun hats. All to entice the fairer sex to shop, with their looser coin purses. Everything was placed very neatly in the shop, which Clyde admired. It was an immaculately clean business front, a level of cleanliness that when compared to the other stores and shops on the famous avenue was applaudable. Inside, the walls were painted yellow and orange, and the ceiling green, with a refined collection of art hung up on the walls. The air was rich with oxygen, due the gazillion house plants they fit in the place. The very atmosphere was refreshing, reminiscent of stepping foot inside the work of Monet. It was a richly classy boutique. Oil paintings, black-and-gray portraits of the old French Quarter, stylish nudes and models, as well as finely dressed mannequins stood in pose, roguish.

Rather than being subject to the endless window shopping of their wives, the husbands chose to wait outside. This gave the housewives the freedom to take their time, and taking things off the racks in armfuls, they'd soon be off to the dressing rooms, spending big money and lining Claudia's pockets. The beauty industry was turning out to be a highly profitable business, but apparently, she was running more than just a classy boutique.

Clyde shuffled in, wiping his feet on the rug at the entrance, so as not to bring in any muck or debris. Walking past the racks of merchandise, looking around, he played the part of the curious customer, all the way up to the front desk.

A porcelain-pale redhead, with a head of hair so wild, rakish, and thin stood behind the counter, greeting him with a big-toothed smile. She spoke to Clyde as he approached the counter. "Hello Monsieur, help you find anything?"

Clyde saw a young woman dressed like any other of these hippie types, informing her he had no intentions of shopping, but had a different reason for being there that day. "Actually, sweetheart, I'm here for something not in the display," Clyde began. "I was wondering if Ms. Claudia is seeing any patients?" he asked, leaning up against the counter, speaking this in a casual whisper.

Her eyes widened, and she shook her head, understanding now what he was here for. "Oh, you're here to see Claudia. Give me one second, sugar." She stepped through the unassuming door behind the cashier's counter, which more than likely led to the back or the basement. After a moment, she reappeared, motioning for Clyde to come with her this time. He lifted the little plank divider separating the counter from the wide-open space of the store and followed her through the door. Inside was a staircase leading down into the basement. The stiff wooden planks creaked and moaned under their combined weight. It was a dimly lit corridor, and she took him by his hand as she slowly descended the steep staircase, which turned his cheeks red.

"My name's Ruby. What's your name, mister?" she asked in a giddy, girlish voice.

"Clyde, sweetheart. Pleasure to meet you."

They continued down the steps, blue hues now coming from under the landing. At the bottom of the stairs was a beaded door, leading to the large basement of the old brick building. Sweeping the multicolored strings of plastic beads aside, Clyde glanced around the room, making quick notes of everything he saw at once. There was a thick, rolling smoke in the air, part incense, part tobacco, with a cup of tea on the side. Elaborately crafted ottomans and plush-looking sofas decorated the space, with cushioned high-top chairs placed around the big bar for seating. The bar itself had on it a variety of spirits; beer, wine, half-drank bottles of tequila and whiskey. He spied a glass case behind the bar which held a decanter glowing green with absinthe, the devil's knockout.

The room was lit with blue light bulbs, long black lights that illuminated the psychedelic colors of the posters and tapestries depicting celestial art, poses of women, animals, and mushrooms. More plants were hung from the walls, and a bust of breasts sat on a marble pillar. Several shag rugs tied the room together.

He approached the centerpiece of the room, which was a round beige sofa, with an ornate Turkish hookah pipe set in the middle on the table, still burning. In the center was the coffee table, a short, hexagonal table with purple felt that had tarot cards still open from a recent spread, empty shot glasses leaving still a small ring of moisture underneath the glass. The ashtrays were full, and he could hear the scratch of a jazz vinyl record playing in the back.

Lying down on the sofa, with one elbow propping up her head and one meaty leg bent, Claudia pulled a great cloud of smoke through the hose of her hookah, then breathed a cherry-scented cloud into the air as she spoke to Clyde for the first time. "Hello, dear," she said in a voice that sounded witchy. "I've been waiting for you."

Giving him a cheeky smirk through slitted, carnivorous eyes, she sat up and turned to spy him like a black widow who'd just caught a fly. She was wearing blue Bollywood pants, barefooted, with black toenail polish that glowed white under the blacklight and gold anklets that loosely caught the eye. She wore a long, flowy white-and-blue blouse, which exposed her midriff and her cleavage. Her long, black curls wrapped on top of her head in a bun, and she wore a terracotta headband, the mark of a more exotic blood. The lady's gold rosary lay next to her Tibetan Mala beads that occasionally got snagged by the crease of her cleavage.

"You've been expecting me, huh?" he started, approaching the circular sofa, looking at the weird piece of hexagonal furniture that the hookah was resting on. It must have been the witch's reading table.

"Well, here I am," he said, pausing near the bar, "Clyde LeBouef, ma'am. It's nice to meet y—"

She cut him off. "Oh, stop calling me ma'am. You don't have to say that, you don't even know me yet. But I know you. Yes, I've scryed you in my crystal ball, Clyde LeBouef, soon you will know who you are too. Please, come sit," and she ushered for Clyde to join her. "I can take it from here, Ruby, thank you."

Ruby went back upstairs to see to the patrons whose money was continuing to burn holes in their deep pockets. Clyde walked over to the sofa, inspecting it as he did so.

"You have to step over it, honey," she said as she lay back down, taking another long pull off the coiled hookah hose.

Clyde tried to break up the awkwardness with casual conversation. "This is quite the place you've got here. I dig all this, uhhhh, you know with like the art and stuff, very cool."

She squinted her eyes and lifted her cheeks when she smiled. "Thank you, Clyde. As for proper introductions, I am Ms. Claudia, it's my divine privilege to meet you as well." She stuck her beautifully sculpted hand out for a handshake.

Clyde grabbed it gently, observing the gold rings she wore, which stood out against her cinnamon complexion, the way his mother's did. Red and gold was, after all, a preferred royal color combination.

"Clyde LeBouef?" she said, holding his grip there, longer than usual, looking deep into his coffee eyes.

He could not break away from her power, convinced in that moment that she had ensnared him in her black-light eyes, smiling a fluorescent-white smile. He struggled to find his voice, but after a second of composing his thoughts, he spoke what was on his mind. "I understand you work with husbands, well, from what my wife told me anywa—"

She cut him off once more. "Would you care for some hookah, sweetie?"

Put off by her habit of interruption, he mustered a polite and friendly response. "Uh yeah, sure. Never done it before, but I'll give it a try."

She giggled excitedly, clapping her hands. "Oh good, good. Here, come take it like this. Yeah, yep, and inhale, deep deep inhale straight to the lungs. Suck it down, dear, here you go, yes, good job."

Clyde sucked up the cherry-flavored tobacco vapor, pleasantly surprised at the taste, and exhaled the thick plume of smoke, which started a spasmodic coughing fit. This brought Ms. Claudia great amusement, as she enjoyed the hilarity of watching somebody with virgin lungs fight through the harsh, burning chokes.

"Yes, Mr. LeBouef, I do work with husbands. It's my life's work. I've been practicing my craft for many, many years now," she said as she sat with her legs crossed in front of her.

Playing to flattery, Clyde thought maybe he could win her over before the session started. "Well, certainly it can't be that many years. You hardly look older than thirty," Clyde said, his attempt at flirtation not going unnoticed.

"Now I see why you've been sent to see me," she said.

Clyde nervously laughed, fidgeting in embarrassment.

"All jokes aside, Mr. LeBouef, what *can* I do for you? What have you sought my assistance for?" She leaned back, taking another drag off her hose, with Clyde taking a pull from his, getting slightly dizzy after the exhalation.

"Well, umm right, yes, well ma'am, let me tell you a little bit of background on myself first. How about that?" he asked, hearing the Creole in his voice he knew he could thank his mother for.

"I did three tours in 'Nam. The first two were rough, but the last one really did me in. I've been back a while now, but it messed up my mind, being over there. Been through hell, and I mean *really* been through hell. And I've been having a hard time of it since," he said, hunched over with his elbows on his knees, clasping his hands in front of him, defeated, here truly seeking help dealing with his lot in life.

"I drink a lot, to forget about it, and my wife wants me to quit, and I know I need to." He hesitated to continue. "It's hard to say, but I'm tired of feeling trapped. I get flashbacks, and I feel like I'm reliving it all over again. It's affecting my marriage, and we've decided that I can't do it on my own. So, I need help, and I don't know if you've worked with people like me before, but I told her I'd do anything you said, and fingers crossed, hope you fix me. I know it's Voodoo, but I'm willing to try it."

Ms. Claudia, a woman who had taken off the chains of living with mere mortals and had the power within to convene with lost spirits, gave a crackling laugh that knocked her head back. She was clapping her hands as she keeled over with laughter. Once she finally composed herself, she gave him his answer. "You may call it whatever you like, Mr. LeBouef, but I can assure you, it's not Voodoo, and yes, I've worked with many others like you." She uncrossed her legs and leaned forward. "After all, all men are the same, are they not?" She smiled. Clyde remained taciturn, undaunted by her games.

"I am a bruja, big difference."

Clyde wasn't exactly sure what the difference was, but whatever.

"I'm free next Saturday, I want you to come around 6:30, and I'll need a ten-dollar cash payment from you at the door.

"Ten bucks?" It sounded steep.

"Oh yes, honey, I'm serious," she said, giving him the nectarine look of a mystifying Calliope. "You can handle that, can't you, baby?"

Clyde begrudgingly agreed to the terms.

"Make sure you're sober. You can see yourself out. I'll see you next week. Don't be late."

Clyde stood to shake her hand once more. She held hers out limply, and Clyde grabbed it limply, gentleman to lady. He thanked her for the road buzz and gave her a bow as he turned to step over the sofa, making his way back up the stairs, letting the handrail lead him on his way up. He opened the door back into the main room of the boutique, and the bright light of daytime assaulted his eyes, constricting his pupils, the harsh glare causing him to squint. People were still shuffling about, and Ruby was in front of him, leaning over the counter.

"Oh, you're back. How'd it go?" she asked, turning around to see the clearly disconcerted, clearly high Clyde LeBouef.

"Went good," he said, tipping his hypothetical hat. "I'll see ya next week."

She smiled too, a bewitching grin that revealed a gold-capped tooth he didn't see before. "Don't be late."

He walked out the door, the chimes eventually falling out of earshot.

Chapter 8

LET THEM GO

Arriving back home late in the evening, Clyde had some time on his hands, given he was off work for the day. Walking through the front door, he was greeted by the smells of a warm supper cooking. The house had been thoroughly cleaned, and things were tidy and in their proper places. The way he always liked it. The home was the reflection of the owner, he believed. Clyde hadn't been expecting company, but his old friend Robbie had stopped by, bringing along James Little and Louis Smith. The trio jumped from behind the wall separating the kitchen and the main room, giving a boisterous shout of "Surprise!"

"Holy hell!" Clyde shouted, his body naturally recoiling from the shock. These men were lucky he was so sharp. "So, that's what the cat dragged in!" Clyde said once he recognized his childhood friends, now grown men the same as he. After giving hugs and handshakes to the old gang, they announced the reason for their visit, which was unexpected but welcome.

"Yeah, man, after I saw ya the other day, I figured since we were in the city, we might as well look you up in the Yellow Pages and pop our heads in! Santina said you'd be back for supper, so we figured we'd wait around if it was cool with her," said Robbie, he'd bumped into Clyde in the street just a week or so ago.

"You know, man, just making sure you're doing good and all," Robbie said, his eyes drifting off toward the others, as they too took in the sight of their troubled friend.

James and Louis were other friends of Clyde's; they'd all been close in high school, running around and getting into petty juvenile troubles. It was nice to see them. It had been a few years, and Clyde hadn't really bothered to keep tabs on everyone since he left Bossier for the second time.

"Welcome home, baby," Santina said, coming from the kitchen to give him a kiss. "Supper's almost ready, I told them they could stick around if they wanted to." She had taken the day off to catch up on the household responsibilities, and to make his return from the appointment pleasant.

"Oh, now ma'am, we told you we couldn't stick around," Robbie interjected, pausing Santina in the midst of offering her friendly gesture, not wanting to wear out their welcome.

"Clyde, we're down here for a few days doing some fishing. I asked if her it was okay for you to come on down with us tomorrow, be at the river all day." Louis said. He was the older brother of James, and the more outspoken of the two.

"Supposed to be a good weekend, from what the weatherman was sayin', hoping to catch some big ones. We can fry 'em up right there," said James, the introverted version of his skinnier big brother.

"Well, long as it's all right with the missus, I would see no problem with it. It'd be good for me to get out of the house, whaddya say, Ma?" Clyde asked.

"Yes, that's fine, just don't have too much fun."

Clyde knew those to be the words of his mother, spoken anytime she tried to convince Clyde to follow the more righteous paths; but knowing full well she couldn't control him, she more or less spoke it to herself.

Clyde knew there'd be booze, and probably a lot of it, but he knew too that he wasn't supposed to be drinking. Then he bargained that it had been several years since he saw his civilian comrades. It would make for a good time and a good excuse to have a little fun. Getting away from home every once in a while was okay, and he didn't want to wither away in his pajamas while there was fish waiting to be caught.

"All right, done deal. Where are you guys meeting up?" Clyde asked, pulling an ice-cold root beer from the refrigerator. They kept more soda in the house these days.

"Well, around 11:30 we're going to be at the park over in Bywater," Robbie said.

"Damn, that's a little early, isn't it?" Clyde broke in, taking off his boots as he sat down in his recliner, root beer in hand.

"Yeah, but we're doing a bonfire too, once the sun goes down. It'll go by faster than you think, boss man," Robbie said.

"All right, yeah man, sure. I'll meet y'all there," finished Clyde, standing up to give his friends their farewell. He bid them proper goodbyes, and then there were only two of them left in the lonely kitchen, preparing to savor their private banquet.

"See, that'll be good for you, Clyde," she said, holding the fork to her lips, taking in a mouthful of the food she'd sweated over the stove for. "They're just trying to get you out of the house."

They took their evening lover's stroll among the cypress and willows outside, hand in hand. Her gentle, thin arms swinging with his, as they conversed together among the cricket chirps, cicada song, and bustle of leaves in the breeze.

"How did it go with Ms. Claudia? I've never seen her. What did she look like?" asked Santina.

"Well, she was different," Clyde began. "She looked like a gypsy I thought, but she's got a really nice place. Coupled with her unique side business, I'd say she's got quite an operation. Nice clothes and gifts, hey, you might dig it," he said, cleverly knowing the ladies in his life to never shy away from retail therapy.

"Next Saturday at 6:30, and don't be late," he said, mocking the bruja's last words.

At the end of their walk, Santina's curiosity fully quenched, they went back inside to tidy up the blankets in the living room, put away the dishes still on the counters, and then brush their teeth before getting into bed together. They grabbed their respective books off of their respective nightstands, and read until they got sleepy, then they turned to get comfortable, saying their good nights. As they swiftly fell asleep under the quilted blankets and the freshly washed comforter, the open windows let in the cool midnight air, with the song of nature, playing low outside their home, filling the space with the soft orchestra of God's creation.

Clyde always had vivid dreams, dreams he could wake up and remember, and if he felt like he might forget, he would write them down in a journal he kept in his nightstand before he forgot them. Unless they were bad dreams; he wouldn't bother interpreting those. He would rather forget it, but the subconscious mind had unresolved trauma to handle with him, and so this night, Clyde dreamed of his past, his haunted memories coming back to him all too clearly.

This dream was of a trip he and his squad had taken outside the wire on a patrol one night. His squad set in an ambush in the worst possible terrain they could find, deep behind enemy lines, hoping that if any gooks came by, they'd be too distracted dealing with the dense brush they were fighting against, and in their distraction, Clyde's boys would quietly dispatch them. This mission stood out in Clyde's memory because here he suffered a terrible scare that caused him immense anxiety. There they were, lying behind their weapons, prone and in their respective spots when they caught eyes on Charlie, moving slowly, almost a similar crawl, silently in the bush. They kept their heads down, listening as the sound of breaking brush grew louder and louder, closer and closer until they were practically on top of their position. Clyde's squad had rigged several claymores, and he lay there motionless with the detonator switch in his hand. It was a clicker, and Clyde was eager to take the safety off and click that sucker three times.

Doing so would send the signal down the det cord and trigger a devastating explosion. Waiting until a majority of the enemy force had been in the snare of the trap, Clyde watched with horror as the enemy troops kept coming, a much bigger force than they could take on. Sergeant LeBouef's heart shrank in his chest when he picked his head off the jungle floor to see there were hundreds of them walking straight towards them. Too many to fight on fair terms. Forced to lie there, still as salt, not even blinking. The enemy regiment needed to pass them, and they needed to remain undetected, or else it would be a bloody firefight. The severely outgunned LRRPs wouldn't stand a chance using conventional methods, and no one was more a master of guerilla warfare than these ones here, so he couldn't beat them at their own game either. They were practically stepping over top of Clyde's squad when suddenly the enemy forces gave halt. He remembered an NVA radioman saying something to one of his superiors, but then it was over, almost as soon as it began.

They never killed him in his dreams, but they freaked him out.

Clyde awoke from this nightmare in a cold sweat, screaming, as Santina grabbed hold of him and pulled him close, trying to calm him down. It took him a second to realize where he was, but Santina had dealt with this before, and coaxing him back to bed after a few minutes, this time, he slept straight through, unbothered and undisturbed in the arms of his wife.

The morning began like it usually did on the weekends, with a pot of strong coffee to rid the morning brain fog, shuffling to and fro, lazily tidying up the house as they scooted their slippers along the hardwood floors much in need of sweeping. The open windows had blown in a gentle jasmine perfume and let in the white fluffies from the fields outside. Clyde didn't have much to do today, and he still had a week until his meeting with Ms. Claudia, so it would be a good day to catch up on the household obligations.

He liked a *clean* house. He was admittedly hard to please, thus very hard to live with and get along with.

Everything had a place; leaving things strewn about aggravated him to no end. He didn't like clutter. Dishes in the sink drove him mad. Clyde liked to finish up the chores early on the weekends. That way he didn't have to think about them for the rest of his relaxation time. He couldn't procrastinate, as this too would just sit in the back of his mind, and he'd fixate on whatever the matter was, whether it be the lawn needing to be mowed, the trash going out, or the house being in need of a cooperative deep clean.

Clyde went out to check the mailbox. It was just the usual bills, junk mail, and advertisements, no newspaper yet, but in the midst of checking his mail, he noticed a stamped letter addressed to him. That was curious but not uncommon; he exchanged correspondence with his dad from time to time, but he didn't frequently give out his address. Checking the sender address, he noticed it was from his brother Dean, who was writing to him all the way from sunny San Francisco, California. His heart jumped to hear from his dear brother again.

Dean had been in the army years before Clyde, but he had still done a tour, in '66. His face was burned and speckled with dots of pale-white scar tissue from standing too close to exploding ordnance, which his doctors determined to be grave enough to send him home. After the war, he came back promising to live on a beach for the rest of his life.

Clyde's mood was lifted at this, as he hadn't heard from his brother in years. Clyde was the youngest of five siblings, and he hadn't heard from any of them. Nobody wrote to him while he was gone, and further distance and divide grew within the once-close family. He didn't take it personally, as is the case with having a larger family. Once everyone gets older and people begin their own lives, eventually those times spent differently in periods past now become long, lonely memories.

The sweltering heat of the day came with the morning sun. Santina was inside, opening all the windows in hopes of letting even a small breeze in their humble home as she prepared breakfast.

"Santina, guess what! I got a letter from Dean! All the way from the coast! He must've gotten our address from Pa."

Clyde sat down, propped up his feet and began to peel back the envelope, pulling out the paper nestled away inside, folded neatly. Eagerly opening it up, he got comfortable and began to read.

June 23rd, 1971

Dear Clyde,

How you doing buddy! I heard you made it home! Welcome back brother. I'm sorry I haven't reached out. I've been busy getting things going out here, I just wanted to write to you so you'd have my address, and to check in with you. I know it was hard over there, but I don't need to know anything, and I don't want to know anything unless you need to talk.

Whatever man, it's been too long, and we need to close the distance. Maybe you can come stay with us for a bit if you need a vacation, hell, if you ever need anything, don't hesitate to write! I love and miss you, I hope this letter finds you well. Looking forward to your reply.

Love, your brother, DL.

"Well, hot damn!" said Clyde, taking his feet down off the table. "Dean wants us to come visit him in California." he said, holding the letter still in both of his hands like a lottery ticket.

"Oh God, that would be so nice. I've never been to the beach!" Santina said, her eyes lighting up over the thought of Azul *Pacifica*. "If I lived there, I would never get tired of the sunshine, or the heat. I'd bake like a lizard on a rock." She laughed, and they laughed together as she brought over a couple of fully dressed plates to the table. She'd even picked up some beignets. "Come get some, it's ready."

Over breakfast, Clyde expressed many thanks for her love and for the meal, and afterward, he went out to the porch to smoke a cigarette and read the paper, which had now just arrived, the paperboy making his usual rounds late as usual. People had no consideration for other people's time anymore, Clyde thought to himself, pulling on his Marlboro Red and rocking back and forth in his rocking chair, reading the headlines, obituaries, and catching up on his world affairs to the tune of passing cars and windchimes.

Clyde hated the news, but he liked to be informed. He hated to see the state of postwar America. Not like the Greatest Generation, who came back from WWII and went straight to the factories to feed their families. No, this generation had the anti-war protests and love-ins, with wildly bizarre drugs surging into the mainland, all circulating around the growing counterculture movement, while the people sang lyrics of revolution. The old-timers were being pushed out, and that's what it was. Their war was better; they worked harder. Each generation has the same to say of the one before. Vietnam was still making headlines, but nobody read them anymore except the families longing for their brothers, fathers, husbands, and sons.

The American dream was a beautiful thing to work for, to strive for, the idea that each man be given his fair shake. But not everyone was dealt a fair hand, and some people were not created equal. Clyde believed in hard work, but he also believed in being highly self-critical. He knew he could work harder, be better, do more. Always pushing himself, always working because he knew people were watching him, people depended on him, and he had the future of his unborn children to think about.

Wrapping up with his morning paper, Clyde fixed himself for the day, getting dressed, and taking care of a few other chores around the house. Early evening, he'd start getting ready for his rendezvous with his buddies in the Bywater, because he couldn't make it earlier; he didn't feel like it. He'd go for the fire.

Three p.m. rolled around, and having had a productive day at the house, Clyde showered and got dressed in his new look. He caved to pressure and bought a pair of bell bottoms, which he loved, since the roomy flare fit nicely over his boots. He wore a small, yellow-and-red Coors Banquet T-shirt and his red New Orleans JazzFest trucker hat. Clyde grabbed his fishing pole and tackle box from out of the shed and kissed Santina goodbye, heading out the door for what should be a *groovy* time. He didn't know; that's just what Robbie had called it.

It wasn't too long of a drive to that side of town. He rolled the windows down and turned the radio up loud, just the way he liked it. The newer rock-and-roll was his favorite, but he liked just about anything, not too picky; good music was good music. His thoughts turned to his upcoming meeting with Ms. Claudia. It was her magic handshake that had vexed him, the way she held his grip longer than usual, forcing him uncomfortably to hang on to her soft hand as she beamed into his eyes with the analytical gaze of a freezing, yet wonderfully warm enigma. When her eyes met his own under proper lighting, a supernova happened. For Ms. Claudia, in the untold depth of all her *brujeria* knowledge, she thought his sallow eyes were like a lake on the moon.

The wind blowing back the loose sides of his hair as he drove, he was on autopilot, his mind elsewhere. Santina and he had gotten along a little better these last couple of days, after an explosive couple of months spiraling further and further downward into deep isolation. He hadn't had a drink in a couple of days, but he knew that was about to change. He was hungry for it, he missed it. Santina was always getting in the way of that, telling him not to, treating him like a mother would. He was grown; he could make his own decisions. He rationalized many of his behaviors with the fact he'd been where he'd been and seen what he'd seen.

Using the war as if it were a good excuse to act any old way he wanted, even if in his own selfish manner it hurt the others around him, in particular, the woman who had sought to care for him all this time. The one who'd stayed loyal and true to him while he was gone. She was good to him, too good for him, but there was something that kept her fighting for them. They were both stubborn; neither one could quit on the other. That was what marriage was all about, working through those grievances and coming out on the other side stronger and better for it.

There was no protest of mind, no quandary of negative solution, not any that couldn't be resolved. He'd stop drinking tomorrow. One last hurrah tonight and he'd be all right; he would just get it out of his system one last time. Swinging his truck into the park and seeing his buddies' old beaters parked side by side, he followed suit and parked adjacent to them. He put his car in park, shut the engine off, and rolled up the old, rickety crank windows. Grabbing his pole and his tackle box from the truck bed, he hiked up his pants a little bit and walked down to the river.

Robbie, Louis, and James were down there with a couple of other people Clyde hadn't seen in a while or hadn't seen before: James's girlfriend, Patricia, a tall, slender, blonde bayou beauty, and her girlfriend Sarrah, a shorter, more curvaceous brunette, with shoulder-length curled locks and a cute nose that had a distinguishable upward tilt. Sarrah was accompanied by her boyfriend, Mel, who was unknown to Clyde, but he was an academic type, from the looks of it. Mel's cousin Chris was a heavyset, blond-haired, ginger-bearded country boy of true Louisiana blood, a sharper Creole than Annette, but he thought more than he spoke, his weight holding him back from being confident enough to speak. A couple of other girls were there too, but Clyde didn't recognize them, nor did he care, as the fiesta appeared to be in full swing already, and he was late for a drink.

They sat in their folding canvas chairs by the water, with their lines cast far out and coolers still empty from not catching any fish. The beer cases were open though, and the cold ones were in their hands already. Liquor was there too, hardly touched, however. They had some music playing on the transistor radio, and there were two or three other trucks parked around them on the banks of the delta, with the tailgates laid flat to provide the party with extra seating. They'd dug out a pit in the sand for their campfire. The muggy air persisted, and the mosquitos were already out. Clyde hated mosquitos, and he hated muggy air. He too daydreamed of beaches.

"There he is, Mr. Clyde LeBouef! Welcome, welcome!" Robbie was exuberantly shouting from the edge of the river, drawing curious eyes and causing a lull in the ongoing sidebar conversation. This made Clyde burn with secondhand embarrassment at being the last to arrive. The ladies turned, flipping their hair, and the gentlemen turned too, without sharing so many words other than simple greetings. "How y'all doing? I see you got started without me," Clyde said as he walked up to the water to greet Robbie, Louis, and James. The latter was already slurring his speech.

"Man, you didn't say it was going to be this many people. Who are these guys, man?" Clyde asked, setting down his box and pole and taking a seat in the sand.

"Oh, they're just my other friends, man. They're cool, don't worry," he said, nonchalant even in inebriation.

Robbie changed the subject. "Here, man, have a shot, get loosened up. Fish ain't really biting. We've been at it for hours. We'll get this fire started after the sun goes down." Pausing, he looked up and shouted over to the partygoers. "Hey! How's that sound to everybody? You ready for the bonfire?" They all agreed, it was time.

James passed the bottle of Jack over to Clyde, who took a couple of swigs before reaching into the bucket to grab himself a cold one. That would do the trick of getting the nervous jitters out of the way. The music was loud. *These new guitar players were really quite talented*, Clyde thought as he listened to the music, which was playing loud enough to draw the resentful stares of the older folks trying to enjoy a peaceful day on the water themselves. Despite the judgment of the elders, it was shaping up to be a good night.

Clyde took an empty chair over to the edge where the fire was going to be and laid claim to his sandy real estate, with James and Robbie pulling up theirs respectively. Louis got to work pyramiding the logs onto the fire, getting his bundle of dry tinder ready to start, with a can of gasoline nearby to get things really started. "So, everyone, this is Clyde. Clyde, this everyone." Louis made the short introductions as he fiddled around with the lumber. "He did two-no, *three* tours in Nam," he added.

This drew oohs and aahs from the bunch, and Clyde felt his chest start to itch and his neck get hot. Giving a sheepish smile, Clyde just sardonically said, "Yep, thanks for telling everybody that, Lou. I really appreciate it." Clyde hated to be put in the public spotlight. Everybody's dumb, curious stares, now they were definitely making premature assumptions about him and the context of his character.

It was uncomfortable, but Clyde, playing it off as best he could, said, "Yeah, but y'all don't need to be shy. I don't bite; least I don't think." He grinned, showing off deep dimples. It was not received with much enthusiasm, more like uninterested fake smiles. The ladies resumed chattering among themselves, and the music that somehow had been turned down got turned back up again. Sarrah's boyfriend, Mel, came up to Clyde with his own malt beverage in hand

and took his shot at making idle chitchat with the revenant sergeant.

"Dang, man, so Vietnam, huh?" he politely began. "Thank you for your service," and he held out his hand. "Name's Mel."

"Good to meet you, man," Clyde said, leaning forward off of the truck tailgate, straightening out his pants as he gripped Mel's weak, academic hand, more attuned to the fine pages of old literature than working. "Clyde."

Shaking hands led to them having another beer, and the two became fast acquaintances. Clyde really appreciated the personal attempt to bring him out of his shell. Mel was a good guy. He was studying to be an English teacher.

They all got out of their chairs and stood a few paces back while Louis poured the gasoline over the fire. He struck a match, and with it caused a stick soaked in the amber fuel to ignite, tossing in with a mighty roar his tribute to the fire gods. An eruption of orange-peel-yellow flames enveloped the air several feet high in a quick burst of chemical reaction, followed by raucous cheers of excitement and praise. Clyde took another shot, helping himself to the bottle this time.

Clyde sat back in his chair, sipping on his third or fourth beer, he wasn't sure. He pondered a moment, searching longingly into the fire, memories flooding the crevasses of his imagination, his mind was in a faraway place. He drifted off into his comfortable stare, recalling certain smells, sounds, recalling his old friends, the ones who carried M-16s in the mud next to him. Those were his *real* friends. Those were good times, even if it was helter-skelter.

Standing around the old square-bodied trucks, the radio was playing a classic, "Have You Ever Seen the Rain" by Creedence Clearwater Revival. Everyone was full of the party spirit, with some other swamp rats bringing over their coolers and chairs and striking up conversations here and there with these strangers. Clyde had gotten up to stand over the fire, warming his cool skin by the flames, the night chill nipping at him through his thin shirt and jeans. Then he had a most bizarre experience, an experience that cannot duly be explained or rationalized by any known science.

Clyde had taken a shot and was chasing it down with beer, but right before he swallowed the beer, he spit it out into a great big mist, which carried so much force in its projection, it caused him to stumble backward several steps, tripping over his sleepy legs. The mist spread out in the wind, blown into the sad faces of the new guests who'd only just arrived, shrouding them in beer spray. Then he felt as though he walked out of his skin, outside of his body, an ethereal, light feeling, watching himself as the others might've seen him, from the third person.

Time seemed to cease progression. All was silent in the world around him, not a sound. His own thoughts were all he heard, and clearly, for the first time in his life. Suddenly, he realized his understanding of his new spatial surroundings was nonexistent, and an old, distorted voice came through to him. But it wasn't himself speaking; it was the husky voice of someone else.

The voice that came through had a ring to it, a voice he could faintly, in his newfound clarity, recall from somewhere. But he didn't know where. The way it carried in that space of time, it sounded everlasting. Clyde watched himself, keeled over at the waist, paused in time as the voice, using him as a vessel, spoke at last.

Quickly, it said to him, "Many, many fuzz will appear upon your face,"

Clyde watched with horror from beyond his true self as his physical body crouched down, over a murky puddle. All the other partygoers remained perfectly still, but Clyde had full freedom of movement in this paused point in time. His eyes jumped back into his true self, as he was looking into the reflection of the water. "Many, many women you will love." the voice finished.

Watching his true self turn his head to the right, he revealed the pale of his neck, which had written on it in a red blotchy marker the phrase "How were women treated in 1972?"

He stood there staring at himself, mouth agape, pondering the weight of the phrase here uttered. He jumped back into his body, back into normal time, and around him, the people were pissed, upset and shaking off the beer spray. Clyde heard the lonely cousin say, "Aw man, what'd you go and do that for?" Realizing then he was not in complete control of his own actions, and not knowing whether or not it was the booze or something else, Clyde gave a few shy and quick apologies before he excused himself and made a mad dash for his truck in the parking lot.

Shaken up and confused, his fingers fumbled with the keys as he tried to get his door open. *What the hell was that?* he thought to himself. Hurriedly getting into his car, he didn't give a second thought to the fishing pole he left behind, which his dad gave him, or the rest of his gear he'd brought and left behind. The others had been just as confused as he was. Had they seen all that too? He hoped not; he didn't know what happened either. He was maddeningly intoxicated, seeing double as he pulled out of the drive and onto the street. The green, yellow, and red lights in their brightness harassed him as he swerved over the median and into the oncoming lanes. All over the road, he tried to pull himself together, slapping himself on the face, trying to sober up as best he could and as fast as he could. But it was no use. He was fucked up.

"Come on, Clyde, come on, man, just get home. Focus, man, focus!" he said to himself, both hands on the wheel, hunched forward, trying his best to concentrate on the hilly backwoods road. Blowing through a red light, Clyde narrowly missed a collision with a passing pickup loaded down with cargo. He cursed himself for once again continuing the vicious cycle of addiction. Santina would be disappointed. Luckily, there weren't too many people on the roads that night, or things could've gone much worse than they did.

In a drunken blur, he gave in to the fact that he did not know where he was. He tried to focus on the road, hoping to see some sort of familiar landmark or terrain feature or something. He was still seeing double. Perspiring from fear and alcohol, he turned right, heading down a long two-lane stretch of road. Clyde saw his opportunity to release a tremendous pressure, trading it for a wild adrenaline instead, the excitement of which would surely silly him sober.

Turning up the radio, Clyde floored it, quickly bringing it up to fifth gear, burning through the bayou like a madman, not realizing his lights weren't even on. Eventually, the two-lane road split off into something he felt looked familiar. After much guesswork and figuring out why it was so dark outside, he at last recognized his own street, and then his driveway, seeing his house with all the lights off. Clyde pulled in and turned off the truck and sat quietly for a few minutes, breathing heavily. The sweat beading off his forehead reeked of cheap malt whiskey. He didn't have the mental flexibility for anything else right now. Shame washed over him, guilty and disgusted with his own weaknesses. He couldn't hold back any longer; he needed help dealing with all the games life was playing with him. He wondered, for what crime was he being punished? Being subjected to live a tortured and mundane existence, knowing there had to be more to it, there just had to be.

The front door opened, and Santina, wearing her nightgown, hair in a bonnet, came out and down the porch steps with her arms folded and still in her slippers. She walked up to the car and saw Clyde inside with an expressionless look on his face, eyes like voids fixed on something and nothing at the same time. One look was all she needed. "Clyde, sweetie, why don't you come inside and come to bed, okay?" she said, standing there in front of the rising red sun, beckoning him to abandon his isolation, and take her hand. She'd make it better.

Clyde nodded, biting on his lips. "I'm coming, baby, thank you." He opened his door, and without words they walked up to the front door. It was a relief to be home. Home was safety, shelter from the world outside that wanted only to hurt him.

Clyde went immediately to the bathroom, washing his face and hands in the basin before retiring to the bedroom. She joined him there, and he took off his clothes, revealing the pale, thin shell of what was once a proud and great warrior. He lay there in the sheets, naked, grimy, and hurt. Undeterred by this, she climbed under the comforter and pulled him close, not caring about the sorry state he was in. She played with his hair until he fell asleep, and while he slept, she prayed to God on his behalf.

Chapter 9

DREAMWORLDS

The week couldn't go by fast enough. The eight-hour shifts at work felt more like ten, not to mention the time he wasted commuting to and from and the time he spent getting ready, packing his lunch, fixing his clothes, making his coffee, doing his hair every single day. It was a repetitious cycle. That apparently every other working adult, who once in youth had great dreams, now forfeited what gave their lives meaning for money. Doomed to work until their bodies break down. If Clyde was forced to work, he would do it in the manner of a put-together, hard-working and motivated young man. He had been on a lifelong quest to prove his worth to the world, and this they saw. Steadily going about his work, no specific tempo or pace, uninterrupted was how he liked it, and he took solace working alone.

Clyde had long been indoctrinated into the machine. He'd been a cog his whole life, doing what must be done, at whatever cost to accomplish mission success. His mission now was to give his employers a fair day's work, earn his keep, and provide for his family, so like he always did when life was hard, he leaned into his work.

Waiting for his appointment with Ms. Claudia was unbearable, having accumulated so many curious questions over last night's debacle. He hadn't planned on getting so drunk; it just happened that way. He could say he was just having fun, but that wouldn't be entirely true. He knew it was more than that. The laughs and good cheer lost their momentum when his evening crashed down on top of him. He likened it to being an outside observer, watching his hijacked reaction to some unknown force that had commandeered the very fabric of his rational thinking.

"Many, many fuzz will appear upon your face. Many, many women you will love." An odd utterance, he didn't know what overcame his mind to manipulate his speech in such a way. The only logical explanation was that it was the result of the building anticipation with his coming appointment with the inscrutable bruja. It could've been that her handshake completed a spiritual conduit, linking him to whatever dark power she used. He was a little scared now, feeling blasphemous for even considering that they deliberate with a heathen. To go through with it would mean to one day ask for repentance under whatever god was the right god.

At work he would think about his parents. Ma and Pa were old, and they'd had him later in life, so much so that Clyde had not known his grandparents on either side; they had passed on long before Clyde was born. All he had known were the black-and-white photographs and old daguerreotypes of his ancient kin. He thought about how short life really was, learning what it meant, that it was something to never be guaranteed. Tomorrow was not a promise, as he'd learned harshly in the war. You never see them again, until it's your own turn to take your dance with Death as he leads you on one last waltz. One day we say our goodbyes to everyone who we have ever loved in this life, but tomorrow, we open our eyes to see them all standing beside us.

Winding down the night, books in hand, lamps lit on their end tables, Clyde and Santina each entered into their separate literary fantasies, letting their minds escape the thoughts they had not yet been ready to confront. Reading was always a great distraction and helped them fall asleep quicker.

Clyde entered deep sleep, his imagination taking hold of his subconscious. Tonight he dreamed he was walking his dog, Cyrus. Cyrus was a good boy, a smaller dog, but a strongly faithful companion. While they were on this walk, out of nowhere, a cub that resembled a cross between a black bear and a panther came from out of the shadows and started to corner scared Cyrus and cautious Clyde. Fearing for his dog's safety, Clyde went to the creature and grabbed it up by its neck with his bare hands, squeezing it and looking into its pitch-black pupils, centered in the bloodshot whites of its eyes. He choked the life from it as it struggled to find a breath. When at last the creature's flame was gone, the pair carried on their walk.

Clyde then found himself in an old Transylvanian castle, with stone-gray walls built by master masons. Superior craftsmanship, now cracked, degraded, and bowed over with time, it was a castle in ruins. The full moon and stars shone through man-sized, arched holes, exposing the bare sky and breeze to the inside room, intact and flat, which had to have been the sleeping quarters. Looking out of the window, Clyde watched in the distance, out on the plain, tall blowing grass, and he saw things in the wind. Things blacker than the night. The creatures flapped huge wings and were flying swiftly toward his castle. He wasn't sure what these things were, but he knew they had to be big. At first, he thought staying in bed and going back to sleep would make them disappear, but he felt their presence outside of the window. They watched him lie there, pretending like he was resting peacefully. Clyde, gripped by paranoia, was unable to take the burning eyes of the resentful creatures. He sat up and looked out the archway window.

A giant, black humanoid bat creature was hovering in place outside the arched window opening, fluttering every few seconds with hairy wings that had veins as thick as his arms. Taller than a man, with strong muscles, a snout on its face, from which its snarling canine teeth were exposed, it looked mad. Clyde didn't dare move, but he watched it as it floated there in open air, looking through at him, looking through his eyes, wanting to speak its grandly archaic language, learned through the millennia it'd spent serving the dominion of the dark lords ruling the nightmarish realm they inhabited.

Clyde, for whatever reason, went outside, to escape the view of this bat creature, but upon his exit from the safety of the castle walls, he found himself dodging the things as they strafed him, kamikaze style, swooping down on him while he ran serpentine to escape the clutches of their razor-sharp onyx talons. Finally, no longer could he flee; he had to rest, and he took a short pause to catch his breath. One of the creatures flew down to meet him, looking at him face to face, hovering in the space in front of him, inside of his bubble. Clyde then knew this creature was the father of the cub he had strangled earlier, on his walk with Cyrus.

It stayed there, spying him with its black oculus. Clyde felt he owed it an apology, and with sincerity and humility, he said, "I'm sorry," as his eyes welled with the innocent tears of a child who's done wrong and feels shame. "I was just afraid."

He meant it with every fiber of his being. His soul cried for taking the life of another living creature. The towering shadow sensed this and seemed to hear Clyde. While still hovering in the air before him, it held out its hand and beckoned Clyde for a human handshake. Clyde and the bat shook hands, and the wraith and its bad company took flight, flying far off back into the black night that bore them. Back toward that full moon, until they were just specks passing through immortal Orion.

Saturday, July 1, 1971

The streets were crowded with people flooding into town for the Fourth of July weekend, aiming to see some fireworks shows, hear some live music, and party downtown in the French Quarter. New Orleans had always put on great fireworks, and the carnies arrived to unravel their big tents of sparklers and games. The big festivals were full of jazz horns and swing culture and hippies and art. People checked into their hotels, getting their rooms, running errands, shopping for their groceries and booze. It was busy all day long, with much activity as the people were getting ready to party the weekend away, remembering their wicked debauchery in the pews the following morning.

Clyde wouldn't be in attendance; he didn't go to church. That was just all for show, people dressing up in their nice clothes, to go down and hear the preacher give his sermon. They would all nod in agreement, pretending that those two hours they gave God each week made them good people, just to fall back into their old ways throughout the week. He had a big night ahead of him as it was. He was getting the Voodoo treatment for his insufferable ways.

He'd gone a few days without a drink, and he had been fighting a headache for the better part of the last couple. That, and a rigidly stiff neck that bothered him every day when he woke up. As his feet pounded the sidewalk, hands in pockets, weaving in and out of the crowd of tourists and locals on the streets, he was just another face in the crowd. People he'd never see again, passing glances to his ragged, shaggy appearance. Hair longer now, and sporting a darker stubble, his pants were dirty and stained from work. His khaki shirt was loosely unbuttoned, revealing sparse chest hair as he swaggered his way down Bourbon Street.

Glancing at his watch, the time read six twenty-nine. He was right on time. Walking up to the stained-glass doors underneath the red canopy, he was grabbed by his arm from behind.

"Hey, man, you got some change?" a beggar asked. One hand held a paper cup, the other reached out and grabbed Clyde's shoulder. His matted hair was wrapped up in a bandana, and he had a couple of teeth missing from a crooked, looney smile. Clyde quickly shook his arm free of the pauper's grasp. "No, I ain't got no change and get your hands off me, dammit! What's the matter with you?" Clyde shot the man a dark scowl and turned back to head into the doors, rolling his eyes as he swung them open and walked inside. He hated when people touched him. Clyde wasn't touchy-feely, least of all with strangers.

Ruby was behind the counter. She gave Clyde a warm smile as he approached. "You're late."

Clyde checked his watch; 6:31 p.m. Fed up with games, he offered a reply. "Yeah, I guess I am."

By a whole minute.

"She's down there waiting for you. Why don't you head on back." Ruby opened the divider for Clyde, and he walked through, wiping his hands on his pants in case she wanted to read his palms.

Walking through, and offering Ruby a courteous thank-you, Clyde opened the door that led to the basement. The stairway was dark as before, but Clyde didn't bother to turn the light on as he passed the short string dangling from the ceiling. Walking down the stairway, he heard music coming from down below. Slowly, the darkness gave way to the blue and black light, the ambience reaching up the stairs, illuminating further the psychedelic hollow of the basement.

He heard a piercing lead guitar coming from the stereo, which created an oscillating atmospheric vibration with its spaced-out instrumental passages. At the bottom of the stairs, he turned to look toward the sofa. Ms. Claudia had set out her *other* baby, her Persian octo-hose water hookah, burning something stronger than plain tobacco. In front of the bar, Ms. Claudia was fixing herself a cocktail as she puffed a cigarette, the glass holder dangling loosely between her wet lips. Her hair was wrapped in a big gypsy head scarf, and she was wearing a loose-fitting, paisley white top, tucked into maroon yogi pants. The arches of her bare feet sank deep into the shag carpet.

"Take off your shoes please, Mr. LeBouef," she said, stirring her cocktail with the painted red nail of her pointer finger. Making her way over to the sofa, she traced the wet fingertip along the different zodiac tapestries which were in different colors, neon greens, bright violets, and blazing oranges. The sun and moon, the stars, all manner of celestial splendor exorbitantly on display in the witch's lair.

Clyde took off his boots and his socks and set them down by the stairs.

"Sorry I'm late," he said. "I would've been on time, but a bum stopped me on the street," Clyde offered in excuse, but Ms. Claudia paid him no attention.

"Do you have what I asked you to bring me?" she said, lifting one leg over the couch followed by the other, taking her seat and setting her drink down on the custom tarot table, taking another drag.

"Yes, ma'am, I've got your money right here. You sure you ain't too high to do this?" Clyde asked as he fished the cash out of his pocket.

"I use my special herbs to enter the fluid state of mind that I need to achieve in order to guide you with clear and precise direction and intention. My mind needs to be entirely elastic to perform this ritual, and you must be receptive to me and my commands. I hope you understand. Here too, I will need you to partake in the herbal rituals. These are not shameful drugs, and it is necessary for you to be as malleable as clay when I put you under."

She handed Clyde the joint.

He'd smoked marijuana before, obviously; everybody had, and what was the worst that could happen? He took a couple of deep breaths of the smoke, inhaling all the way down deep into his lungs.

"Hold it in," she beckoned to him.

He held in the smoke for a few seconds and slowly let it out. Next, a great coughing fit consumed him, his lungs and throat burning as he coughed. His head suddenly got hot, and he felt his ears ringing. His novice reaction brought a big smile to Ms. Claudia's face as she burst into laughter. Clyde handed it back over to her after calming himself down from his coughing spell. Once the harsh aftereffect subsided, Clyde then felt very good. He felt a warm tingling sensation in his head, and he felt all his aches and pains begin to dissipate. He wasn't at all worried or upset anymore.

The uptight mannerisms he'd constantly held on to loosened their grip. He felt himself relax for a change, and it was a nice feeling. He heard the music in the background, each layer of it unfolding to his ears. He thought the lights and tapestries resembled art, and as she sat next to him, she started fiddling with something on the shelf underneath the coffee table, and Clyde realized there was something a whole lot stronger inside the weed. Moving the hookah to the side, she cleared a space on the table and pulled from underneath the table a blue cast iron cauldron.

"What's that, Ms. C? An indigo chili pot?" He laughed to himself over his own wit.

She raised a curious brow at him, unamused, knowing he was feeling the effects of her *special* blend.

"Yes. It's an indigo chili pot. Hand me that vial there, please, Mr. LeBouef."

Looking next to the hookah, he grabbed a vial of reddish liquid, inspecting it until he was personally satisfied that it was in fact *not* blood of any kind, since it was too thin. He handed it over, and she dumped it inside the cauldron, which she'd placed onto a hot plate plugged into the wall via an extension cord. She grabbed the hookah by the neck, and the hoses drooped as she carried it over to the bar, taking care to cover the coal passively burning in the coal tray.

Behind the bar, fiddling with several jars of what appeared to be herbs and various witchery ingredients, Ms. Claudia pulled a piece of cheesecloth from a drawer and laid it flat on the bar. Placing handfuls of different materials into the cloth, she knotted the heavy sachet together and came back over to the sofa. The water had now began to bubble inside the cauldron. She tossed in the herbal pouch, and Clyde sat quietly, stuck on the soft couch cushions, looking around the room in a melodic daze, euphoria, and feeling a warm bliss washing over him in slow, metamorphic waves.

Ms. Claudia sat herself cross-legged on the sofa next to him. She laid out several objects on the coffee table and took a quick inventory of her supplies. "One sprig of lavender, two drops of *extracto corozo*, three leaves juniper, dried and crushed thistlewart, basil and bay leaves, a strong Nepali incense. Complete with one vial of Sin of Man." One by one she tossed these items into the cauldron. Now he really wondered what was in the vial. After the initial reaction, the boiling water, mixed with the sachet, and her whole fresh ingredients, created a strong, aromatic fog in the space around them. This concoction continued to bubble and boil, and she took great care to stir the contents thoroughly with a small, slotted spoon. Taking it out and shaking it off, she set the expired sachet on a napkin on the table. The leftover fluids soaked the felt beneath as she replaced the lid of the cauldron, trapping the fumes, letting the bubbling concoction further strengthen.

The atmosphere was cloudy, and as their breathing air was further diluted, Clyde felt his claustrophobia creeping in.

"Okay, Mr. LeBouef, how are you feeling currently?" she asked.

Clyde looked at the cauldron, watching as its lid rattled from the built-up steam pressure. "Well, I'm hot right now, but I think that's just because of this thing."

"All right, well I want you to lay down, okay? Make yourself comfortable."

Clyde then awkwardly curled himself along the sofa.

"Here, have a pillow," she said, handing him a smaller throw pillow.

Making himself comfortable, he rested his hands on his stomach and lay there flat, with one leg propped up. She came around the other side, so she could sit nearer his head. Bringing her legs up Indian style, she sat and reached over, removing the lid from the cauldron. A fog rolled over its lip and down its short belly, onto the table and down to the floor. The fog then climbed up Clyde's legs, coming past his waist and over his chest.

The fog enveloped his torso, and then his head, and the hot steam reached high into the air. She wafted it in his direction and told him to take long, deep breaths of the strange smoke. "Keep your eyes closed, please, until I tell you to open them. Concentrate on keeping them closed, keep breathing, breathe it in."

Clyde did so and kept his eyes closed, concentrating on breathing in deep volumes of air, in through his nose and out through his mouth. She continued fanning the fog his way. The music playing in the background seemed a lower volume. His body was floating for a second before the herbal fragrances and the heat of the cauldron, now simmering low and controlled, grounded him back into Ms. Claudia's hold.

"I want you to let yourself relax, love, okay? Lay back down, focus on those long, slow breaths. Feel yourself, really feel yourself, feel the rise and fall of your chest, with the lifeforce of God that flows in your veins from the heartbeat within you. Let it slow you down, then you'll be at ease. Let your worries vanish, and focus on my voice. Focus on being here, present with me. Give yourself to the will of my voice, submit yourself to the feminine divine," she said, waving her henna-painted hands over his face, which looked blue under the glowing blacklight tubes, an incandescent royal purple and not black. Clyde felt lackadaisical, loosely in touch with his old war worries and marital concerns. He watched the insides of his eyelids, as a dark blue veil unscrolled over his field of vision, slowly pulsing. Breathing slowly in and out, Clyde let himself go, feeling in tune with a more tribal rhythm. The music was now a steady hum he was following closely, to keep one foot in the door of real world.

"You're going to only respond when I ask you a question. Do you understand?" Ms. Claudia said as she unplugged the hot plate, taking a sip of her drink, which had now been watered down by the melted ice. She lit another cigarette.

"Yes, ma'am, I understand," he said, now hearing a piano delivering lower-pitched scales of a sordid variety.

She then placed her hands on his head and started to run her fingers through his hair, easing him into a state of even deeper relaxation and comfort.

"I want you to think of a place that made you happy, and I want you to hold that memory until you feel like it's right there. Begin."

Clyde, then thinking on her question, began to search within the wide expanse of his mind for a place where he felt happy. He struggled at first to find this place, but when it entered his head, he remembered it clearly.

He recalled a Christmas morning from childhood, coming down the stairs in the middle of the night to see all sorts of gifts under the tree sparkling beneath the twinkling lights wrapped tastefully around a live Christmas tree, with ornaments shimmering alongside the gold and silver tinsel. The room hued in reds and greens, and the snow whites and pale blues of Christmastime, the most wonderful time of year, the excitement he felt, the eager anticipation. Christmas Eve was the longest night of the year, feeling like it'd never come to pass. With the eager child waiting for what felt like an eternity, finally the wait would be over, followed later by a huge banquet dinner.

That was a happy memory for him. He held it there, put himself there as he continued to breathe the fog in slowly, relaxed and thinking of nothing else now but a happier past.

"Do you have it?" he heard her say.

"Yes," he said, eyes closed, completely still.

"I want you to focus on my voice now once more. I want you to relax now, Mr. LeBouef. This relaxation of yours is the greatest feeling you've felt in a long time. You're remembering a scene from your life that brought you great joy. I want you to take this opportunity to drift into an even deeper slumber. Follow your happy place; this scene will open the way to the dream of which you'll learn to be, the dream of your life."

Massaging his scalp and running her soft, slender fingers through his long hair, the oil of her hands mixed with his greasy flow, creating a soft, easy trail of positive energy, tangible, its flow traceable as it followed her fingertips, and moved onto him. Her touch sent whizzing electrical currents through his body, empowering him. He felt alive and ready to be shown the way of the bruja, if she could even be called that.

"I'm going to count backwards from ten, Mr. LeBouef. When I get to one, you will be in a different place, a place you do not recognize. You'll begin to dream, as if it were a movie, and you, my dear, are the star. I'll be here taking notes and asking questions, which you will hear deep inside your unconscious mind. You simply answer when asked, and continue watching the movie, the movie of forgotten time. It holds the key to the answers to the questions you ask. Are you ready?"

"Yes."

With her enchanted touch, she whispered some incantations and gently ushered him toward a state of hibernation. She started her count, her voice, that of an angel, guiding him on his journey into the unknown. As she descended backward from ten, he began to feel sleepy, and as he listened to her, he fell further and further away from himself. His connection to the real world began to escape him. He followed the fading echoes of her voice until at last, the sleep she spoke of took hold of him. The bruja would now reveal the truths he sought.

Part 2

CRISTOBAL TRUJILLO

Chapter 10

DARK ROYALTY

What once could've been said, can now never be heard. His eyes like a thousand mirrors, acting as high-powered lenses reflecting out into the world.

"Reckon yourself ready to enter the archaic chambers?" echoed a wispy voice, far back in his subconscious mind, coming forward as though brought on by that which is unknowing and confounded. He heard Ms. Claudia from the floaty, amorphous headspace he was now occupying.

"Follow my voice, Clyde. Concentrate. What comes into your vision? What do you see?"

The line of questioning subsided, and Clyde was unsure of exactly what he was feeling. He saw no visual reflection or refraction, nothing at first. "I can hear you, but I don't see anything yet. It looks dark; I see darkness. I'm scared to go in." This darkness was where the visions of the old ages would begin to manifest, drawing themselves upon the slate canvas, devoid of light. In the darkness was where the vision was gathering itself, and in the darkness was where he looked, until at last, he saw it.

Beautiful galleon ships, gliding across the blue seas, with giant red crosses stitched into the now-dingy cream-colored sails. The ships moved under moonlight, which barely illuminated the ghostly armada out in the vast, open Atlantic. The sounds of waves crashing against the rotting wooden shipboards, no doubt strongly tempered by the furious seas after a long and arduous journey. These vessels could take a beating, and they could maneuver with ease. Numerous times they'd narrowly dodged watery graves, sailing through powerful tropical cyclones. The waves had never known man to be capable of such navigational prowess, for these had survived every test the seas had thrown their way.

La Madre Rosa was the name painted on her bow, a marvel of nautical genius and design. She had been crafted by the finest shipmakers in Spain. No detail was skipped over. Her handrails were carved of the finest cherrywood, with the beautiful wood grain shining through the coats of stain. The ship gleamed, freshly swabbed by the humble sailors, whose charge it was to maintain her decks in the highest order.

The intricacy of the craftsmanship knew no bounds, from floor to ceiling, her quarters were finely decorated with ancient Greco-Roman sea iconography: Poseidon and his trident, the nymphs and their unmatchable beauty, singing their siren song to the sailors, forever lost in the deep. Trims of gold, bronze, and silver ornately decorated every seam, hinge, sham, doorknob, and rail post. A more beautiful ship was never commanded by anyone else. She was engineered for the specific purpose of sailing across the open ocean to the New World.

Under a blanket of millions of stars with not a cloud in the sky, she navigated her way slowly through the choppy seas, with white-capped waves battering her as she was tossed around by the currents of a coming storm. Lightning could be seen far off in the distance, with Thor's hammer striking down, creating great booms of thunder. The flashing of lightning struck fear into the hearts of those out in the open air on deck. A long journey on the seas it had been, and this would be just one of the many storms that had plagued her voyage across these uncharted seas.

This scene had entered Clyde's mind, as he was deep now in his immovable, lucid state. From behind, he heard that voice. "Go now, inhabit the flesh you've known before." A vacuum pulled his mind into its new vessel, and for the first time since going under, he'd awoken and was looking through a different set of eyes, as if they were his own. Looking around, the scene was familiar to him now.

As if he were a bystander, he stepped inside one of the ship's cabins. He watched as a man rose from his bed, flipping back the wonderful maroon silk sheets. He then felt that he was the risen man. The sheets were soft, he recalled, as he'd been sleeping just a few short seconds ago, soft against his freshly shaven face. In fact, he had been completely comfortable up until now. Five lashes for the fellow beating on his cabin door.

"I'm up, goddammit! Give me a minute!" he shouted toward the door.

Being tossed side to side in the cabin by the waves that were battering the ship on the outside, he moved on sea legs to his wardrobe. Throwing on his robe and stumbling to the door, hanging on to his bedpost for balance, he went to open it, but the wind blew it wide open as soon as he turned the knob.

"What news have you for me so grave you'd think it wise to bother me this late at night! And in weather like this? Are we not on course?"

It was the first mate. At first glance, Clyde immediately recognized him as the honorable Lieutenant Enrico Cardenas.

"Captain, it's land!" Enrico shouted, a look of triumph spread across his face, dripping wet with rain from the storm. His eyes were beaming in excitement as he came through the open door and pulled the captain close into a soggy embrace. The captain didn't mind the wet lieutenant. Spotting land after all these months was the news they had been waiting for. "That is to say, my friend, we survive this thrall of vicious weather, given to be certainly our last test of the seas. I'll be up shortly. Have all hands on deck. We pull into land at first light. Make haste, will you!" the captain ordered.

Enrico sprinted across the ship, heading below deck, rousing the men from their slumbers, if the storm had not woken them already.

Running back to his wardrobe, the captain pulled out the first pair of breeches he saw, and the first cotton shirt, followed by the knee-high leather boots his father had made for him. He didn't need much to guide them into land. They'd learned their lesson on the last expeditions. Keeping everybody together during the storm was paramount, and he had to be out there directing the traffic of the five-ship fleet.

Stepping out of his cabin and onto the deck, immediately soaked with furious rain, he walked down the length of the ship to the stairs that led below deck. Flipping open the curtain, the captain began to shout, stirring the stragglers from their sorry slumbers. It was all hands on deck now.

"Oh, never mind the water falling from the heavens, you abhorrent wraiths. Get to your stations! Land ho! Answer the storm with bravery! Move now, and let fear not grip you! Rise to the deliverance of our great Lord! Fly you now! Move, move, *move*! We're making land!"

The men below deck started running up the stairs in chaos and disorder, still pulling up their trousers, half-asleep and groggy from their interrupted short rest. The feelings of lethargy were gone almost immediately upon hearing that land was close. Thunderous cheers and shouting overtook them. In the morning light from where they stood on the deck, beyond the eye of the storm, they could make out the great coasts of the New World. It was the first any of them had seen this place, including the young captain.

Clyde looked around, through the captain's eyes. He was not controlling anything. Nothing he was speaking, nothing he was doing. He was merely attached, watching this scene unfold as if it had been scripted and rehearsed. The great flashes of the storm seemingly drew closer, as they moved closer and closer to land. Making their way through the eye of this great storm, the smaller ships followed closely behind the leader. All were built with tremendous craftsmanship, but they were not made to withstand these treacherous waters for so long. None had been lost yet, but that could not be said for some of the men who had not finished the journey alive. The sea was unforgiving, and on the weak of mind and spirit, she bore little indeterminacy.

The captain climbed hand over hand the roped web that led up to the crow's nest. With a telescopic looking glass and a compass, he swayed back and forth in the wind, having trouble on the ropes getting the footing required to propel him upward. Desperately he fought the howling winds, climbing toward the Crow's Nest to grab hold the picture of his long-awaited glory. Conquistadors, Spanish soldiers, and explorers, fueled by cupidity, their discoveries within this unknown place would bring worldwide renown to their expedition. That glory would become his. Sure enough, the continental body could be seen in the distance through the tempest fury.

That famous land, found by the great explorer Columbus, was now a land of active conquests for Spain. The captain eyed her coasts, with a glance toward those mysterious rocks and cliffs. This was where destiny, the decisions of the Lord for the story of his life, had brought him. Swallowing his tremendous pride, he pulled out the looking glass, one hand holding the roped web, and the other wiping the rain off the fogged glass, he placed the blurry lens to his eye. Through the glass, under the rising sun, the coasts became clearer. The land they'd left Havana for in search of was here in front of him, no longer a myth, legend, or fantasy, no longer just stories, but reality.

Those stories of great Cortes he'd heard his whole childhood; it was then that his dream of being a conquistador began. The stories moved his imagination since he was a boy, always wanting to hear more about the fabled warriors.

The conquistadors were the warrior elite of Spain. Proud knights of old, famed legends of glory, war, and gold. His chance to place his name forever among those legends had finally come. Uncertain what the Lord would have in store for them next, what great trials awaited them, what forces they would battle with, and where else they would fight except into the deep unknown. Where would their great battles be, and who would praise them when they came home? The untold heroics of these men would need to be told; they would need their great successors to honor their discoveries, their brave journey, and their selfless sacrifice.

"Cristobal, hold on!" he heard the crowmaster say. "Rocks!" he shouted. Dendrick Rodon had been temporarily distracted watching the captain's ascent, and in his few seconds of distraction, failed to see the coming obstacle. By the time he saw it, it was too late. Dendrick held fast to the hogshead, but the captain was thrown about, losing his hold and falling to the deck below.

"Holy shit!" shouted Dendrick from above.

He was crude for a man of the blade, less of a gentleman than the others. Enrico ran from the aft to the bow in a hurry, looking to the captain, while a few of the sailors tucked away their faces to hide their laughs over his tumble. The adrenaline absorbed the brunt of the pain.

"I'm fine damn it! Go see to the ship! Make sure she's still worthy, go!" He shook himself off as he stood. Once the ship had regained her bearings, Lieutenant Enrico Cardenas could be seen running up and down the slippery shipboards, assessing for damage, while rallying the men and issuing his captain's orders. Cristobal climbed *back* up onto the roped web and up towards the crow's nest once more. The terribly sorry Dendrick Rodon started apologizing for failing to alert the captain, but Cristobal had already forgotten, as he marveled at the sight of the huge continent taking shape before their very eyes. The Americas were drawing closer with each passing second. The rain now softening, the morning sun coming up over the skyline, illuminating the great golden coasts of this new world, the pink and purple wavelengths fissured the sky, and the carmine fire of *el sol* began to burn hot.

All the hurrahs and cheers of his men were like putting laurels on his head; everyone was lifted high in morale and eager to get off the ship and onto dry land for the first time in months. Fighting cruel seas, sickness, and the lack of nutritious rations to keep their strength and drive, the terrible toll of loneliness and homesickness afflicted all. That, however, was their own decision to make, and they wanted to be here. They wanted to explore, to find glory, to conquer. In the name of Phillip II of Spain, Captain Cristobal Trujillo was the spearhead, responsible for getting from the shipyards in Spain to their port stop in Havana, and then on to find the New World for themselves. The king himself personally blessed Cristobal and his men on the morning of their departure. This was their chance to seize glory and greatness for the empire and for themselves. Driven by their intrepid desire for wealth, their greed was the fire that forged their blades, cooled in blood.

Or so was their reputation.

Clyde's dream vision then gave him the memories of a childhood not his own. Again, through the lens of someone else's eyes, he recalled the biological parents of his old life, who in their youth and eagerness, had conceived him when they were not yet capable of raising him. They gave him up to the church as an orphan, walking away from that Toledo cathedral, ignominious and ashamed.

Growing up with anger, against his will, he spent his early years in seminary, devoting all his waking hours to prayer and learning all things holy. He loathed it, but as an orphan, it was the best he could have hoped for, and he looked up to the fine padres of the institution. The Lord's light brought him comfort, and it was there he took solace on those lonely nights in his room, when thoughts of wonder and questions he was too young to be asking started to come into his head. Those cold nights shivering under the thin woolen blankets made him tough, and it was then that Cristobal's conquistador dreams were conjured up.

Fortunately, he didn't spend his whole life there. At eight years old, he was taken from his orphanage, a humble, God-fearing boy, to be the first child of two parents who greatly yearned for a child of their own. His adoptive mother suffered from a barren womb, but her heart was full of much love, which she gave to Cristobal as soon as the padre brought him in, as if she just knew he was the one.

They delighted in being his parents, fostering with their good charity an unfortunate soul such as he to raise as their own. Instead of being a poor leper of society, a life of opportunity now awaited him. Love him they did, showering him with affection, fostering his growth in a way that the Church could not, keen on giving him the gift of education. They sought to advance his literacy and his learning of the old histories of Hispania. He was filled with words by the time he reached puberty, simultaneously trained vigorously in royal etiquette. He was expected to function as a member of their class, while making himself appealing to the higher classes.

These wealthy elites who ran their government held the key to his opportunity to fulfill his great dream. Decorated military officers, soldiers, public officials, governors—he cared little for bureaucracy and politics, calling it idle work of the lamest variety. When he was sixteen, he left the villa of his adoptive parents and enlisted into the Spanish Army. Cristobal studied the history of their country's military exploits with his father in his study. Reading the old tomes made him swell at Spain's proud achievements. It was then he knew he wanted to see war. Particularly, to be a conquistador, which after hearing the stories, knew what legends were made of, and he wanted that for himself, for his own life story.

They bid him a sorrowful farewell, and he was off. His desire to learn and eagerness to prove himself saw him finally fit to become a soldier. With this new title, he came closer to his great dream of becoming a conquistador. He wanted to be just like the famed conquerors of the New World, even if the largest empires of the Yucatan had already been toppled by the likes of Hernan Cortes, Pedro de Alvarado, and Vasco Nunez de Balboa. Cristobal would use his imagination, and picture himself coming onto shores to swarms of natives with spears defending their homeland from the Spanish warriors, with himself leading the charge. In his head, he fought with veracity, and he let his dream guide him in his youth. In the dilemma of the heart versus the brain, he followed his heart, which told him to serve.

He spent his early years as a common infantryman, sharpening his teeth in the Iberian Peninsula.

These memories flooded Clyde's unconscious mind as he drifted through these different visions. Recalling all aspects of a new childhood, a new adulthood he had never seen before. Ms. Claudia's voice came from beyond. "The ship, Clyde, get back to the ship. What's happening as you reach the beach?" Her ethereal voice reached over from the real world. Clyde was devoid of time and space; such concepts didn't matter, and while he struggled at first to find it, the unknown metaphysical forces that be allowed him to navigate his way back further into his ancient memory, seeing now for the very first time, the golden shores of the true Americas.

Chapter 11

THE NEW WORLD

He shouted, "Guide us straight into the middle of the *golfo*, best you can!" Simultaneously, the colors of His Majesty King Phillip II of Spain began to fly in the harmonious swells of turquoise waters, moving along the Western Pacific Crest, the warmer waters being closer to land.

Cristobal had been given his orders directly from the king. Being the young captain he was, he had undergone much specialized training to get an opportunity such as this. He'd purchased his own weapons: a rapier with a beautiful gold handguard, and from a Turk, he acquired a fine scimitar of Moorish origin. His armor was a gift from his adopted father after he'd finally earned the title he had worked so hard for. In hopes he'd bring honor to the Trujillo family, Don Roberto gave his adoptive son his own old morion, with a cardinal plume, signifying his own status as a captain and member of the warrior class. It was Cristobal's high honor to represent the family as one of the esteemed conquistadors, the knights of Spain.

He made ready in his captain's quarters, donning the armor over his breeches and blouse, fastening his sword belt, making sure both were seated where they needed to be. He grabbed his morion off the bedpost, stuffing his other plumed cap under his breastplate. He tidied up the quarters one last time, taking a good look, because he knew he would never see the comfort of ships again. Even for the others, it would be months, maybe years before they returned home, if they returned home at all. He'd already spent hours packing different satchels with various essential captain's equipment: Journals, soaps, snake oils, herbal remedies and salves, as well as spare clothes, bedding for camp, fire-starting materials, ammo for his arquebus, and several books. He carried his own load, no different from anybody else.

Having double checked all the various things on his prerequisite departure list, he believed himself ready to embark on what would be one of the most famous expeditions of conquistadors in the New World since Cortes. Cristobal was a warrior of the Lord. He believed in the cause, and taking a knee on the side of his bed, in full armor, made the sign of the holy cross and prayed to his Heavenly Father.

"O blessed Father, Lord Jesus Christ, I ask you to bless forward our footfalls in this strange land, walk with me, and lead me so I might better lead these men to you and away from the nine circles. We are the pilgrims of restitute days. We ask for shelter, for glory, for your light. Grant us passage. In the name of the Father, Son, and the Holy Spirit, amen." Rising to stand, Cristobal turned and headed out the door of his cabin, morion in hand, bags over his shoulders and on his back, his mission not only being one for Spain.

Last night's storms were now a memory, but nothing the experienced sailors under his command couldn't handle. They'd seen much worse. Of course, Cristobal himself was well learned in navigation, using the stars, the charts, and his compass. They'd been able to successfully sail on course for the last several months. However, *La Madre Rosa* was not the lead ship; she was a galleon nestled among the other five ships— one other galleon, her sister vessel, and three additional galleys—the quickest of which was commanded by the leader of this naval expeditionary force, captain Fernando de Malaga. The ships were rowed by the lowest enlisted soldiers and sailors and navigated by the ships' officers. Conversely, it was Cristobal's company that was the precious cargo, for they were the reinforcements. The crew under his watch had done much better than he expected, no worse for wear than any other band would be after such ventures. They had deaths, tossing their deceased overboard and to the depths of the ocean floor. The ships were horribly unseaworthy after the voracious crucible of sailing the rugged Atlantic, then worse off once they reached Bahamian waters, to be pounded continuously by tropical storms and cyclones ripping through the coasts of the unknown American mainland, the Indies Isles, and the Golfo. Seeing spectacular displays of nautical expertise was routine, as they had been in the sailors' perfect element for months.

Soon, though, they would be in the land of the Indians. The same lands that bore forth the legends of the famed Aztec jaguars. The southern continent for the last twenty years had been slowly explored, conquered, and taken under Spanish influence, with the pages of future history books being written daily. The game was now one the conquistadors were familiar with—soldiering, and suffering, doing both in silence.

The sound of the seagulls overhead filled his ears as they drew nearer to land, now seeing a long stretch of beach in the distance. Cristobal walked up to the bow of *La Madre Rosa*, observing all the sailors engaged in their nautical tasks, dreaming the same dreams as he, of kissing the foreign sands, liberated at last from the confines of the hundred-twenty-by-forty-foot ship. Ocean madness had claimed a few sorry fellows, unable to cope with the futility of their cries, unable to escape the horrors of nightmarish winds and fifty-foot-tall waves tossing their tiny wooden ship on the water as if it were a matchbox.

They speculated on the sordid variety of sea life they would soon be cooking up on fires along the beach, as many of the sailors were highly capable fishermen, coming from places like Valencia and Mallorca. They eyeballed their straight-line course, unsure of the true antemeridian line. The sailors shouted to one another from across the water, signaling crude gestures and jests, but it was all in good play and all in good spirit.

Cristobal's orders were to link up with an already-established Spanish Expeditionary Force camp, not too far inland but its precise location still vague. Pulling out his looking glass and peeking through, he spied the general lay of the land, and the questions of strategy that filled his head distracted him from the relentless noise that accompanied large groups of tightly wound, strung-out men who would kill to look at a woman. The land pulled him back in, the great mystery of it. He faced a long strip of island, running parallel the coast, which would be a nuisance to navigate, since it wasn't directly connected to the mainland. Navigating the ships through the various tighter inlets would be even more hazardous, as they couldn't tell the depth of the shallows until they were nearly right on top of them. The rising sun made the water a mirror, firing her whitecaps, rushing waves carrying them closer and closer to the white sands of their sons. Astonishingly, it was harder to see in waters so clear after months of looking through sore eyes at the same muddied and monochromatic seascape.

Looking for the southernmost edge of the unnamed barrier island, Cristobal determined they'd skirt its coast until they found a place suitable for the flotilla's landfall. After a few hours more, they reached a fair spot, appropriately before sundown. Climbing his way up again to the crow's nest, Cristobal met with his sentry posted at the top, who after spending all night fighting the storms from above, had crashed out in the bottom of his crowmaster's bucket, dead asleep in the middle of the day.

Cristobal applauded Dendrick Rodon, who ignored the dirty looks of the upper castes, which felt him too poor to think so highly of himself. He possessed a grandiose personality rarely found in people trodden down by society. He claimed he could see farther than any other man, allegedly having the sharpest eyes in all of Spain. He did have several reputable people corroborate these claims, reciting spectacular feats of ocular exhibition which proved his ability beyond the glimmer of a doubt. His family was afflicted by extreme poverty and hunger, a result of their birth, not choice. From a young age, he and his brothers were forced to hunt for small game to supplement the family's meager diets. Hunting in the Castilian Woods honed his vision and propounded his grit against the rugged terrain of the inland Spanish forests, battling winter snows and training his eyes to fight whiteout. Life would see him made into an excellent conquistador, strong and quick-witted.

He had earned every right to think about himself the way he did, and he regularly reminded them that he came from nothing. Dendrick Rodon built a reputation on the gifted eyes he was given by God, and this made his services highly requested across the whole of the Spanish Armada.

"Dendrick, do you see it starting to break up there? Look, there, farther south," Cristobal said, pointing, and handing over his looking glass.

Dendrick, taken by surprise, awoke startled. Coming to his *wits*, he asked the captain apologetically once more to repeat his question, which he did.

"Aye, it's breaking up, all right, but it's going to be a tricky one, Captain. Uhhhh—" He put his hands on his hips and looked out, nodding his head. "I think we can do it."

Taking back his looking glass, Cristobal held it up to his eye once more, training the lens on their objective. He looked through the telescope for a few seconds longer, then pulled it away from his eyes, pointing with his index finger. "Guide us to those beaches off of that horn, on the other side."

"Aye, sir, I can try."

"I trust your eyes. Get us there safely."

With that, Cristobal stepped over the bucket, climbing down the webbed rope one foot at a time, the fluttering red cross sails flapping with the south-southeasterly gales blowing off of the golfo, sea spray coming up and over the rails as the tide picked up near the approaching land.

"Make ready, we're hitting the sand in an hour," said Cristobal to Enrico, who was overseeing the current state of things, making good on the manifests, inventories, and other logistical headaches that Cristobal wanted nothing to do with. Grabbing the hard-working sailors by the shoulders as he passed them along the railing, Cristobal congratulated them on a job well done and told them they should be proud of having achieved what so few had ever done. The crew were mostly from the poorer castes, so this was their chance to pave a new future for themselves, in a place of boundless opportunities, as conquistadors or as sailors.

The water slowly changed from a deep blue to an emerald green, lightening up as the boats began to draw nearer the shore. Glowing shades of jade and blue, the setting sun blanketing the tired world with purples, pinks, and oranges, stretched over what could only be called God's master canvas. On those long and stormy nights, when hope was mostly lost, they had no other place to turn to but their faith, and to each other.

"Haul in the sails!" Cristobal shouted. It was echoed across the vessel and across the water to the other ships behind them. The sandbar was fast encroaching; such beaches Cristobal hadn't seen in his whole life. The undiluted face of raw nature plain ahead, the sweltering heat of day doing all but giving remission. It was a huge mass of land, truly a new world in every sense. The crew gave each other praises once more, raising their cries and prayers to the Lord as they inched into the shore break. For them it meant rest, the arduous work now nearly completed. The propinquity of returning home would not be talked about until measures called for such discussion. In the meantime, the only standing order Captain Cristobal had to go off was the more important objective of finding the bigger Spanish base camp. From there, the expedition would be in somebody else's hands.

The wind pushed the ships slowly into shore, landing on the sandbar of a long beach, the evening waves lapping easily into the sand and pulling themselves back out, a steady rhythm, accompanied by the hum of birds and gulls overhead. The galleon came to a stop, no longer able to go forward in the narrow longshore.

"Drop the anchor! We've made it!" Captain Cristobal shouted. The command again thunderously called across *La Madre Rosa* and echoed throughout the battered remains of the fleet, docking adjacently along the coast. Shortly thereafter, all the ships were gently rocked in the cradle of the ocean, at last, solid ground before their very eyes. To walk on land again was enough to make a man cry, and more than a few shamelessly did so.

Cristobal gave a great sigh and a quick prayer of gratitude for the conclusion of their voyage. The hard work they were about to be faced with was not far off, so for the time being, the men could celebrate the evening away with hot food, wine, and a good night's sleep, camping out under the stars, giving their horses the chance to feed and drink as well.

Cristobal leaned over the railing of the ship, looking down at the waves washing over the sand, watching the pull and release of the turquoise tide.

"Alright, let's get ready. Enrico, fetch Dendrick, bring the sea captain too. His men will need special orders. Take four other conquistadores for security. We're stepping foot ceremoniously into this New World. Gather the padre; he will offer up our gratitude directly, for the blessing of our travels, and for the glory of our successes."

The future, unknown. The vastness of this place, unfathomable. Looking out at the thick, lush forests, the mountains, and high rising valleys, the rivers that the ocean must have fed could have been forever countless. It was a land of abundance. An astonishing scene to behold, this was the culmination of years of dreaming and manifesting that dream. Fighting through months of seasick nights, living life at the mercy of a temperamental Mother Nature. Bearing witness to the Roman Neptune's boastful wrathfulness.

Easing himself over the railing and stepping into the rowboat, their weapons and gear in tow, the small party jammed themselves into the small craft. Captain Cristobal at the front, eyed the shores with a steely gaze, full of wonderment. They were lowered from above by shirtless sailors chewing on the tobacco leaves they harvested in the Havanese plantations. They rowed for a few minutes, anxiety and excitement now overtaking their emotions. This part of the empire was still virginal, the history having yet to have been written. It soon would be.

Clyde had witnessed all of this as if in a dream, watching as if he were there, but living it vicariously, feeling as if it were his own actions and words happening in real time. A voice far out in space called to him.

"What do you see, Clyde? Where are you? Who are you? Who is with you?" Ms. Claudia asked from beyond.

Clyde, who was in a deep trance, with eyes closed, lying on the circular sofa in the middle room, heard this in his dormant hemispheres and gave a weak response, speaking through the narrow opening of his lips to her in a crying whisper. "It's beaches, the most beautiful beach I've ever seen in my life. Ships. Huge ships, lots of men," he said, his face twisting into a terribly agonized heartbroken expression, on the verge of tears as he felt pain deep inside himself for some reason.

"Captain, they're calling me Captain."

Ms. Claudia, who was cradling his head in her lap, massaging his temples with her fingers, shushed him back to his dream, running her fingers through his hair as he lay there immobile. "Be not afraid," she said in a whisper, into his ear. "Go to it."

The rowboat at last would go no more, its part in this drama now over. Stepping off into the shallow water, which warmly ran through his leather boots, they sloshed their way up toward the sand.

"Be fair to us," Cristobal said as he stepped onto solid sand, looking everywhere, gazing in every direction, along the long and expansive coasts. There was more green than the eye could see where the jungles began.

Then Cristobal gave a victorious cry as he turned to hug his lieutenant, Enrico Cardenas, and the other conquistadors. He gave a hug to the sailors' captain as well, Fernando, congratulations for successful seafaring and captaining. The two officers, one a soldier, one a sailor, patted each other on the back, laughing aloud, and sporting huge grins under their waxed moustaches.

Reaching down and splashing his face with seawater, refreshing his cracked and dry skin, Cristobal turned to face their personal steward of faith, the holy man who had come with them from Cuba. The priest, or as they called him, the padre.

"Padre, please, come say a prayer over us and this land. Say a few words for us to our Lord now," Cristobal said as he motioned for the father to step forward. "Certainly," the padre said in an older, broken voice, the saltwater glistening off his beard and mustache, smiling in delight through great white teeth. They all took up hands and formed a circle together.

The father began his prayer.

"It is in Jesus Christo's name we give our thanks to you, O Lord our God, for guiding us to the safety of your creation and delivering us from the perilous seas that sought to destroy us for so long. Bless these men, Father. In your name they've traveled across oceans, fought sickness and despair. Missing their wives and their children, Lord, they are here to do good work O God, to do their empire and king a great honor, in exploring this foreign world you've delivered them to. Give them your strength and your wisdom, and walk with us all as we lean on you for everything we may need. In the name of the Father, the Son, and the Holy Spirit, all say amen."

"Amen."

Cristobal then gave the orders to have everyone come ashore and set up camp. The sun would soon set, and one by one the rowboats began shuttling sailors and conquistadors to the shore to join them. More than a few excited men didn't care to wait, jumping ship directly into the saltwater, which quenched their sun-baked skin as they swam up to the sand, crawling on hands and knees to the hot beach, kissing the ground below them, tasting the soft white sand on their lips.

Chapter 12

LANDING PARTY

Fires began to glow along the beach as more men and more supplies made landfall. Sleeping on the sand would be a nice change, with the coastal breeze and sea mist cooling them off in the dark of night. Food was cooked over the fire—lamb and beef, potatoes. Fruit, too, was passed around, and wine sacks were shared until they ran dry. Merriment quickly filled the shore. The spirit of good company and good drink working their magic, bringing out songs and verses from these good men. Captain Cristobal made his rounds to each campfire, striking up conversations with the myriad characters under his command.

Officers stayed with officers, sergeants with sergeants, the lower ranks with lower ranks. Dividing themselves into sailors and conquistadors. "Do not let the men to your right or left be strangers. We are all now the only family we will know," Cristobal said to one group. "Go and make friends, talk, play, drink, be at ease. The worst of it is over!" Encouraging some joint companionship, it was a true sentiment; they would be all each other had out there, and there was no place for grievance upon your neighbor. They were the closest thing to family for thousands of miles.

Instruments were brought out, and music was played on string, wind, and drum. The fires simmered down to low crackles as the men cared less to tend to them, but being tired and weary, preferred to bed down peacefully with casual whispers shared among themselves. Cristobal laid his head down on his satchel beside his most loyal military comrade, Enrico. The two of them talked quietly. Cristobal, with a mind that never slowed down, considered the logistics of his company by firelight, going over his personal ledgers, seeing their stock and inventories, creating ration plans and orders of movement. Tomorrow they'd need to finish unloading everything before pushing into the jungle and finding the already-established Spanish basecamp further inland.

The stars glimmered with the light of a waxing moon, as the ocean waves in their unrelenting rhythm crashed sequentially on the sands. "You know, Enrico," said Cristobal, taking a bite from his apple, "Nobody has brought me my horse. You charged someone with her care, correct?"

"Aye, Captain, got a man on each ship keeping an eye on them. She'll come ashore in the morning," the lieutenant said.

"Good. I'm going to write in my journal for a bit. We'll wake with the sunrise, my friend. Go get some sleep now, brother." He pulled from his satchel a brown leather journal with cream parchment pages. Pulling out a quill and using a seashell to hold the ink, Cristobal turned onto his stomach and began to make notes.

23 Junio 1543

I am kept in the good company of the brave men who traveled here with me. Of the original 250 expedition members, we've lost 24 on the voyages over. What this place here is, I cannot say, nor is it within my humble heart to question the shores which God delivered us to. The hardest days are ahead of us I believe. Many who came with us have no intention of returning home. For some of them, there is nothing to go home to. The great thirst for adventure that ravages the minds of young men makes them easy prey to the dangers and trials of a life never before seen. Nobody can say for sure what the New World holds for these men. I have felt the pangs of displacement. I pray and seek to maintain a clear and undiluted mind, for the lives of the many that are on my conscience, just finished celebrating their achievement, but the work is far from over. On first impressions, the mission is intimidating, it is no small charge, and If I perish here, no one will know my name or who I was or the things I liked or held most dearly in life. My face will disappear from time, like so many others who dreamed of having the opportunities we now possess. It is our duty to carve our own names by force into the annals of history, to make ourselves and our stories known to the world. The true glory in life is not wealth but in building a powerful legacy, giving yourself time to borrow time from the great beyond. That is all. Tomorrow waits.

The sweeping waves crested the coast with a robust energy and constant display of awesome nature. Nightfall had come, and on the sand they slept. The good dreams of adventure, being satiated in this most fitting manner, quenching their thirsts finally on the sweet reward of their toils. It was quite interesting to Cristobal, this strange chance he had been given in life. He'd come a long way from being a simple orphan. If all went according to plan, tomorrow they would fully unload their belongings and equipment from the five sailing vessels, bidding their farewells to *La Madre Rosa*, leaving her there to rot away abandoned until they returned.

It was not more than twenty years ago when Cortes landed in this place as well, bringing with him the full wrath and power of Spain. It was serving in this capacity that Cristobal regarded as his greatest life accomplishment. Drunk off of it, he knew the glories would be thrown upon his feet. The parades, festivals, and parties would all be great too. Should they be triumphant, they'd even be rewarded with land of their own to settle, which many of them planned to do. Conquistadors earned a special privilege, having fought and bled for their country, so the Spanish government saw to their good treatment and due reward.

On the contrary, the dishonor of failure was a terrible fixture to wear next to one's name. The bells of shame he would have to wear, should their spoils not meet the expectations of the Spanish throne. King Phillip II had a clear purpose and direction when it came to settling New Spain, making the further reaches of the empire, those yet to be explored, something new and modern, taking advantage of the region's abundant natural resources. The plethora of different spices and the new species of wild game to hunt led to intently researching the densely rich native fauna. Since the early conquests, a period of science and discovery had been initiated, hidden away from the church, of course. The Indigenous possessed much knowledge of these sacred botanicals, many of which had clear medicinal implications, and the Spanish sought to acquire this sacred knowledge for themselves.

Sunrise stirred all life to rise, men and creatures alike. Stretching in the dawn of a new day, a refreshed feeling was shared among them. Dusting himself off, Cristobal sat up, looking out toward the ships still rocking where they were anchored.

"Enrico, get everyone up," Cristobal said, looking over his shoulder to his sleeping first mate, who stirred a little but was hoping for a few more minutes of shuteye. Cristobal rubbed the sleep out of his eyes, feeling the dew on his skin with his sandy hands.

"Get the supplies off the boats. I want every last scrap of food taken from the holds. The horses are to be freshly watered and fed. Everyone is going to sweat today. We'll stay in camp for one more night, then we're off in the morning."

Rising to stand, Cristobal reached out a hand to help Enrico get up. Enrico was now alert and listening to his boss's orders, adding it all to his never-ending list of things to do for the captain. He helped Enrico to his feet. "We've got all day to sort it out, brother," said Cristobal.

There was already movement among the men, who had woken up early to bathe in the ocean, splashing around naked in the sunrise, enjoying the morning freedom. They let their freshly beaten clothes dry in the western winds. Overall spirit and morale seemed good among the men as Cristobal looked around. The crew, now notified of their tasks, started to break away from their little campsites and moved onto the ships to begin the disembarkation procedures.

Cristobal spotted their Cuban priest returning from a walk down the beach. The padre, barefooted in the sand, let his robes hang down at his ankles as the morning tide brought the seafoam in and over his toes, grounding himself to his new earthly surroundings. Walking up to one another, Cristobal halted the padre as he drew nearer.

"Padre, a word?"

The old gray friar simply nodded, placing his hands at the small of his back as the two of them walked then together.

Cristobal pointed to the jungle. "You see that, Padre?"

The padre held his hand over his brow to block the glare, helping him see what it was the captain was talking about.

"*That*, Padre, is what we need the Lord to guide us through. *That* is going to be treacherous. This way, Padre, please, join me."

He obliged, the two of them turning toward the forest, walking up the sloped surface leading away from the beach toward the unbeaten bush. Pausing to glance behind him, Cristobal pointed to the crew. "Those men will do anything I tell them to, not because they have to, but because they are free men; they can come and go as they choose. It is because of their loyalty that they stay. Loyalty for their country and their king."

They walked up to the wood line, shuddering at the dark jungle they would need to pass through. Sliding his hand along the smooth skin of the palm trees, Cristobal continued. "You see these *palmas*, Padre? Feel the warm sun on your skin? We are here. We've made it, but to be present is a choice that we must consciously make, or else we'll miss the whole thing. We'll miss the point of this whole experience."

The padre listened as he walked along with the young captain.

"Let us both take scrupulous notes. You must scribe your daily observations, detail the journey's twists and turns, and let not one detail of our future dealings go unremembered. You will tell our story, should anything happen to me. I trust you. Tell our story justly, and as true as you can," the padre looked at the captain as if to ask a question, but the captain had one last directive to give.

"Stay close." He added.

Finishing his monologue, Cristobal looked at the padre, reading the man for a flicker of emotion beyond the stoic glare of an impregnable moral fortress as such he was, looking for affirmation.

"We will be blessed, my son, and you will tell the story yourself," the padre said with a humble bow, his gray brows lifting with his heartfelt expression. Having heard all of that, Cristobal felt at ease; the padre's polite response naturally incumbent with the manner of his profession.

They turned to head back to join the rest of the men unloading crates of gear, barrels of rations, various livestock, mules and horses. The beachfront was now humming with the officers coordinating the young conquistadors and sailors, seeing that the work gets done timely and efficiently.

"Captain, she's being brought out now. Want me to saddle her?" Enrico said as he came over to join Cristobal and the padre.

"No need to bother, my friend. I know she'd rather I do it. I will take her for a ride shortly," he said, watching the horses being led off the gangways. They brought her off the ship; she was rambunctious and needed to blow off several months' worth of accumulated steam. She only cared to hear the voice of her master, who had always treated her with fervent tenderness and deep respect. A remarkably blonde paso fino steed, she was of the purest breed and could run like the wind blew, which, unlike Dendrick Rodon's claims, the question of her ability could not be raised, as the reputation of her exploits would be famous one day. She was as loyal as the best street-begotten dogs and incredibly smart for her kind, understanding many different commands and phrases. Cristobal had worked very hard to teach to her.

Simora was her name, and she had been a gift from an old Hidalgo Cristobal met on the road to Madrid several years back. Her coat was a golden blonde, with a white blaze starting from the top of her forehead and going straight down to her nose. It was a special marking of her kind, for a special kind of steed, for it was she who carried on her back a champion of New Spain.

She couldn't help but share in her master's stubbornness as well, ignoring his commands to come, she sloshed her way through the water and up the beach, drinking freely from the ocean. Cristobal, finally tired of yelling for her, gave a sharp whistle instead and watched with excitement as she turned around on a dime and began to trot his way. Clamoring up to him, the saltwater sparkling off her mane and short brushed hair, she nuzzled her snout to his forehead as the two of them met. She was a truly faithful companion, with an unbreakable bond that only time and trust can build. Such a giving and reciprocal relationship was hard to find in the realm of humans.

"Welcome to your new home," he said in a silly, pacifying voice, stroking her muzzle as she neighed in contentment.

"Go, drink, *vamos.*"

She recognized the words using her higher horse intellect and trotted back over to the water, taking off in a great gallop to join her equine comrades and the few conquistadors taking their siesta up the beach, doing what men and horses do, horseplay.

The rest of the afternoon, Cristobal made various checks on the progress of the unloading of the different ships, making sure the important equipment was all accounted for. One of the sailors, a stoutly built, mustachioed man, was laboriously inspecting several firearms and munitions crates. Cristobal, now unencumbered by his armor, approached the working fellow to ask for a report, which the sailor, who didn't recognize the captain due to his lack of uniform and insignias, struggled to regurgitate the unorganized figures from his ledger. The arms master also apparently had a terrible stutter, and Cristobal decided to leave him be, since he felt bad watching the poor bastard. He already knew what he was supposed to do anyway. He sailed with their sister ship, which was the galleon that carried the armada bigwigs, the true navigators.

Seeking out the quartermaster of their sister galleon *La Estrella Rosada,* Cristobal found instead the captain, who was his bitterest rival, Captain Fernando. He contemplated his pride for a second, choosing to swallow his ego and embarrassment and ask the sailor's captain for a replacement compass, after his was smashed when he was thrown from the rope webbing leading up to the crow's nest. Tapping his fingers on Fernando's arm, Cristobal asked his question.

"Would you be able to outfit me with a spare compass, friend?"

Fernando, who in plain clothes resembled just another one of the ragged sailors, kept in reserve the clear seriousness and cold intensity of a highly capable naval commander. "Yes, I would, brother. I have several. Here, have this one." He pulled from his waistcoat a fair instrument, with the needle quickly settling on true north. The properties of geomagnetism had yet to be fully understood, with the magic of the devices remaining a mystery to those who were not trained in their use. During the transaction, the stuttering arms master passed by, recognizing now the leader of the conquistador party.

"Oh, Captain! I'm so very sorry! I didn't know that was you. Do forgive me. I have a spare compass, several in fact," he said, fumbling with his satchel for a few moments before he looked up at Cristobal, who was holding his newly acquired directional instrument. Fernando was all right for that one.

Everyone was on everyone's nerves once the work began. Playtime being over, Cristobal needed time to think, and he figured what better time to think than while exercising the lethargy out of his horse.

"Simora," he said, slapping her neck in playful jest. "Are you ready to spread your wings on this world?"

The atmosphere was one of optimism within the camp, as the group of more than two hundred took over the beach. The weather was nearly perfect. Turning to his gear, he began to work the bridle as he searched for his saddle, somewhere among his piles of disorganized gear. Curse the incompetent fools who'd dispatched his personals from the ship while he was away performing various *recondos* throughout the immediate area.

Giving her a strong slap on her hindquarters, Cristobal and Simora swiftly took off, as fast as she could, working out the stiffness in her rigid muscles after months of no exercise and poor diet. She took off at an almost uncontainable pace, which took the rusty captain a second to gain control of. Off she ran, kicking up sand and splashing water with each measured step, sending herself into a full sprint along the length of the beach. Feeling the wind on his face, the spirit of the old expedition was alive in the both of them, master and beast. Racing along the coast, they ran for several miles in one direction, and examining the greenery, Cristobal looked toward the dense fauna. Seeing all the brush they'd have to blaze through was daunting, but something that would need to be done.

Searching for a better, more suitable avenue of approach into the bush, the only real way to make a true determination would be to turn Simora around and ride back toward the ships the *opposite* way, scouting the same beach over again from a different point of view this time, just in case he missed anything the first time. He made mental notes of any suitable breaks or trails, which would eliminate wasted time spent dead reckoning through the heavily vegetated terrain. Cristobal's mission was to deliver the company from his authority and into the hands of *the comandante.*

This could have been the first time this part of the mainland had seen such travelers, but the base camp, according to the briefing Captain Cristobal sat in prior to their embarkation, was that it was not too far off into the jungle, and the expeditionary forces were already expecting reinforcements. So, by procedure, they'd have scouts of their own dispatched to search for them. The only caution was that the expeditionary force they were to supplement came from the opposing side, attacking the brush from their position already within the mainland, not from the coast, as was Cristobal's case. The forces Cristobal was to supplement had come up from lower New Spain, on an expedition north to further stretch the empirical boundaries.

Constant exploration had been taking place for the better part of the last three decades, and with the conquering of such empires as the Mayans and the Aztecs, there were still warring tribes that needed to be cleared out from the newly acquired territory if the land was to be made proper Spanish property. There was heavy fighting going on in the south, and the push from the Southern Americas up north was proving a tough task. Despite the Spaniards' clear advantages over the Indigenous population, the native warriors had a strong reputation for fearlessness and tenacity. Their ranks possessed skilled archers, spearmen, and hunters, who knew the land better than anyone, forging a tribal society in that harsh expanse of inhospitable wilderness. Not to mention the various elements in which the different tribes operated. They had adapted naturally to the world around them, changing in time as the world had done over a period of uncountable seasons.

The reports varied in their consistency, but every tribe had its own unique signature. The people did follow some measures of structure and organization. Clan-style hierarchies of power, orders of power based on blood and land. Their religious practices were far from orthodox, given the knowledge of Indian barbarism in the south. Their modes of life were primitive, mostly agrarian, living off of the land. The things they did bring to the table were excellent understandings of the physical and nonphysical world around them. In the New World, with their highly capable agricultural skills, they aligned their knowledge of the land and seasons and combined them with an advanced understanding of mathematics and cosmological sciences. This way they were able to provide themselves with their basic staple foods.

What terrible grief it was to have to eradicate the people who lived here. It weighed on Cristobal's heart, and he resolved to be as diplomatic as possible, wherever possible, to spare unnecessary blood. He thought this as he rode past the sailors, carrying the rowboats to shore on their shoulders.

The sun was starting her evening descent, and the colors of the sky were even more extravagant this evening than last. Amethyst, citrine, and pearled reds, with turquoise seams, woven together between the scattered cumulus clouds, with their silver linings that just barely poked through, silhouetting the countless shapes, which on the lower levels broke down into wispy cirrus, now blown easily on lazy gales. It was unlike any display he could recall seeing in days before, receiving the omen as it sanctified their cause and journey.

She carried him far and fast, as his own indifferent thoughts occupied his mind, failing to realize he had overshot his destination, Cristobal brought her to halt. "Whoa, girl, easy now, easy." She paused, standing there sticking her head down toward the ground. Cristobal scanned the area around him in a full circle, taking in the surroundings in a deeper sense. Stopping to look, listen, and smell, he heard the bird choir singing many different parts in their mixed tonalities of song. In his stillness, he heard the breaking brush, the snapping of twigs and branches, which he took for indication there was bountiful game, which meant food was a resource they had available to them.

He hoped there was a decent amount of fresh water stemming from the different tributaries and inlets further inland. They would need to cut into the jungle and head straight east, while sending out scouting parties of their own to locate the main Spanish force with whom they were to make their rendezvous, reinforcing the veteran expedition and further exploring the wild territories and lands north of the capital.

Turning back toward the ships, Simora now comfortably trotted along, happy to once again be free and left to do what horses do. At the site of the offloading, Enrico was directing the men, making sure that all the equipment was together so it could be better organized, and the weight evenly distributed to the men and mules for the journey inward. Various piles of gear now lay scattered across the sandy beach, and with dusk approaching, they'd make camp here for one final night before heading out for good. It would be a long time, if ever, before they would see these ships again.

"Captain, welcome back. I hope the fresh air did you good. Don't forget to have a bath. The water feels nice too, very warm," said Lieutenant Enrico. He nodded over to some sailors, already thinking their work was done for the day. These goons were passing around a wine sack.

"Maybe they could be of some use and catch us something fresh for tonight?" said Cristobal.

That sounded good to him, and it sounded good to Enrico, and orders were orders. Enrico promptly went and offered some encouragement to the several happy sailors. They started casting lines and nets seeing if they might procure anything besides the basic rations they'd been surviving on for months. When they landed in Havana, they were treated to all their favorite Spanish and Cuban food.

Enrico Cardenas was an energetic officer, one who took his job very seriously, but also a man with a good sense of humor, who did his very best to see the good side of things, even when the circumstances were grave. Cristobal had picked Cardenas for his proven battle ability and penchant for leadership. He was like Cristobal, but younger and less disgruntled. He had come from a poor family as well, a common theme shared among conquistadors. His family struggled to make ends meet with their small parcel of land, so he resolved to join the military at his first chance, so he might send a portion of his earnings back home to his people to help them along. They didn't have much growing up, but they were never without. Enrico's mother was a good woman whom Cristobal had the opportunity to share plenty of meals with prior to their sailing from Spain. A few days before they set sail, Cristobal was in charge of hosting a farewell banquet for the families of the departing.

Cristobal, having selected a great many men personally from his command for this expedition, had figured it would be a kind gesture to invite the parents and spouses of his men to a formal dinner party, so he might set their minds at ease about where their sons were going and under whose thumb they'd be pressed. In a centuries-old Segovian castle, waited on by servants, they enjoyed a delicious candlelit feast, with a wonderful assortment of foods and delicacies provided for by the government. Such food some of the peasants had not seen before.

Cristobal looked dapper in his captain's dress uniform, medals and ribbons gleaming under the soft light of the room. The golden hour outside glittered through the several stained-glass panels adorning the castle walls. The long table was quickly crowded as the several courses were brought out. The seats were all filled with guests, each partaking in their own particular fancy, whether that be eating until they couldn't bear to anymore or drinking until they achieved the same. Prior to the feast, Cristobal offered a speech, which he had neither rehearsed nor prepared for. He raised his glass and offered up his inspiring words, followed by the warm captain's toast.

They had all felt homesick early on as the vast emptiness and monochromatic blue seas began to be the only thing they saw, day in and day out. Each man grappled with this his own way, the captain too, who took to his quarters in his spare time, digging his head into his nautical charts or into some dusty volumes from his shelf. He sought to distract himself from his own life, the one he was leaving behind, back in Spain.

Fires began to illuminate the beach, as the men settled themselves for the night. A long day of hot work in this western sun was taking its toll, still, most were in high spirits. At Cristobal's encampment, Enrico, the padre, the crow master Dendrick Rodon, and the sailors' own captain, Fernando, were all seated by the warmth of slowly smoldering flames. The padre had been seated several feet away when Captain Fernando invited him closer to the fire.

"Padre, come now, do not think you are a stranger in the mix of these conquistadors and sailors. We are all men and children of God. Come make yourself warm. The evening chills are not yet at their worst," Fernando beckoned to the old friar who, in his robes, politely smiled and offered his gratitude, scooting along the sand, closer to the blaze.

Captain Fernando was meant to be Cristobal's counterpart on this expedition. He was an extremely skilled navigator, with a great knowledge of all nautical schools of thought. The seas were his life; from a young boy on the shores of South Spain, the salty water of the Alboran Sea flowed in his veins. He himself had been on several voyages to exotic places, Portugal, Morocco, and Algeria, to name a few. He understood how to handle logistics, how much supplies and food were needed, seeing to even rationing and fair distribution of work and rest among his sailors and subordinate naval officers. He ordered his subordinates around with a humble voice, but he was a gravely serious man. He was also the one who paid his sailors' wages, seeing personally to the treasury.

Cristobal had taken a dislike to Fernando early on in their journey. In Cristobal's mind, as the commander of his company, he was the leader of the primary ground force, which made him the sole leader of them all. Fernando's purpose was getting them there. The conquistadors boasted a great pride in their war work, and it was not only their egos that had been bolstered by this, but rather, they all carried an overzealousness of the heart. Fernando was very well liked by the sailors he commanded, on account of his fair and reasonable approach. But one pitfall to this was that Cristobal's own men had more than once been out of line in addressing the naval captain, taking him for a pushover and failing to respect the rank that he had rightfully earned.

Captain Cristobal felt no remorse in dishing out punishment as he saw fit, and such a display of indiscipline was cause for a great thrashing of the lash, by his own hand. Fernando wouldn't take up for himself like that; he didn't enjoy inflicting pain on others.

Huddled around the fire and sitting cross-leggeded, they stared into the orange flames, which slowly turned the locally acquired firewood to charcoal. Things were quiet now in the beach camp. Enrico broke the peaceful silence to inquire about their plans of action.

"Captain, how do you feel about what's next?"

Cristobal couldn't help the long pause he took before answering that question, because he felt it was too broad. How could he say what was next, for something that was the culmination of his life's work? The dreams and aspirations he'd worked toward for so long were finally here, but how could he confidently say that he knew where it was all going to lead them? Working toward his dreams, as his dreams were fueled by the desire to fulfill his purpose. To say that he took this opportunity seriously would be an understatement.

He had found several decent potential entry points, but cutting through the brush with their amount of gear, bodies, and animals would be difficult, not to mention the noise they'd make would telegraph their presence easily for everyone within earshot. The several inlets and cutaways off in the distance opened up to several large lagunas, with a sporadic brush, palm trees lining the shoreline. The vegetation was largely untouched, and they couldn't say for certain that on this strip of the beach, humans had landed before. The stars shimmered above the fire, smoke rising between the low-moving clouds of a cool autumn night. During the day, the blistering heat from the high afternoon sun baked everything it touched, while darkness brought extremely low temperatures, bordering on freezing.

Trailblazing a fresh route would not be easy, but he only needed to make it to the base camp. Then Cristobal could relinquish some of the duties to the officers who had more to lose. "First things first, we need to find the rest of the expedition. Once that's established, our further outstanding orders will be seen to in order of precedence," he said, straight to the point as always and leaving little room for the imagination.

"We set out at first light. Don't stay up too late." Looking to Lieutenant Cardenas, he said, "Hope that answers your question."

A good last night's rest was a plan everybody could live with.

Chapter 13

AWAKEN

"*Wake.*" Clyde heard it from deep in his consciousness as he sat there by the fire, in the company of these other strangely familiar individuals. Yet in a second, he came to, quickly recognizing the surroundings where he'd left his true consciousness. Behind him, Ms. Claudia was rushing back to the couch from the bar with a large glass of water. "Drink, baby, drink," she said as she pressed the glass to his lips, tipping his head back gently. He swallowed to the last drop. He then sat up in a vicious coughing spell, heaving air in and out as he coughed violently. She smacked him on his back repeatedly, with blows much stronger than her feminine image foretold. Clyde was drenched in sweat underneath his T-shirt, his hair soaked, and his skin felt clammy and gross. Darting eyes wandered the room as he worked through the crushing his lungs endured with every contraction. He glanced at the clock; it was midnight.

"What in the world did you just do to me? How has it only been five hours?"

She was again on her way back from the bar, this time with a cold wash rag for Clyde to press to his forehead. "Here, hold pressure on this." She placed it to his brow, and he held it in his hand and pressed, squeezing a few droplets of the cold water down onto his cheeks, still waiting for an answer.

"You have just had a glimpse of your former life, Mr. LeBouef. You have seen something not many people ever get to. Did you like what you saw?" she said, taking a seat next to him, pulling out a clipboard and hugging it closely as she shot him an inquisitive look.

He wasn't expecting therapy afterward. "I don't think I can put into words what I saw, but why'd you wake me? I was making good progress!"

Clyde wiped his brow with the rag, and his face flushed red with rehydration. Slowly he was coming back to his senses and surroundings, and he began to calm down.

She leaned him back, looking at him through the black and blue lights of her lounge's neurotic decor. "You were a conquistador, Clyde, on a great mission in the New World. You come back here next week so we can do this again. Don't bother paying me. You were very receptive to the conditions I put you in. It'll be easy to put you under again."

Taking it all in, Clyde was still stuck in place on the sofa with a glazed look in his eyes. The pulse in his head started to thump with the familiar beat of an oncoming migraine. His mind had been put through a mental Olympics, stretching the very fabric of his thoughts. He'd been somebody else. This was not the Voodoo that Clyde had heard about growing up. There were no spells or violent possessions of the body, no thrashings or mysterious incantations. Yet, despite a bruja being what she claimed to be, this could not be the work of dark brujeria either. But what she did was not Voodoo. It was a puzzle.

"You want me to do this over *again?*" Clyde asked, surprised by how nonchalantly she considered him repeating the demanding psychic sequence.

"Well Mr. LeBouef, sometimes the more trauma a soul has been through, the more journeys are required. If in your previous life you felt you were carrying with you unresolved thread lines at the time of your passing, then those would need to be remedied in your next incarnation, for your soul to move on, for it to grow."

None of this made any sense to Clyde. He didn't know what all this talk about incarnations, or past lives, or "going under" meant, but he did know that with his own eyes, he'd seen places he'd never seen before. Then the mystery of wondering who was he living that experience through? Who was Cristobal Trujillo? Apparently, he was him. He spoke Spanish fluently. How could that have been? Many of these questions had no answers yet, and that would hopefully be made clearer in their next "session." He was trying to process it when the vivid memories of the voyage and the beaches began to fade.

Ms. Claudia was turning off the blacklights and unplugging different things, preparing to close up shop for the night. The indigo chili pot she'd taken over to the bar and set in the sink, straining the fluid through a colander and catching the raw botanicals she had used, throwing them into the trash. Covering herself in a patchwork shawl and fiddling around with the set of keys she had in her hands, she started toward the stairs.

"Mr. LeBouef, I know you have many questions, and that's good. You now have something to think about, but please, I have to close the shop now and head home myself. Get your things and let's go, okay sweetie?" Claudia said, ushering fragile Clyde over to her.

Clyde grabbed his socks and went over to put on his boots, pulling the first one on with ease, but having to smash his foot down to seat the second. She went around him and started climbing up the stairs.

Clyde couldn't help but wonder what the rush was, but he followed right behind her up the narrow staircase, the full glory of her backside swaying side to side in front of him. He peeled his married eyes back and focused on watching his footing, pulling himself up by the handrail. Walking out the door that opened behind the counter, they passed through the divider and out the front, onto an oddly quiet Bourbon Street. Clyde was present, clearly hearing the pitter-patter of raindrops landing in the puddles before them. Ms. Claudia turned around and stuck her key into the lock, closing the store for the night and putting to rest another day.

Clyde broke the silence. "Well, when should I come back?"

"Next Friday, 6:30," she said, clutching her purse in front of her, her black hair casting a glare under the streetlight. "We'll do one more session, and I know that will answer some of the questions you have. You have much to think about. Take some time to reflect, and come see me next week. That sound good to you?" Ms. Claudia asked.

Clyde, eager for answers, confirmed his appointment. "Sounds like a plan. We'll catch you next week," he said, and the two of them parted ways, walking in opposite directions. Clyde walked away with scattered thoughts flashing all over his mind. He did recall the storms on the seas, he did recall landing ships on a beachhead, in some oddly familiar location he couldn't quite place. He remembered the horses, the curious beasts walking up and down the shoreline, kicking around in the sand, or playing in the water.

He too had been one of those curious creatures, walking barefoot on the soft white sands on which they walked, soaking up the satisfaction of a job well done. It was no easy thing to navigate such waters. The waters of the Atlantic were choppy to start, and those unpredictable waters meant storms. The weather could change in an instant.

The terrible feelings of homesickness, almost everybody got the opportunity to know that, but Clyde, in his own life, hadn't been too concerned with being homesick during Nam. He missed the comforts of home, sure. He missed his wife and the home-cooked meals she prepared for him, a far cry from the disappointing rations he was used to. The comfort of a hot shower when he wanted, or using a toilet, were things he did not take for granted. Santina made him feel as though he didn't need to be afraid, and Clyde appreciated a little more after this session the home that she had tried to make for him. He cursed himself for being so damned hard to please. Despite her hardest efforts, he made her feel as though she was never doing enough.

Nobody understood Clyde; he was as lost in life as he was lost in himself. The many complicated facets of his being were too unique to be comprehended by himself, let alone anyone else. He was just different, and it wasn't his fault; he was the product of his environment. The experiences of both his life as Clyde LeBouef and Captain Cristobal Trujillo would make him question whether he was to be the hero or the hanged.

Clyde drove home, passing the different corner bars and restaurants, which were unusually empty. Friday nights were usually for bad choices, but tonight Clyde had been through enough. He felt groggy, like a blurring fog had rolled over his brain and clouded his thoughts.

He gripped the steering wheel, no radio, no music, nothing, he was sure Santina would be awake, waiting for him. He made it home with no problems, pulling into the stony drive and taking quick note how the porch lights hadn't been left on for him. She was probably sleeping, he thought as he turned off the truck and headed up the porch steps, the creaking deck boards breaking the silence. He opened the screen door and went inside, taking off his boots and standing them up next to the door. Santina had fallen asleep on the couch with the TV on.

She looked peaceful lying there, her eyes closed, her hair brushed and neatly tucked to the side. Clyde moved through the darkness toward his recliner, only seeing by the light of the static war between the black-and-white dots on the screen. From beside the armchair, he pulled out a huge crocheted blanket, courtesy of Santina's *abuela*, and draped it over her, being careful not to wake her. He took a long glance over her, watching her sleep, watching as the air she breathed was drawn inside. That same breath he had longed to be. Being drawn in, to sustain her, to give her life. How he wanted to water the ground she walked on, so that countless flowers might grow on the trails she had trodden. Looking at her, he realized he wasn't the best husband, and he didn't give her the affection she deserved or the love that she needed. It was hard for him to let that softer part of himself through, being too used to protecting himself. He was the most courteous and polite young man to everybody he met. To the strangers on the street or the people he held the door open for. Clyde was nice to everybody. Everybody but her.

Clyde knew this, and those bitter realizations choked him up. He took himself to the bedroom and got undressed, climbing into bed after making sure the windows were closed and locked. There Clyde rested, closing his eyes, but sleep did not come to him. There were far too many things he had to think about. Sleep was hard for him to find anyway, too paranoid about intruders, but this first session with Ms. Claudia had given him a new rabbit hole to fall into. He tossed and turned, unable to shut off his mind from all the questions he had, questions like what it was she put him through and what it was he'd seen, the things he saw a mystery themselves.

He did his best to try to recall everything that happened after he'd gone under, but even more time had passed, and he was hazy in recalling the details. Remembering his presence as he was there, when in that other person he felt what they felt; he knew their memories, he'd already known he was Cristobal Trujillo. He couldn't bring to the surface the details he had seen in those familiar faces, faces he had once known so well. He was there, in that place and time with them. He thought, as he tossed and turned, that even the memory of a smell, a sound, a subtle reminder might jog his recollection of those vivid visions further.

Clyde recalled reaching back into that space in his mind, in the depths of his subconscious. He remembered the incense mixing with the concoction that bubbled from the witch's cauldron, enveloping the room in a heavy, smoggy air. He remembered she had eased him over to the other side.

Clyde LeBouef, someone who, in the deepest sense of it, was having brilliant thoughts, finally at home, catching up from a fever that had debilitated his function for three days post-Voodoo journey. Each night he restlessly tossed and turned. Cold sweat evaporated off his skin as he shivered in bed on an eighty-degree Louisiana night. His wife was at his bedside, diligently taking care of her sick husband, tender as always, as she nursed him back to health. Feeling like she had asked a lot of him, she felt guilty too for his current condition. Clyde was not ready to talk about it. Missing work for three days would be a hassle to explain to his bosses, but Clyde in the aftermath was dealing with horribly bad migraine headaches, the kind where the throbbing pain was at his temples and the nape of his neck, and pinching it to relieve the pressure did no good. The stinging brightness caused him to squint, as he tried to keep his eyes covered and block out the outside noise. "Good Lord, make it stop," he'd say, but after three days had passed, his symptoms lessened, and his emotions began to stir in a new way.

Not dread or worry, instead, he was the reverse of himself. The light seemed to shine brighter at dawn this morning, the warmth coming back to him now. Once-cold fingers and toes were now feeling fine again. It felt good to feel the warm, muggy air. He saw more clearly and moved with ease, pain free, free of those shell-shocked tremors and cold stares. When he went over to the mirror and looked at himself, he saw more age in the eyes. It was the look of the lost vagabond. Hair disheveled, overdue for a shave, he heard the clattering of pots and pans down in the kitchen, guessing he wasn't the only one awake. Santina was up and about, doing last night's dishes. Clyde looked around; the house was a wreck because Santina had to worry about dealing with him in his invalid state for the last three days and had little time to mind the house. She felt guilty for having sent Clyde to see Ms. Claudia and undergoing who knows what kind of dark witch magic.

As the delirium of the fever high wore off, Clyde looked to Santina. "How long have I been out for?" he asked, while rubbing the fog out of his eyes.

Standing over the sink, apron and rubber cleaning gloves on, with one hand holding a sponge and the other holding a bottle of soap, she held up three fingers. "*Tres dias.*"

Holy shit! Three days! She said it too matter-of-factly for it not to be true. He had to get to work immediately and report that he was, in fact, absent due to being sick, comatose the last three days.

They were going to look at him like a madman any way he tried to explain it; there was no way he could mention to them the fantastically real pictures and scenes he had envisioned and vividly lived. The glossy teal of the open ocean as it morphed into twenty shades of emerald closer to shore and over the reefs, finally lightening up to the crystal-clear waters that sparkled over the sandy beaches the ships had anchored themselves to. Hitting the coast, and negotiating powerful tropical storms and hurricanes of the fiercest caliber, being pelted with thick rain and golf ball–sized hail, the strong winds easily slapped them around on the slippery boat decks.

He looked in the mirror and felt something different; it was no coincidence that this character Clyde had portrayed was a character himself, as real as the living people of today.

The skinny man raced around the home, grabbing pants here and socks there, donning a dirty work shirt on his way out of the door, since no one had done laundry in three days for some inexplicable reason. He needed to get to work and find someone he could explain his *unique* situation to. This was not necessarily a medical emergency scenario, but he had to try his best to give a rational excuse and not admit the truth—that he was possessed by some strange occupational force of the mind, something that had gripped him and was too real to deny.

He walked out the front door, down the porch steps, and over to his truck, which at first refused to be cranked over but relented under persistence. Clyde turned on the radio, rolled down the windows, and started racing down the street like a madman, blowing through several stop signs, red lights, and flashing signals actively blinking for school zones. He was being reckless, but it was hard to care when he was so scared he would get fired and made an example of.

Furiously he beat his thumbs against the steering wheel, painfully watching the clock on the radio change minute after minute. It seemed like ages before the dead convoy began to inch along, a typical workday morning rush. Clyde made his way further along until he reached the manufacturing plant where he worked, parking his truck in a hurry, and jumping out. Clyde ran through the parking lot and immediately through the turnstiles, in through the front double glass doors. Quickly, he made his way to his supervisor's office and knocked on the door several times.

"I'll be damned if you're not alive! Got worried about ya' after your old lady called and said you were ill. It's been what, three days?" Mr. Blackrock said.

As he opened the door, Clyde stood there, looking defeated, dodging eye contact. "I know, sir, and there is no excuse for that. I'm very sorry, I've been sick with a horrible fever that just broke this morning, and I haven't been able to do anything for three days."

Clyde offered his excuses, but Mr. Blackrock, with arms crossed over his ugly light-green shirt, tucked into his khaki pants, and wearing those thick, black-rimmed safety glasses, sat in his rolling chair looking at Clyde as if he were an insolent knave needing a spanking. It boiled Clyde's blood.

"Hey, if that's not good enough for you, sir, get me a union rep. I don't need to prove anything to you."

Mr. Blackrock's jaw dropped in astonishment. "Excuse me, Mr. LeBouef? Are you fit for work this morning? Have you put a couple back already?" He came at Clyde with a sharper, accusatory tone, which Clyde really didn't take too kindly.

Fed up with the games, Clyde simply shrugged his shoulders and laughed a little. "I'm sorry, sir, I don't know what's gotten into me. Please, forgive me," he said, holding back laughs in what was supposed to be a serious conversation. "If I'm not fired, I'll get my stuff and get to work."

With a barely audible grunt, Mr. Blackrock gave his approval, and Clyde went over to his locker, making himself ready with all his tools, gear, and protective equipment.

The day dragged on as Clyde's head thumped with a pulsing migraine, which was made no better by the loud machines, beeping horns, shouting, and overall chaos. Eight hours never felt longer. Finally, the work bell rang, and they were all running toward the door. People actually would take off running, and Clyde always joined the race and took off too, making a beeline for his truck, firing it up, and racing through the streets to get home in time for supper.

Clyde washed his hands and face and made himself ready at the kitchen table, where his plate of food was waiting for him. They shared their meal and caught up on the day's happenings, the slightly different daily encounters and conversations they'd each had with the people they interacted with each day.

After their meal, they took an evening stroll around their yard, letting the dog run free and careless in the slightly grown-out pasture grass of their property.

At night he dreamed he was part of a patrolling detachment, a reconnaissance unit of several conquistadors, eight of them wandering along a well-beaten goat path deep in the desert somewhere. Not minding their footing and scanning the ground as if they had lost something they needed to find. "There's surely a few more around here. Everybody just keep looking," Dendrick said excitedly as he led the pack from the front, his horse trailing behind him from the rope lead wrapped around its neck. Cristobal held over his head the arrowhead that one of the men had found, and Dendrick, eager to capture another trophy to take back home with him, had encouraged Cristobal to allow a brief dismount to look for more of the indigenous arrowheads, to take them home to their families.

Waiting for the rest of the week to pass was like waiting an eternity. He bided his time and spent it thinking about his future appointment with Ms. Claudia. With each focused recollection, these feelings were becoming more tangible and detailed. Thoughts long forgotten, even those things which we take to our graves, were to be uncovered. It was like living someone else's life, and only the devil could do something like that. Clyde took to the Lord sweepingly, pleading for his deliverance from that Voodoo evil. He asked for whole and total forgiveness. He bartered his soul's salvation, apologizing for being so curious as to go and enter into a pact with witchery. Praying on his knees at his bedside in the mornings and the evenings, vowing to go to church on Sundays, Clyde felt bad for his transgressions and felt scared the Lord might now enact some wicked punishment upon him.

Life kept on, however. The days passed, and Clyde was again somewhat excited at the thought of it. The tune he'd sung the last several days was about how badly he had messed up, but as the day drew nearer, he began to anticipate it eagerly, and all those curious questions he had asked himself now made themselves known to him and his curious nature.

The story couldn't end there; there was far more to see, he believed. On the day of his appointment, Clyde wished Santina well as he threw on his sunglasses and took off in the truck. He lit a cigarette and turned up the radio and with the wind behind him, drove down the streets of downtown, like he had done so many times before.

He parked his truck in a smaller public lot, off one of the side streets, where he locked it up and turned to walk himself into the mix of strangers. Emerging from the alley, he joined one of the sidewalks and began to navigate the asphalt maze. He kept his hands in his pockets and tried not to make eye contact with anybody, avoiding any sort of attention. He'd pause and watch a street performer maybe, or stop to listen to the preacher man and the bum, confessing his woeful state, acting normal, but what was normal?

They were just strangers; they passed each other by without a second thought. Each individual, a unique set of their own miseries, and faults. The troubled men, who worked too much, the unloved wives, and mothers. The forgotten grandparents, who only wished to see their little ones one more time. The kids, with no worry but when Christmas vacation was.

Then there was he, on his merry way to do the bruja's bidding. Her spell worked on him, as he let himself be tormented by thoughts of her, but he remembered Santina, and how after his first appointment, when he was struck with a fever, she'd cared for him while he couldn't care for himself. He remembered she had done that his whole life. She stood by his side through all the bullshit of his life and had vowed to do it forever and again. Santina was his best friend, and he owed it to her to find the answers to the questions he couldn't ask himself.

Clyde wandered into shops to take a look at souvenirs or gifts, with nothing catching his eyes as he passed by the various storefronts, decorated to be appealing to the tourists. Wasting time until 6:30, which was now fifteen minutes away, Clyde began his trek over to that side of town, and at 6:30 sharp, found himself passing under the red canopy and in through the door, spying Ruby hanging some merchandise on one of the racks off to the side. What he thought looked like women's blouses.

He spoke from the door. "Hey, Ruby! You mind if I head back?"

She looked up over her red-brimmed, red-lens glasses, her bright-red lipstick contrasting distinctly against her pale skin and red 'fro.

"Sure thing, baby, you know the way." She smiled.

Clyde nodded and made his way to the divider, passing several patrons who'd been perusing the aisles and shelves, appreciating the racks of splendidly colorful garments and accessories.

Heading through the door and down the steep basement steps, he pulled on the drawstring knotted to the light bulb chain, illuminating the narrow basement staircase and making his way cautiously down, entering the basement through a newly installed beaded curtain that Ms. Claudia must have hung up in the last week. The look was the same, the same blue and black lights, the Lava Lamps, the posters, tapestries, all manner of deco-francais on display in this uniquely decorated office.

But where was the witch? She was nowhere to be found; the place was empty. Clyde took his shoes off, recalling that she had asked him to do this last time. Then, from the other side of the room, she emerged like a black widow, coming to feed on the poor fly that had wandered into her web. Her hair was in pigtails, black curls, and her baby hairs were gelled down against her forehead, looking quite exotic.

"Mr. LeBouef, welcome back," she said, extending her arms for a hug, which he didn't know was happening for a second. "Please, join me on the sofa. We'll get you under right away," she said, with the demeanor of a friendly nurse, bringing him back for a routine procedure.

Clyde was ready. He hustled over to the couch and made himself comfortable, lying down on it.

"Hang on a second, sweetie. I need you to hit this, remember?" She passed him a joint, freshly rolled, and good smoke by the smell of it.

Inhaling the vapor deep into his lungs and holding it there, he then let it out and began to cough a little. An embarrassed smile spread onto his face. Ms. Claudia laughed too.

"I can tell you don't do this very much."

She brought over the cauldron and set it on the table, where the hookah usually sat. She then threw in the several ingredients whose names Clyde couldn't recall. There were herbs, powders, full-sized ingredients too, roots or something. Soon, a frothy smoke began to flow from the top, spilling over the side. The foam evaporated into a fog that rose to the ceiling, filling the room with swirling odors and an air that made everything hazy and blurry.

Ms. Claudia then began her dialogue, which Clyde found to be more ominous sounding.

"Have you noticed anything different about yourself?" she asked, as she went over to the bar, lighting a few more candles to add to the ambiance.

Clyde thought about it for a second before answering her. "Well, I was sick for three days. Migraines, cold sweats, troubled thoughts."

"Troubled thoughts?" she said, in a stately way.

Clyde had noticed a change in himself, in his less agitated, more understanding demeanor the last couple of days. While still frustrated over the fleeting images he had seen during his first experience, he preferred not to elaborate. She saw through his fragility.

Ms. Claudia came up from behind the sofa and took turns whispering strange incantations into each of his ears. She spoke a tongue he did not recognize, and he did not see her eyes roll back in her head or her tongue split itself into two, as she licked up the side of his cheek. Clyde listened along, waiting for her instruction. She started her countdown, this time in what he recognized to be Spanish. She started softly, and he felt her gentle breath hit his ears, which put Clyde deep into the familiar stupor before she hit *ocho*. Her voice went from her normal soprano, down an octave with each passing number, until she hit *uno*, when at last she spoke in a husky voice. A voice of consternation, certainty, and goodwill. Dark, empty, and hollow, all was black, all was quiet, total darkness. This was the last thing he heard from the physical world.

The next thing Clyde would see would be the unfolding epic of the captain, Cristóbal Trujillo, as he begins his great expedition and links his reinforcements with the commander of the Spanish Expeditionary Forces. A man who would play a much larger role than Cristobal could ever imagine. A man who would teach him more than any man had ever taught him before. A man whose name was legend, spoken alongside the famous "Cortes the Killer." A man who possessed grit and determination of the highest degree. His name was Comandante Javier "Rodendros" Redondo, and he was the supreme commander of the whole expedition.

Chapter 14

THE SECOND APPOINTMENT

Cristobal led the way, chopping through the dense brush with his machete, the sweat cascading from his brow. They moved in straight-line succession, one after the other within the vegetation. It was the only way to make sure nobody got lost en route to the rendezvous. Had it not been for the tremendous plumes of smoke off in the distance, Cristobal might not have known where to go. Even still, it took them three days of dead reckoning to reach their point. They maintained their discipline as best they could, trying to avoid sharp snaps and cracks of dead twigs and branches.

He did not wish to sneak up on the encampment. Cristobal, sensing they were close, halted their advance. "Enrico, you stay here with the men. Bring Simora to the front, I'll be riding her out to meet the Comandante. Have Dendrick mount up, and bring the sailor captain to the front as well. We're going to make contact."

At Cristobal's orders, the line of men and animals stopped their advancement and hunkered down. Dendrick Rodon brought his nag, alongside the soon-to-be-famous Simora, up to the front of the formation. Captain Fernando was already mounted, bringing up the rear of the company, making sure nobody ran off or deserted. Simora, unaware of the dangers of their predicament, came alongside the file, the loose and overhanging vines of various bushes and trees scraping by her wayside. she paid no mind to this mild inconvenience. She was a Conquistador's horse; she knew her place. She walked with the leader, which made her a leader as well.

"There she is, my sweet girl," Cristobal said as she dipped her head down to meet his, and they nuzzled for a second in a warm exchange.

"Let us make ready, Simora. Saddle." Cristobal saddled her up, while Dendrick tended her bit and bridled her. Cristobal straightened the reins and took control of her.

"Yah!" he commanded. She tossed her mane and moved forward a little. This let her master know it was time for him to get ready to ride. She'd be disappointed they weren't going for a long run through the sand.

Waiting for Dendrick Rodon to make ready, Captain Fernando put forward his thoughts.

"So, we're near the encampment, are we?" he smugly asked, standing his nag next to Cristobal's Simora. His was an unimpressive one, with a lackluster brown coat that hadn't been brushed through in some time.

"Yes, if I'm not mistaken, we're probably within a thousand paces of it, maybe more. The three of us will ride out, and God willing, hope our friends found a clear spot to pitch their fires. We're close. Stay behind me and Dendrick, and if I give the signal to halt or be still, do so without hesitation. We may hear them before we see them. It is the bulk of the expeditionary force, after all."

Captain Fernando gave an *aye* at this and tipped his visor down over his face. The three of them were now ready to step off.

"Enrico, should we be lost, listen for a whistle, then whistle back. Do so till we've rejoined you, should our success not be immediate."

Enrico gave a nod and stepped out of their way, taking up a comfortable lean against his lance, plunging itself into the moist earth.

The three of them trotted off into the brush, with Cristobal taking point. He swung his machete through the brush, blazing their trail. The others also chopped their way through the thick vines and branches that hung on all sides of them. The mosquitos had now discovered the fresh blood that had entered their arena and were making a feast of conquistador and sailor alike. Everyone was at the mercy of the insects in this miserable jungle. Halting every once in a while to listen and smell, to take in their surroundings, Cristobal thought he heard something but couldn't say exactly. So they carried on slowly, making idle progress through the undisturbed flora.

All around them were frightening creatures, some of which the old ones could not even identify. Was that a leopard or a panther? What in fact was most definitely a jaguar. Rare and ancient creatures, no fiercer was there than the cat. Horridly sized spiders, which made their already pruning skin crawl. Thick, sturdy timber, the sheer volume of which could not be fathomed. The place was awesome in every way. The horses were led by their masters, who gently held the reins.

No sooner had they begun to second guess the direction they traveled than the path began to break apart, no longer well trodden, but now toward an opening, with considerably more daylight penetrating through the dense canopy. Moving now with a rejuvenated sense of purpose, they rode into the light, sweeping the brush and vines to the side to step inside a clearing. The plants lay crushed, splayed in a circle. Standing within the circle, they looked up to see there was a hole in the jungle canopy above, letting broad daylight into the middle of all that darkness.

Easily several men's length far and wide, they were in the center of it, soaking up the sunlight's rejuvenating rays. Coming to their senses, they'd forgotten which direction they'd come from. Cristobal then gazed at the obvious broken brush they'd left behind in their wake, and from there they carried on north-northeast, back into the darkness.

"We're close, I can hear them," Cristobal announced to the group, and he beckoned them further, creeping up to the barricades of an even bigger clearing. They crossed a creek that ran horizontally against their steepening incline, climbing uphill for several minutes before the jungle floor, soaked in wet leaves and debris, bottomed out. They reached a massive opening in the brush, where Cristobal saw felled trees, campfires, small tents, big tents, horses walking freely in their limited pasture, conquistadors tending their equipment, or passing the time with games and drink, among the other typically noisy happenings of a military outpost.

They rode their horses from out of the brush up to the barricade line, where a sentry was posted for security.

The chattering Spanish voices of soldiers and friends were all enjoying the companionship and feasts that only a successful hunt would merit.

"Dendrick, wait here. When I wave you off, go gather the rest of the company," Cristobal told the crow master, whose razor-sharp memory and attention to detail were unmatched. Nothing ever escaped his ever-searching eyes. Not that this was a difficult command.

"Yes, sir," said Dendrick.

He held up his horse while Cristobal and Captain Fernando continued through the clearing. Cristobal jauntily rode Simora, a display of an officer's disciplined horsemanship.

The sentry, who now could distinguish friend from foe, called out to them. "Halt! Step no further! I'll bring the comandante!"

They halted, Cristobal swallowing hard, as his comandante carried an intimidating reputation, very well known for exploits during the original New World conquests.

Rodendros was a nickname given to him early in life by his mother, a play on the word *rododendros*, Spanish for rhododendron, and his last name of Redondo. The leader of the Spanish Expeditionary Force, Comandante Redondo's face was still charmed by youth, yet the wrinkles of his brow and his deep laugh lines suggested someone more advanced in age. He had tested himself his whole career as a conquistador, fighting in several campaigns, long before joining Cortes. He had the prestigious honor of being part of the original crew that first came over to the New World, and together, they toppled the greatest civilizations the ancient world had ever known. This made all others obedient to the comandante's word; the fame and renown of his heroic exploits. He'd been made rich through his plundering and royal commissions and grown more comfortable in his older age, dedicating less time to training and more time to smoking the native herbs. Spending the last several years enjoying the rank and reward of his post, with his retirement not too far off, the comandante had been requisitioned by the king to head back into the field and push the northern line.

The comandante threw back the leather flap over his tent, ducking his head under the short ceiling. He had requested those reinforcements more than a year ago. His forces had slowly been shrinking in size; it was once an intimidating sight, the comandante and his elite conquistadors, who had been so withered and reduced in their number, horribly by rampant sickness, fighting with the Indigenous, and desertion, that only a quarter of the men they set out with remained. The comandante's forces had left from the capital, journeying north over snowcapped mountains and through densely vegetated Latin American jungles. For months they made tremendous progress, before finally the comandante had to send word for reinforcements.

Born in 1475, the comandante was sixty-eight years old, with a head full of wavy silver hair and a matching mustache, which he kept pristinely oiled and twisted in his signature handlebar, held together with native myrtle waxes he acquired from the Yaqui. The comandante was dressed down, the opening of his frilly white shirt revealing his Aztec medallion, which he claimed to be forged from pure Moctezuma gold, worn on a strand of turquoise, coral, and pearls.

Cristobal observed the source of their smoke signals, which the whole of this region had to have seen—still-smoldering piles of lumber the men had chopped and harvested from the clearing to make camp. Smoke poured up into the air, and Cristobal had been fortunate enough to see the signal from afar. Cristobal could smell the roasting game and burning tobacco, and judging from the look of the wine sacks that were being passed around, they either had a good trade route to New Spain, or their hunting and rationing skills were superior. Cockily he walked, the spirit of the Dionysians on his back, when with his signature cheeky smirk, he stepped in front of Cristobal and Fernando, who'd dismounted their steeds since they'd been waiting.

"Trujillo?" Comandante Redondo shouted from a good ways back as he walked up to the barricade, holding his hand over his brow to block the sun, and to make sure his eyes weren't betraying him, but that his reinforcements had indeed arrived.

"Captain Cristobal Trujillo, Señor Comandante. We're sorry it took so long," Cristobal said, standing upright and addressing his superior with proper discipline and military courtesies.

"Relax, friends, you've all come an incredibly long way. Please, no salutes or formalities," the comandante said, spreading his arms wide open with welcome.

"Comandante, I'll send a runner back to the line," Cristobal said, turning to see if he could make out the crow master, back in the bush. He was sure Dendrick Rodon had been watching the whole exchange from the tree line.

"Well, make haste! You can smell the game in the air, can't you? *Rapido!* Bring me your hungry and thirsty!" said the comandante, sending them away.

Cristobal turned back around and whistled loudly. Off in the distance, Dendrick Rodon whistled back, setting his steed into a quick trot back the way they came. The barricades were opened, and the two of them let their horses go in to graze and drink freely.

"Who are you, friend?" the comandante asked Captain Fernando.

Captain Fernando was the most senior ranking naval officer assigned to this small Spanish expedition. He was in charge of all nautical logistics and naval command. He charted their courses, read their maps, navigated by way of the stars, and could accurately predict the weather of the seas before the storms had even happened.

"Well, Comandante, I'm the-"

Rodendros cut him off. "You know, Chalchiuhtlicue is the Aztec goddess of lakes, rivers and streams, but you sail the seas, the domain of Poseidon. You must be a true navigator and star man. Please, Captain, the work you have done cannot be praised enough. Your country thanks you, as do I," he said, placing a hand on Fernando's shoulder as he stood there dumbstruck from the flattery.

"Please come, feast with us. We'll help you with everything immediately!" said the comandante, ushering Cristobal and Fernando to follow suit. They walked with the comandante, watching his ragged veterans dig a couple of hogs out of the ground. Delicious ashy smoke rolled out, and their mouths watered as they walked by.

Cristobal was taken aback with the high praises the comandante was throwing at the feet of his counterpart. Surely, he couldn't be mistaking Fernando for being the leader of this expedition? Of the voyage, surely, but the final say in all matters since leaving Spain, to the arrival in the New World, fell to Cristobal. His ego was bruised, but he followed the comandante into the command tent, which was dimly lit by candlelight and the minuscule daylight peeking through the door flap. There was a small bed of coals burning low in the middle of it.

"It's already a furnace out there, but at night it gets very cold, with a nip that'll bite flesh. Also, the fire keeps the bugs away," Redondo said, swatting away a mosquito and taking a seat in a plush cushioned chair behind a crudely cut table. "Take a seat, *hermanos*, let's talk."

Comandante Redondo motioned for the men to sit on a couple of tree stumps that had been brought in exclusively for that purpose.

He tossed a freshly splintered log into the coals, and tiny embers were carried up by the smoke. "Gentlemen, the area we're moving on is north-northwest of here. Your crew were meant to be reinforcements, to supplement our current force, which is 136 men strong. We started two years ago in Santiago, Chile, with five hundred."

Hanging on to the words of the comandante, Cristobal couldn't help but feel a great admiration for the man. He spoke strongly, with a Castillian tongue, disarming and proper. Cristobal felt timid in his presence, but still he listened, being sure to maintain his pomp for the sake of ceremony. The noise outside increased as the rest of Cristobal's company beat their way through the brush and into camp. The supply officers were outside directing the flow of men, livestock, and equipment. They shouted their instructions, directing the eager fellows, who at long last could get a good night's sleep without having to pull guard or mind the fires for a change.

"I want to tell you a quick story. Don't worry about them. The *sargentos* can handle it," Redondo said from behind the table.

At this, Captain Fernando stood up and dismissed himself abruptly, apologizing but explaining that he needed to be out there coordinating his sailors, which the comandante understood. Cristobal tried to chime in with his remarks, but the comandante started talking again.

"When I first joined Cortes, now two decades ago, I did what you young men are doing now. You are giving me your faith, trusting me that I'm going to make the right calls out there. Should you find yourself questioning an order, if you think my word is not good enough, then simply remind yourself of my deeds; where I've been, and what I've done. Then your mind can be at ease, knowing I'm going to do my absolute best to teach you everything I know."

The easy flow of his words, the calm demeanor in which he casually spoke, he was very impressed already with the famed comandante, able to focus on the man's character, feeling like this audience, and those words, were meant to be said. It was as if fate brought him this familiar shade, to whom so much admiration was given already.

"When do we set off? I'm ready, you just say the word, Comandante."

Redondo allowed himself a chuckle.

Suddenly, Fernando burst back in through the tent flap. "We can start on the smaller inventories," he said to Cristobal.

The comandante looked sad for a second, as he was reminiscing on his glory days, conquering with Cortes.

"Very well, you've got things to do, I understand. We leave the day after tomorrow. Any man who wishes to stay may occupy the camp, but remind them not to run themselves short of rations, and keep diligence on the ships. The coastline is a three-days walk from here, so once a week send a party to check on them. They'll be your only way of return passage, if you are to return at all. Go, do your checks; make your final preparations. We won't see this part of the continent for months, maybe even years."

Cristobal stood up from his tree stump seat to exit the tent.

"One more thing, Captain."

Cristobal turned to face Rodendros, who held a rolled-up scroll. "This is the best we've got. Make yourself familiar with the lay of the land. We've much navigating to do yet, and these new territories will need borders and names."

Nodding in acknowledgement, Cristobal thanked the comandante for his time and made his way out of the tent. The air smelled new, it smelled good, with a musk that hung heavily upon it. After months of gathering much familiarity with it, he could taste the sea spray on the air, blown inland by the gales that came down from the open northern plains.

Cristobal spent much time out in the wilderness, cutting his teeth against the hot steel of his past wartime conquests. His few encounters with combat were mere scuffles when compared to the experiences of his superior, the comandante. He envied the man, for being born before he was, for getting his chance to be a part of history.

Stepping away from the tent, Cristobal joined Captain Fernando and Enrico Cardenas. The rest of the company were busy laying out their gear, belongings, and rations, as well as different stores of wines, tobacco, and medicine. Cristobal also took stock of their munitions and arms: swords, arquebuses, lances, and crossbows. They were on the cutting edge of modern military weaponry.

The horses, mules, dogs, and other various animals and livestock they'd brought were taken, and several slaughters commenced, to build rations for the journey inland. They also saw to the horses, who were far too valuable to neglect. If they were moving at a good pace, they could easily cover ten miles a day, but the nags needed to be able to graze and drink and acclimate to the new weather and altitude before they set out running them wild across the Americas. Most of the men worked late into the night, but the hardest work had yet to begin.

In their tent, Cristobal and Fernando were on opposite sides, setting up their bedding, which was no more than a couple of furs and wool blankets. Their gear was spread out on the floor, scattered about the way that boys do. The two of them were prodding each other, trying to learn more about one another through stories of childhood, military service, and family.

"Fernando, we've got a long road ahead of us, let's keep a watchful eye out there over each other, agreed?"

"Agreed."

Cristobal then held up the scroll the comandante had given him. "If you would double check my work on the map later also, I would be most appreciative."

Cristobal extended his arm, which Fernando took and clutched.

"As if you were my own brother. Do not doubt this." Fernando said.

"You don't need me to check your work. My work is with the sea; I'm afraid a flat pond hardly compares to hills, valleys, or mountains. Trust yourself; you'll do fine."

They exchanged warm glances and made their way to their makeshift beds. The rest of the men bedded down under the billions of stars that dotted the clear night sky. Free of the stifle of the jungle, no longer sweating or being eaten alive by insects, but enjoying the cool wind in the wide-open clearing. Fires burned low now, and exhaustion took its toll in the form of deep quiet, nothing but the snores and nocturnal creatures to be heard in all of the dark.

Among these nocturnal creatures, Captain Cristobal Trujillo sat up in his tent, sprawled on the ground; The several furs, which he flattened out as best he could, served as a flat working surface for him to examine the map the comandante had given him. Slowly unrolling the scroll across an old deer pelt, Cristobal suddenly burned with humiliation, like he was at the butt end of a cruel joke. The map was blank. Nothing could be seen except the slight holes and perforations that peppered the parchment. The horror quickly turned into an acute panic inside of Cristobal's head, as this was surely not a task that *he* should be responsible for.

However, he could not refuse orders, and this was more than an order; it was a heavy responsibility. The freedom to draw in the lines of the map, to give new places names, to claim sweet virgin territory for the empire, this was an opportunity like no other. Cristobal's name would be etched forever into the annals of history, for this was what being a conquistador was about, the adventure, the honor, and the glory. Lying down in his tent by candlelight, he hovered over what he now knew to be a blank piece of parchment. He hung his face in his hands. "God help us all." he uttered. Cristobal rubbed his fingers down his face, feeling the stubble as he brushed down. "We are in your hands now, Father."

The father! He suddenly remembered he'd forgotten all about the padre!

Hurriedly, Cristobal grabbed a pair of breeches and slipped on his boots, stumbling out of his tent shirtless and holding a lantern over his head as he walked across the field to the first fire pit he saw. Moving the lantern around, he checked the campsite, but the padre was nowhere to be seen. He moved up and down the line until he found the spot where indeed the padre was.

"Padre, a word before we sleep tonight?" Cristobal asked quietly as he gently stirred the father to rise, softly shaking his shoulder.

"Yes, my son, of course. What is it?"

"Would you say a blessing over us? And ask for his grace of us?" Cristobal asked in hushed tones, leaning over to speak closer to the padre's ear.

"Yes, my child. Here, come close." The padre pulled him into a cherubic embrace. The old friar, who'd made ready with his frugal belongings already, was the living example that one didn't need much to do good work, and his presence among the men was uplifting enough to drive them on when it was hard, offering prayer and a friendly face when needed.

"Our Lord God, we give thanks, and the holiest of praises unto your name. The safety you've granted us, oh Lord, we ask for continuity. That you bless us with that armor for a while longer, for we know not what toils will come against us. Walk with us, Lord, protect us, and protect these men. They are fathers, brothers, husbands, and they are sons themselves. Grant them safe passage and bless their hearts. Let them be delivered from sin. Guide us, Lord, lead us by your divine light as we march surely into the unknown. We are grateful and give you all the glory, Father God, and in Jesus's name we pray, amen."

"Amen."

In unison, Cristobal was joined by another voice, and turning his head, he spied a shadowed figure lying off to the side. The crow master peered from under his cap, a trickster, cunning, and highly intelligent. Cristobal told him to go back to bed. The young captain, feeling better about receiving those fresh blessings, went back into his tent to try and catch some sleep, but instead he found himself awake, tossing and turning, thinking about Fiorella, his love back home in Spain.

She was the handiwork of God's most artistically capable angels. There could not have been a more beautiful woman to him. Her skin, which was incredibly smooth and free of blemish, glowed in a darker shade of cinnamon spice, which complemented her greatly, as she had tremendously dark features. Her hair shined like the glistening black coat of a panther, with a set of light-green eyes to match. When she looked at him, for a second, he'd be wrought with shock, for to sight a creature with this level of masterful, unearthly design, one had to have been shown a degree of divine providence.

Cristobal fondly remembered her infectious laughter. She enjoyed a good bit of mockery, but someone of her class could get away with it, part of her upbringing in the higher classes of Toledan society. Her aristocratic parents, affluent and well-to-do, had only raised one child and named her Fiorella, after her maternal grandmother.

She'd grown up playing with the other kids in the commons, and despite being of a different class than he, Fiorella and Cristobal enjoyed many a fun afternoon, playing games in the summer sun until it was time to go home. The division of the people into different classes could not corrupt the innocence of childhood. Toledo had been a thriving city since the conquests, great wealth being brought back in the form of gold, jewels, and resources. These things flowed through the streets, but for Cristobal, growing up in an orphanage, he didn't see the spoils of their country's glories, nor was he allowed to stay with her outside for very long once her parents started to gather more prominence.

He loved their conversations, and they shared a love that bloomed early, with the two souls, who could not have been any more different, denying society's crooked class system. They had no right to determine who they could love, and deciding that they were meant for one another, they promised each other they would find a way. As they grew older and were beginning their new chapters of adulthood, the call to service had been louder than her calls for him to stay.

She cried at night for him, but he was gone, for who knows how long. He thought of her in the same way, and one thought did burn within him while he was gone; the feeling that he somehow had let go of his one chance at love. He did love her, but it was his own decision to walk away. Her memory was one he'd carried everywhere, and Cristobal, who was a man of chivalry himself, dedicated his arm to the service of his lady, Fiorella. He fought for her and fought the painful remorse he felt over leaving her. He was punishing himself to prove something unknown, like she'd somehow see how hard he was working to be the man who was deserving enough of being hers.

Those hard battles fought, those hard decisions and long nights freezing in the harsh winter snows or burning in the blazing sierra summers. Lost at sea, guided only by the lights that the sky provided. The hazards of this life were enough to make the best men snap with insanity. Long periods of dragged-out dement, getting up close and personal, you looked the man you killed in his eyes, and you watched as he drew those last breaths. It was hard to watch the way their eyes got so wide, and a twisted frown of shock came over them as they uttered their last guttural sounds.

Cristobal had begged atonement for these sins, but he was always reassured by the Church that God smiled on his warriors, for what they did was in the name of the Lord, and there they could not be wrong. The glory of his majesty's empire, the Spanish crown, which beamed its golden deliverance over the land, only spurned the violence further, now bearing Cristobal Trujillo down toward his destiny, out there in the unknown of the New World.

First, they awoke.

Chapter 15

EXODUS

They planned to step out from camp early in the morning, after several meetings had been arranged and completed, things decided on, things that the upper echelon of command needed to configure. Comandante Redondo had clear instructions: seize as many lands along the northern boundaries of the empire as possible, without causing too much of a stir with the Indigenous peoples who occupied them. They had already learned much about the native people in the last twenty years of conquests since Cortes first came years ago.

This was how Comandante Redondo came to know the only Indian among them. He was, first and foremost, the comandante's translator and Indigenous correspondent, whom he consulted with on all manners of local customs, language, and relations. His name was Aatuani, a tall Indian, who had hardly any visceral fat on his body. His skin was dark, and he had long hair that he wore in a braid. His eyes were dark, and his convex cheekbones gave his face a sharp, angular look. Cristobal was also surprised to see his teeth were white and clean.

Aatuani spoke several dialects of native language and was taught Spanish by missionaries later on in life. Now, he had been taken in by the comandante, which afforded him a much better lifestyle than he had known before. There was no question of the loyalty Aatuani felt for his master; he'd left his homeland to work with the conquistadors, which Cristobal thought was mildly opportunistic but not uncommon.

Comandante Redondo put on his morion and sword belt and mounted his horse, Luchzuochu. Aatuani was at his side, dressed like a savage. He wore only a brown cloth around his waist, walking barefoot everywhere he went. He carried a long spear, which mostly served as a walking stick. He swore no true allegiance to either side and didn't help when they found themselves in combat with one another.

Not wanting to betray the trust of his people, Aatuani explained to the villagers back home that he was simply serving in a diplomatic capacity, to keep the bloodshed in their lands contained. He claimed he would barter their good relations, and if they could communicate with the strangers, they could bargain and trade with them too.

What a blessing it was, though, Cristobal thought, to have with them in their party one who spoke the Indigenous tongues and the language of their own mother country. It really was remarkable what they had accomplished in the short decades since the first invasions. Aatuani let the comandante and Luchzuochu lead the pack, and he fell behind the marching column to walk beside Cristobal and Simora, using his spear as a walking stick.

"Hello, Captain. I am Aatuani, and you?" he said, friendly and in decent Spanish.

"Cristobal Noriel Trujillo. Tell me, friend, how is it that you are a savage, yet you speak our tongue? It's no wonder Rodendros has you hanging around!" Cristobal said, keeping stride with the much taller Indian. "I am the captain of those conquistadors back there, and their lives are in my hands, so you listen to me; you're going to do translation work for me and help me fill in some of the blanks on my map here, do you understand?" Cristobal said, looking sharply at the Indian.

"Yes, I understand, Captain."

"Comandante, have you a heading for us?" Cristobal asked, getting himself as comfortable in the saddle as he could while wearing a full set of armor.

"North-northwest the whole way. Keep us in line," the comandante said, running his hand along Luchzuochu's black mane.

The sun was out now, and the temperature was steadily climbing. The long column of men penetrated deeper into the jungle. Rear sentries had been placed to watch their backs at all times. The men could easily cover ten miles a day, but since they were hauling a great deal of equipment further inland, their pace would be slowed, due to their encumbrance and general ignorance of the land.

"Rodendros, I'll take us. I'll walk in front," Aatuani said, the native translator motioning with his bony fingers like they were a pair of walking legs.

"Aatuani, friend, north-northwest," Rodendros said, reaching down from his horse to hand Aatuani his compass.

In truth, Comandante Javier Redondo, who through his enduring long periods of wartime service, was now very down-to-earth and seemed to be more present and less brainwashed than Cristobal and his peers, blinded by their desires for glory and riches. Unlike the spooky legends of the old conquistador days, those veterans who had torn the jawbones off of the high priests, the ones who had learned to disconnect themselves from gore happening around them, knew it wasn't what it was made out to be.

Rodendros made eye contact with Cristobal and nodded toward Aatuani.

"We happened upon this one farther south of where you found us. We thought he was suspiciously curious, lingering about. He approached us from out of the shadows one night, which gave us all a great scare, and after we violently detained him, we made sure he hadn't brought any of his friends. Hearing him speak Spanish, though, I knew he could be of use. I offered him a handsome reward on behalf of the crown for his natural abilities, should he let us borrow them. Once his service with us on this expedition is finished, he will be a rich man indeed."

His voice was husky, clearly someone who enjoyed tobacco. Rodendros was capable of managing at least one vice. He was most sober at any given moment, not wanting to degrade the quality of his character through troublesome meanderings. His gray hair hung down the sides of his face, and through slitted eyes, he examined all before him. They looked ready.

"Lead the way, Aatuani," Rodendros said, waving him off.

It was a rocky start; at first they had to go very slowly, crawling along through the thick foliage, stepping on the dead wet leaves, slashing the brush with machetes and swords or risk getting themselves caught or tangled up in the mess of vine. Then there was the nearly impossible task of guiding the nags and mules, which were so loaded down with equipment, Cristobal felt true pain for them. Days passed this way until the vegetation finally slowly started to break up. Cristobal followed behind the guide, with Rodendros behind him. Cristobal also had his compass out, making sure their guide didn't stray too far off azimuth. They passed through the nightmare of a jungle in about a week, with many upset men throwing curses toward the New World for giving them a fresh rash of blisters, because of their inability to tell which plants were poisonous, or because they woke up riddled with mosquito bites, which for some would be a death sentence. They passed through waist-high water in stagnant black marshes, which brought on dysentery and fevers a few weeks later.

After passing through to the other side of the bush, they were greatly relieved to see the wide-open plains before them. It was a breathtaking view, abandoning the dark, grim, verdant jungle. The canopy opened up, and the blue sky now hung high over them, with huge pillowy clouds spread far and wide across the horizon. They rode out of the darkness and into the light. It was inspiring to see the vastness of the New World displayed before them. It was a beautiful land, and it went farther than the eye could see. Cristobal took the precious moment to heart and allowed himself a moment of silence to pay his reverent respects to the gracious ones above for giving him this privilege.

From off to the side, Aatuani came to the front of the formation, realizing they'd been brought to a dead end. "I'm sorry, please, let me go look for a way down."

"Pass it down, we're halting here for now," Cristobal shouted back toward the first few men of the file, who happened to be Dendrick Rodon's squad. The crow master's gifted sight was more than useful, and to his detriment, it usually earned him the position of point man.

The sailors had been dispersed, mixed in with their more combat-capable counterparts. Lieutenant Enrico Cardenas and Captain Fernando were in the middle of the formation, enjoying an enthusiastic conversation a little too loud for Cristobal's liking. They received the order, and several minutes later, the command made its way down the line and back up to Cristobal in the front.

Cristobal, Rodendros, and Dendrick Rodon all dismounted their horses and stepped off toward the edge of the cliff, looking out at the gigantean lands before them. It wouldn't be easy to descend, and Cristobal strongly opposed the direct approach. But Rodendros saw it differently, as did Dendrick Rodon.

"If we're careful, we can make it down," said Dendrick.

The comandante, equally mad, fed into his delusions. "Look out there. You see how it sort of breaks off? That kind of looks like a path, does it not?" asked Rodendros, resting his leg on a fallen timber.

Dendrick held his hand over his eyes, squinting but believing the comandante to be correct.

"No, that definitely looks like a path. I think you're right."

"Aatuani, that over there," said Rodendros, pointing with his saber. "What about there?"

Aatuani scurried over to where Rodendros had pointed, and in a few seconds, he was off into the shadows. Everyone watched as he made his way down, following the rustling vines and fronds with their eyes. The overgrowth had hidden from Dendrick the broken trail, which could potentially be used to descend if not traverse the cliff face. Aatuani came back shortly thereafter, excitedly motioning for them. "Yes! Yes! Come on! The trail leads to the switchbacks!"

Rodendros gave a laugh. "Cristobal, you see how excited this one gets. It warms my spirits to see him so gay."

Cristobal looked over at the straight-standing native, with his black hair and high cheekbones, jumping up and down in excitement.

"He is different," Cristobal said.

The trail was barely visible, but it was clearly broken, and Aatuani led the way for Dendrick Rodon, who demanded to see it. The crow master, whose eyes never missed a mark, was swift to compliment the comandante's keen observation. The comandante decided to rest and told the three of them, Cristobal, Dendrick, and Aatuani, to go recon the switchbacks and make sure that it was in fact a negotiable pass.

Aatuani opened the way to the hidden passage, holding up a few of the camouflaging fronds that had occluded the trail in broad daylight. Under the native's outstretched arm, Cristobal and Dendrick cautiously ducked, walking into the bush for hopefully the last time.

Behind the fronds was a clear trailhead with a strange totem marking its beginning. It was a simple wooden post with a blue talisman hanging from it, feathers of an unknown variety weaved within a web of shells and beads.

A path was now visible. The way was down, but the trail descended sharply, with narrow switchbacks clear up and down the steep, inclined cliff face.

"Let's follow these and see where they go." Cristobal said.

Aatuani nodded, confidently he took point and took the first steps out onto the switchback path. They had plenty of room, but getting horses and supplies down would be tougher. They could do it if they hugged the wall, and finding an alternate route would mean losing precious days of rations and time by backtracking, which was unacceptable.

Cristobal sat there for a second, contemplating what to do next. Dendrick Rodon stepped in front of Cristobal, following behind their native guide.

"Right, let us follow this a ways," Cristobal said, snapping himself out of it.

"Captain, by the looks of it, I would wager this was once a common trade route. This trail and these switchbacks have been here for quite some time, by the looks of it. Either they used to walk this way or they still walk this way, and if they still do, then that means this savage is walking us right up to their front door," Dendrick said, looking over his shoulder at Cristobal as the three of them shimmied along the narrow ledge.

"If he planned an ambush, don't you think he'd have done it before the reinforcements arrived? Don't you think?" said Cristobal.

Dendrick snapped his head forward, following carefully after Aatuani as they took short, choppy steps downhill.

"Look at the man. He has no concept of such things. He does not understand strategy or foresight. He is a creature of the land; the land is what he knows. He has no conception of our methodology or approach. We just pay him well," Dendrick said, sounding unconcerned. He then went quiet, not wishing to berate the comandante's confidant to the point of reaction.

They reached the edge of one narrow ledge and turned around to come back, zigzagging down from one to another, down the face of the sparsely vegetated cliffside. They walked down several levels, not realizing they were at such a high elevation merely a few hours ago. About halfway down, Aatuani motioned for them to stop. "Look!" he said in hushed excitement.

Cristobal looked to his left, and there was the mouth of a cave, going straight into the cliffside, opening up into what appeared to be a cool, moist limestone retreat, hidden from the heat of the unrelenting sun.

"Yes, let's go, but first," holding up a finger to pause, "a torch." Pulling out a wooden shaft, he used his flint and steel and set to work igniting the fat-covered torch. After about a dozen tries, he succeeded in igniting the torch top, and the flames sprang forth from it. It would serve the purpose of illuminating the earthen orifice.

"Don't be too proud of yourself, Captain. I'm sure this one can rub two rocks together and make fire," Dendrick Rodon said.

What would have been a private victory was now sullied by Dendrick's true yet hurtful words. Cristobal's smile disappeared.

Carrying the torch, he walked into the mouth of the cave, Dendrick and Aatuani following closely behind. Sharp stalagmites and stalactites were everywhere, dripping with cool condensation. The temperature had dropped tremendously. It wasn't a very large cavern from the looks of it, but when seeking shelter in a harsh storm, or just to find some shade, it was comfortable enough. A small crack in the limestone was dripping water like a spring, and Aatuani went and pressed his lips to the stone, drinking from the Earth tap.

Cristobal stepped cautiously deeper into the cave, using his torch to light his way as best he could. Dendrick shuffled his feet along the broken rocks, feeling the grit of the walls with his hands. He went to share the basin with Aatuani, cupping his hands under the stream and using the water to splash on his sun-scorched face.

"We'll call this one 'Cristobal Cave.' You like that?" Dendrick said, rubbing a hand over his dripping-wet face, once more drawing amusement at Cristobal's expense. Cristobal rolled his eyes, further examining the cave. He then happened to run his torch close enough to a small alcove, which exposed something hidden. A slanted slab of stone was covering up a secret channel.

"Hey, come here, look at this!" Cristobal shouted, his voice bouncing off the stone walls in all directions. The others followed the torchlight and joined Cristobal at the stone obstruction.

"Help me move this aside," Cristobal ordered, and the other two placed their hands with his on the slab. Heaving with all their strength, they managed to walk it side to side, clearing the way to what appeared to be a narrow passage.

"We don't go," said Aatuani, hunching down at the mouth of the corridor.

"Of course we go, you fool," Dendrick said, holding the torch, the glare bouncing off the native's high cheekbones and oily forehead.

"No, I won't. We don't," the guide insisted.

"Aatuani, why don't we go?" Cristobal asked, drawn to intervene.

The native then stood back up, and taking pause, gathered himself, before going into a surprisingly impressive Spanish monologue.

"It was many moons ago, in the land of my fathers, long before I walked among the living. My people revere a once-great tribe. A nomadic people, our ancestors, the ancient ones, who walked these long plains and taught us our ways. These caverns are not where men should dwell. These caverns are for the spirits. The spirit travels on, and these caves are their way."

This of course went against every sort of theological philosophy Cristobal had been brought up with in the Church. However, it was clearly important to their guide that they return the way they came, as he would not carry on deeper into the cave. They took their last glances before heading back by torchlight to the entrance.

Walking outside, they stepped into a cold night. The sun had set much faster than they had thought it would.

"That's odd. We arrived midday, did we not?" Dendrick asked Cristobal, who, feeling the biting cold, was now entering a frantic state.

"Good Lord, the comandante is going to be furious! Have we really kept him waiting this long? Come! Come! We must leave at once!"

Behind Cristobal, Dendrick and Aatuani followed, climbing the narrow switchbacks up to the landing where the comandante and the rest of the company were waiting. Cristobal pushed the air out of his lungs as he ran up the switchbacks, and after climbing several levels, they climbed over the threshold, but they struggled to find where the trail fed back into the clear portion of the landing. Retracing their steps by the quickly dimming torchlight, they stumbled through to the unmarked trail. Dendrick tripped over a thick tree root, falling face first into the ground and eating a mouthful of dirt. He gave a weak groan before standing back up.

On the other side, the comandante was standing in front of a huge bonfire, which was sending large plumes of thick smoke into the air. Cristobal was gasping for breath and wondering how he had lost track of the time. He didn't feel as though they were in there for very long.

"There you are, young captain! Your arrival was anticipated hours ago. What the devil was the disturbance?" Comandante Redondo asked, tearing a piece of flesh from the bone of a wild animal that they had cooked over the fire.

Cristobal was searching for the words when Aatuani broke the silence. "The switchbacks are passable but very dangerous. And there was a cave," said the guide to the comandante, who looked over at Cristobal.

"So, you just stood outside of it for a while?" the comandante asked.

"We went in and looked around, then turned around," Cristobal said.

"Well, if it was nothing worth mentioning, then that's all you needed to say. Captain Cristobal, in our friend's culture, caves are looked at as portals to the spirit world. It is highly sacred to enter one and should only be done when performing ritual or seeking shelter from the elements. When we traveled with Cortes, we explored our fair share of them, and we too felt the immense power of these ancient places. I'd rather avoid them as well," said Rodendros.

"We can make it down, Comandante. The cave is about halfway down, straight into the side of the cliff. I say we move everybody down the switchbacks tomorrow and set up camp after everyone makes it down. After that, it's wide open, far as the eye can see," Cristobal said, now collected.

"Great plan, my boy. Now get some rest and unwind. Help yourself to some food. I'm going to retire for the evening with Aatuani; he'll be our point of direction. He says he has something very special to show us," the comandante said, placing his arm around Aatuani and walking with him back to the command tent.

Cristobal wondered what that meant, *something special to show us*. What did that imply? Cristobal put the thought aside as he, Dendrick, and Fernando, who'd been waiting with the comandante, all nodded their acknowledgment and gave their salutes before heading to the back to the junior command tent.

"What do you think he wants to show us, the guide?" Dendrick asked, lifting the flap and ducking under it.

"I couldn't say for sure," Cristobal said, lifting his hand to hold the flap open, "but the two of them are quite fond of one another," Cristobal replied.

Dendrick shuffled over to his gear, taking off his armor, setting down his weapons and morion, and Cristobal did the same, stripping down to his britches.

"Oh, of course he's waiting on the comandante's every wish. He lived a savage life before, and he's living like a king now! Why mess up a good thing?" the crow master said as he fixed his bedding for the night.

It was true, though, Cristobal thought. How had he come to learn their Spanish tongue anyway? It was unsettling to think they had no privacy from their guide, their only link to the foreign world, thus, they could not manipulate him, for fear he would hear their plans and abandon the party, or worse.

"Well, only time will tell if this one can be trusted. Until then, I trust what the comandante says. It's better than walking blindly in the wild. This one can show us the way of the land, for he is a steward of it," Cristobal said as hung up his outer garb to dry. Fernando was crouched over, lighting a lantern and giving some light to the small space. He planned on working on some maps of his own.

Cristobal pulled his thick leather journal from the satchel next to his pile of gear, which was crudely thrown to the ground. Spreading out on the ground, they made themselves comfortable and took to their separate notes by lantern light, penning their thoughts for the evening. Cristobal's thoughts drifted around, unorganized and scattered. His head was everywhere, and he felt off after the anomaly in the cave, the quick passage of time that had occurred within the sacred hollow. Cristobal shut his journal after a few minutes, his eyelids suddenly feeling heavier. He set it to the side as he prepared his bedding the best he could to make himself comfortable for the night. Fernando scribbled a bit longer before blowing out the lantern and closing himself up in some blankets. It was cold, and they could hear the wind whipping around outside, battering their tent. The weather had held pretty well up until then. Fernando insisted there were storms about.

Cristobal tried to sleep but found himself tossing and turning in anticipation of tomorrow's movement. Getting down the switchbacks should be no problem, as long as everyone took it slowly. Outside, the last conversations fizzled out as men took to their sleep and the sentries posted themselves at their designated security points, keeping a watchful eye over the horses, gear, and conquistadors that were hunkered down for the night by cliffside and starlight.

Chapter 16

SO YOU WILL WANDER

They descended the switchbacks slowly, which was extremely dangerous, as the ledge could barely fit a man. But with cunning and the strategic way the comandante divided up the equipment, every man carried a single piece of the animal's gear; this way the beasts could walk naked on the narrow ledge, guided by the man in front by a rope around its neck. They remained very calm driving the beast down the narrow zigzags. When they made it down, with minimal incidents, they spread out, letting the horses graze and water right there along a small creek that ran before the wide-open plains. Their eyes glazed over, taking in the scenery. Comandante Redondo led the group, with his native companion beside him.

He didn't need a compass, for he knew exactly where he was going. This was his land, and he needed no tools to show him the way. The stars were his map, and the blowing of the dry wind his directory in the harsh, arid environment. Many nights of clear skies blanketed by billions of stars and planets offered him the opportunity to refine his cosmological proficiency and better understand the heavens, in the way his ancient ancestors did, for in Aatuani's culture, they revered their ancient ones.

Aatuani shared his old technique with Rodendros, in exchange for further lessons in Spanish, as well as lessons on cultures and histories from other places in the world.

Their mutual transferences of knowledge, skills, and abilities led them to develop a great friendship, talking for hours on subjects such as the Spartans, Romans, and those old philosophical contemplations by the likes of Plato, Socrates, and Marcus Aurelius, whom the comandante adored, reading every word of *Meditations* once a year. Maturing in age, they could learn from each other with mutual humility. So great was the comandante's character, the men never questioned his directives. Javier Redondo could be gravely serious, but in the moments when joy and laughter overtook the man, his howls of amusement could be heard by all.

The weeks had been long, and they journeyed from dawn to dusk each day, covering a vast amount of ground quickly on the plains. They took copious notes, drew sketches and diagrams, made many plant pressings and collected various samples and seed pods for cultivation. They studied the unique game they hunted, and Aatuani identified every native plant or animal the comandante inquired about. He knew everything about this world, for the guide was a steward of it. They rested their tired and famished bodies when they could, eating from the rations they replenished as often as they could by hunting the scores of wild game, which were abundant here. The dangers were often pointed out by their guide, who would stop to point out a rattlesnake or scorpion. Pointing out the poisonous flora was common, and all of the men eventually learned to distinguish the poisonous from the nonpoisonous plants, as well as which ones carried unique medicinal properties. Aatuani was an expert in the use of such herbs, able to whip a salve or balm for the conquistadors' blistering feet.

They negotiated obstacles constantly—a creek that needed to be crossed, a steep ravine that needed to be outskirted. The rains had not come in some time, and the further they traveled west the many shades of greens and browns began to change as the landscape started to shift. Before long, the plains slowly began to change too. They had come across the ocean, chopped through hellish jungles, traveled across high plains, ascending and descending valleys and cliffs, and now they were approaching the edges of an expansive, daunting desert, which stretched as far as the eye could see.

Cristobal used his compass the whole way to make sure they stayed on course, and many times he was astonished when their native friend would lead them off course around an obstruction, only to then get them nearly perfectly back on track. The guide possessed a natural sense of direction, moving effortlessly through any type of terrain in any kind of weather. The season was also changing, going from those late days of summer to cooler, longer autumn nights. As the temperature changed and the nights cooled, the morale improved. The conditions the conquistadors had to contend with were lessening in their severity, and most men were in good health as well, with the exception of a few men lost to accident or sickness. Some fell victim to the creatures, bitten by a venomous fang, or stung with a poison stinger, or in a spell of hunger, ate the wrong mushrooms. This was a most terrible death for the men to witness. Writhing in agony, muscles clenched to the point of pain and terrible discomfort, a great shaking of the human body, uncontrollable and violent. They would foam at the mouth like rabid dogs before the light left their eyes, leaving a shocked grimace where one would once smile.

Comandante Redondo worked closely with Cristobal along the way, riding his steed next to the young captain and sharing hours upon hours of conversation. Mostly it was one sided, with the comandante unburdening himself of all the lessons he'd learned in the last forty years of conquests and war.

Under a half-moon they set up camp near the bottom of some stony crags in the underbrush of sweepingly tall grasses. The horses set off in different directions, grazing and taking advantage of the lunar pull to head for the hills, as they must have been terribly thirsty. The springs and streams had become harder to find, and Cristobal ordered the men to collect as much water as possible at every available opportunity.

The heat drew every ounce of moisture from their skin, which chapped and cracked in the sun. Every day they would sweat out all the water they had drunk and then become dehydrated and need more. Some suffered terrible madness, excruciating headaches, and fever. Aatuani would work up a tea for the afflicted. His native medicine did work, and to the surprise of many, brought more than one man back from the brink. He would hunch over a bush and gather the edible berries or point out trees that were fruit bearing or wrapped in a special bark that contained strong anti-inflammatory properties. "There was magic in the medicine," he'd say, as Comandante Redondo would eagerly scribe in his notes all that he was absorbing from Aatuani.

Rodendros was always hungry for more knowledge, another thing Cristobal greatly admired about him; he had lived life the way he wanted to, and when life needed him to make a choice, between using his heart or using his head, he listened closely to his heart.

By now, the seasons had started to change. They kept track of the passing days, took notice of the green leaves that had begun to crisp in the fall, leaves that turned different hues of reds, yellows, and oranges. The birds sang mornings full of long songs, and the men were able to draw morale from the cooling temperatures. During the night, it would get incredibly cold, especially as they picked up more altitude, leaving the plains and approaching the desert. The cooler weather gave them hope that at least their daytime traveling wouldn't be so miserable. Tired of bushwhacking, any small comfort they got, no matter how small it seemed to be, was good enough to stifle their gripes for another day.

The sun went down a little earlier, and around this time, Cristobal would begin preparations for his next day's tasks. He planned their physical and weapons training time and expected each man to carry his own weight. Overseeing the implementations of the Conquistadore Standards of Conduct Code, coordinating with the various levels of leadership their orders and pieces, and keeping the integrity of the whole formation were just some of the things he had to do on his own time. Making sure there were never any breaks in the line, and making sure Enrico, Dendrick, and Fernando weren't letting any deserters skip away unseen, he always monitored everything from his position in the formation.

They had walked for a full month, and the nights were getting frigid. It was the best they could do, as they trudged across those open plains, to make do with single-log fires, so as not to give their position away. The security measures were mostly Cristobal's taskings as well, but it was a duty he never took lightly, and he'd learned in the past the lessons of strategy that would serve him well here. He knew how to set traps and carefully rig them beyond the boundaries of their camp. The sentries posted were always to be awake and listening. The comandante had requested not to be awakened unless it was a dire emergency, and it was Cristobal's task to determine what constituted said emergency.

The sailors complained more than their conquistador counterparts, tired of the food, tired of the constant walking, shirking their duties. These things Cristobal observed, and he could only assume they were reflecting their leader, Captain Fernando, who thought his rank kept him free of the shit duties. They also moved slower than the rest, but who could blame them? They were men of the sea. They were fish who'd jumped onto a boat and were now being dragged through jungles and endless plains with winds that would howl in the daytime.

In truth, the expedition had been going too well for too long. They had lost a few more men along the way, battling fever and unknown sickness. They quarantined the sick or left them for dead.

As they often had to move through different types of diverse regional biomes, the temperatures were often fluctuating, however, they were approaching the autumnal equinox, which meant the harvests would be taking place soon. Cristobal and Fernando sat by the fireside listening to Aatuani, who after warming up to the men, and the men warming up to him, was trying to have a normal conversation.

"The place of my people, the place I'm taking you, was once a great empire, like the Romans."

Taken by surprise, Cristobal looked at Fernando, the sailor's brown eyes wide in disbelief, baffled as to how this native knew about the existence of the Romans.

"Not only do you speak our tongue, but you are versed in the ancient histories as well? First, my friend, you must tell us how you came about learning our language," Cristobal asked, genuinely curious, and impressed with the guide.

Comandante Redondo shuffled over groggily to the group, having woken in the middle of the night to relieve his bladder. He stood over the flames, warming his hands as the heat blew his way, the gusts of fall air coming from above hinted at the coming freeze.

"Don't worry, friend, tell them where you learned your Spanish from."

Aatuani cleared his throat and looked into the fire, taking his time to slowly, and in fluent Spanish, tell them the story. "I was taught very little at first, by Christian missionaries who were passing through our villages with the first white men. When they overthrew Moctezuma, I was just a boy. We were eager to make peace between our peoples but were doomed to conflict. I watched the ships take Tenochtitlan, I saw Cortes parade the corpses of the high priests, while looting gold that was not theirs to take. They came with fire, diseases, and smoke."

Redondo, who stood with his hands clasped behind him, listened, and with remorse said, "We forced them to learn our language, even if it meant beating their native one out of them. It was blasphemy; they bowed before false idols, and they needed to be cleansed. That is how we saw it anyways," the comandante said, feeling for the upheaval of his native friend from his home, closer to the Yucatan.

Rodendros continued, "I observed a magnificent culture, a people of true genius, who were capable of much more thousands of years ago, with their simple and primitive tools, than we are today. The people prospered and built massively powerful empires. I came over with the first wave, landing at Veracruz and trudging through the jungles of the Yucatan. It struck great fear into my young heart. When we saw the cities, rich with fantastic spoils, we jumped. I, in my own avarice, knew we would leave no survivors, for there was too much wealth to leave behind. I laid eyes on Moctezuma, the great one. It was while we had him bound, I realized I will never respect a man more than I do him, for he was quite valiant in the face of complete and total annihilation. The people too, if they'd known who we really were when they'd seen us, they might have been quicker to accept our original advances for peace."

Cristobal and Fernando rested their elbows on their knees. With dropped heads, they listened to the quiet conversation over the crackle of fire. Redondo bent down.

"Gentlemen, do you remember our conversation, when I said Aatuani was showing us something special?" asked the comandante.

"This place that we are being led to is where our friend laid down his roots after the rape of his people."

Aatuani carried the torch. "It's true, I swear my life on it. A kingdom used to exist there. A great carved city of the earth and rock. It was the home that we had been called to. We were nomads at first, moving around from place to place, but the longing for our lost home was strong, and so we settled in the desert. A dry land, dry for many years now, no rain, which was why the majority of them left the great ruins. They dispersed in every direction across the land, looking for water. I too wander in search of those waters, to drink from and to clean myself. The others went in search of new lands to farm as well and hunt on lands untouched. The scavenger birds would fly over our heads and circle us, seeing our starvation-stricken forms. They lived there for more than forty generations, a thousand years. My first home was destroyed by war, and my second home, that of my adoptive people, was plagued by famine. I bear no grudge over my brothers and sisters for abandoning such a place in search of fertile earth or flowing waters where they could raise their young with all they need."

Dendrick Rodon had walked up on the ensemble. Curious, he took a seat on the ground next to the comandante.

"Through the seams of the many lives we have lived before, I know all of you from somewhere." He paused. The fire crackled in front of them, where they sat under the billions of stars that watched from across the universe.

"Many years of walking it would take for you to reach my home of origin. This place, though, the home of my adoptive people, they walked for entire generations to find it, and they still roam, though they are no longer living. A thousand years we lived in this place, thriving, learning, living together. The wildlife flourished, and the hummingbirds hummed when the sparkling waters rushed freely across the plateau."

Aatuani continued his story. The men took their sips and drinks and adjusted their postures for prolonged listening. Cristobal sat next to Fernando, who sat beside Dendrick Rodon, who'd joined their company for the night. Dendrick was a senior squad leader, and that meant he could join command meetings.

"Continue please, my friend, your people," said the comandante.

"The sun and moon guided my ancestors to this place. What you called the North Star we called something different. We studied the stars for many seasons, observing the equinoxes and the solstices, refining our mathematics, and of course, we sowed our own seeds and raised our own crops. Perfecting our agriculture in those harsh sierras was hard, and after years of failure, we managed to grow corn, squash, and beans with what we knew of the land, being grateful for what she gave us, what little providence she could."

Aatuani spoke, and everyone was mesmerized by his fluency. He had total control of it, and they were all remarkably impressed, for he was a true savant.

"We went hungry many times. During the drought, game was scarce. The women of our people, they were strong. The great mother we respect in all forms of life. With the wisdom of our women and the strength of our men, we built a society in the canyons. We wished to be like the birds that come and go with the seasons, and to be also like the seasons that also come and go."

Dendrick had to speak. It seemed the suspense was too much. "To the point, humble friend, please."

Rodendros was quick to intervene. "Aatuani was here first, therefore he is my guide, and *I am the* humble friend, crow master."

There was no arguing with something like that, an affirmation as solid as the stone. Redondo continued.

"Brothers, Aatuani is taking us to the ancestral holy place of his own kin. My friends, I've personally seen what majesty these so-called 'primitive' people are capable of. We could teach each other, learn much by coexisting together. The things we would take back to Spain would be far more valuable than gold or silver. We would have knowledge and maps," said the comandante, looking to his officers. "We could name the rivers as we crossed them."

Cristobal's ears perked up at that, tearing his gaze from the flames to look over at the comandante, with the fiery shadows dancing across his thousand-yard stare.

"It is in keeping with the spirit of the old expeditions that we are to explore and stretch the canvas of the Spanish flag over the whole of this land, however long it takes. We cannot do that by getting fat in the city. We will go to this place our friend here describes, and from there, once we've had our fill, we shall set out once more, across the mountains and to the ocean that surely lay on the other side. The danger is there, and it will take years. I understand those who choose to go their separate ways, but one thing at a time, gentlemen. That being said, I'm going to sleep. Come, Aatuani friend, time for bed."

Redondo pulled Aatuani toward him with the motion of his hand, and Aatuani nodded sheepishly. He propped himself up with his walking stick, the dirt and ash caked on his face and hands. In his simple cloth, he followed the comandante to the command tent, where the two of them could enjoy hours more of mutually enriching conversation.

Fernando was the first to break the silence. "Seems like an awful lot of things being planned by the comandante for this mission. We were told two years maximum, which includes time at sea. Sailors are not necessary for *conquistadors* to perform their charge. We transported you here, we resupplied the ground force, but we are not going to be here for more than a year."

Cristobal puckishly chuckled at that.

"Fernando, friend, if you miss your bed and your cookies and your nap time, then just say so," said Dendrick.

Fernando gave him a special nonverbal gesture to show his reciprocated amusement.

They shared a laugh over the dying fire. Cristobal figured it was a good time to address the question still up in the air. "I am like you; I do not know whether trusting this guide is the right thing to do, but I also know that I want to do those things the comandante spoke of. I want to discover new rivers and mountains. Walk across the sierras and through those jungles again, as horrifying as it was. I've wanted this my whole life, so I will stand beside the comandante."

The group nodded their agreement, and Cristobal stood to leave, not before Dendrick Rodon grabbed him by the arm and finally let his true thoughts be heard. "I'm going to turn in as well, but listen, Cristobal. If this is a trap, or the guide is playing us, then chances are we won't see it coming. We need to be eyes open at all times. I'm going to talk with the others about it. Let's be smart, let's have a plan, and be ready to fight, because the odds are his friends won't be as well tempered as he is."

Cristobal heard his friend and gave him a hug. "I understand brother. Get some sleep, we'll talk more about it in the morning."

They all went back to their tents to spend the night as they'd spent it many nights before, alone in thought; under a tent or under the stars, it mattered little. They were far from home, a whole world away, but another day closer to their destination, which hopefully wasn't too far off, as it was soon to be winter, and the cold nights had yet to fully set in.

The night hummed low, as the song of different insects and animals echoed in the quiet darkness. The conquistadors and sailors had become closer since they'd been traveling together the last several weeks. They'd had time to get to know one another more. Many of them were hand selected for the expedition, either by word of mouth or might of arm, a few coming from the same units. Everyone dreamed of coming over to the New World, but it was also a monumental sacrifice to come here.

Cristobal was unable to sleep, lying on some old antelope furs with only a thin woolen blanket to keep him warm. In the darkness, he lay down with open eyes as he thought of Fiorella. The love he'd left behind, her memory kept him sane. The thought of having a family one day and becoming a father himself was a fantasy he enjoyed playing in his head.

He couldn't help but curse his foolish last words to her.

"Don't forget about me." Of course she couldn't; she had loved him too, and how she cried for him the nights he was gone. How she hugged his legs as he tried to walk out the door. She did not wish him to go, but he had to, and it hurt him too, because he didn't wish to go either, but rather he was called to this life; it was now all he knew. In his imagination, he'd play out the parades and festivals that they would have in the streets upon their arrival back to the motherland. The marigold glories that would be thrown at their feet. The laurels placed atop their heads. Being worshipped like the great conquerors and heroic Cesarean Knights, those figures of courage, honor, and bravery, would've been even more fulfilling than being a father. His name etched into history, forever and always; that kind of notoriety-driven dream can drive a man to insanity. Fiorella would've been proud, he thought, if she could only see him now. If she could only see how far he'd come.

Chapter 17

VIDA LIQUIDA

It hurt Cristobal's heart to think about home. It was a soldier's calling to go to war. Selfish, she had called him, accusing him of only ever thinking about himself. He thought of the reward. Success in the New World would mean everything for the family. He felt proud, being sent off on his first campaigns, several years before, where luck had kept its watchful eye over him, keeping him safe from danger. Of course, there is no such thing as luck, but the many hours spent training hand to hand in the melee, and the long marches had prepared him for the rugged life of soldiering. In those days, they had to earn the privilege of riding a horse, which was why his relationship with Simora was so strong.

A conquistador's first horse is a special one. The celebrated beasts would carry them stoically, giving Cristobal and his men a critical advantage. They could outmaneuver the enemy with horses. They could attack with more ferocity and speed, which let them overtake their adversaries using horse-mounted assaults; fighting with crossbows, swords, and lances, they would fight wave after wave of enemy combatants. Some of the horses did escape the Spaniards because they were not being watched very well, but Cristobal did his diligence when he tended to Simora. Her blonde mane never went too long without a good brushing. She was a friend, far from home. She was symbolic of the neutrality of nature, how there is inherent good inside all of God's creatures. The universe had brought the two different species' souls together at the same time and given them the same shackle of circumstance.

"In keeping with the spirit of the old expeditions," his comandante's words.

It had been months since they landed on the shores of the Golfo, and they were taking things slowly, as the increasingly dry climate pulled every last bit of moisture from the air and from their skin and bones. The clear shift of temperate zones had seen the plains turn into a rocky, barren waste of desert, with long serpentine dunes, towering tabletop buttes, sheer sandstone cliffs, and deep fissures of the earth, a maze of unending canyonlands.

How things managed to grow in this place was a puzzle. They had scarcely seen any sort of creek, river, or lake in several days and were starting to run low on their water. They'd lost once more, a few more men, to desertion, illness, dehydration, or starvation. The padre had played the role of medicine man, but he put to rest more than he was able to save. These kinds of losses were expected. It was no small undertaking, and the threats here were unlike the ones of their homeland. Certainly, they had been fortunate until this point to avoid combat or confrontation with any sort of Indigenous. The clear advantage of their guide meant they followed in the footsteps of one who walked the way the enemy walked and spoke the language of their opponents. Their dealings with Aatuani were as far as they'd seen any interaction with a savage go. That, however, was about to change.

The skies here were bluer than they had been before, with huge, lofty clouds. The ground was fire, a red sandstone, with sparse vegetation dotting the landscape. Cristobal couldn't help but feel for the shriveled-up, sad bushes that were fighting with their whole might to survive in the chiminea that was this unknown desert. For miles and miles, Cristobal could see the towering mesas and buttes, which protruded from the earth like reverent monoliths. It was a daunting challenge, facing the desert that lay before them. Here the sun would hold no grudge and would be indiscriminate with whoever it chose to afflict. By now, the men were more acclimated to the heat, but it was their water supply that Cristobal was worried about.

"Comandante, we need to look for water before we go wandering further into this place."

Comandante Redondo peeked over his shoulder at Cristobal, who rode atop Simora behind him.

"Young Captain, do not worry yourself with water. Aatuani is familiar with the area. He says there is a river nearby."

Aatuani walked in front, looking back to confirm Redondo's words. "It's true, Captain, a river flows just before the real desert begins. There we can let the animals drink to their hearts' content, while we bathe, swim, and drink ourselves."

"And fill up our water reserves," said Cristobal, idling atop Simora.

They kept on, the horses dragging their feet against the gravelly and coarse sunbaked dirt.

"Let us see it, Father," he muttered, swaying side to side as Simora lazily walked ahead.

They had been running low on their game reserves as well, but food wasn't so much of a problem yet, as the men could go days without eating. Cristobal sweated through his armor under the heat of the sun. He couldn't stand to wear it. The metal burned the skin of his neck, and his cotton rags for clothes underneath were withered and destroyed.

They passed large patches of cacti, towering green totems that made Cristobal feel uneasy as he stood in their tremendous shadow. How anything could maintain itself in this stricken place was beyond him. As if reading his mind, while they carried on toward the river, which was yet to be seen, Aatuani directed his attention back toward the young captain.

"Captain Trujillo, the place of my people looked far different in her prime than what you see before you. Our home was once one of marvel, its construction a generational effort, ongoing for hundreds of years. We grew crops in this place with no water, yet we fed thousands with our harvests, and our women bathed our young in the rivers, and we washed the feet of our elders at its banks. Water once flowed through here like the Great Lakes to the north."

Cristobal felt off about the place, for he knew that they were trespassing in lands where their presence was not wanted. This, however, was not his decision to make, and he was of the mind that their mission was a numinous one.

Comandante Redondo gave his opinion. "These lands, while now barren, once used to have great cascading *lagunas*, with lush vegetation encompassing the wildlife that ran abundantly here until the long drought spell began. Everything dried up without the rain. Dead animals could then be found on the banks of the shriveled-up streams and dry riverbeds. To tell you good men the honest truth, I'm not sure myself if there are going to be flowing rivers here, but Aatuani says there are. We shall pray with the padre tonight over it."

Aatuani walked with his back straight and his head high, his black unibrow furrowed as he led the pack toward the sun, reaching its pinnacle in the afternoon sky. His great walking staff served its purpose to propel him across the hot sand, which he walked atop barefoot. "My people left long ago, you know this, but a few of us devotedly stayed, to remain watchful over the spirits that still reside there. Making sure the portals remain closed."

Cristobal raised a brow, and reiterated the word. "Portals?"

"To the spirit world, Captain, the place of your father's father's father," said the comandante.

This type of talk confused young Cristobal, who was strongly bound to his faith. He had never perceived the rationale of other theologies. There was one way to salvation: the light of the Lord and faith in God. Anything else was a blasphemy to the Lord's holy name and an insult to any God-fearing Christian.

Dendrick Rodon called a halt.

Knowing him to be the most likely candidate for quickly identifying an approaching threat, Redondo kept his squad on point for weeks.

They all paused, pulling up the reins and signaling down the line to hold things up.

The conquistador, who had seen something glimmer in the corner of his eagle eyes, felt it warranted pause. Comandante Redondo got off his horse, furiously walking over to Dendrick, who was bent over at the waist, crouched and looking at something. He held in his hand something shiny, small, and black. "Arrowhead," he said.

He held it up for all to see. The first sign of civilization in this region. It was a small, obsidian arrowhead, delicately notched, so much so that its razor-sharp edge was still viable after countless centuries buried in the dirt.

"The river is close. We must not stop," he said, clutching his fist closed over the artifact.

"Arrowheads, you say?" said the comandante.

"Cristobal, there's surely a few more around here. Everybody just keep looking!" said Dendrick, brushing his hands through the sandy dirt.

The comandante ordered everyone to spread out on their hands and knees to look for more of them.

This was against Cristobal's better judgment. He did agree having more artifacts to bring home would greatly authenticate their story, because these were not the Mayans or the Aztecs. These were new and unknown native peoples, running around together in their tribal systems, stewarding the New World from coast to coast presumably. The proof of the great society they searched for had yet to be seen, and they would need all the help they could get in justifying their excursions, should the ruins fail to have such things as gold or jewels. They needed to prove the importance of their discovery, since it was not the traditional conquest. This mission was more in line with an exploratory assignment.

"Aatuani, how far are we from the water?" Comandante Redondo asked.

"Not far, maybe half a day's walk. These canyons will start to open up soon. If there is water, it'll be low."

"Do not wander too far. We know not who patrols these trails. Somebody controls the river," said Rodendros.

The men began to stretch, and the order was passed back that they were taking a breather. Using short, choppy steps, Cristobal and the others began to comb through the sand and earth, some on hands and knees, others bent ninety degrees, scanning the sparse brush for any sort of anything. After twenty minutes, Cristobal finally found one. He was amazed for a second as he held it reverently in his hands, feeling the ridges where the glass had been flaked and chipped off, feeling the smoothness of it after unknown centuries being sanded down by time and erosion. The lethality of such projectiles was famous, and in the days of the old conquests, the Indian archers would do serious damage to the invading forces by way of the bow and arrow.

The conquistadors, however, had the advantage of technological superiority. They were plated in armor and mounted on horses. They possessed crossbows and arquebuses and were thoroughly adept in combat themselves. They were a tough breed, some of the finest men in Spain, a proud legion of fiercely aggressive debutantes, possessing a collective narcissistic charisma, a group ego they carried from the time Cortes made their cause a worldly matter. Everyone across the world had heard of those battles and wars in South America. The New World appealed greatly to all, but someone had to do the dirty job of cleaning it up.

Of course, cleaning it up would mean there would be wars to fight with the native populations, but wars and long military campaigns were far too costly, and the comandante knew this. This was also his play with Aatuani; by maintaining a good relationship with one of the natives, he'd more likely be able to barter for peace and diplomacy. Aatuani had become the comandante's private confidant and inside operative, which meant the comandante had a secret way into the Indigenous circles.

Having friends helped, and Cristobal and Fernando had begun to enjoy each other's company more, bonding over the mutual stresses the comandante gave them. Fernando knew his job; Cristobal could not argue this. Watching his peer, in trade and in age, harrowingly take the helm and guide them on surely one of the most perilous sea voyages of all time warranted Cristobal's earnest respect.

After suffering relentless storms in the open ocean, fighting through powerful cyclones in the Golfo, it was a miracle they'd made it there alive. Cristobal felt that Fernando, in his line of work, had it easier than he. He thought Fernando was given more room to grow into being his own officer. Cristobal was the same rank as Fernando, and yet was still in this belittling learning process, where he was subordinate to the comandante. Cristobal put his ego aside; it was the curse of youth, wishing for the time to pass. He knew he still had much to learn in his career, and he hung on to every word the comandante said. Suddenly, Cristobal realized something in the midst of his daydreaming. He had broken through some brush and could hear the sound of moving water coming from below. Needing to see if his ears were playing tricks on him, Cristobal scrambled down the loose rock with calculated steps. Peeking over some smaller cracked boulders, he looked down, realizing that this slope turned into a ravine, with water running along the bottom of its concourse. It wasn't as big as he thought it would be, and it actually appeared to be rather dried out, but it would be enough for them to live another three days. The sun had gotten thirsty as well, it seemed.

"Damn it," he said.

Cristobal scanned down the drying riverbed, taking his time to analyze the scenic picture. When at first it seemed like he was struck by a trick of the ears, now it was a trick of the eyes. He froze, motionless, holding his breath so as not to make a sound. He spied a beautiful siren along its banks, beating some rags against a wet stone, while her wavy black hair hung low beside her delicate arms. Slender, she wore very little, her bosom kept under cloth. He heard the sloshing beat of the sopping rags and observed as she collected two large pitchers of water, a terribly heavy load for such a small woman to bear. The pitchers were clay-colored vessels, with black and white painting on the outside.

Choking on his Adam's apple, Cristobal swallowed hard, but still he did not dare move a muscle, for fear of giving himself away. The woman went about her business, slapping her rags, and Cristobal was working on his plan to escape unnoticed when he heard his name being shouted out in the distance, atop the ravine.

"Captain Trujillo! We're leaving!" Comandante Redondo ordered from above. Cristobal was crouched, watching the woman; when she heard the shouts, she looked straight up at him. Paralyzed, he held her unblinking gaze, unable to move as she eyed the peculiar white stranger across the river, in his funny clothes and plumed cap. It was over; he was caught.

"Captain, you down there?" Rodendros shouted from the top. He looked down, also shocked at what he saw.

"The river! Sweet Jesus! You found us some water! Thank you, my God, good God! Everybody! Quickly! Into the ravine!"

The woman abandoned her pitchers and took off running down the bank of the withered riverbed. Cristobal stood there, unmoving, his tongue in his throat, mute and needing to take another look at the native woman with his own eyes to make sure she was real. He heard the others coming down the slope, sending loose rocks careening down and thudding against the gravelly, dead riverbed. Despite its lower level of volume, the comandante got a running start and belly-smacked himself into the shallow water. The men ran up to the drying riverbed and scooped mouthfuls of water with their hands, doing their best to drink themselves silly, in need of dire rehydration. The horses too joined their masters in quenching their thirst.

Cristobal walked into the river, which wasn't very deep, knee high for the young captain, and waded to the other side while the others made their way down. He approached the stone upon which the woman sat, where she was beating her rags against the rock. On closer inspection, Cristobal saw the different shapes and patterns drawn on the bodies of the pitchers. In black paint, he saw what he would call a bird, surrounded by zigzag lines, circles, and other strange motifs painted in a pattern along the vessel's exterior. The inside was the color of the naturally resourced clay, a fired terracotta. The pitcher was incredibly smooth, clean, and free of any superficial visual deformity.

The other was equally marked in strange glyphs; an ant, a snake coiled around a tree, the Tree of Life perhaps. The water was filled to the brim, and it was quite heavy to move. It was a prize catch; these were artifacts of superior quality, but it dawned on Cristobal he'd have to be the one to explain where these pitchers had come from.

"What are those?" Redondo shouted from the other side, where the rest of the party was descending.

"There was a woman here!" Cristobal shouted back. "She left these!"

Comandante Redondo audibly gasped and threw his hands up, cheering in joy.

"A woman, you say! Where did she go!"

The comandante ran across the water as fast as he could, so he could hear the young captain better, and to come and inspect the vessels for himself. "What was she doing? What did she look like? Where did she go?" The comandante hurled these questions toward Cristobal, who tried to answer them as best he could.

"Well, Comandante, I made it down to the bottom without her hearing me. She was over here. She filled up these pitchers of water, and she was washing her clothes when she heard you shouting up there for me. Then she looked up at me and took off running up the river."

Comandante Redondo absorbed this for a second, trying to hear himself think among all the noise the men and animals were making. It was beginning to infuriate him.

"Quiet!" he shouted, his voice carrying throughout the whole canyon.

"We are going to follow this north from now on," he said.

Cristobal wasn't sure he heard the comandante correctly. "Comandante, we have Indigenous people on our backs. We need to be smart."

Rodendros looked at Cristobal and cocked his head, raising a brow. "I'm sorry, Captain, let me rephrase my directive. We'll camp here tonight, drink this riverbed dry, and in the morning, we'll follow it north, to see where it leads."

Cristobal heard the orders but felt like they were sitting ducks in the bottom of the open ravine. Pushing the thought aside, he did as he was told. They began to make camp, setting up their riverside campfires and cooking down some of their game reserves. The sky was clear and the sun beginning to set, the wispy cirrus clouds blowing gracefully across the sky, with a light breeze that was blessing the men out in the arid desert dusk.

The days would be blistering hot, but at night the temperature dropped. Some nights it felt good; other nights, the cold bit down through to the bone and made one shiver senselessly. It was a good night tonight, though, not too cold, and the air could be heard whistling through the canyon. Nighttime here was interesting. The worry of grotesque creatures kept many of them awake, traumatized by their jungle excursions. The desert creatures were similarly bad.

The stars were spotty, cloud cover burying the small ravine in on itself. The lighter shades of blue were simmering down into a brassy grayish hue, while tangerine oranges, flamingo pinks, and purple haze faded into a ceiling of stars, planets, and galaxies. Earth, of course, was the epicenter, which the known universe revolved around.

Aatuani heard Cristobal mention his encounter with the Indigenous woman. He took alarm at it and was unsure why the comandante had been so quick to push it off as hearsay. He approached Cristobal as he was helping Fernando set up their tent along the waterside.

"Captain, might I have a word with you briefly?"

Cristobal looked up from where he was crouched over, to see the tall, half-naked native man leaning over his walking stick.

"Of course, I can spare a minute for a friend."

Aatuani crouched down too, to be eye level with Cristobal. "These vessels that you see, my people are the ones who made them. It was our traditional, generational work. They could be decorative works, like these water carriers you see here, or they could serve in a utility manner. We made large-bottomed pots and used them to cook our beans, long tray dishes and deep bowls to eat on. Hand painting the vessels was another skill which needed to be passed down. It was taught to us by our fathers, as theirs passed down to them. We would trade our crafts, be them hand woven or clay, with the different peoples up and down the rivers and trade routes. That was further west."

"These are fabulous relics! We must bring these with us! These will go in the museum of our findings!" said Cristobal.

But Aatuani was quick to put out his fire. "No, Captain, please. We must not take these. They do not belong to us," the Indian said politely. "We can leave them here; she will come back for them."

Comandante Redondo scuttled over and shut down the argument for good.

"Those are coming with us, my friend. A treasure so easily abandoned could not have been much of a treasure at all."

Aatuani looked down the length of his staff in defeat at the comandante's orders. "The woman will tell her people. More than likely, she's already made her way back to her village and spread the word of our arrival. Do not be frightened; they will approach us in peace before they resort to arms. We will be ready for them. Until then, there is nothing we can do to stop what God has preordained of us. Get your rest." Weighing the gravity of the situation, Cristobal agreed with the comandante. Worrying would do nothing but distract them and make them lose sight of their target, make them lose their focus, where razor-sharp awareness was key. The threat of confrontation was out there and real, and it meant that Cristobal and the others needed to be on guard, keeping their heads on the swivel, as there were natives about.

"Step up security on our flanks. We need guards posted and roaming on sentry duty the whole night. We cannot fall victim to surprise," Cristobal said. The comandante approved of this, as did Captain Fernando and Dendrick Rodon.

The goings-on inside the camp were quiet, and the men moved with care, so as not to disturb the peace. They had been given explicit instruction to maintain their low presence, which meant no talking. They were to gently stoke the fires, to not send ambers shooting up and out of the ravine, and they were not to make any loud noise. Everyone did well, for the most part. The sailors thought they could manage to sneak in a few cheerful drinks and conversation, but Captain Fernando stifled their bandy voices.

The conquistadors were on alert and quiet in their riverside camp. Fires lit up and down the riverbed; shadows of flickering flames danced up the sandstone cliffside, working their way up the ravine. The smoke floated up, and the fires continued to burn low for the night. They were all fast asleep, as the night swaddled them.

While the men slept on their riverbank encampment, Comandante Redondo stirred uneasily. It was true, their location was highly exposed, but the men and horses could no longer go without quenching their thirst. It was critical to the survival of the expedition to find water before their gourds ran bone dry or the horses tipped over from exhaustion. Self-preservation meant they needed a resupply, and it was too late to leave now anyways. Comandante Redondo trusted the quiet cover of night to provide a sense of security. Every noise, every snore, every bit of movement he heard made him grimace and cringe. It was still entirely too loud in the camp for his liking.

Aatuani had been watching his friend stir in that uneasy fashion for some time. He shook the comandante's shoulder. "Rodendros, you okay?" he asked.

Rodendros rolled over and sat up, looking over at the guide in the near dark. "No, my friend, I'm not, but I'll be all right. Never mind me."

Aatuani raised an eyebrow and lifted his hand to request more information, but the comandante lay back down and spoke not a word the rest of the night. His captains had been busy themselves, with Cristobal and Fernando taking the watch during their roaming guard shifts.

Cristobal put on his armor, grabbed his weapons, and made his rounds diligently about the riverbank camp, stopping to kick out a fire or hush some of the enlisted. Cristobal swallowed his pride and resumed being an officer. Cristobal moved up and down the whole line and was pleased with the noise discipline, so he made his way back to his tent and stood the sentry post, keeping his eyes on the whole picture. He listened to the sounds of nature and enjoyed the hollow crispness of it.

He breathed in the cold, dry air, which had a good taste, and as he exhaled it through his nostrils, he felt alive. Here he was finally; after years of dreaming it into existence, he'd been given a coveted role in one of the great expeditions. This was history, which they wrote every day they stayed out here.

Things couldn't keep going this well, Cristobal thought. They were bound to run into trouble at some point, but he did not fear that, for God was on their side. Taking it day by day and hoping for the best was the best he could do, but he always expected the worst.

A great remnant of a city, Aatuani said. A place where people thrived, in the unsurvivable. A drought that stripped the land clean, her water drawn away. The idea that a flourishing society could exist at another point in time in this place seemed far-fetched. How could a place with blistering daytime heat and canyons that fissure the earth, abundant in dry creek beds and prickly cacti, harbor and sustain natural life?

Cristobal thought, however, that if at another point in time, it was a thriving region, it couldn't be the same now, not since the drought. This was why he assumed the place Aatuani spoke of was the abandoned remnants of a city. It was hard bargaining to say whether any sort of riches were to be found there. He was doubtful their spoils would be of any real material substance. Cristobal was not going to let his chance at glory be another misallocation of the Spanish crown's resources, a waste of time. He could not let that be the case.

Then too, if their mission was to gain territory for the new Spanish colonies, then they would need the absolute freedom to discover and explore and be allowed to take their time practicing their careful cartography, which was still a crude if not mostly unreliable science. Wars were to be fought, new places to be named, trade routes established, opening lines of commerce through the various settlements that would spring up in the wake of their successful conquest. It would've been an impossible task without the conquistadors, so either way, their presence was required. The comandante needed those reinforcements desperately, and things might have been different had they arrived earlier.

Each day that passed, Cristobal felt as though maybe they might prove something significant to history. That thought was like a drug to Cristobal. He smiled under his morion visor and leaned coolly upon on his lance as he quietly amused himself with thoughts of bravery and glory, shaking his head over how carnival life could be. Here they were, exploring the northern edges of what would one day become rightful Spanish land for their sons, grandsons, and great-grandsons, hopefully for a thousand more years.

There were a great many scholars among them. The padre, being an excellent scribe, sat in with the comandante at the end of each day, so the comandante might relay the day's occurrences, and the padre might add them to the histories.

Fernando was an excellent nautical navigator, expertly skilled in the use of his tools—sextants, astrolabes, and the compass. He was the expedition cartographer, and he took his work very seriously. The likes of Columbus and Magellan had inspired the young man, and he dedicated many hours of his time to his craft. His men loved him for his dedication to their way of life. Fernando's mind was a sponge, and everything he read stayed with him; his own understandings of the different schools of thought were far beyond his peers'. He would not only maintain accurate sketches of their many changing surroundings, the mountains, rivers, and canyons, but he also kept a detailed log of all entries into the different subschools of their discovery: important findings relevant to distance, direction, and description. Numbering in his journals, he'd keep track of the changing weather conditions, differences in the air pressure, and altitude. Differences in vegetation and wildlife. Captain Fernando was well received by his men. He was fair and had the knowledge to back up what he said. It was no small feat to navigate an ocean, let alone to maintain an accurate logistical report of their rations, equipment, and personnel. Which was why the comandante praised the man on their first meeting, because he understood Fernando was a man of many talents.

The skilled war master, Javier "Rodendros" Redondo, excelled at everything he set his mind to. To be in his position, with his wisdom and experience, one had to put themselves through a great life of pains and struggles. The blade he carried in combat had seen the triumphs of the old expeditions, and the hardships he endured for years side by side with Cortes, in places like Cozumel, where Redondo fought up the steep Mayan temple stairs and into the inner sanctums, where he massacred as many of the heretics as he could, more than two decades ago. They had gone up against the mightiest of all New World empires, the Aztecs, and it was a hard fight getting them to relinquish their vise grip over the land. But they'd done it then, and they'd do it now.

All conquistadors knew of him; he had carved his name in stone twenty years ago under a waterfall rumored to bless the women with abundant fertility. Ten years later, an Incan high priestess called his name from the fires, and he was carried to the Andean Mountains of Patagonia, spending the next several years as a nomad, wandering up and down the western Chilean coast of the South Pacific Ocean. Rodendros was not boastful, nor did he care to speak much of himself, but he was a conquistador through and through, and everyone knew that, which was why he had incredible standing in the whole Spanish government. His strategies were battle tested, and his men showed great prowess on the battlefield, helping him again and again add city after city to the list of ransacked and burned places he'd left behind in his wake.

Aatuani approached Cristobal as he stood sentry, still deep in thought, leaning on his lance. Cristobal was scanning up and down the riverbed, straining his eyes to search for any bit of movement or life out there in the cold desert night.

"Friend Cristobal, do you know what happens now that we've been seen?"

Cristobal looked through his morion, and eyeing their native guide, he searched for motive.

"I believe you know."

Aatuani cleared his throat. "These people, my people, are not violent, but if threatened, will defend themselves. If you've been seen, we can only assume that from now on, we will all be watched very closely. They'll keep eyes on us from a distance, until we get too close and they feel it necessary to intervene. I will do my best to keep the peace."

"So, they're going to keep us out?"

"No, they're going to stop us from stepping onto sacred grounds."

"Sacred?" Cristobal asked.

"Yes, the places that were forbidden most to go. The ritual chambers where we sent our loved ones to the other side, where we welcomed all new life, where we cried together and laughed, then wept moreover at the impossible beauty of it."

That gave an alarm, because for a fleeting second, it sounded like Aatuani was not supposed to be bringing a group of foreigners to this sacred location, and if this sacred location was within the ruins, or nearby, then they potentially ran the risk of conflict.

"Why are we not allowed there?" Cristobal asked, shuffling his steps as he adjusted his posture on his lance.

Aatuani leaned the same casual way upon his sturdy walking stick. "You are white men; you are not like us," he said, explicit and forthright, then he waded into the shallow riverbed back toward the comandante's tent, where he'd presumably stay for the night. Cristobal looked up at the rim of the ravine. He didn't want to imagine it, but he pictured the shadowed enemy peeking over the lip and watching down on them, with hateful, resentful eyes.

The night passed uneventfully as Cristobal pulled sentry duty for two more hours and then woke up the crow master for his shift. The morning came, and after an exhaustingly dull night of surveillance and personal introspection, Cristobal roused the men at sunrise. Like a beacon of hope, the sun rose above the ravine, casting its fiery rays down.

Men stirred from their slumber, making their morning conversation. From where Cristobal stood, it looked like Enrico Cardenas was dragging his feet this morning. He shouldn't have been so smug, for he enjoyed special privileges, being Cristobal's second in command. That would need addressing, as he was an officer as well, and Cristobal expected him to hold himself to the same rigorously high standards as he did himself.

Cristobal laid down his lance, took off his morion, which he'd dutifully worn all night, and left his sword belt behind. From the southern side of the bank, Captain Cristobal called out to Enrico from across the way. "Cardenas, I need your report!"

Enrico, looking up from the saddlebags he was working to get closed, quickly made his way over to Cristobal. The rest of the men were packing up their belongings and getting their horses ready. Not all of the equipment could be brought down, and for the stuff left at the top, there were guards pulling security around the clock. The main purpose of this excursion was to resupply the water and drink their fill, which they did. Enrico came through the water, his pants a different shade of color from his shins up.

"Enrico, are you doing all right?" Cristobal asked with genuine concern for his friend, who looked rough, the beard on his face overgrown and bushy.

He looked surprised at Cristobal's words.

"Captain, I know the comandante thinks I've been easy on the men, but I don't wish to make their anguish worse by being a bastard toward them too."

Cristobal nodded, thinking of a good answer for the troubled lieutenant.

"Yes, Enrico, I understand, but just because you are maintaining good order and discipline, that does not make you a bastard. They fully know the obligations of their profession. It is not your place to spare anybody their feelings. The men need to be addressed, for we have reason to believe that we are now being followed. By who, we do not know, but we need to mind our security and each other. Lean on each other now more than ever, Enrico. Do not let anyone break from the formation for any reason. Wander too far, and they'll find themselves abducted, off to get sacrificed or some other unholy fate. We'll skirt the river as far as it takes us. At least we'll know there's water," Cristobal said, disseminating to his officer the plans that he and the comandante had worked up together.

"I'm also thinking, keep your eyes on our guide. The comandante trusts him completely, but I question his generosity," said Cristobal, who then let Enrico go about his way, the officer resuming his responsibilities in organizing their company.

The paranoia was evident in Cristobal's voice, as he was nervous, expecting his first real encounter with the strange natives, natives who may or may not prove to be hostile. The fear kept him looking over his shoulders. They continued to pack up their gear, refilling their limited stores, and scooping up last-minute handfuls of water straight into their mouths. After the horses were done drinking, they led them back up the ravine carefully and slowly, making sure to use extra care, since they couldn't afford broken legs this late in the expedition. They rejoined the rest of the element atop the ravine, where they could look back down and snake their eyes up the winding curves of the river. How pitiful it looked. There had been no rain in these parts for months, maybe years. All the vegetation felt the strain of dehydration, holding on to every precious ounce of the lifegiving liquid.

Chapter 18

HAZARDOUS BEGUILEMENT

In its prime, it would have been a very strong river, with a powerful current and rich white sparkles that danced across its rushing blue sheen. Eons of erosion had shaped it so, carving itself slowly into the canyons, its winding curves and low valleys the result of unrelenting time. Shrubs and bushes conservatively dotted the riverbank, which was steeper in some places than in others, but as they looked out from the top of the ravine and down the snaking skeleton of what was left of the river, as far as they could see, it seemed to run straight through the earth, splitting the land in two.

It certainly might have been a lush pool at one point, but now it was a shriveled-up shell of its former self. The life that had thrived around it was now choked off, dying, or in pain. The men, however, were rested, their thirsts quenched and their morale improved since their much-needed reprieve. Comandante Redondo led the way, with Aatuani walking in the shadow of him and Luchzuochu.

They only carried with them the essentials, leaving littered in the ravine what they could spare, and walking north, skirting the canyon that carried the dry riverbed bed below, eventually opening up into wider channels, near the colder base levels of the canyon, where the hot air met the cold. As they covered more and more miles, the hollow canyon widened and grew. Cristobal realized then that they had only stumbled into a smaller tributary of a much bigger river.

Now they looked out at the deep bowl-shaped canyon, with a powerful rush of raging rapids at the bottom, surging north, through broken levels of cracked earth.

They rode their horses safely along the edges of the canyon side, peering down into the great chasm, seeing the heavy flowing river crushing the sides of the canyon walls below, forcing itself through the rock with tremendous power. At the bottom, its cascades were a sight to behold, and their foolish thinking that God would let them die of thirst made them grovel in the dirt for forgiveness.

Where there was water, though, there was life. Which could be taken a number of ways. Fresh game for them to hunt, fresh fish to catch, but also, the competitive outsiders. They would need to deal with the Indigenous, seeking either their blessing to use this water source or striking them down in cold blood for it. This river was the life-sustaining force of this dry, dead world, but it also could be used another way. Its flows could be used to penetrate deeper inland, utilizing the lazy-bodied sailors, who at this point were just serving to deplete the conquistadors' rations quicker. Directly ahead of them, some miles off, they saw sheer, jagged cliffs jutting out from the surface of the earth and rising up like great monuments of this foreboding desert land. To their right was a thousand-foot cliff drop down to the grand rapids below, where the river of this great gorge ripped through the sandstone. They rode on, following its winds and turns, taking in the scenery a job in itself. They serpentined with it, symmetrically following in parallel the flowing waters, Captain Fernando de Malaga with his compass in hand, taking copious notes and sketching several different maps at once. The wildlife was more evident now, and the men took turns shooting darts at any wild game they could find.

Cristobal could see the colored flowers blooming on the cacti. The mesquite brush prickled them and was annoying. Different shapes of exotic foliage and vivid flora impressed them, from the wide and shady fronds to huge agave and sagebrush. After the drought, what was left was a skeletonized version of thriving shrublands. Those blue-sky days punished the land and all who walked its surface. The conquistadors no longer needed to search for water, but were it different, and they were a thousand miles south with no water in sight, then they'd be condemned. Water was crucial to their survival, and their survival meant they could see their mission through. Out there in those arid terrains, Simora gallantly carried her master across streams and up steep mountain slopes. She trudged on in agony, despite her being run through. She knew no complaint, only to work harder. Cristobal loved her greatly, and she was gently cared for, a model of her kind. She strode onward, toward the front of the formation, as they'd now spaced themselves out, creating distance between each other, in a strategically spread out column.

Comandante Redondo led the way, with his native guide close by. The two of them walked together. Aatuani stamped the butt of his staff into the earth with each step he took. The two of them were chattering, but Cristobal wasn't really paying attention. He was taking in the landscape, the unspoiled wilderness of this New World.

The crow master rode toward the front of the line, a look of worry spread across his face, which was cast bronze by the sun. He quickly exclaimed that he'd spotted scouts trailing them, due south of their position.

Cristobal felt the adrenaline begin to course through his veins. Recalling the young woman he'd seen at the river some days before, he worried the retribution for that encounter was now here for them.

"What did you see? How many of them were there?" Cristobal asked.

"Couldn't have been more than six. They moved fast, switching cover quickly. they've probably been tracking us for days."

Aatuani chimed in when he heard this. "They are watching us from a distance. They are not going to attack. You were not supposed to see them. They are harmless; the people of this region seldom attack unless provoked. Remember, every tribe is different. There are some out there who would enjoy the capture of their enemy, scalping you where you sit if given the chance. Your Cortes conquered the people in the south, and the news of that conquest spread as far north as we. My people will always search for the peaceful answer, but after hearing the stories of the horrific wars your people fought, we'd prefer to keep our distance."

Comandante Redondo affirmed this. "My friend, if you say we don't need to worry, then we won't worry. You just keep us on track to reach this lost city of yours."

The winter chill had set in, more noticeable at night than during the day. Presumably the summer months would be considerably warmer. There wasn't much to say of it, other than at night, if the fire burned too low, the cold shook Cristobal awake, feeling it in the toes first, then up the body it crawled, until the conquistador's motivation for existing was scarcely available. On they rode, covering many more miles a day, winding their way up the natural shape of the great river. The sporadic brush on the banks of the tributary they'd drunk from had now changed, as did their plans.

The river they now saw was massive and powerful, its great mouth pouring out into several waterfalls collapsing down into sharp rocks with descending levels of terraced rapids. Taking long glances through their looking glasses, Rodendros, Cristobal, Dendrick, and Fernando found themselves in a hazardous beguilement. The accurate mapping of a river such as this was one of the things they were directly responsible for. This land and all its new, undiscovered waters and territories had to be conquered, charted, mapped, and named. This was their true purpose, but the comandante had another objective. His aim was to bring his forces to the doorstep of the abandoned ruins of Aatuani's people and see with his own eyes what rumors the Indian spoke so passionately about.

Without a proper way to navigate the rapids, they would be forced to remain on foot, exposing themselves to greater risk of danger in the canyon plateau instead of using the flow to push their company deeper into the mainland. On the ground, they'd deplete their rations long before the conclusion of the momentous undertaking of mapping the uncharted river.

It needed to be charted, at the very least, with as accurate a sketching as could be made. For this, Fernando had done fine work, and he would check in with the comandante occasionally to make sure his work was well regarded. They needed to map the river, but they were in a hurry toward the secondary objective, getting to the ruins of Aatuani's *adoptive* home, to see the architectural marvels he claimed were carved into the cliffsides of the mysterious mesa plateaus.

Then, a moment of illumination struck Comandante Redondo. What if the sailors stayed to map the river, with Captain Fernando overseeing the thorough completion of its exploration, while he branched off and took the conquistadors to the forgotten city?

Comandante Redondo called a halt, and the whole formation came to a stop. Looking out over the canyon, watching the river rip through the rock, its fury capable of sending morbid shudders down even the strongest man's spine, he told himself he wasn't afraid of it. But he was, and he was no sailor. Curse his being human, feeling that fear, which made his gut wrench. He knew he'd come to the crux, and a life-or-death choice needed to be made. Call it self-preservation, but he made up his mind rather quickly. The late hour of the day was showing, and God had chosen to paint the dry skies with vivid violets and soft peaches, with the silver-lined clouds shimmering in the distance, making the whole of his impasse now even harder. Over that picturesque site, the comandante looked down a thousand feet below to the rapids and rushing current. The white foam ran like blood veins along the top. Comandante Redondo, now resolute in his standing, declared that history would now write itself.

They'd split up.

The answer was simple, and there all along. Leaving Fernando there to conquer the river, the conquistadors would go onward to the place of Aatuani's ancestral people.

Cristobal studied the comandante as he sat there, blankly looking out at the huge chasm below. He seemed to snap to attention once he'd been hit with his stroke of brilliance and turned his mare quickly to face the others.

"Fernando, Cristobal, let me explain the dichotomy of our predicament. We are here so that we may seize new land for the empire. Part of that means we are to, as best we can, map the lay of these new lands, charting the rivers and mountains as we see them. We cannot ignore that duty. Should an expedition come behind us years from now, to this exact river, right here, to this very spot, they should have an adequate map to follow and guide their way."

Cristobal sat atop Simora, listening to the comandante's words. He could sense where this was going. He could see the logic in it too. Each sentence compounded what he already knew to be true. If the comandante were to split them up, then Cristobal would finally get a legitimate chance to make his name the stuff of legend. It would be his turn to step into the light, leaving behind a name people would remember.

"However, we cannot ignore the claims that our friend here has made. His claims of civilization, a people who banded together in these barren, dry wastes, and made it a thriving home for a thousand years. They are not as old as the Mayans or the Aztecs, but I believe they are certainly related, and if that is the case, then the impact of our actions onto the face of history itself would be decided by our very meeting. Coronado had an old word for these people. He called them Pueblos."

Giving a slight pause, Comandante Redondo looked to Fernando, who sat there stupefied. This would be a career-defining opportunity for him as well. The rare gift of having the ability and freedom to do such free exploring was what every navigator dreamed of.

"Fernando, what this means for you is that I am henceforth dismissing you from my services and charging you the new task of mapping this great river and its many tributaries, by any means necessary. We will be back to help you once we've sorted out our alliances with the Indigenous. Cristobal, you will gather what's left of our men, take supply of all our stock; we'll divvy up the remaining rations with Fernando and his boys. The success of both these separate expeditions, Fernando's great river journey and our own journey to the great native ruins, hinged before on our ability to stick together out here. We'll no longer have that luxury."

So, it was true, Cristobal thought, as he felt the weight of those words, felt the gravity of their meaning, he suddenly felt more alone, as the heavy responsibility was being placed on his shoulders. It was what he had wanted the whole time.

He'd be a key decision-maker now, and he needed to carefully weigh the consequences of his actions before he took them. Fernando heard his orders and was thrilled to make it happen. Ready to get back to doing what he was meant to do, by any means possible, which was an instruction that he interpreted as meaning his only real constraints were the limits of his imagination.

That surely meant to include the fact they were in the middle of the desert with no big trees or materials to build boats from, and salvageable building materials were scant. Fernando and his sailors had a lot of work to do. Regardless, in the daunting face of an impossible challenge, Fernando accepted his orders and shook the comandante's hand from horseback before heading off to rally his sailors for their new mission. The comandante made one more request of the young explorer, sailor, and navigator.

"Fernando, this river shall be named for me."

He nodded and rode away.

Cristobal rode up to the comandante, who was dismounting Luchzuochu.

"This is where we'll make camp tonight. We'll figure out the details in the morning. Go and tell your sergeants to rest the men and horses; food and drink for everybody. In two days' time, we depart this place."

Cristobal gathered Dendrick Rodon and Enrico Cardenas and began to break down the comandante's orders to the other squad leaders, who set to work with their conquistadors setting up camp. Meanwhile, Fernando had traveled down the line to meet with his sailors, so he could give them all the good news of their new directive. Once they'd made camp and set their fires, as they had done so many times before, the clang of armor could be heard as the men downgraded, the rattling of the steel plates, and the flopping rucksacks hitting the ground. Their last night of joint-service comradeship and laughter began, and tents began to pop up in their usual fashion, with the men not caring particularly how loud they were or who it angered. They'd all endured the hard road together.

Not everyone was lucky enough to have a tent; it was usually for the higher ranks to enjoy, but Cristobal did his part visiting with the men. The good care of his conquistadors was most important to him. He wanted to be a good leader above all else. He wanted to stay out there and chat with them about their wives and their children, or with those happy to have neither. He had learned what each man hoped to do and dream. Out there, it was just them. They leaned on one another when the times were hard, and when the heart felt sick.

Aatuani was gathering some firewood with a few of the men from a short grove nearby. Fernando and the sailors were organizing themselves once again as a unit, with him disseminating his own specific orders to his subordinates, who began to sketch and make plans of their own. They had much work to do, but they could do it from right there if they so chose. They had a dangerous mission, which would require much preparation and planning. Comandante Redondo sat on a large sandstone, riffling through his many journals full of notes on language, culture, drawings of creatures, rubbings and crude replicas to supplant the many glyphs he'd seen.

He worried splitting their forces in half would strain their resources, but Comandante Redondo was the most likely man capable of pulling off such a crazy maneuver. He had forty-plus years of expedition and combat experience, not to mention his own elaborate experience with the natives; he knew what to do. Cristobal fell in line; if he had better ideas, then he'd have better let them be known, but the comandante's decision-making was superb and had never given Cristobal reason to question before. The objective was to find the ancestral city ruins; anything beyond that was out of the scope of Cristobal's focus and above his pay grade.

It was a night like countless other nights; Cristobal didn't particularly care to keep track. What was the point? They still had a long way to go. Either way, it was better this way. The sailors weren't trained tactically the same as the conquistadors, and without the sailors getting in the way, the better their chances of successfully using the maneuvers they rehearsed as a singular fighting unit.

Removing his saddlebags, Cristobal felt the increasing pressure of his new role. He was now going to be center stage in this unfolding drama, and that was a heady feeling. He smiled to himself and shook his head at his ironic peril, knowing it was what he had been dreaming of since he was a boy. Luckily, he wasn't alone. Rodendros was the best mentor Cristobal could've hoped for. He knew what it was like to have what Cristobal wanted, and his name was famous, with his deeds reverberating across living time for a reason.

The natives further south were different, Rodendros explained it, but Cristobal knew that already. The conquests of old contained fascinating lore, such as the conquistadors' ships, encumbered with stolen Aztec gold, sank themselves from the extra weight, dragging many cursed souls down into the depths. The men who, in the consequence of their own greed, drowned in Lake Texcoco with pockets full of golden doubloons. The bountiful riches of the Mayans and Aztecs, the fantastic temples, the feats of the most astounding academic capacity, were undertaken with an ingenuity that is unmatched even in modern times.

None of that could be seen here. None of that had been seen since arriving on these shores. Just thick patches of endless brush, wide-open plains, large valleys, canyons, and deserts. The landscape they'd surveyed thus far was still unlike anything they'd seen. Cristobal felt he drank from the pool of fortune, being given this opportunity; it was a tremendous honor.

The camp was visibly divided into two halves, the river party and the ground party, which was completely understandable, given the nature of their quests. Left or right, whichever fork the other could have been, they were not, and they'd have to come to terms with that new reality. The hierarchy was consolidated, and the camp was buzzing over the changes. Cristobal sat in his tent, writing in his journal to Fiorella.

Fiorella,

Another night I prepare to lay myself down alone, consumed by tormented thoughts. I have felt those pangs of hunger, and the pain of a tired and broken body. I worry about my future, for it is uncertain. The men are

*tired, as am I. Redondo rallies us onwards. The curse
of spending my youth indentured to somebody else, I
wish we had not to toil with labors, for I'd spend every
night under these new world stars with you, our fingers
entwined in one another's, in a pasture of one of these
great plateaus which we've marched through.*

*We make our way now to our native guide's ancestral
homeland. We've skirted a great river, which we've left
Fernando and his sailors behind to map thoroughly. We
will come back for them. We shall find them on the river
once we've discovered the native ruins Aatuani enticed
the comandante with. We shall see, my love.*

Cristobal shut his journal as Aatuani flipped over the flap of
his tent and stood in the opening.

"Captain, would you like to take a walk?"

Cristobal was curious and intrigued at the proposition, so
he agreed. Seldom had the Indian come to him for a word
in confidence.

"Certainly, friend, let's walk," Cristobal said, as he stood.
Aatuani stepped aside and held the flap back for Cristobal
as he walked out, free of his armor and wearing his simple
garments. Free of the weight, a reminder of their forbearance.
He stepped into the cold desert night, faintly lit by stars. He
drew a deep breath and felt it glide out of his nostrils as he
tasted the dry, dusty air.

"Do you know of the Trojans and the Greeks?"

They walked through the middle of their cliffside camp,
looking to their right to the canyon below, the chasm barely
visible save for the darker shades that were only visible once
their eyes had finally accommodated, then able to distinguish
each distinct layer of sandstone the whole way down. They
walked the edge north. Cristobal was again caught totally off
guard by the grand scope of knowledge the native possessed.

"The Trojans? My dear friend, what speech has Rodendros
made you subject to now?"

Aatuani used his staff to gently ease him along, as they
could sense there was no rush. They had been curious about

one another for some time, but Cristobal had a hard time trusting the guide. He knew the comandante gave credence to Aatuani's good name, but just because he vouched for him did not mean Cristobal was properly convinced of his intentions or motives. Easing their pace to a crawl, the gravelly crunch could be heard as the ground compacted over the red landscape where they trod. Looking back, Cristobal glanced at the others, making ready their preparations for war, sharpening their blades, wiping clean their armor, and tuning their bowstrings. Fernando eagerly gathered around his men to run them through their tentative plans. This was their purpose as seamen, to be of use on the water. The inland conquest was no place for them, and vice versa. Either party would likely hinder the other and add liability to the success of both. In this case, they were better off going separate ways.

Comandante Redondo was making himself comfortable by a pathetic-looking fire, feeding it bone-dry grass and sparse kindling, with some of the pokey, scrubby brush to help. It burned long enough for Rodendros to go scrounge around for real firewood that he could use. There were trees in the short grove, but after man had picked them over, what was left were weak, skinny trees, with leaves that had been scorched off from the heat of the burning river valley. He laughed at his lame fire, with its single flame burning low and slow.

Cristobal and Aatuani walked and talked.

"Rodendros has talked with me about many cultures in our time together. The Mayans and Aztecs, yes, the wrath of the Mongols, the intelligence of the Roman strategies and the skill of the gladiators. I am most curious, though, about the story of Troy. The story of the Trojan Horse, are you familiar?"

Cristobal looked at Aatuani and wondered immediately what he was getting at. He did seem to be genuinely curious, and Cristobal did not put it past the comandante to talk about such things with the native, whom he trusted entirely, but did not expect that his stories would cause Aatuani's imagination to run wild, hearing the stories of the old mythologies and heroes.

Aatuani had been wandering his whole life because he'd been having the very same dreams himself, of finding a world different from his own, but he wasn't in it for discovery. Aatuani was looking for a home and had been looking ever since Cortes burned Tenochtitlan to the ground. Comandante and Aatuani had spent unknown time together. Cristobal wasn't sure whether or not he had been with him for several months or several years. But one thing Cristobal could say definitively was that the guide had not led them astray once, and so long as he played the part of negotiable translator to any potentially hostile parties, then Cristobal had no problem letting him take point.

Unable to relax most of the time, many years in combat had taken a toll on the comandante, and he didn't make it known to anybody, but one had to assume that when you've written as much in your life story to fill the halls of a hundred libraries with stories as he had, you'd have something more to say. Deeper, hidden beneath the whites of his eyes, was a doorway to his past, and the gray beard that had overtaken his once-waxed mustache gave testament to his weathered and rugged manhood. A leader of leaders, the comandante had already been much celebrated in his life, his glories and fame reaching back to early days on the Spanish Countryside. He was an educated man and knew many things, yet he didn't communicate with everybody the same. He didn't give away all his cards, and he was always one step ahead of his opposition.

Cristobal played on the guide's curious nature, exciting him with his own depiction of the relic civilization.

"Yes, I'm familiar with it. It was a brilliant attack. They used the enemy's vanity against them. Sneaked into the city, right under their noses and won the war consequently. The warriors' skills in those days were unmatched. They had the heroes of old, Hector and Achilles. The Greeks were interesting in that they had many gods they worshiped, whereas we only worship the one," Cristobal said.

The wind blew slightly, the same dry breeze, but the temperature had dropped, and it would soon be nightfall. They stood there having their conversation, the guide leaning on his staff, the dirt and grime dusting his knees and thighs with an ashen powder. His long bare legs exposed to the air; it was a wonder he managed to not freeze those cold desert nights. His long black hair, which used to be nicely braided, dangled about in a big tangled mess that hung down the sides of his face. Aatuani had obsidian eyes that were cemented in the present. He was connected to the Earth in a special way.

"We used to worship many gods too, until your people came here many years ago to teach us of the ways of your Christ. It was through the missionaries I learned to speak your tongue. I was always meant to be a translator for the Spanish. After they'd arrived, my fate was sealed. But my love was always of traveling the land. Now, I'm going to share the glory of my home with you, so someone from another world might appreciate our thousand-year struggle." Aatuani paused, giving the captain a troubled look.

"Come on, Captain, let's get back to the fire. It's getting cold," the guide said as he hugged himself, shuddering from the chill. They turned to make their way back toward the canyon camp, being careful not to step too close to the edge, for fear of falling a thousand feet into the raging rapids below.

It was getting cold; the winter months were starting to set in, and that kept the days cooler, and the nights incredibly cold. The small fires the men made did little to combat the frigid weather, and many hugged the man next to him to share in his warmth. Cristobal was cold, and after another long day of travel and planning, he was dog tired and went to spoon with Dendrick Rodon and Enrico Cardenas under the infinitely complex constellations of God's unique creation.

The conquistadors would follow the river north, following the interior of the land, and blazing a trail through unknown sands. They left a majority of their unneeded supplies with the sailors, who had decided they reverse course *back* for several days where the canyon originally bottomed out. From there they would establish base camp and set out to explore the waters from that point. Fernando was resolute in his new project and had set to work straight away, seeing the shipmaster and figuring out what they would need to build vessels that floated. Building materials were scarce, so they would need to rely on their own wits to make it possible.

There was not much eaten, not much spoken; it was a quiet night. Stirring restlessly, Cristobal was ready to break out of there already and make it to the ruins, to see the fulfillment of his dreams, to see the great wonders of a distant civilization. The way their thousand-year society must have had to adapt to survive the harsh struggles of life out here in the scorching plateaus of this desert arena was more than worthy of scholarly research. It garnered them much respect in the young captain's eyes. Cristobal thought about it; tribes of Indians flocked together, men who were strong banded together, tall and proud. Cristobal had heard through his eavesdropping on the comandante that the Indians raised fierce warriors. Excellent spearmen, and archers, warriors of a succinctly high caliber, strategizers and tacticians alike. There was much to be wary of when it came to the local Indigenous. Cristobal thought how fortune had spared him combat up to this point. It was a run of good luck, although he knew there was no such thing. He knew, however, that he couldn't run from it for much longer.

Chapter 19

THE ANCIENT ONES

The two parties bid their farewells the following morning, as a thin layer of dew clung to the cornices of the low-lying sandstone floor. The sun had barely begun to rise, but better to get a head start on the heat and move while the air was still cool. Cristobal was up before dawn, making his own preparations. Simora waited outside his tent, her reins knotted to one of the stakes. What would become of Fernando's voyage would be unknown for the foreseeable future, and Cristobal had his mind fixed on his new directives. He could no longer speak for the naval captain.

They would further penetrate the desert interior, forgoing their one and only assured source of water, in search of the ruins. Aatuani was taking point with the comandante, but who was leading the way? This place was known to their guide, but should they wander into territory where he could not barter their safe passage, then they would need to resort to the use of arms.

They moved at a quicker pace, unburdened by their stock of rations and munitions, which all had carried in the beginning, but now, the remaining rations matched up with the remaining bodies, and everyone had enough not to starve. They'd also abandoned countless other valuable pieces of expedition equipment. Aatuani had been given a horse to ride, and he rode his with such natural ability, the others were amazed. The remaining company of men and horses trooped the red

Earth, blazing through miles and miles of the same terracotta plateaus. They rode on, Aatuani leading the way hunched over his horse as they trotted along in a full gallop.

Aatuani looked over his native shoulder, his hips bouncing up and down as the horse carried on at full speed. He lifted his arm and pointed his finger at a large, towering butte, a monolithic, rectangular-shaped behemoth of compacted red sandstone. A tall chunk of mountain, square and flat at the top. They had begun to see more and more of them. They stood alone in the landscape, dotting the horizon.

Off in the distance, they approached the larger mesas, giant flat-topped hills. Navigating those insane inclined cliffsides was out of the question, as they were not prepared for such mountaineering. Cristobal looked at the various scenery, taking in the experience that he knew he would never again have—to discover the unknown, to be like the legends of the past, who had unlocked the ancient secrets of the world. The glory would come in magnitudes.

Cristobal kept Simora up to speed, riding beside the comandante. The comandante, a naturally gifted rider, had utmost faith in his guide companion. They shared many nights together in their long travels, and friendship was something that made the loneliness of those cold nights more tolerable. Comandante Redondo hadn't known a family in the last forty years he'd been in service to his country. His family were the people carrying swords to his left and right.

Through the most austere conditions, he'd triumphed again and again, and Cristobal was his pupil, absorbing his words and committing his lessons to memory. Cristobal dreamed he would one day carry the comandante's torch, earning the high praises and esteem of his countrymen. They sped on, across the plateau, making great time, forgetting the worries of the river party behind them. Captain Fernando was capable of the job, and Redondo knew that, but Cristobal saw it a different way.

Was it not selfish of them to carry on toward this vainglory and abandon the seamen to fend for themselves without adequate arms or security? They would be out there on their own, and should Cristobal and the rest of the conquistadors not return from their adventure, then the sailors would be in dire straits. It could have been looked at as a mission they were doomed to fail from the start. Cristobal worried for Fernando, but he would not worry himself over matters that were now already decided. Onward they burned, until the twilight carried forward golden streams of beautiful indigo shimmer.

The coolness in the air chilled the sweat they had poured out all day, and soon they shivered. They slept long enough each night to dream warm dreams of home, where their loved ones embraced them over the warm hearths and stewpots that their beloved wives had labored over. They hurriedly raced the days away, running the beasts into the ground and losing a few from running them so hard and long. The padre fared among the worst when it came to the long horseback journey. Constantly complaining of his back pain or saying that his hips felt like they were going to fall apart.

Enrico Cardenas maintained the rear security and rode beside him, so as not to lose the poor padre along the way. For several days they rode on, forgetting about the river entirely, as their water stores were full. The comandante brazenly pushed their pace, and they carried on deep into the dry lands, far from the worries of the real world. They entered survival mode and were barely stopping to eat because they were so focused. They could rest once they made it to the ruins.

Comandante Redondo's gray beard was ashy and pale from riding through the dust bowls of the breezy valleys. They were approximately fifty-six riders strong, and the comandante had allowed Aatuani to guide them toward the safety and shelter of a towering mesa. The comandante led the way up the steepening cliffside, following a trail that led up the east face. It was no coincidence that Dendrick Rodon had spotted it. The crow master had used his eyes to sight several avenues of ascent, but once on the other side of this large mesa, Aatuani claimed they would cross over into the land of his ancient people.

They made their way up and over the rugged terrain, confronting the loose fallen rock, which sent grapefruit-sized stones careening down toward the men below. The smooth slabs made it hard to maintain grip or traction, which posed an obstacle crossing the narrow mouth of the trail leading up the side of the mesa. They then formed a single-file line of men atop horses and started to climb up the steep slope. Looking high up into the sky as the angle of the climbing horse threw them backward, they struggled to maintain their hold of the horses as they climbed up the side of the mesa. Slowly, one by one, they inched forward up the slopes, fighting for traction. The horses struggled to maintain their grip and their balance on the slopes but were doing the best they could. This scared Cristobal more than sailing through tropical cyclones, thinking that at any moment, he could be hurled backward off the side of this mesa and tumble to the rocks below. He closed his eyes and prayed to God one last time. It was silent, and the air was still as they climbed. Cristobal held his breath, waiting for the worst to happen.

Then it started to level out, and after several minutes of climbing the trail, they'd broken through to the pinnacle and were climbing over the brim. Dismounting the beasts to walk them over the lip, they let them run free at the top, shaking off the crippling anxiety they must have felt as well.

From the top of the mesa, they could look down and see the whole wide lay of the desert land that was behind them, beside them, and before them.

"This is it. The land before you is the land of my people," Aatuani said as they gazed out at the vast view before them. Deep canyons fissured the huge plateau, rigid and unstable rocks giving way every minute crashing down, echoing through the wide ravines and alcoves surrounding. The sparse distribution of natural vegetation was an indication that the drought was still clearly affecting this region, which was hot and dry and looked very much the same as the other side.

Cristobal, knowing the work was far from over, felt encouraged that they had reached a tangible milestone. There they found themselves, overlooking the plateau, watching as the various yet-unidentified bird species soared and glided through the air effortlessly. He longed for this moment, which combined fear, anxiety, excitement, and adrenaline, which pumped his body full of blood and made him feel alive, while at the same time, fighting a nervous churn and rumble in his stomach. It was a lot to process as he looked out at the plateau, but he held it together, even though he felt as if the ground was spinning. The comandante snapped him out of it.

"Unbelievable, my friend. Truly, this is an unbelievable sight to behold. Such pure wilderness, unrelenting and harsh. No wonder you were driven from your lands," he said, looking at Aatuani. "Anybody who could make this place a home for forty generations deserves respect." He paused, then gave the rest of his orders. "We need to get off this mesa and carry on west into those cliffs over there."

Looking out, Cristobal could see tall spires on the other side of the plateau, jagged sandstone cliffs jutting out from the ground, easily a day or two away. It had been a long time since any game could be hunted, and the men desperately needed to eat something fresh. Cristobal tried to rally for his men by getting them to make camp there, but having fresh game to eat was a creature comfort that came second to finding the ruins; that was paramount to anything now. Once they discovered their great mystery, they could relax.

They rode their horses down a switchback that was narrower than the first switchback cliff with the cave of distorted time. They took their time and made their way down slowly, carefully in single file. Taking in the view of this place on the way down, Cristobal wondered where out there could there be such a place. He hoped it wasn't far but held no false expectations. As far as he was concerned, this was his career, and he was in it for the next forty years, same as the comandante.

Coming to the bottom of the plateau, they began to disperse freely. Cristobal rubbed Simora's head, affectionately praising her for carrying him across the winds safely every time. She was the best horse he could have ever asked for. She let out a great neigh, showing her mutual amusement and affection.

Aatuani waited for the rest of the conquistadors to make it off the mesa. Dendrick Rodon had come down last, spending every minute possible on that high vantage point, taking in the surroundings with a memory so keen as to remember the differing landmarks. If there were none to be seen, he would make them himself. The crow master took great pride in having better eyes than most, and he diligently used every opportunity to exercise his gift. The top of the plateau gave him a view of everything, in each direction. He saw they were not on the tallest plateau, nor the tallest mesa. They were on a flat of mammoth canyons, dry creek beds, and various labyrinthine channels that could not be crossed directly or indirectly.

Enrico Cardenas waited for Dendrick at the bottom, the ever-watchful and good lieutenant noticing the change in Dendrick's mood by reading his perturbed expression.

"What did you see?" he asked the crow master.

"It's still a day or more to the cliffs."

Enrico smiled. "Is that it?" he asked, amused.

Dendrick glanced across his shoulder as they mounted their horses, waiting for the rest of the party to regroup.

"I don't think this place welcomes us, friend. I felt something when I looked out across the plateau."

Enrico dropped his smile, taking on a concerned tone of voice. "Well, what did you feel?" he asked.

"Worry."

They rallied together at the bottom, Comandante Redondo shouting for the men to ride on, and again, taking off at a full gallop, the tired horses gave everything as their masters pushed them further and faster than they thought themselves capable of. They took a few breaks to rest the poor creatures, who were nearing complete exhaustion from having been pushed so hard. Since the great split, Cristobal hadn't given much thought to what Captain Fernando was doing downriver.

They rode over several dunes and took in the natural wonder of the different formations. The way the stone had been shaped through countless centuries of time, the wildlife among them seemed content enough, but it was hard to imagine setting down roots in a place where the daytime roasts you year round and the nighttime is just as unappealing, with its ugly creatures that crawl around on furry legs with stingers or fangs. Snakes with venom strong enough to kill a man. The day before last, while they had stopped to rest, one of their good men stepped onto a rattlesnake on purpose, to see what would happen. The stupidity drew no pity from consequence, and he lay dead after several minutes of struggling on the ground. The padre gave the conquistador his last rites, and the light of his life was no more, called home to the Lord for an act of impulsive stupidity.

Cristobal thought of Fiorella. He thought of the day he'd come home to her, with her unable to stand the delay of his arrival. They'd walk in the parades that would line the streets of the capital city, the triumphant return of their expedition party, successfully having conquered new lands for their empire. They would be praised, glorified, and well rewarded for their painstaking sacrifices along their famous desert trail.

The conquistadors spent this night a bit differently than they spent previous nights. The seasons had changed before their eyes, watching all sorts of new varieties of flora change their colors in the autumn. The jungles they chopped through, the vast forests of green they navigated themselves out of, constantly fighting with the bush itself. Had it not been for the luck of having such an experienced guide and translator, they would have been relying on their own navigating and map reading. It also would have taken a considerable amount of chance for them to find the ruins they were seeking. Were it not for their guide, they'd have not heard the rumor at all.

Comandante Redondo was part of Cortes's first conquests and was with him the whole way; Aatuani at the same time was just a young boy, begging for food in blustering markets, a stone's throw away from where the human sacrifices' hearts were being carved out of their chests. They had been riding on the same strand of fate their whole lives, and they never knew it until fate herself brought the two of them together. How he came into his service was still unclear, but they were fortunate to have him, as he had been a trusted member of the expedition since the start, except for the choppy sea voyage.

Aatuani brought the horses to a stop. They'd run into a gorge, which prevented them from reaching the cliffs they'd seen from the top of the mesa. They negotiated the rugged and rocky terrain thus far, but this was a sheer cliff, with sharp and menacing rocks at the bottom, no water at its base, and the longer you looked down, the darker the abyss became.

Comandante Redondo dismounted the tired Luchzuochu, who was blowing hot air out of his great nostrils, and Rodendros, with legs still asleep from riding, hobbled back a ways before regaining some grasp of his balance.

"Well, Aatuani my friend, we cannot cross this gorge, so you must lead us a different way."

The guide idled atop his horse, looking to the other side.

"It's not the gorge that's stopping us," Aatuani said, pointing his finger across the chasm. "It's them."

Cristobal snapped his head, and adrenaline raced through his body as his heart fell deep into his stomach. It was a sight he had dreaded since their arrival, but his eyes did not lie to him. The comandante looked as well, and even he was silent, frozen not with fear but anticipation.

Chapter 20

STRANGERS OF THE

SOUTHWEST

On the other side of the gorge, nestled tightly within the compacted walls of the adjacent cliffs, were several shrouded figures, wrapped tightly in drab, striped ponchos. Their faces could not be made out at a distance, but they stood stoically on the opposite side of the gorge. Several taller warriors flanked the shrouded figures. They carried spears and shields, painted with a geometric pattern. A few also carried bows, Cristobal noted.

Motioning for the others to be quiet, Aatuani let out a beastly call, a high-pitched howl that carried across the gorge. Lifting his spear and pumping it in the air several times, he made himself seen to the figures across the way, who were standing their ground, unflinching. They slowly came through the corridor, toward the light and toward the strangers.

Aatuani spoke to them in his own language, delivering his words in a tone that sounded like a question. His kinfolk were now moving from their shadowy cove out into the open, into the warm embrace of daylight. Their approach gave Cristobal a shudder; feeling the supernatural aura they gave off, he stood frozen, watching the interaction unfold. Comandante Redondo stood behind Luchzuochu, eyeing the natives under his morion, watching his guide handle the very situation he was here to handle.

The figures stepped closer to the edge of the gorge, now practically a stone's throw away from the expedition party. The leader of the party stepped forward, making his way forward using a walking stick ornamented with eagle feathers and colorful beads. He returned the guide's great call, which Aatuani again gave back in unison, this time with the elder and his entourage. Shouting at the conquistadors across the gorge, his native tongue was strange, like nothing Cristobal had ever heard. Aatuani spoke his language with the comandante in their private lessons, but seeing him use it to communicate with his own people was interesting.

The two Indians spoke to one another familiarly, with the elder speaking to Aatuani with great waves of his arms and frustrated tones. Harsh tones then, as it seemed Aatuani was defending himself. The two other elder figures shuffled forward then to stand with their brother, their sandals scuffling the sand underneath. Their long black hair could be seen from afar, thick braids that hung down from their heads. They wore ornamented headbands, with more feathers and beads, and they carried with them staves, which they must have used to get around better in the constant inclines and dipping valleys of the plateau. They didn't appear to be too large in stature; they were of average height, but Cristobal knew better than to judge his enemy on appearance. The reputation of the New World warriors far preceded his own arrival to the place. They had stepped out of the shadows to join their elders on the edge of the gorge.

They were taller than their elders, and they carried their weapons with prowess. Their pitch-black eyes rested atop their high cheekbones, underneath protruding brows. They were strongly built, with the dark complexion characteristic of their people. It was as if these men who spoke this different language, who dressed differently, and thought different, were actually not so different than he'd been led to believe. He wasn't intimidated anymore, seeing that these men were not the warriors that he'd been meant to fear and respect. If anything, they were messengers, carrying with them a cruel totem of refusal. They didn't want foreign invaders freely stomping over their sacred lands, and that was understandable. The conquistadors needed to make it to the other side of this gorge, one way or another, and should they stand in their way, it would be nothing for Cristobal to cut loose every man who carried an arquebus and crossbow.

Aatuani had kept speaking with the three elder figures on the other side, each one attempting to drown out the other. Then Aatuani shouted a long, haunting string of deep chants that echoed down the canyon, causing rocks to drop on cue as the soundwaves reverberated off the sandstone walls.

The other voices lulled, and Aatuani spoke up, firm and direct toward his people, standing directly on the edge of the gorge. He seemed to be explaining something, speaking with his hands and motioning toward the fifty armed men idling behind him on horseback. The breeze blew their hair across their faces, and their ponchos flowed in that same breeze. Cristobal now examined them closer, trying to infer what he could from the language he couldn't understand.

Aatuani held up his hand and shook it toward the strangers. Then he dismounted his horse, muttering under his breath in his own language. He walked back to where the rest of the party was waiting, and the comandante asked him what was being said between the two parties.

"Well, what are they saying?" asked Rodendros, who'd taken off his morion and was adjusting his sword belt behind Luchzuochu.

"They won't let us cross unless they know our true intentions for being here," said the guide.

Redondo laughed. "Well, tell them that we are simple explorers, lost in a land that is unknown to us."

Aatuani looked across, back toward the cliffs. "I'm going to go talk to them. I'll be right back," he said, as he turned to face the gorge.

Taking off into a full sprint, Aatuani bolted toward the edge of the gorge, carrying his walking staff in his hand as if he were a Greek javelin thrower. He held it high and it cut horizontally through the air as he ran toward the gap he was attempting to vault. At the last moment, he jammed his staff down into the earth, right at the edge of the gorge. The length of the pole lifted him over the chasm below, and his running start threw him over to the other side. He landed in a roll on the ground, his walking staff traveling behind him. A cloud of dust and dirt blew up where he landed, and the team on the other side held their spears up at length to keep the acrobatic Aatuani at bay.

The comandante's jaw dropped at the display of athleticism and bravery his guide had just shown, but what was he going to do now that he was over there with his own people? Rising to stand, Aatuani held out his hands and spoke in softer tones his own language, still being held at spearpoint. The three elder figures looked at him as he spoke; they nodded and shook their heads, actively listening to the guide plead his case. Aatuani held out his hands toward the spearmen, and they lowered their spears.

A good sign, thought Cristobal.

His back was a little scraped up and red, covered in a lighter brown dust from where he landed. They all stood there, listening to the guide. The conquistadors stood quiet and helpless on the other side, shut out from the conversation by the language barrier alone. Cristobal watched the interaction with unblinking eyes, as did the comandante, as did Enrico, as did Dendrick Rodon.

After several long minutes of quietly watching for something to happen, Cristobal saw Aatuani fall to his knees and kiss the sandals of the shrouded figure who had stepped up first to speak with them. Aatuani rose to his feet and made a grateful gesture toward the poncho-wearing elder men. He turned and ran back toward the conquistadors, vaulting the gorge the same way as before, and no less impressively.

Aatuani stood again and dusted himself off.

"Those men are the wise ones. Sacred sages of the old ways. They've learned the story of our people from their mothers, grandmothers, and great-great generations down through time. One thousand years of stories of my people, our legends, and spirits. They know the land innately, their lives spent here on these high plateaus. They reside besides the Kachina, our spiritual beings that watch over our families and crops."

This spooked some of the men. Talk of ancient spirits, that was a magic of a darker variety, and something they would refuse to hear. Audible cries of *blasphemy* could be heard from the back. Enrico Cardenas quieted the men's superstitious caterwauling to let the guide continue his refrain. To those devoted Christians among them, it was a highly unnerving thing to say.

"They've permitted us entry, so you may do your exploring, but they want you to abandon your beasts to run freely. The land will provide for them, but a life of servitude and exhaustion is no way to spend a life given graciously by God."

Comandante Redondo let out a raucous laugh, a boisterous fit that drew out trickling laughter from some of the other men. Cristobal even bashfully tried to tuck his smirk away.

"My friend, abandon our horses? Have you gone mad? The only way we've crossed this country so quickly is because of these creatures. Yes, we run them ragged, but they are not without food and water. These beasts are well kept, you can assure them. We have to carry on with them. Letting them go free is out of the question," the comandante said, standing beside his very own proud Luchzuochu, who had seen him through many years of trial and war.

"Rodendros, if you want to carry on into the country of my people, you will need to honor their ways. We must go forward without the horses or take our chances another way. On foot, we will travel through the secret channels of eroded stone and earth, and in the water of these old gulches and streams until we reach the source. From there, you will be able to see for yourselves the wonder of my ancestors, who continue to teach us from the beyond, through our wise medicine men, the keepers of the light of this place."

Comandante Redondo knew, unfortunately, that the tone in his friend's voice meant he was serious about abandoning the horses. It was a hard bond to sever; some of these men had been with these creatures for many years. It was a heartbreaking thing to contemplate, and even Cristobal, who had so proudly paraded his beloved Simora in the streets of Toledo, was not yet ready to cut her free. Setting aside the emotional attachment the conquistadors had for their horses, how else would they expect to return from this place?

Cristobal was along for the ride, not making the decisions, not fighting with Rodendros over things. They were going forward, and the outcome of their party would be dependent again on the decisions of the comandante, Javier Redondo. The appeal of the ancient ruins and lost riches was great and pulled at all of them, ravaging their imaginations over what they would do if they came into possession of a small individual fortune. Thus, they were all faced with a moral dilemma. Was the risk greater than the reward? These matters were blurred by a greedy fire that burned in man's eye, a fire for wealth, and power. It was a poisonous thorn, some driven mad by it, others bereft of it. Truthfully, it was the gold and glory they sought; that was all they had ever sought. Cristobal had heard of the Spanish ships that sank because they couldn't carry all the gold they'd hoarded from Moctezuma, and that was the kind of hero folklore he wanted to be part of, oddly enough.

His family would've been set financially for generations, but he had a feeling that the place Aatuani was taking them possessed no gold or riches but was rich in something else. Cristobal could step outside his strict Christian upbringing and ideology to ponder those things the others would consider supernatural, magical, or blasphemous. He thought about the impact their discovery might have here in the Americas over the long term. Maybe the payoff would come at another time, when he was long absent from this Earth. He did not know, and his mind raced trying to justify and rationalize a million different courses of action and outcomes.

Comandante Redondo ordered Dendrick Rodon off his horse, and his feet hit the ground with a hard thud where his boots landed.

"Cut the horses free. Hurry up. We'll make the return passage on foot." said the comandante, removing a knife from a sheath on his hip and cutting off his reins and his saddle, tossing them over into the gorge below.

The natives on the other side watched the comandante's gesture, and with subtle nods, they turned their backs and wandered back into the shadows from where they came. Aatuani rode without equipment, but he slapped his horse on its rear, and it took off as fast as it could, understanding the chance it was being given, galloping off into the wind.

The rest of the men followed suit, jumping down and retrieving whatever gear they'd stashed away before setting their horses free. One by one the horses started to wander off. Some were looking for somewhere fresh to graze or drink, while others just stayed put unmoving.

Cristobal felt especially sad setting his girl free, but he choked down the tears and wished Simora well in life as he sent her on her way. She could roam freely until the day when the earth she grazed on and trotted on so naturally in her prime called her home. Simora was her name, the great blonde beauty, who after this would be made famous by her conquistador, Captain Cristóbal Trujillo.

The horses were left to their own devices; the land would provide for them. The saddles, reins, bridles, and bits were all tossed into the gorge, and the men stretched their weakened legs for the rest of the journey forward on foot. If they thought they were roughing it before, now they were really going to feel the crushing weight of fatigue on their malnourished bodies. They adjusted their boots and threw on a few extra layers for warmth while the comandante and Cristobal worked out a contingency plan with Aatuani.

"Okay, so we climb to the bottom of the gorge and follow the streams to the source? Right? That's what you said, is it not?" Comandante Redondo asked. Then he asked, "Are those men going to be down there waiting for us? Are they seeing us to our destination? Or is that for you to make happen?"

Aatuani leaned on his staff and glanced at Cristobal before looking back toward Rodendros. "They won't be waiting for us; they'll already be there. Finding the way into the ruins will be our task to take on alone. Several days of walking, maybe more. First we climb down, then we thank God for getting us down safely. Then, and with the elders' blessing I've procured, we may follow the lost path to the ruins of the ancient ones."

Chapter 21

THE HOLLOW TRAILS OF

SKULLS AND SNAKES

The trail, which led to the lower levels of the gorge, was not obvious to them at first. After carefully investigating their locale, Dendrick Rodon noticed a section of the cliffs that bore strange petroglyphs, deep carvings in some places, and lighter etchings in others. He brought this to the comandante's attention and that of their guide, who ran over to Dendrick quickly, his slim frame gliding through the air.

"These marks were left here centuries ago; this is the work of my people. The entrance is nearby. It'll lead us underground," said the guide.

They saw depictions of animals—deer, birds, wild game—as well as stick-figure people atop these creatures, with warriors holding shields and spears. The crack of the stone sliced the image in half without affecting the larger picture. These sacred communications from the past carried weight on Cristobal's soul, as he stood there trying to replicate the images freehanded into his journal. He would decipher them later.

"Look here, what's this?" Comandante Redondo said, throwing back a slab of stone that opened up to a short, dank corridor.

"That's it," Aatuani said, nodding to the comandante.

"Take us down," Rodendros demanded.

Horses could be heard braying nearby, yet to fully wander off into the free country. They had to crouch low, as the tunnels must have been dug for people with shorter stature, or to act as a deterrent from enemy forces coming to their land with ill intent. The temperature dropped dramatically as they exited the daylight of the desert and wandered into the dark unknown of this passageway. Aatuani lit a torch and took point as they passed through the forgotten channels. Torches were lit down the line, and as the men crouched through the corridors, their torches illuminated stranger glyphs painted on the sides of the stone passageway. Red, black, and white paints were used to tell the old stories.

They gazed at the wall art, emblematic of a people who, advanced in their intelligence, had a deep understanding of the world around them and were highly capable storytellers, sharing their story by whatever means they could. They passed down the story of their survival on these high plateaus, riddled with danger and relentless drought. Surviving there was no small feat and the intelligence he'd already seen exhibited by Aatuani. The native's knowledge and understanding of the land and all the creatures and plants living within it was enough to let Cristobal know that these Indians were an advanced people who knew much more than they spoke.

They soon broke through to the daylight, after following the shallow descent of the hand-carved trail that led to the gorge floor. The men could be heard grunting and shifting as they squeezed through the narrow clutches of the corridor. Most of them were thin enough, but their armor made it hard to maneuver, the iron plate scraping against the rocks as they held their breath in vain. After much painstaking effort, they were at the bottom, watching their horses look down at them from above, confused as to where their masters were going. They extinguished their torches and made a left turn out of the passage, heading north along the bottom of the gorge. Night was encroaching, but they intended to push on.

Comandante Redondo broke the silence, with his sturdy voice carrying his orders to those who listened, which was everyone. "Don't put those out! Light those torches and draw your swords! We're pushing on. The trail is not yet lost to darkness!"

The order killed the men's morale. Onward they pushed, into the cold night, the temperature plunging so low that the men could not only see their breath as they exhaled the crisp winter air, but crossing through the shallow beds of water had soaked the already paper-thin leather of their boots, and the cold air on the outside froze their feet on the inside.

That did not matter to the conquistadors; the tough men ignored the pain and stayed on alert as Aatuani led the way by torchlight. They climbed along the trails, which now were much harder to discern from the normal terrain. Scrambling over cracking boulders and loose granite inclines, their guide knew the land, and he knew where they were going. He measured their distance traveled between their distance going by way of an internal compass that was innately attuned to the stars. That was his map, and he followed the points of constellations like Orion, Ursa Major, and Sirius intuitively, with a deeper knowledge of his place in this world than most. Aatuani blazed on into the night, as the sorry band of cold and hungry conquistadors followed behind, running on fumes, as they lacked the proper rest and nutrition for such a trek. Weakness affected them, and the morale withered away as they fought the malaise of sleep deprivation and hunger.

The hours of darkness passed slowly. Cristobal kept his eyes on the man in front of him as they followed the trail off into the night. He stepped where he stepped, and if there was an obstacle to be negotiated, the man in front turned around and helped the man behind. They moved quietly and suffered in silence, keeping their thoughts to themselves. They struggled to keep their traction on the slippery rock as they walked carefully over it, losing their balance and confidence more than a few times in the moonless night. Here was where the guide flourished, as he wore no boots or greaves, but barefooted he preferred, and he seemed to walk sideways at times. They could hear the different creatures of the night, busting through the black screen, further frightening the men who, in their sleep-induced paranoia, could not react but simply shivered nervously to themselves as they pushed on. They walked for hours this way.

The torches eventually burned low, and the men now stuck close together one in front of the other as they followed behind the guide, who from the front of the pack, slowed down his pace to give the conquistadors time to scoop up their diminished spirits and catch up to him. Rodendros took notes of his surroundings as best he could, while his eyes continued to accommodate his night vision.

They entered a large, flat plateau, which if his eyes did not deceive him, was surrounded by sheer red cliffs and drops on all sides, the bottom of a large, bowl-shaped canyon. The size of it was unknown. Nobody except the crow master could see that far. The wind had stilled, and it was quiet. Redondo shushed them further, and Cristobal could have heard a drop of water. The animals stopped their nocturnal song, the chop of wind no longer hammered their freezing ears, and the atmosphere around them was calm. As they stood there, firm in their silence, listening to the ominous void, Aatuani's tired voice came from the shadows.

"We're almost there. If we keep going, we can make it by sunrise!" he exclaimed.

Rodendros finally allowed himself to spill a few curses at the circumstances of their tormented night hike. The others weren't thrilled either, as it had been over thirty-six hours since they started, and right about now, most of them were missing their horses. There was no time to worry about that. They were on the heels of a centuries-old discovery, and they would be the first to glorify their findings. This was a personal conquest for many of them. Cristobal was doing it to prove to himself, and to his family back home, that he had what it took to carve a legend out of his own name. He could not rest, knowing he'd be forgotten; his name had to live on. It must.

Cristobal's thoughts moved to his Fiorella. Where was she right now? What was she doing on this night? The same night which he had been given, they could both look up and see the same waxing gibbous moon. He hoped she was at home, warm by the hearth, with her family around her, since family was all they really had. She was a good woman, and he swallowed the pain that came with the call of his duty. Stepping away from home was different for some; some of the men didn't have families or lovers waiting for them. More than a few men couldn't have cared less about getting back to the ships or getting home. This place was a new beginning, a pathway to greatness that few were ever afforded. In the service of their crown, and in the noblest profession of all, the profession of arms, combat was their career, and they had yet to wet their blades on native flesh. There had been no need for it up to this point, and their scattered confrontations with the natives had proved rather peaceful. Cristobal did not get the sense that he needed to be looking over his shoulder every minute of the day, because whatever happened was what God intended to happen. There is no escaping the ending written for us.

The seconds became hours, and the hours became the old days. The sun started to lift itself high into the sky. Their eyes devoured the daylight, and their spirits were again rekindled as the heat of day began to warm their bones against the muggy morning dew. They continued to climb through the rock, pushing themselves further into the canyon, which had opened up into a low valley where sparkling water ran through smaller creeks and streams, which they drank from freely. They quickly rehydrated themselves and kept going a few more hours through the deep-ridged canyons, coming to a long valley, where they skirted the bottoms of the towering mesas as they walked.

Then they lifted their eyes, and off into the distance, they could finally at last take their first true look at the ruins they'd been promised. Carved into the side of the canyon bowl far above them was a feat of architecture so astonishing, they could only stare at it at first, trying to figure out what to make of it. It was a magnificent complex, and from where they stood, it looked as if maybe it could have functioned as an incredibly old fortress. Carved into the canyon wall was a rough complex of various-sized dwelling rooms and ritual antechambers, all connected through intricate weaves of native adobe craftsmanship. There were many individually separate rooms, with the ruins ghostly and quiet. At the bottom of the canyon floor, the conquistadors were congratulating one another. Comandante Redondo ordered the men to help him lift Aatuani into the air. Calling him his brother and shouting many affectionate curses and praises at his Indian friend, the comandante and several others let out tremendous, echoing howls that rattled the canyon bowl. Cristobal simply stared up at the wonder of it, hundreds of feet up into the air, wondering who the hell lived in this ancient and forgotten place.

How in the world had people built such a complex so high off the ground? Had they climbed the near-vertical face? An absurd notion, but its location was invariably highly strategic, tucked away in a great alcove. Its geography provided shelter from the elements and was nearly impregnable. The men had to settle themselves for the comandante to think straight, but he was more excited than they were. Dendrick Rodon traversed a boulder so that he might get a better look. He squinted his eyes in the rising sun, fighting back the glare and drowsiness of a night spent exhausting themselves. He clung to the rocky crag with torn-up hands, withered by months of expeditioning.

"They carved it from the stone! It's a fortress!" the crow master exclaimed, thrusting his free arm in the air with his bloody fist clenched, signaling the great victory for the conquistador party. They had never seen anything like it before.

Cristobal watched the grandiose gesture, and his poetic mind gave him a quick verse, which he softly spoke. "Left to be eroded, and crumpled by time, their story a memory, in someone else's mind."

Aatuani was a rebellious spirit; he enjoyed the Spanish wine and merriment. He had been with them for months and had kept true to his word, which surprised Cristobal, who at first had a hard time acknowledging the justifiable purpose of his accompaniment. But his innate ability to read the land got them from place to place, taking them from the hellishly thick and unending jungle brush, where they were getting eaten alive by spiders and mosquitos, through the swampy marshes, to the open valley plains and deserts. He had guided the way and got them here, for better or for worse.

The large number of men they lost along the way due to illness and accident was obvious when Cristobal looked at what was left of their party. Their already-depleted number was cut in half by splitting from their nautical counterparts, a move that crippled their strength. They were weak, hungry, and desperately needed to rest, but rest was an afterthought. First, they needed to figure out how they were going to arrive on the same level as the sandstone city. Comandante Redondo began to plan immediately. He ordered the men to relax, and it was an order; he knew they needed it. The men took seats on the cool ground, catching their breath and basking in the afterglow of their discovery. The whole party would be known, the name of every man, down through the ages.

A story is often remembered by its characters, and the characters of this story were as different as they were the same, but to appreciate the expedition as a whole, there needed to be embedded within the conquistador party a mystery member.

Somebody needed to play the witness.

The men gathered under an overhanging crag, which provided them a wall to lean against and keep their backs to, should any predatory animals or Indians with bows get any ideas. Not that they could put up much of a fight in their decrepit, malnourished forms. Many fell asleep immediately.

Out in the open air, with the freshly risen sun warming their cold toes, ears, and fingers, Comandante Redondo and Aatuani gazed up at the ruins; Cristobal and Dendrick too. They couldn't make sense of it. Why put so much effort into making a place as advanced as this, to then leave it behind? Surely the terrain was unforgiving, and any period of time without sufficient water for crops or the people's general consumption would have led to intertribal fighting or conflicts between the warring clans.

"It is so unique that such a place could be carved right there into the mountain, with human hands deliberately laboring for unknown centuries over this feat. Nothing like it have I ever seen. Even the Aztec, with their great temples and pyramids, would have had to salute the work of their cousins in the north," Redondo said.

Cristobal gave in. "This site needs to be treated with respect; many suffered in this place."

"Suffered?" Aatuani said. "No, Captain, my people prospered, for a long time. We suffered mostly in the end." He looked away forlornly.

The comandante entered back into the dialogue. "This place is not totally abandoned, is it, my friend?" Redondo said, proceeding to ask Aatuani to explain the circumstances with the men at the gorge.

"Those men are to us what the padre was to you, holy men. It was through them I had to barter your passage. They wish for peace, they wish not for blood," he said. He looked solemn, but his words seemed genuine.

It was a great privilege to be allowed into such a place, and Cristobal knew that. He felt the reverence of the atmosphere, a charged feeling he could not explain.

Aatuani continued. "Only a few families live here. We keep a watchful eye over our home. The women, children, and elders live inside, keeping to the privacy of their chambers and eating what little we can sow. Drinking water when we can spare it. Someone has to take care of this place. Its purpose must not be lost."

Redondo and Cristobal listened, and Cristobal wondered what he meant when he said its purpose must not be lost. What purpose? There were many questions to be asked, and they accepted any information from their guide that they thought would assist them going forward on future conquests. Cristobal questioned too if he and the comandante were on the same page as far as what their *true intentions* were, should the elders ask them separately. Did they seek to gather glory for the empire, or to gather material wealth, riches, and glory for the self? Vainglory, the worst kind of glory. Only time would tell what God planned for them, and for their futures, and for the futures of their kinfolk. Cristobal needed a private audience with the comandante, so they could be in agreement.

Dendrick Rodon had gone to look for some game, and he had managed to slingshot some weasels and other small sand rodents. He'd also come back talking about the splendid variety of lizards he'd seen scurrying about, with many different bright and vivid colors adorning their scaly, dry skins. They didn't have much to eat, but hunger was nothing new to them. They had on many occasions gone days, even weeks without solid food. It had cost them greatly, in terms of their strength and spirit, but their effort was the very thing that emboldened them, for nobody else was capable of the things they were doing. They were the trailblazers of future conquests and expeditions here in the New World, and the immense weight of the watching world was on top of him. It was on his shoulders that his own sons would stand. Cristobal knew they were writing history each passing day, and that the best option for them was to turn and leave these people in peace, but Aatuani was already smoothing things over with the elders. They'd be all right, he thought.

Cristobal sought to get the comandante's attention, but he was too busy strategizing their approach up the face to the alcove above, wherein lay the impressive ruin complex, carved into the mountain. They were going to have to climb it. At least that seemed to Cristobal to be the only way. That was a long climb too, and he swallowed nervously at the thought. He instead took out his journal, which he'd last used to pen an entry for Fiorella.

He sketched the visible face of the mountain, and while examining it, determined it would be nearly impossible to ascend. The problem was in relation to their current positioning; they could not see the expanse of canyon spread out before them. They were just ants on the surface of it. The size of this whole plateau was a mystery, and one could get lost in the myriad trails that cut through it every which way, some leading somewhere, some leading nowhere.

Aatuani spoke up, coming over to the comandante and Cristobal, who were observing the complex together.

"I know the way up, but I've only been down once. I have not returned to the sacred cliffs since I first left."

Comandante Redondo's eyes lit up in great excitement, because that knowledge would make his life tremendously easier.

"You do! Fantastic, my friend! We must head up at once. We must see this up close! Your service to the crown shall never be forgotten, my dear friend. You will live a handsomely rewarded life. By my arm, I swear it!" said Rodendros, hugging the guide tight. Aatuani was his closest friend out there, but he was also the closest friend the comandante ever had.

Cristobal sensed the missed opportunity, but he did not wish to interfere with the comandante's celebration. He kept quiet and made himself ready to receive his next set of orders. They at long last could finally head toward the crown jewel of their achievement, the tangible, visible remains of a colony long lost to time. Three centuries or longer it had been abandoned. The ghostly atmosphere made one feel as though it had been only recently vacated. The hairs on Cristobal's neck stood upright, as he felt as though they were being too noisy in a place where they did not belong.

Call it healthy paranoia or a tinge of expedition fever, or maybe it was the long withdrawal from the pleasures of society, like their tobacco or their women. Not having those fixes made him want to snap. They had come all this way, abandoning the horses that carried them this far, and they were now at the mercy of the mesa's strange inhabitants. Strange in the sense that Cristobal, who was a young and eager captain from Toledo, had never seen such people before. They were much different from he, their appearances the opposite, from their complexions to the build of their frames, the Indigenous obsidian hair, bound like ropes in noble braids. There could be no denying the connection observed between Aatuani and the ground he walked over with bare feet. The grasses, stones, and sands reached through his soles and guided him supernaturally across the vast wildlands of the Americas. The land was their way, living a life free, on the same magic winds that blew the birds of migration south of the equatorial line.

There were many admirable traits to these people. Comandante Redondo always regarded the Aztec with incredibly high esteem, reminiscing about the Aztec jaguars he fought next to the Temples of the Sun and Moon. In those days, the sword was king. Senselessly killing, no pleasure or pain to it, for the comandante, it just was. The pathway to peace had to be across an ocean of destruction and strictly enforced population rehabilitation. They were here in the name of Spain, but they were vulnerable and weak, and fighting was to be avoided at all costs. They needed to negotiate alliances with the different tribes in the region, and they needed to be able to find this place again, should they need to.

Aatuani led them up a path that climbed up through to a rough incline of loose boulders and unstable, slick stone. The handholds they used to lift themselves up and over were shoddy at best, and looking down at the ground below was an invitation for dread to strike Cristobal's heart. He treated it like his last hard climb, the last obstacle blocking him from the glory of their great discovery.

They climbed late into the afternoon. Passing the lounging snakes with caution, fighting to maintain their breath as they gained altitude. They were choking on shallow air, trying to fill their burning lungs with it. For some reason, that same air also had a good taste to it, like one could taste the earth from where it came from. The minerals were richly packed into it, and in his head, he enjoyed the thoughts of the tasty wind as he punished himself for not keeping up with the comandante and Aatuani as they led the way.

Dendrick Rodon was in the back with Lieutenant Enrico Cardenas. The two of them, who had been strangers before this expedition, were now good friends, who had shared many long nights of conversation together. Talking about their similar circumstances at home, neither one had family to speak of. No wives or children; they were young, and adventurous. They did not wish to be tied down and domesticated this early.

They took care to help one another, ready to catch the man in front if he started to slide down the cliff face. Losing their footing, grabbing on to loose roots or vines, they slowly, methodically pulled themselves higher. At last, they reached a flattened terrace, which was not very wide but flat the whole way across. There were crude ladders that climbed up several more feet to another level of the terrace, which stepped up again to face level of the canyon side. From there, they continued negotiating their way up until they'd come to something comparable to a walking path. This path climbed up nearly vertically, and they climbed it slowly, being sure to take their time. This close to the end, they could spare no accidental deaths.

They approached the alcove ruins from the left and were now able to make out the details of what it was they saw from below.

As they climbed up the final stretch of the dusty path, they crested the top of a small berm. From that vantage, they laid their eyes on the full grandeur of the ancient complex. It was much bigger up close, and the men gasped aloud, sharing praises of amazement with each other.

"It is simply astounding. My friends, *this* is the work of the masters," said the comandante, gasping for breath himself.

They stayed behind the berm, making observations of the ruins from afar. Dendrick Rodon came to the front of the formation and joined Cristobal at his side.

"I cannot believe it, to see with my own living eyes! Do you see the people? There's movement over there, look!" said the crow master, as he pointed over the berm toward a depression in the floor of the complex.

The comandante squinted his eyes, and Cristobal followed Dendrick's index finger as he aimed toward the ruins. They were just dark figures from where they stood, people walking about, carrying baskets of grain, pitchers of water, and sitting outside the various dwelling entryways. Inside, the chambers of the complex were pitch dark. Architecturally speaking, it was a powerful monument, and the Spanish government would immediately recognize the complex as a true natural landmark of historical and cultural significance.

"Only a handful stayed behind; they refused to be driven from their homes. Keeping the traditions alive has proven to be the hardest work, and now the work we mind the most. Sharing with one another fantastic stories direct from the mouth of the ancient ones. We are the keepers of the lost legend."

Cristobal listened to the guide and felt very honored to have been brought to such a place. They were guests in this enchanted reserve, and they would come in peace or not at all. This was his resolve; he would not take life that was not his to take in a place he was brought by invitation.

His longing for home grew stronger, and his lust for glory faded a little, seeing the people peacefully go about the day as they'd done for a thousand years.

Chapter 22

OAXACAROA

The comandante, Cristobal, and Dendrick took turns passing each other the looking glass, processing their predicament from the cover of the berm. Their approach was an important one, because while they were superiorly armed for an altercation, the party agreed that diplomacy would win here. The people did not seem to pose any threat; they were women, children, and old people, and the few men he did see were busy tending to their crops, which yielded little but disappointment. Cristobal saw a people who moved at no particular pace, who moved with no clear intention. On one hand, they toiled with the rest of the ancient workers of the world, the Egyptians, Romans, and Greeks. On the other hand, they lived their lives sowing repeatedly doomed harvests, walking around the empty chambers like ghostly apparitions inside a maze of confusing sandstone corridors and abandoned chambers for the last millennium.

Aatuani spoke up, pulling back the conquistadors' attention. "I will go to them. I will make them ready. Please, wait here. I will give the signal when it's safe for you to reveal yourselves. Do not make a noise, do not move, be very quiet," he warned.

It wouldn't be appropriate for them to startle the decrepit elders or scare the daylights out of some small children tending their chores and helping their gray-haired grandparents. Aatuani jumped over the berm, his quick movement startling the others as he took off, leaving a cloud of dust going up the trail. He climbed up toward the complex, and they could see him gaining ground, but he soon disappeared from sight. They all looked at one another, wondering whether the Indian would come back. They sat there anxiously, the minutes taking their time, the seconds pulled and stretched. Cristobal felt sick, lurched over that berm. *This is it;* he thought, he was nervous, his mind racing between thoughts of war and peace, or the limitless varieties of every situation in the thinkable between.

Most would argue that without the willing arm of the warrior, peace could be no guarantee. Certainly, it could not be guaranteed under the pen, because the pen served nothing here. This place was a secret, a virginal myth, unknown to the world, but it wouldn't be for long, not once the conquistadors made their recoup. It was now *their* grand discovery and triumphant victory, in the name of exploration and conquests alike. The comandante was practically seething as he dug his knees into place and kept his low profile.

At long last, the conquistadors heard Aatuani's famous horse whistle. They poked their heads up and fixed their eyes on the void he disappeared into. Seconds passed, but then they saw him, walking at the front of a group of several Indigenous. They quietly shuffled behind him, no one speaking. Their quiet energy disarmed Cristobal, knowing he would not need to fight, for they came with no warriors to protect them and were unarmed themselves. Comandante Redondo stood up straight and tall before stepping over the berm. In full conquistador regalia, and with his arms outstretched, palms facing the sky, he approached them, as if it were he who was the prophesied bearer of unity through peace. He matched their dusty pace, and when they stopped, he stopped.

Behind the berm, the others took their chance to stand up and make their approach as well, backing up the comandante as he kept on toward the group of natives. Enrico signaled the formation behind them to make ready, and he jumped over the berm to join the rest, prepared to give the order, should the need arise. Cristobal swallowed a hard lump in his throat; the nerves had his knees shaking. He kept his eyes fixed on the guide, Aatuani, as the native brought forward his people. The guide stood in the gap of the two parties, the length of his wingspan the only space separating the conquistadors from the Indians now. The tension was so thick it could have been sliced with a saber.

The comandante was cradling his morion in his arm, wearing instead his ceremonial tricorn, plumed with the feather of a Brazilian peacock. Next to the comandante, Cristobal stood, feeling shabby in his armor, which was dirty and scuffed, beaten by the seas, jungle, and desert. The clean-cut young captain who had left a year ago now had a bushy black beard, with roasted-coffee eyes that now penetrated everything around him with complete attention to detail.

He looked over his shoulders before, but he didn't now, standing there in the open breeze, eyeing them. Aatuani stepped forward, toward the conquistadors, nodding to the comandante before turning back to address his people. Though he did not speak their language, Cristobal could see the scorn being delivered at the hands of the tribal elders. Aatuani stood there in the middle, mediating a one-way conversation between the two. The comandante stood there with his hands at the small of his back, waiting politely for his turn to make a warm introduction and a good first impression.

Cristobal picked out a few words of Spanish during the native's conversation with the elders, since there were no native equivalents. That let him know they were talking about Rodendros. Aatuani motioned for the comandante to step forward, which Javier did, one hand on the hilt of his blade, the other on his helm.

At that moment, three familiar figures in drab ponchos appeared. The deep-set eyes of those who were knowing looked straight through the conquistadors' shallow souls. The sages, possessing the wisdom and secrets of a thousand-year history, passed down from generation to generation, radiated a powerful energy Cristobal felt from afar. They were charged by the supernatural, and as Cristobal looked at their deeply wrinkled foreheads, their deep crow's feet, and the liver spots which marked their advanced ages, the old ones' onyx eyes seemed then to be endless voids of undeliverable knowledge.

They stepped to the front of the crowd, where they stood opposite Aatuani and the conquistadors. Reverently they stood, unfazed by the armor-clad strangers, with their advanced crossbows, steel swords, and crazy, glory-hungry eyes. Cristobal was entranced by whatever native magic they'd hexed him with, unable to move, unable to shake the impending sense of doom.

The comandante addressed them first. "We are not here to cause harm to you good people. We are here to explore," he said, with a note of subtle humanity and empathy.

"If you are the watchers of this place, then know, we do not seek its destruction, but rather, its eternal preservation," said Rodendros, speaking with the shortest of the three elders, who stood between the other two.

The elder in the middle spoke for them all, distinguishable by the colorfully beaded and feathered headband he wore around the crown of his head, his gray poncho dropping down past his knees, revealing dusty ankles and leathery feet cramped into woven yucca sandals.

Aatuani prepared himself to translate, and the elder stepped forward, speaking low and slow, the ancient vibrations of his people.

"My name is Oaxacaroa. I speak for the people. We do not want bloodshed. Our numbers are small, and our people are either too advanced in age or too new to this world to lift hands in defense of violence. We will welcome you here, on the grounds that you respect our home and all who dwell within."

Aatuani finished translating for the conquistadors, and Comandante Redondo nodded his affirmation. Oaxacaroa continued, and Aatuani translated further.

"Keep at bay your negative thoughts and inhibitions; our people are not to be trampled over by white men. The days of our prosperity may be long over, but the history of our people's struggle will live on for generations and generations, long into the future, long after we are gone. That was how important the work they did here was."

Cristobal watched the frail elder speak; the other two stood stoically like statues at his side. The rest of the natives were huddled behind their intermediaries, listening to the smooth beat of Oaxacaroa's voice.

He wore a long braid on each side of his face, the gray ropes he kept tucked under his beaded headband, and they easily reached past his midsection. He was different from the others. In Cristobal's eyes, he almost seemed to glow. Cristobal could tell his people loved him; he watched the bystanders listening, daring not speak while he spoke. Oaxacaroa carried the authority of his people, governing what was left of their society after the majority of his kinfolk had abandoned the place, due to a drought that would not end.

Aatuani continued to translate, as Cristobal focused back in to listen to the guttural noises and myriad unknown syllables of their native language. The guide and the elder continued the dialogue.

"We will feed you and allow you to rest. We will shelter you here, and you may take as long as you need, but you cannot stay." He paused, as if he had more to say, but then Oaxacaroa, the other elders, and the villagers all turned, and everybody began to walk away, back up the trail toward the ruins. Cristobal watched them walk up the gravelly concourse in utter shock. They'd been invited in through the front door, to come and have a look around the place for themselves.

Aatuani motioned for them to follow, and the comandante and Cristobal followed suit. Young Captain Cristobal felt the pull of his life's destiny before him. Enrico roused the rest of the formation to file in behind. They walked in the sun, up the trail to what looked like a huge stone palace, carved right into the side of this natural alcove, which was covered from above by an overhanging lip of its own. It was a fortress, a product of native genius and design. It was utterly impregnable, and without the hidden knowledge of its existence, would be nearly impossible to discern from the landscape with the naked eye. They could not see any other way up, since its main edifice was several hundred feet off the ground. They preferred not to use the frayed ropes and makeshift ladders that ran up the side of the terraced alcove face.

The incline was steep, but when it finally flattened out, Cristobal arrived to witness the majesty of this place. From where he stood, he could observe the whole complex. Taking note of the many different rooms, chambers, and walkways weaving the place together, the stone from which it was carved and built ensured it was made to endure time. The complex was huge, and unlike other great Spanish cultural discoveries, this place was, for the most part, abandoned. There were hardly any people to stand watch over the place, let alone people to stop them from taking it over. It was a chilling thought, turning on the people. Cristobal felt hesitation, unsure of whether he should keep going or turn back, in fear of offending whatever ancestral spirits presided over this place.

Oaxacaroa spoke, and Aatuani instinctively began to interpret.

"Our ancient mothers left us to find food for our people, but they never returned. One day it was, when the heat had driven me mad, I had a vision of my family and friends, living happily elsewhere, while I suffered here, in the homeland of our people. It was then I knew, I must maintain the watch, because though I knew no one would ever be coming back, I felt I would one day be asked to defend it, and that this was the destiny of my life, to protect and keep the history of our thousand years of struggle and survival."

His words were heavy as stones; everything the wise man said was. There were no questions in his speech, his manner was imperturbable, and it allowed Cristobal to feel disarmed by his wise energy. The other side of Cristobal was unsure; it didn't seem right for them to be there. He now wondered if he could even strike down an old man like that. Whatever native spells or curses Oaxacaroa could possibly utter over his name, whatever enchantments or befoulments he could play did not scare Cristobal, for he wore the holy armor of God for protection. When he prayed, he spoke directly to the Lord above, declaring with authority his willful strength and power over any and all demons that would stand between him and their glory. He would strike down all who opposed with utter and complete barbarity, and the Lord would sanctify their epic; because like all things done in Christ's name, their cause was blessed, and their glory was his glory too.

Chapter 23

THE COMPLEX

The people were not thrilled at the arrival of their guests. They had been undisturbed, unbothered, and living in peace on the high plateaus for a millennium. Yet, the conquistadors vehemently felt that they were being granted an illustrious honor. This was not the kind of place one would come and make themselves at home, The comandante knew that, and Cristobal knew it too. The delicate state of the ruins meant they needed to be light-footed when moving about the complex, being careful not to disturb the loose stone walls and foundations. Cristobal watched as the locals went back to their daily tasks, the men spoke together in semicircles or walked together up the various steps and slope sides of the rock complex. He saw a few natives shucking maize, taken by the basketful from one of the dark rooms within the complex. Presumably that was where they stored their food, inside where it could be kept cool. The elders sat around together, telling old stories, watching the little ones run around and play, as if they didn't know the situation was developing.

Cristobal felt he was behind enemy lines, and he wondered if the others felt that way too. They all acted normally while receiving a tour of the complex by Aatuani, who carefully instructed them on introductory cultural courtesies and such. It would take little for the situation to turn sour. One threat or drawn weapon could lead to slaughter, and Cristobal didn't wish for that. He kept his guard up as he carried his gear into the first available rooms within the complex. Cristobal wanted to lay down and sleep from exhaustion, but he knew he needed to organize what was left of his element outside. They filed the rest of the men up the trail and into the courtyard. Not wishing to disturb the quiet peace of the place, most of the conquistadors set their minimal belongings against the alcove walls before they entered into the actual complex grounds. They were wary of the place after the talk of spirits earlier and felt more comfortable sleeping outside on the cold, hard ground than inside the complex with whatever spirits were in there. Aatuani expressed to the comandante that he too should sleep with the men outside of the actual rooms and antechambers. Rodendros would have none of it. He would sleep in a room; he wanted to "feel the place."

Comandante Javier "Rodendros" Redondo, was an enigma. You wouldn't know that he did what he did just by looking at him, and the normal feelings of man could not sway him. He kept his temper and lusted for no woman. He indulged in drink sometimes, yes, but in the name of brotherhood and kinship. While his men were suffering, he suffered too, but he suffered in silence, which was the way of men in those times.

They hung their morions on the jagged edges of the massive crags that surrounded them. The complex, which was hand carved into the stone, was so impressive in size that Cristobal could not stand to wait even a few hours to explore the dizzying maze of connecting rooms and corridors. They would need to be thoroughly investigated and charted after a day or two of mandatory rest and relaxation. Aatuani appeared to be bargaining with the older women, who were fixing food for everyone. They hadn't planned for forty-plus grown men, starving and emaciated, to arrive unexpectedly on their front doorstep. The women too initially were cold and bitter about the conquistadors' presence, but after much back-and-forth with the women, and speaking to their good, motherly hearts, Aatuani seemed to change their minds on feeding the starving Spaniards. He gave the ladies several kisses and, content with their responses, went to greet a few of the men who were closer to him in age.

Cristobal and the comandante watched him from the shade where they were sitting, both in mutual amazement that they actually found the place. It was cold outside, made worse by being in the highlands. The complex was already situated far above sea level, which meant the air was thinner up there. Their lack of acclimation and the strenuous night trekking up to elevation took a heavy toll on several of the men, who'd developed severe headaches and terrible nausea as they made the incline approach. Their weak, tired bodies rejected the place before they'd even arrived.

Enrico Cardenas was missing his friends and came to sit with Cristobal and the comandante, who were now entertaining Dendrick Rodon's pessimistic realism. The crow master was voicing some concerns he'd kept quiet about, but now that they were here, he felt it proper they discuss and strategize about their next moves, voicing their thoughts and grievances as a team.

Enrico warmly greeted his tired friends, who were shaking their heads, listening to whatever Dendrick Rodon had to say.

"Look here, can you not see the vulnerability of our predicament? We are trapped here, and for what? The ashes of an ancient people long forgotten? For a place nobody will know we even found? We won't be able to share the story with anyone if we don't make it out of here, Comandante."

Dendrick was emotionally perturbed, and the comandante could tell, as could Cristobal, watching the ever-vigilant crow master express his troublesome worries. If Rodon was complaining, that meant it was serious. Even though he possessed an oddly grand interpersonal disposition, Dendrick Rodon earned every accolade he ever received. He spent every minute of his life observing the world around him; he knew when something was off.

He continued his tirade. "Three weeks. We can stay here three weeks; anything longer than that and we're asking for trouble. We don't know these people, Rodendros, and you more than any of us should remember the savages in the south! If we aren't careful, they'll carve our hearts from our chests and hurl our lifeless bodies from these clifftops like they did the men on Templo Mayor!"

The comandante rose to his feet, hearing the crow master's words and remembering full well the atrocities that took place over a four-day sacrifice to the gods. Looking over his shoulder at the largely unexplored ruins behind him, he made a decision. "We will depart this place when it is time to depart this place. There is an opportunity here to learn from a world completely unknown to us. Step aside from your faith, man, for one second, and put yourself in the shoes of the great expeditioners—Polo, Niccolo, Columbus. It was our predecessors who made this dream possible at all!"

The comandante's attempt at exploiting the international fame of such characters was futile. Their discoveries altered the fabric of history for the rest of time, and what had they done? Dendrick Rodon wasn't having it. Enrico watched passively, and Cristobal sought his opportunity to address the matter. Dendrick was a highly experienced conquistador himself, and his words did carry weight.

They had served together a long time, and Cristobal knew Dendrick stayed a pauper for most of his early years, staving off his ravaging hunger with spoiled or rotten leftovers, saving the freshly stolen bread and meat for his younger brothers and sisters. He cared for them because his father was a drunkard, in and out of the brig for most of young Dendrick's upbringing. His mother had passed early on from the flu.

Dendrick had the most genuine attitude of anybody Cristobal had ever met. Following his orders without gripe or complaint, he executed his responsibilities professionally, and he led a most lethal squad. One wouldn't think the laid—back Rodon capable of it, but he among them had killed more people than anyone else. Second to the comandante, that is, who claimed to have killed thousands of Aztec and Mayan warriors in his days fighting alongside Cortes, from the shores of Veracruz to El Dorado. Dendrick had long suffered from a broken soul and was tormented quietly night and day by the tragedies he never spoke about.

They weren't planning on violence, however, and the conquistadors wished the need for blood would not arise. Dendrick made it clear he did not trust the Indigenous folk, and before he went back to his stony crag to rest, the crow master left them with these words, spoken as hollow as the valley they climbed through to get here. "They may have left their marks on the face of time, but what did they leave here with?"

He turned his back to them and went to rest before the meal.

The comandante invited Enrico to sit among them. Enrico mentioned they hadn't seen Aatuani very much since arriving, but the comandante assured him he couldn't have been far. He was far more than a guide, Cristobal thought. Aatuani had led them to this place in the middle of an entirely unmapped continent. He had ushered them through the New World with the kind of familiarity that only comes with being born of this land. His knowledge of the stars, and the way he looked to the cold, dark skies for direction. Through his bare feet, weathered and callused after the tens of thousands of miles he'd wandered in his life. The spirit of the guide was one he embraced with his heart and his soul. It was his being and his purpose.

Rodendros addressed the curious lieutenant. "Aatuani is representing our cause. If he is preoccupied, you'll have to forgive him, Lieutenant."

Enrico acknowledged the orders with a nod and sucked lips.

Comandante Redondo continued, addressing the group. "Three weeks is what the crow master wants, but I cannot upheave the roots of this expedition because of one man's paranoia. Should anyone else not wish to be here, they can try their luck out in the wastes below!" he fumed, much angrier than before.

Cristobal finally broke his own long silence, trying to mediate a peaceful exchange. "Comandante, I think we must allow ourselves to be free in this place, as they are. We must talk to these people, learn their language, hear their stories, and try their foods. Let us learn the rich culture of these ancient folk. We should be bringing the olive branch of peace to them and not place our basket of hope in our guide's claim to guarantee it for us. Let us break our own bread with them this night, spend an evening of good intention with our hosts, and in the morning, we'll be much better off because of it."

It was a terrific suggestion, and the comandante sat on those words for a few seconds. The circle was quiet, waiting on Javier's final say. He thought about it for a few more seconds, looking out, off into nothing.

"All right, Cristobal, that's a fair idea. Aatuani will deliver them the news. Going forward, I want you all to go off in search of their histories," said the comandante. "Men, we need something to prove without argument that it was us who were here first and no one else. Our findings and work in the coming weeks will give our endeavor strong acclaim. Let us collectively see to it. And be smart about this; keep your weapons close. If it feels off, it probably is. Do not let down your guard. Three weeks, now let us see if these native women know how to feed their hungry men."

Cristobal wasn't expecting much by way of food. His appetite hadn't quite come back to him since he developed altitude sickness on the climb up. Regardless, he would try to keep something down. Their emaciated frames were pitiful, and their sun blotched skin was loose, hanging from their decalcified bones. There was no fat on them to keep them warm, so they shivered in the cold, not realizing the alcove, which the ruins were carved into, blocked much of the outside elements already. They stayed warm by the fireside, a ritual they performed as often as convenience allowed and necessity permitted.

There wasn't much in the way of food. Corn, beans, and squash were their staple foods. There was small game roasting over the flames, giving off a scent that made the conquistadors salivate. Nearby, one of the older women was tipping a hand-painted pitcher, filled with water that sparkled as she poured it into the clay cups. They were served a brothy, aromatic soup, served from a large, two handled cauldron that was brought out by two strong, tall Indian warriors, holding the heavy vessel with sheer grip strength alone. The vessel was so full, it splashed over the sides as the two warriors carried it over to the larger fire being started in the middle of the courtyard. Most of the people had gathered there over their community meal with their paler guests. Into their cups, the elder lady poured them another round of beverages. This time, it tasted like an incredibly bitter tea, which most of the men choked on while swallowing. The Indians laughed at this.

The pottery was made directly from the clay of the earth, with hand-painted depictions of nature, man, and beast. Cristobal observed the works and noticed that the great paragon of the hunt was a common theme, highly dominant in their art. They had seen similar glyphs in caves and on the sides of cliffs, mesas, crags, and on hidden slabs of sun-scorched sandstone. They were passed terracotta bowls with black-and-white spirals painted on the inside. Women entered carrying woven baskets and pottery relics, which seemed to be for ceremony. He saw a large empty vessel, painted on the inside with serpentine curves, weaving parabolic lines along the base and up the sides.

There were large vessels full of corn, which were wide near their base, with thick handles for sturdy carrying. The planters that decorated the various chambers and walkways were each different, with no two being the same. With natural pigments, they painted a cactus with black-and-white geometric shapes, or paintings of antelope or bison being chased by the hunters, who leveraged their smaller, slower human stature with the spear. They threw this weapon with such skill and lethality that its obsidian-flaked spearhead pierced the heart of the creatures and gave them a swift sleep. They knew where to hit, so the beast did not needlessly suffer. They understood the value of life in all living things and honored the sacrifices such creatures made with their own prayers and offerings. It was a craft in which they humbly excelled, as generations had expertly passed down the artform.

Cristobal observed these things with astute attention to detail. The anxiety of his heart did not let him for one second let up from observing his own surroundings as the men filed by for a bowl of warm, brothy soup.

The smaller dwellings in the observable area surrounding the mesa were made using sunbaked bricks from the very mud of the mesa herself. That was not the case here. This was the tedious work of hand on stone. The many rooms, which were connected by shallow walkways and enclosed corridors, were all held together with larger, cylindrical rooms in the levels below, which depressed deep into the earth. These were ceremonial pits for ritual, the special chambers, which Aatuani made known to them as they shared their bowls of vegetable soup, tipping back their heads to drink down the broth. They were thankful there was a lot of it, as it did wonders for the soul. They all filed by the gracious mothers who offered them a simple, warm meal.

Saying their thanks, the men dispersed and went off to their separate corners, banding together under the alcove as a company and sharing their chow together. Life appeared to have no pace at all. People weren't in a rush here because there was nothing to do. Living life harmoniously together and getting a little older each day.

Though there were fewer than two dozen of them now, the native population of this specific location, according to Aatuani, was around 150 people or so, with thousands more populating the surrounding areas of the region in similar types of architecture, singular dwellings and carved complexes similar to this one. According to their guide, his people spread out once they realized there was no end in sight to their great drought.

Untethered to the hassles of the modern era, the natives flourished in the realm of their own existence, while back home in Spain, there was a renaissance happening. A powerful movement of art and music, sweeping through and inspiring the greatest thinkers, artists, and poets to ever live, to unleash their talents onto the world. The polymaths, who were so skilled in their study of arithmetic, anatomy, and astronomy, that the old Moorish sages, whose critical understanding of numbers, metrics, and medicine far advanced the knowledge of the magic-carpeted, gold-tasseled Arabian world of the East, would have to tip their hats in respect.

So too did the highly important work of the Spanish and Italian empires elevate humanity, schooling the world with one masterpiece after another. The paintings were the work of the finest artisans to ever hold a brush. Crimson, Cristobal's favorite color, and cyan shades of azure, peppered the verdant greens they used to paint landscapes with such realness, the people applauded the artists in the streets as they unveiled their works to the public. The pain you could see as they dotted white the pupils of their muses' eyes. The art spoke to them, conveying every conceivable emotion, and emotions between emotions. It spoke to the incredible talent and intellect of the entire country, a country that was blossoming thousands of miles away, while they were here, under the awning of this awesome Indigenous architecture.

In Cristobal's own observations, the people were highly skilled in their labor of the land. An agrarian people, they tended their crops daily, and in the winter, they made themselves busy with their crafts; pottery and basketweaving. The children played together while their mothers watched. The elders with their guards were seldom seen, but they were there. Cristobal also could count on his hand the number of times he'd seen their guide since arriving, but he soon appeared, coming up to Cristobal and Dendrick, who were busy themselves looking for weak points in the defenses and security of the complex. There were many rooms for one to disappear into, many shadows to conceal one's nighttime movement, but the high altitude and natural topography of the place made it nearly invisible in the dark.

Aatuani, Cristobal, and the comandante all participated in a ceremony in the biggest of the circular chambers. It was a pagan ceremony, which made them stir with unease as they were blown with strange smoke from the pipes of the wrinkled ones and passed around clay cups of an extremely earthy tea, which they were highly encouraged to drink. As the ceremony went on, the conquistadors found themselves in a state of uncontrollable laughter. They inhaled the vapors deeply, which preceded them by moving toward a crescendo of euphoria. There were ancient chants and dances performed by all those of able body and voice. The land was a landscape to behold, as a bright red sun went down over the cliffs, casting its glow over the entire mesa. It was a magical scene, which set a fantastic backdrop as they drifted away into ethereal trances, letting the spirits of the sun and moon whisk their energies inside of them.

The cold attitude of the people changed from that morning, and Cristobal felt oddly close to this place and to these people.

He felt truly that it was his purpose in life that brought him here, and he felt tremorous nerves inside his body and mind as he fought the splendidly colored hallucinations of the bitter brew. Unsure what the future would hold, he was afraid of what he could not control. Cristobal sensed his spirit calling out for God, asking for forgiveness for his sins and wrongdoings. He asked for protection and for guidance and for the Lord, but then, he wondered, where was the padre in all of this?

He felt like he'd completely forgotten to visit with the padre the last several weeks, and now he was unsure of even the last time he had seen the man. This thought quickly spiraled downward into the thought of, *What if something bad happened to the padre and I hadn't noticed?*

A feeling of panic struck him, as the others were laughing and shouting and raising a fire right there in the middle of the room. He felt fear as his heart beat faster and his thoughts were quickly shrouded in a dark pessimism. Sensing his trouble, Oaxacaroa took Cristobal by the hands and looked into his eyes. He looked at Cristobal while he spoke to Aatuani, who sat shirtless across from them, on the other side of the flames. He spoke with a smile and warm eyes; his hands felt rough, callused and weathered from seventy years or more of rugged agrarianism.

Cristobal looked away nervously, seeing depictions of lizards and snakes on the walls and in the shadows of the fire. He started to shrink down into himself, fearing the judgement and evil eyes of others.

"What did he say?" he asked as he looked to the guide, hands in the clutches of Oaxacaroa. The laughter in the room made it hard to hear anything, but Cristobal focused on the guide, and the background noise became a focused, low hum. The rattles, drums, and sticks kept the ancient beat, the smoke-induced psychosis gripped him as he waited for the translation.

Aatuani sat shirtless across from them, a spiral painted in the center of his chest in red mud. White stripes were painted under his eyes, and he wore a large eagle plume in a headband of his own intricate beaded design.

Aatuani spoke from across the flames, in a space that seemed like it was shared only between the guide and the young captain.

"Many, many fuzz will appear upon your face," said the guide, taking a pause for himself, continuing with hollow, unblinking eyes. "Many, many women you will love." He smiled a crooked smile that Cristobal felt he'd seen before. Oaxacaroa looked sympathetically toward Cristobal, knowing the young captain was out of his gourd on ancient compounds and elements. His onyx orbs glowed hot orange from the flames of the fire, and Cristobal rolled his eyes back into his head and fell into a deepening whirlpool of colors that came from a vividly magical palette, with dancing brushes that painted for him never-before-seen shapes and patterns. Things were moving in ways that were not normal. The omens and portents made sense, the beat of the drums, and maraca-like rattle instruments propelled the energy upward with the cloudy, perfumed smoke that evaporated into the air.

The comandante was just as entranced, unmoving, and mute. He sat there with his mouth agape and empty eyes that seemed to be wet with tears, watching the flames rise, and following the beat where it went as it pounded faster and faster. He was experiencing something for himself, as was Cristobal, as were the rest of the men, their minds being opened by these people.

Oaxacaroa, in his pastel ceremonial dress, brought forward to Aatuani a bowl. An ordinary bowl, unadorned and naturally colored, the same reddish color that plastered the whole plateau. Aatuani reached over and grabbed it from the elder's hands, continuing to shake his head to the rhythm of the rattles. Grabbing the bowl with both hands, Aatuani clutched it close to the center of his chest, over the spiral. He lifted the red dish to his forehead and closed his eyes, uttering a quiet but audible verse.

Raising it high over his head, he took off in a sprint and jumped through the flames without losing so much as one drop. Once on the other side, he kneeled and drank from the bowl for several seconds without pause. A brown sap slowly streaked down the sides of his mouth, down his neck, and onto his chest. Through the fire, Cristobal felt he resembled a *demonio*, a foul, shaded entity from another world. The madness was visible, as the crazed rhythm of the tribal noise came to an abrupt stop. He looked little like the guide they started the journey with, but in that moment, an embodiment of that which was inside of him, as human then as Adam during the Creation. Cristobal held his arms to the sky triumphantly. The ceremony concluded, and they left the room of visions to get some sleep for the night.

A night of insomnia awaited Cristobal and the comandante, as they staggered back into their small stone room, where their bedding and equipment cluttered the floor. Their teeth were chattering as the sweat from their bodies began to freeze, and they both desperately clung to one another to keep warm. In his head, Cristobal battled the motley beasts of his imagination for hours. He lay there awake, thinking of all that had happened to him in his short but courageous life. He saw himself there, on the other side of the fire. He saw himself putting an end to this madness. The sooner it was over, the sooner they could get back to Spain, and he could have a life again. It was then that Cristobal resolved himself to seek the Padre out, because he was going to establish his peace with death officially and make his last confessions before it was too late to do so.

Chapter 24

THE VENUS COUNCIL

Cristobal wandered off into the night, stumbling, tripping over every rock and scraping up his knees and elbows in search of the good padre. Needing the spiritual body cleansed immediately from whatever *brujeria* magic they had undergone, he needed absolution, for Cristobal was drunk. He was mumbling short, incoherent ramblings to himself, completely unaware of his surroundings or direction. "Please, Padre, where are you, Padre? I am in need of you."

Bumping his shoulder as he staggered through a dark corridor inside the complex, he mumbled some more.

"They're coming," he said, and stricken with emotion, he fainted, knocking his head against the wall on the way down, taken by sleep to the more vivid dream worlds of his youth, where his imagination always took him to the furthest reaches of his mind. Cristobal went deeper.

He slept for several days, following the ceremony, and he had learned this from the beautiful young woman who was fanning him off with hand-woven yucca pads as he was awakening. He recognized her instantly. She was the young woman he had seen when he stumbled into the tributary in search of arrowheads, which the men did find many more of. Cristobal had spotted her first in the lower ravine, kneeling on the stones beside the creek, where she was bathing her feet and beating her rags. As he opened his eyes for the first time since he hit his head, she greeted him with the first friendly smile he had seen, and to him, it was the most beautiful thing in the world.

She waved the yucca fan on him, and the cool air felt good on his face as he lay there in the nude on a makeshift mattress of furs and blankets. He saw in her gentleness a great humility. The warm smile she gave him was one of timid innocence, and he was thankful to her for tending to his care.

"You are most kind for doing that," Cristobal said as he slowly came to, sitting up on his elbows and fighting off the groggy haze which was his karma for the night before. She was thin, and so very dainty. Her black hair was long, and in a tight oiled braid running down the middle of her back. She turned away, appearing to leave, but Cristobal held her up.

"Wait! Before you go, what is your name?" he asked, pointing at her with his finger, then pointing to himself and saying "Me, Cristobal."

She looked at the ground at first, shy or dumb he couldn't tell, but either way, he was taken with her.

"Soyala," she said, and he repeated it to himself, once again thanking her for caring for him in his sickness. She was in the middle of pressing a cold rag against Cristobal's forehead when the comandante barged in.

"Good God, man, what the hell became of you!" he said in grand jest as he entered the chamber. The chamber was warm from the small fire burning in the middle of it. Most of the rooms allowed for such things; heat was necessary for survival. The comandante was full of life once more, and it was good to see him so well and rejuvenated, but Cristobal felt like he needed to make right the improprieties of his past.

"Comandante, would you bring the padre? I think I'm dying." He hushed his voice. "I think they poisoned me," he said, looking over his shoulders and making sure nobody else was nearby to hear.

"Poisoned you? Impossible. I feel incredible, my friend, absolutely golden. And the padre is no more, unfortunately, I'm very sorry," said Rodendros, bowing his head as he sat on the edge of Cristobal's makeshift mattress.

"I can give you your last rites if you so wish," he said, pulling out a piece of paper from his breeches.

"That won't be necessary, Comandante. Apologies, but what happened to the padre? When? How?" Cristobal asked.

Comandante Redondo then went into detail of how on the night of their thirty-six-hour trek up the side of the canyon and into the plateau, the padre had somehow fallen from incredibly high up, without a shriek or a gasp or anything. Every man kept his eyes to the ground, watching their own footing, and suffering in individual silence while the padre plummeted to his death, hitting the rocks below, nothing but a hard thud to be heard afterward. Too eager to reach the object of his dreams, Comandante Redondo pushed them onward, unknowingly abandoning the body into the night. To dust he would go again.

"For God's sake, Javier, the padre needs a proper burial, or we'll be damned, you hear me! Cursed!" Cristobal shouted, frightful over the wrath god would have on them for treating a holy man with such little remorse.

"You're already cursed, my friend. You heard the old man at the fire, didn't you?" said Redondo; then he stood up and walked toward the doorway. "Besides, in regards to the padre, I've sent three to find the body and bury it properly. Speaking for myself, I've already asked the Lord personally for his humble forgiveness. Please, Captain, do not worry yourself with my divination. That is my business and mine alone. You understand me, boy?"

Cristobal was stung, but he did understand. He had no right to offer advice or orders to the comandante. Rodendros had seen it all, done it all, and been everywhere in between. The comandante turned to leave the room as Soyala was coming back in with a pitcher of drinking water for Cristobal, whose high cheekbones were prominent because his face was sunken in, but the jaundice glow was covered by the beard that he'd grown.

He again thanked the young native for her gracious hospitality toward him. She gave him a cup of fresh creek water, which he drank in gulps. She poured from the pitcher several more cups until the pitcher itself ran dry. He got up and gathered his clothes and belongings. Getting dressed, with his back to her, when he was finished, he looked at the woman one more time before leaving, taking with him a portrait burned into his eyes at that very moment. Bowing low to her, he made certain she knew of his respect and gratitude. He walked out into the daylight; the camp was moving about with all sorts of different tasks. Enrico and Dendrick Rodon were working on their sketches of the place, discussing in the open air their differing opinions on directional feuds or distances between this point and that point. They were discussing the buttes, which stood tall and skinny, like small mountain statuettes. The sun washed him in its warmth as he walked further into the daylight.

The comandante was speaking with Oaxacaroa, picking his mind for any ancient wisdoms he'd be willing to part with. Everyone was busy—everyone but him.

Tedious work was now underway, and Cristobal walked around the camp in a foggy haze, seeing the conquistadors make good on their orders from the comandante, to get to know the people, to ask them questions, to fight the language barrier, and to exchange gifts. They all had mingled with the women and their husbands, their children, and elders. With only a few families in the place, it was easy to spread out and lose sight of them, but they were gracious and welcoming to the Spaniards, which Javier half-expected anyway, due to the fierce reputation they'd built decades before.

The conquistadors sat and watched with admiration the native potters and weavers, exhibiting their generational trades to the many who were so surprised to see these primitive people be so capable.

They'd sit and listen to the many stories from the wise ones. Oaxacaroa brought forth the legends of their spirit, Kachina, and the sacred lands, fascinating their minds, while others only took notice of the younger girls who were dancing in free merriment. Cristobal remained stoic, reading their expressions and watching as their tongues wagged slowly. Afterward, Cristobal went to see the comandante, who was taking a break from public relations, retiring to his room inside the complex to finish the work he needed to get done within.

Cristobal went inside, and navigating the confusing corridors and chambers, called out for Rodendros, who was standing in the middle of one of the corridors further down, with a torch in one hand and a piece of parchment covered in scribbles that resembled something of a rudimentary floor plan. The comandante had been determined to investigate every square inch of the place while he was here, and he stayed awake for several days off of some sort of magic cactus, going from room to room, counting his paces entryway to entryway, exit to exit, room to room, and passage to passage.

After a few days of this, it became from exit to entry, exit to passage, passage to entry, and passage to passage. Madness drove him deep over the edge, and with a torch in one hand and parchment in the other, he'd hold his quill in his mouth with his teeth. Then he'd lay the parchment flat to the sandstone wall and sketch the general shape of the room and its approximate location to the room or passage adjacent. This is what he was in the middle of doing when he heard young Cristobal approaching.

"Yes, Captain, over here. How are things?" said Rodendros, drawing a square next to countless other squares and circles on the parchment.

"Good, Comandante, things are well. Dendrick Rodon and Enrico Cardenas are moving quickly on the exterior site, and strategically speaking, it's a dream come true. This place is damn near unconquerable."

Rodendros continued his work, counting in his head to remember hard the sequence of paces which he'd recalled up until this point.

"Well good ... good." said Rodendros, with a blank, tired expression. Under the torchlight, Cristobal could see Javier's distracted eyes, his black pupils double their normal size. He was somewhere else entirely, so focused on his parchment paper and his work, thinking about his retirement that wasn't far away. The comandante must have had a million other things going on in his head, because he wasn't here with Cristobal.

The tragedy of living the life of the comandante was that the magic of this splendorous place was lost once he'd found it, once he realized there was no gold or riches to plunder. Rodendros had seen the majesty of the ancient temple pyramids during the Mayan and Aztec Wars; nothing after could ever compare. While this was another exotic place for him to add to his lengthy list of places traveled, the reason he was working so hard was so he could justify the expenditure when his superiors asked him to.

But to Cristobal, this was the highlight of his career, only wishing instead that he'd been able to slay more opponents in battle. This journey had carried him across the seas, into a virginal world. New lands they were able to sail to and see, and for that opportunity, he was grateful.

Aatuani, having smoothed out relations with the elders after the ceremony, fell back into the duties of his house and his responsibilities here at home, taking care of the frail ones and going out to hunt in the canyon, often returning more empty-handed than when he left.

Their ritual medicines were potent, and their knowledge of the herbs and plants led them to become healers of hearts, able to ease the spirits and soothe the worst afflictions. When the conquistadors first made their arrival, the old mothers quickly helped to ease the headaches and nausea of the men suffering from altitude sickness. The labors they toiled at were necessary for an agrarian people. Aatuani set aside a few afternoons and took some time to give instruction to the conquistadors on things such as dryland farming; how they use the time of year to keep up with their rotating crop cycles, marking religiously the equinoxes and solstices, which for them was an important time of the year, telling them when it was time to reap, and when it was time to sow. Much of the success was dependent upon the rain, of which there was little, the main reason why their number depleted over centuries past.

Although rain couldn't be foretold by the cosmos, many of the ancient ones spent their whole lives observing the patterns of the moving stars, planets, and constellations, for answers and secrets to their human existence. Each had a unique Indigenous name. What was Orion for them was something different to the Indians. It was the most natural marvel one could behold out there, back then, in those simpler times. Their knowledge of the world beyond them was the result of a thousand years of living with the world around them.

The days passed, and Cristobal took the time to slowly observe the routines of the people; there seemed to be more and more of them showing up each day. Families with their young, coming from far and wide to view the strangers. They all came in peace, bringing gifts of native jewelry, play stuff, and small trinkets for the Spaniards, who were very grateful for the hospitality. They brought food and drink of their own, which they willingly shared, and the conquistadors found themselves interacting more freely with the newer arrivals, sharing meals and using nonverbal communication to express themselves to one another.

Several men were taken with the younger women who had arrived. Dendrick Rodon, a known womanizer, loved to admire a woman's beauty. In every shape and form, he loved women. The work seemed to be getting done, so Cristobal let it go. What that work was, Cristobal wasn't sure. He seemed to be disconnected from emotions, his thoughts scattered, watching the native girls brush through each other's hair. The maternal affection reminded him of his family at home. He missed Fiorella; he wasn't sure he remembered what her voice sounded like. even the memory of her infectious laugh was slowly fading as his memory and concentration eluded him.

The exhaustive investigation of the complex was an undertaking overseen by the comandante with the help of Cristobal. Cristobal busied himself each day with keeping detailed logs of the day's discoveries, the unusual findings, basic translations of language, as well as copying the nearby petroglyphs down as identically as possible, scribing next to each with their own ancient interpretations, as well as his own. Some days Cristobal sat with the outcasts, getting his counsel from an old hermit, lost to lunacy. He listened with the same attention he gave the comandante, because even the craziest of fools might say something that makes sense once in a while.

Aatuani would check in with his conquistador friends every once in a while to make sure they were doing all right, but he was often seen colluding with the elders, casting his shadow over them as he entreated their favor. Dendrick Rodon kept his eyes on him; he was uneasy watching the Guide and wanted to stay true to the three-week time limit he suggested to the comandante. The figure was not made up out of thin air, The crow master's logical nature told him that for fear of running their rations too low, and fear of wearing out their welcome, they needn't stay any longer than that.

After a fortnight in the ruins, the once-empty complex was crawling with life once more, and Cristobal voiced his security concerns to the comandante. Rodendros had not left the complex since arriving, rarely seeing the light of day except to relieve himself. Even though they all coexisted peacefully, Cristobal knew they were in a vulnerable position; he knew they couldn't get too comfortable and that they needed to get back on their heels toward their next mission, to make it back to Fernando and the sailors they left on the river.

A variety of Indigenous people wandered about the complex, many shapes and sizes, with the same sandy red complexions, the same black hair, the same dark eyes. They treated one another in a fashion that seemed as if it were a reunion of incredibly old family and friends. Most were unbothered by the Spaniards, the language barrier preventing many different emotions and feelings from being properly communicated. Cristobal thought over what Oaxacaroa said to him at the fire. It was a queer combination of words, but if it was indeed a curse, it would not outweigh the power he had in using the name of his Lord, a light that conquered all darkness. He disregarded the elder's words and put them off as Indigenous ramblings. The remaining company, after a few more deaths, now numbered about thirty men, working day in and day out to document every aspect of the conquistadors' findings. Each proactively occupying his own time with the native peoples, the complex, or with the very nature that surrounded them.

They huddled together for warmth under the great overhanging lip of the alcove, looking out to see the full moon and a million stars beyond. They had no name for the place, and they could not squeeze the ancient name from the elders or the children or anybody they asked; it was a protected secret. There were countless other mysteries Cristobal wondered about these people, but they were getting along better and better each day, and there were times when Cristobal felt that he shared a sense of common humanity with these tribal people. There was no hatred for the stranger; there were no ill intentions. Was this mission in keeping with the spirit of the old expeditions? What was a conquistador without conquest? Was his service diminished because he hadn't been there twenty years earlier to make his name alongside Cortes and Rodendros?

Many would consider him lucky, having missed the destruction that came with war, but he didn't see it that way. His hunt was for glory, to be immortalized like the old heroes, and the comandante swore they would have it, as he had his own turn, many years ago.

Rodendros and his guide would often walk together, talking like two pillars, one of marble, and one of granite; different, but not so much you couldn't see that they were both pillars all the same. It was an unexpected friendship they shared, but Cristobal knew God had brought the two of them together with divine intention.

The nights would grow cold, and Cristobal would entertain the image of that native girl, the one who cared for him in his stupor, the one he'd seen by the water. He thought she was graceful, like a bushy-tailed doe in the tall grasses of the Spanish countryside. He pictured bringing her home, to show her his world, and how different things could be for them both. It could never happen, though, and was sadly a fleeting daydream. His heart belonged to Fiorella; it always would. Her love was enough to quench his earthly desires.

Another week had finally come to pass, and they were now at a pivotal point in the operation; they now needed to consider leaving the comforts of the complex and moving on to wherever the winds of chance carried them next. Despite the natives remaining cordial, Cristobal felt they had worn out their welcome, and he convened a council with Comandante Redondo, Dendrick Rodon, Enrico Cardenas, and Aatuani.

They gathered in one of the rooms inside the complex, and they all brought forward their cumulative works to show the comandante what had been achieved in three weeks' time. Each man laid down something different. The winter air blew a nice breeze through the openings in the walls; some pathways and openings led nowhere, creating pockets of still, warmer air. The builders, however, did everything with intention and factored into its construction such a way to allow for the proper ventilation and air circulation of the interior. The complexity of its design was one of the more speculative facets. Various cosmological alignments could be observed at particular times of the day, each day. They observed the rotation of the seasons, using it to manipulate their harvests, and year round, the people observed the movement of the larger celestial bodies from different vantages throughout the region. There was much to be said about what these primitive people had accomplished.

Cristobal was keen to elaborate first; he'd been patiently waiting for his moment to have the floor. In the recessed circular room, they gathered near the center, looking out at a remarkable view of Orion as he descended from ancient Olympus. They spoke in length about the strategic pros and cons, the secure position, but the scarcity of available resources. These people were almost completely reliant upon their crops, which hadn't produced much in the last hundred years or so. It was a terrible period of drought, and Cristobal had the privilege of observing several rain chants and dances in the last three weeks. He'd observed their culture through a veil of reverence, taking in all that was different and unique about them, and committing to memory his experiences. They only scratched the surface, though, because they were now involved in what could potentially become a yearslong expedition, and Cristobal was thinking they might yet be able to conquer something worth conquering, but not these people. These people, from the outset, treated them with neighborly grace and hospitality.

Their ceremony, with the elixir of dreams in the room of visions, had shown him a different perspective, as he was then on the outside looking in. From out there he observed his changing life and felt fearful of those changes. He trudged forward toward the beast of his own natural ego, fighting the battles of the world and wondering how it could be such an ugly place. It opened his heart to fear but also to courage and the hope that courage would win, so he might one day fulfill his glory dream.

"Comandante Cristobal has a ring to it, doesn't it, friend?" Redondo said, shooting Cristobal a glance from under the hoods of his eyes, with a familiar cheeky smirk that somehow validated him. He was happy to share what he had learned thus far, learning not by embedding himself within their circles but using his scrutinous eyes to pick apart the shared routines of these simple people. Cristobal was frivolous in his observations, and he had determined that he knew enough about them to know he didn't want much more to do with them. They were a people left behind, and to stay here while the finest movement of art and philosophy the world has ever seen was springing up all over Europe would be an unfortunate thing. Meanwhile, these native peoples were stuck barely scraping by with their dilapidated homes, low-yield harvests, and primitive modes of living. The drought was reason enough for the conquistadors to leave this place, having satisfied their discovery and expedition spirits over the last three weeks. How could they continue to survive these prolonged periods of no rain? How could they continue to live in a place that was primarily arid and devoid of life? What future, if any at all, did a mostly barren, sandy red waste hold for them? Even the complex in which they were now convening, which was worthy of being one of the ancient wonders of the world, was not sufficient to keep them there, battling the elements for a thousand-year struggle. The lack of material riches made its luster lack even more. These things the men discussed at length with each other, expressing these concerns and questions over a stone table set under a skylight opening.

The natives and their small number seemed content filling their pitchers from the nearby creek, but with their tribal relatives in town, how long would their supplies last? They were riding out the poor conditions in the name of holding their stake over their homeland, which was completely expected and understandable. They claimed to have been there for forty generations, but there was no way of saying for sure the true extent to which this culture receded in time.

The comandante brought Dendrick and Enrico forward, and the two laid forth a large canvas, stretched over a crudely constructed frame. The canvas, made from tanned goat hide and shaved incredibly thin, depicted the complex and its full sweep of surroundings. Set in the middle of the canvas, their ink drawing depicted the many different rooms, chambers, and levels of the complex from beyond its walls, showing the topography of the land behind and beside them. This was one of many sketches and drawings the two brought forth. The cartographer and the crow master, using their compass and their eyes, pieced in their very location under the stars and folded it into the master map.

Another charcoal drawing showed the way the alcove hung overhead, providing their natural cover from the wind, storms, and elements. Strategically tucked out of sight, nearly impenetrable, and highly defendable. The detailed work of the architects was highly praised among the men, with the conquistadors giving glory to Aatuani's revered ancient ones, whose work stood strong, enduring the rigors of time.

It wasn't the most detailed map in the world; it certainly was not as detailed as they would have liked it to be, but with limited time, it would serve as firm documentation of their discovery, and that was enough for the comandante, who thanked the men for their hard work, letting them know they had done more than was asked of them.

Comandante Javier Redondo was now a mortifying shell of the former glorious conquistador of legend. His breeches had grown baggy, his armor and gear two sizes too big, as he'd grown so thin. His ribcage pushed out against the skin as if it could burst through at any moment. Rodendros's gray hair had grown long and wavy, and his beard was thick. Physically he looked frail, but that did not stop the others from looking at him as a strong, straight-standing father. The comandante spoke well, and when things were hard, it was he who pushed himself harder.

Rodendros stood over the table, looking at the pieces of parchment, the arrowheads, pottery shards, and beaded jewelry that Dendrick Rodon had "acquired." Among the mix was a beautiful coral necklace, a gift Dendrick planned something special for.

"Captain Cristobal, what do you make of this?" he said, hanging his head between his arms as he stretched them over the crowded stone tabletop.

"Was it worth it to you?"

The comandante lifted his head, and Cristobal was paralyzed in the grip of his tortured gray eyes. He was a sage of his own in that moment, wise too like these strange medicine men. He had weathered more war than most people dream of seeing, which is why Cristobal stumbled over his words at first. He was nervous under that gaze, in that cold stone chamber, with only a skylight and a couple of candles burning. Cristobal wanted to be honest with Rodendros, and with the rest of them, who were waiting for his answer.

"Of course it was," Cristobal managed to say in a strong voice, knowing that the comandante was weighing his response, searching for a weak spot in the armor, as he'd always done.

"I think we need more swords, sir," said Dendrick Rodon, who was breaking his temporary conversational abstinence.

"There's something going on in this place that these people don't want us finding out. Now we can, and I think we should, mark this place on the map and move on," he said, trying not to get worked up about it. "Or we can keep pretending that we're not disappointed there wasn't any gold."

The truth of his words affected everybody, including the guide. The crow master, taking stock of his audience, shrunk down a bit when he looked at the faces of his cohorts, particularly Aatuani, whose Spanish was remarkably good. Obviously, he had heard Dendrick's words, and from across the table, shot the crow master a bone-chilling stare. Aatuani had perked up first, though, when he heard Dendrick's mention of reinforcements. The comandante shook his head. "Why would we need reinforcements? Have these people not given us shelter, food, and hospitality? Have they not granted us the very honored privilege of taking a short glimpse into their simpler way of life? Look around you with those powerful eyes, crow master. Have you not observed the way the sun shines over this place? I'll have you know, it is by a most intelligent design that this place is constructed. I measured room by room the full concourse of this structure, and I can say we've only scratched the surface. This place has centuries of mysteries within, mysteries as curious as the people who've inhabited it!"

The council agreed on another thing, that the short weeks they had spent there in the ruins were a vacation compared to the odyssey they'd endured to get there. Some of the Indigenous questioned the merit of Aatuani's loyalty; they wanted to know why he had brought these foreigners here. They could only assume he was selling them out so that he might exploit their vulnerability, and in doing so, earn himself some kind of reward from his new Spanish friends. The guide reassured them, though. He told them he knew what he was doing, and when the elders raised their own concerns about the strange visitors, he called them old and crazy and said they were imagining things.

It wasn't uncommon for people out there in the sun for so long to go mad. Cristobal had personally seen several people suffer from severe heat illness on this expedition. The comandante then held up his hand, delivering his final judgment.

"Reinforcements wouldn't get here for months, maybe years. We'd sooner move on and find them naturally occurring in the wilds. Taking the fortress is out of the question, and if that means you men feel that I misled you, then I'm sorry you feel that way.

"But I have given it much, much thought," he said, pausing to look away before breaking the news to them. Bringing his eyes back around, he spoke to each man singularly. "We're moving out, and that means walking for weeks, gentlemen. We'll go back the way we came in, with or without Aatuani, until we reach Fernando and the boats." The comandante finished, giving them a chance to digest his decree.

"I think it is time for us to abandon this archaic place." he said.

Chapter 25

MAY YOU LIVE FOREVER

The council began to wrap up their proceedings, with each man on the same page regarding their objectives. They would not idle for long, another day or two, before they made their way back toward the rushing river on foot. Comandante Redondo had already acknowledged that it was a risky journey, that most if not all of them would not survive, but he was resolved in his speech that he would not let the men go without their leader. He had brought them here, and he had to do his best to get them back home. These men had wives, children, and parents who loved and missed them, and the other lot, who didn't have a soul to care for, well, they were free to stay if they wanted, but they wouldn't be gone back for.

Aatuani stood up, realizing the meeting was over, and boldly stepped in front of them to ask why they wanted to leave so quickly, as they had only just arrived.

"Rodendros, there is much more to learn about my people. You can take our story to the rest of the world! You'll be famous! Stay longer, wouldn't you please? Our talks have been my favorite. I've so enjoyed our talks! I've much more to learn about the Romans, Trojans, and Greeks!"

Redondo smiled at his friend's enthusiasm. "I'm sorry, my brother, but our time together is coming to an end. Believe me, I have learned from you, my friend, more than I can yet see."

Aatuani came around the table and gave his friend a hug. "You have taught me so much, Rodendros. Thank you for appreciating and respecting our sacred lands. We will throw a celebration, with lots of dance, song, and drink to send you on your way!"

Comandante Redondo smiled apologetically toward his friend. Aatuani's hands were tied; he knew it was time for them to move on.

Javier looked at the sad, dark-eyed Indian, a being of another world. A mirror into a different time. They could never exist together, not at the same time anyway, for unknown to either the comandante or the guide, this fate had been written for the last forty years. The guide, watching the destruction of his Aztec homeland at the hands of Cortes and Comandante Redondo, who torched the fruit stalls with the people inside, and in the streets, fought a heartless fight against fierce warriors with obsidian stone axes and clubs, made for inflicting massive melee damage. They would have too, if not for the Spaniards' skin of steel and superior weaponry. The blending of two cultures from two different parts of the world was a symbolic milestone of diplomatic progress. Their mutual resolve to maintain peace had spared both parties bloodshed, and they were blessed to have been fed and comforted the way that they were.

The men enjoyed those incredibly slow three weeks, savoring each day to bathe in the sunlight before bundling up next to the fire at night. The spirit of the old expedition was alive, and Cristobal's growth along the way could be seen in the depth with which he now looked at the world. Things were no longer simple to him, but fighting against the harsh wilderness and elements, the deaths and hardships endured, dodging his own death at every turn, made a man out of Cristobal. He was under the tutelage of his wise comandante, who took the young captain under his wing, schooling him on widely diverse military matters in their spare time, offering every strategic lever he possessed. The comandante was satisfied having someone to teach everything that he'd learned in his forty-year career of great conquests.

A celebration sounded more than good, and right outside the stone chambers where the proceedings of their enigmatic council had just taken place, it sounded as though a large celebration was already taking place. Cristobal and the others first heard loud, deep drums, which could be heard thumping beside the rattles and chants of sacred derivation. They walked outside into the open air; it was nighttime, and the moon was full and high as gray, wispy clouds blew across. Aatuani was standing there with a crowd of natives behind him; the many new faces had come from every direction to the place they once belonged, to lay their own eyes on white men for the very first time.

"We're celebrating from now until you leave, Rodendros. May you always remember your time here. And you too, young Cristobal, I wish you all good luck," Aatuani said, clasping his hands in front of him and nodding. The people behind cheered as he stepped forward to give each of the conquistador leaders an embrace of wholesome sincerity. Dendrick Rodon and Lieutenant Cardenas were included; none could be left out, for they fought the same battle together on those rugged plateaus, and in those mesa-laden valleys; they fought the battle of the heart.

Aatuani continued, stepping back to see the four in front of him. "I'll go say my goodbyes to my other friends, but do drink and eat. I threw this feast for you, friends!" he said, smiling at them before departing back into the stone chamber that they'd been reclusively wargaming in for the last several hours.

At least that was how Aatuani interpreted it all. It sounded to him like they had been searching for riches all along and were saddened when the fruits of their journey brought forth no abundant wealth or vast fortunes. The comandante made do with the finality of their discovery; he'd already led a life of glorious achievement, and this expedition would be a nice addition to his already impressive resume, a career-closing move that would allow him to ease himself into a lazy, fat retirement, spending time with his family back home in the land of rabbits.

It was not enough for Cristobal, however. He didn't want to party. He didn't want to drink any more of their exotic hooch or eat their staple foods with them. He wanted to move on to the next big expedition, the next great quest. He was searching for the quest that would bring him his eternal fame, a fame that reached beyond the grave and carried him high up onto God's shoulders in the sky. Cristobal enjoyed the journey, and it was a long and arduous one, but now that it was coming to an end, he was unsure going forward about staying a military man forever. He missed his love, Fiorella. So much so, since he'd arrived, her sweet memory, which was once emblazoned on the walls of his mind, what he saw in every waking moment, now became a distant memory, faded under the heavy duress his new life demanded from him. He didn't have time to be sensitive or romantic; his men needed him. He could not be a dedicated family man *and* a conquistador; it would have to be one or the other, and it was not fair to her, nor did he have it in him. So quickly, he thrust himself into his new world, and it was then their fault he was swept away from her.

Cristobal spent many of those long, empty nights fighting with himself over this dilemma. A fork in the road that would alter the course of his life. He was young enough that he could do anything he wanted. He already served his crown and his nation, and for the people at home, he'd gone through immense suffering; battling starvation, illness, danger, and fear, but triumphing over the low odds, making their journey a successful one, and finding what they set out to find were the things he achieved. Capitan Cristobal Trujillo overcame every challenge put before him, yet he was admittedly still not satisfied with the merit of his own accomplishments. They were not glorious enough.

The men scooped up their papers, journals, sketches, writings, rubbings, and other artifacts they'd brought forward for presentation to the comandante, and stepped out into the moonlit night.

The people could be seen everywhere as the men stepped from their seclusion and into the fresh breeze of the plateau. Several ceremonial fires, the biggest they'd seen yet, were lit in the middle of the circular subterranean levels, with people dancing, chanting, and playing in the light and heat of the immense glow, the shadows of the flames flickering on the cavernous walls. The smells of roasting game were a pleasure to the senses, and they salivated over it, smelling the aromatics that had brought Columbus here in the first place. The wild, blazing sunset painted the perfect backdrop over the canyon below, and when Cristobal looked out at the wide-open plateau from within their alcove, situated hundreds of feet in the air, his heart was inspired once more to carry on the flame of the great expeditions. He would keep going, keep searching for his Cortes-like glory; he would not cease until he could return to Fiorella, a champion and a hero.

Only when he was satisfied he had done enough would he return to her, then retire from the service and spend his life glued to the hip of his better half. That is, if she bore the truest virtue, attached to no other, abstaining from the desires of the flesh. He didn't dwell on that for long. Fiorella would wait for him; he knew she would.

Cristobal paid no attention to the drunkards already making raucous and acting fools, the women laughing at the inebriated Spaniards as they carelessly and freely indulged in fun with the people. The elders sat nearby, in simple chairs, made from the same stumps and tools that had been used for generations, presumably. There were outlandishly costumed characters at this feast as well, wild figures dressed in all sorts of colors. They looked like carnival characters, with bright plumes of feathers adorning their crowns, with beaded bandies covering the bare-breasted women, whose innocently naked existence had called the men forward like the sirens did the sailors.

They were distracted by that, but the comandante had made his way over to Aatuani, who had gone to paint his body for the occasion. Thick smoke was rolling in the air, fragrant with herbs and stinging with its smoky denseness. The two of them began an exchange, which Cristobal strained to overhear due to the noise of the festivities. He opted to read their body language instead and try to read their lips, making out their words as they were spoken.

They looked squarely at each other before grabbing one another into a brotherly embrace. The two men, who under other circumstances might have been old friends somewhere else before, hugged one another tightly, speaking into each other's ears, at peace in their private bubble. Cristobal carried on and let the friends share their goodbyes.

Dendrick Rodon was organizing his gear in a cubby nearby where he had stashed his belongings away from the rest of them. He was tightly bundling his journals, maps, and sketches. Tucking away the arrowheads he collected neatly into a pouch where he kept some other small items—seed pods and interesting rocks. He'd even managed to extract from the grand chamber some ancient and cracked pottery shards. He'd found a small, ornamental doll, propped up in the corner of one of the complex chambers, which he'd quickly grabbed and stowed away on his person, not caring for the consequences of thieving something. Dendrick Rodon was settled in his thinking that something didn't feel right and that he'd needed to gather his things, should he need to make a quick escape. The crow master listened to his intuition; he looked for the signs and felt for the anomalies. He listened to his gut long enough to know when something seemed off.

He'd taken rubbings of the glyphs, copious notes, and made his own astute observations of the people who were hosting him. The crow master too had grown thin, his body feasting on the reserves of his once-muscular frame. He was unkempt, but he was still very much alive. He would not turn his nose up at instinct, because he who doesn't listen to instinct is a fool taking chances. What was worse was that given the dilapidated state of his knapsack, he had no way of carrying his bundles of maps, sketches, or manuscripts, or the pottery shards, or even the turquoise jewelry he had stolen in broad daylight. A week before their council, the crow master took it upon himself to seek the service of a young woman in the mesa to weave him a basket to carry his belongings in. He gave her three pesetas for it.

As the potters worked the clay, so she worked to hatch together a sturdy frame from desert willow saplings, weaving a yucca basket around it. With long strips of tanned leather, she fashioned him shoulder straps, which were highly innovative and comfortable. To kill his own food while on this long-distance escape, he would need to hunt with his crossbow, and with eyes as good as his, he shouldn't have any problem scavenging his way back to Captain Fernando on the river. Also, a crippling factor was the lack of potable water, of which he'd been unable to stash a sufficient amount. Earlier in the afternoon, before the council, he sat by the creek, drinking himself silly, trying to absorb the water like one of those bloated desert cacti he'd seen along the way.

No, Dendrick Rodon could tell, the people had not been acting right. And where were all of the village's combat-capable men? All he saw were women, children, and old people. Call him paranoid or suspicious, but that was the nature of being a conquistador. Nothing like the stories he had heard in his youth, either, because he too grew up with a similar dream to that of Cristobal. But as he grew older, the glory that Cristobal sought after and spoke endlessly about no longer fascinated Dendrick, and he was just doing what he had to, so he might one day live well off his military pension, his days of war long behind him. He busied himself in his secluded cubby before preparing to go and face the crowd of savages one more time.

What started as a handful of small families at first had nearly quadrupled in size over the last three weeks, with people coming from far and wide, temporarily repopulating the place. They brought things to trade with too, like exotic furs, spices, and tobacco.

People came from all over the entire region to see them. To look at these strangely dressed white men, who spoke a different tongue and carried fancy, shiny things of their own, like their sabers or gold medallions depicting the Holy Mother. Always wearing the sacred cross of Christ, another example of their differences; the deities and spirits whom people like Oaxacaroa and his elder folk seemed to convene with. Gathering around their fire, chanting into its flames, speaking directly to the spirit world, which the Christian conquistadors considered to be the work of el diablo.

The cultures could not have been any more different, and that was all the more reason for them to abandon the place and make it out of there while they still could. They were on the eve of their departure, and upon reflection, Cristobal

considered their time in the complex critical for building the
unit's cohesion and confidence, allowing them to work better
on their future expeditions. He also was relieved to establish
friendly contact with the Indigenous, but there was much
more of the region to explore yet, and they still had to get
back to Fernando and the ships. There was much more to see,
much more to do, and much more to learn.

While the celebration was happening, the men gathered
their belongings, trying to be quick about it, because in the
morning, they were off again, back into the canyonlands.
They needed to continue stretching the Spanish borders
and exploring this New World, deliberate in their efforts of
spreading the Word of God. Most of the Indigenous spoke
no Spanish, but Aatuani assured them that they already had
found God and would not budge from their old ways. That
happened early on, indicative of their inability to coexist,
putting the last nails in the coffin over any hope that these
natives could be reasoned with or communicated with. Not
without the assistance of their guide, who had still not said
whether he would be joining the conquistadors going forward.

Spanish culture was going to sweep across these plains; it was
only a matter of time before they broke the native resistance,
eventually submitting their lands to the invaders over time.
Over the last three weeks, some of the conquistadors took
some of the younger girls in the mesa for their own, doing
what they could to make sure Spanish blood ran through
the veins of the Indigenous for generations to come. The
mixture of Spanish and native blood would be a way of
securing peace, so it was encouraged to take a concubine for
the night. Cristobal knew too, that if for generations to come,
their royal blood mixed with these exotic people's, then they
would solidify their rightful claims to the land, by the blood
of their fathers, by naturalization. Caring more about the
countless red-skinned beauties before them, the conquistadors
buckled under the pressure the muses put on them. Women
always turned them upside down. The ones who developed
attachments cared more about fostering romance over finding
and exploring the ancient complex, which they thought to
be too slow moving and not as important. The great pain of

man, that in their daze, they never stood a chance against the power of the feminine divine.

Cristobal was unfazed by the women of the party. His own native romance wasn't around at the moment, so he instead let himself spend one last night enveloped in the shadow of all his effort. He looked long at the complex, lit by firelight, burning the image into his memory. This magical place locked away centuries of mysteries and secrets that were so tightly kept. The only ones who know their great histories were either long dead or soon to be. All that to say, they were not telling outsiders more than they needed to. They had reason to shelter themselves; the natives were more than aware of what their cousins in the south endured decades earlier at the hands of these very same men.

They met along the same star lines and trade routes; they exchanged rumors, news, and goods with one another, supporting each other through the terrible conquest and diaspora of the Yucatan peoples. The peninsula had fallen, and the Spaniards, in their greed, now came north.

The people bartered their sublime pottery away, for other, more critical necessities that they could not get in their corner of the desert. They would trade their baskets, which were crafted by women who weaved their work with care, imparting their maternal love and wisdom into every piece, every piece a piece of themselves. Trading their precious baskets and clay-fired gifts for tobacco from the plains or mangoes from the tropics. Trading and haggling were talents passed down through the many generations. The women of the culture were highly regarded; these were people who praised and honored their mothers. A mother's womb was as sacrosanct as a seat next to the Creator himself.

Drifting through a carnival of wild dance as the people sang loudly their songs for the rain, Cristobal recalled the extraordinary pictures in the room of visions, visions beyond his sense of reason and beyond the boundaries of his reality. The inner connectedness he experienced as he shivered, scared and alone in the cold, marooned darkness. The warmth of the fire served as his only beacon of hope on those nights he spent, like the ones he spent so many times before. Not only did Cristobal make his peace with his own inevitable mortality, but he sought to right a terrible wrong.

He had not borne a child yet with Fiorella. He had hardly known the woman who he pledged to marry; they were just kids when they married. It wasn't long after the reception that Cristobal had left for his training. He loved Fiorella, but the chances of his making it home to her seemed to diminish more and more each day. Life was just too short, and there wasn't enough time.

The attitude among the majority was to stay. Enrico Cardenas and eleven other conquistadors volunteered to stay back and maintain a hold over the complex while the comandante, Cristobal, Dendrick, and the others journeyed back toward the river to find Fernando. The epiphany that he did not need to prove himself to anybody lifted a great weight off Cristobal's shoulders. Cristobal made it known to the remaining company that they could follow him if they so chose. From there, they would again join forces with the sailors of Captain Fernando, and once the mapping of the river was complete, they would sail it back to the coast, and after a months-long death march through wild and untamed jungles on bruised and battered feet, they'd return to the freshwater inlets and lagoons near the barrier island where they had first arrived. The scourge of their heroically brave undertaking, at long last, complete.

Off in the distance, sitting alone like a precious doe, Cristobal spotted the object of his desires, the tender woman, Soyala, who in his terrible state, fanned him with the woven yucca pads on a bed of furs and sticks. Her light illuminated the landscape of his lonesome heart from across the flames, causing in him a feeling of shy, boyish reservation. He would not look at her directly, but in his periphery, to see if she was looking at him. He deliberately paid her no attention. Brazenly, she reached out to him through the smoke, surrounded by the breathing fire, which glowed and made music of its own. This angel offered her hand to him, and in his dreamlike state of pure, vulnerable love, he asked her to be his. In a confident voice, she spoke to him as she leaned in further, her face inches from his.

"I already am," she said.

"If you listen to the fire," he said, "you can hear it speak to you." Listening to the fire speak to you, now that was something she had never heard before.

It was in that fire, on that night, that Cristobal looked inside himself, listening beyond the noises of the outside world and focusing on the symphony that surrounded him. The rich sounds of wood crackling and popping, the sizzling hisses, it was in there that he saw through the mire of his own existence, that he consequently understood how incredibly dangerous this profession truly was. Foolish, even, to partake in such a life-or-death expedition as this one had certainly been, he was extremely grateful, and beyond thankful for having made it through it all. He sat there before the flames and gave his glory to God, because in his heart, he knew that he had done his best, and God was who he owed it to anyway.

Soyala and Cristobal would spend early mornings walking innocently on the short trails that ran beyond the complex, down into the mesa. The elders shook their heads at her, sitting with the Spaniard. Then they were received by Aatuani, who was whispering into their ears. She saw no reason why she should look down on them, ragged as they were. She felt bad for him, and beyond the dirt and grime were the remnants of a handsome captain from Toledo, and that she could see perfectly fine.

Feral in her possessiveness, Soyala's only knowledge of this strange and fleeting lover was his name, which he had graciously taken the time to write down for her and the time to teach her how to say it.

"Captain Cristobal Noriel Trujillo." It took her only minutes to perfect.

He knew as much about her as she did of him, their communication not needing to be expressed with words. He bid her sad farewells after their morning walks, when he went with the comandante for the day's work. Cristobal quietly daydreamed about sharing a life together, and neither one knew the other was thinking the same. It didn't take long for Cristobal to take her as his concubine, sweeping her away while he was on one of his roaming guard shifts. Their midnight encounters would turn into episodes of intense fire and passion, as the two of them rolled around, naked on the warm blankets and furs that lined the floors of her room within the complex.

Soyala bathed him in the hot springs, washing his hair and his beard with fragranced soaps, again, goods that were traded for. She applied salves to his wounds and fed him better than any of the other women did. Soyala's thinking was, she needed him to be strong and in shape, so he could carry her away, far from her life trapped in monotony, stuck forever in the confines of these small ruins, in this lonely desert, with dreams of a world bigger than the one she came from. Her family was unwilling to let her depart. The sacred oath their people had sworn meant she could not shirk her responsibility to care for the sick and old people of her home. It was the duty of each member to protect and safekeep the ancestral secrets. To ensure the preservation of their people and remember well the hard lessons the universe taught them. Repeating an oral history for a thousand years, passing it down from family member to family member, and generationally too, each suffered through the prolonged periods of famine and drought. The crops would no longer thrive as they once did in the days of old, due to the rains not coming for many, many years, but since the sacrifice of suffering was made when they swore to be the stewards of the land, they sealed their fate when they laid their roots down in the sand.

Cristobal spotted Soyala dangling her feet from one of the terraces. She was far away, and he could barely discern her figure among the surrounding chaos. The ruins were alive with people; women, children, and more of the men had shown up over the last few days, and as Aatuani promised, there was abundant food and drink, and many enjoyed the ritual smoking of the potent native herbs. It was always an enchanting experience, the resonant incantations and song, the dance and the flames, roaring up into the air. Their rituals were different compared to those of the Christian faith, it was a cultural awakening to be part of these gatherings.

Aatuani sat with the indomitable Oaxacaroa, joined by his fellow sages at the fire. They observed the gradual impairment of the Spaniards' faculties. The conquistadors had been freed, finally letting loose their spirits with the people whom they'd lived with and learned beside for the past month. They danced shirtless with them and joined in with the native shouts and wolf howls. The elders watched without passing judgement on them, for they hadn't a need to judge. The darker ambitions of the spirit, greed, lust, and envy, were unheard of in those ghostly canyons. There was no ruling class to laugh in the face of the poverty-stricken, for nobody here possessed any great wealth; they were all equally poor and with minimal possessions. Those minimal possessions they did have were crafted by the labor of their own hands. They devoted their waking hours to tending their withered crops, unfettered when the early harvests yielded little. Their evenings were spent together with family, and their nights were spent in observation of the celestial bodies or paying visit to their ancestors through a thousand-year-old ancient dream technique.

They were always hard-working people, that was evident. Unfortunately, however, they were at the mercy of the elements, and if their drought continued, then their way of life too would be in peril. Aatuani had ambitions of leading his people; he would not let them starve, nor would he see his people torn down the way the Aztecs and the Mayans were torn down.

A few years after the conquest, after being subjected to harsh reform at the hands of Christian missionaries, Aatuani found his true home in the north with his cousins who'd been living on the high plateaus for generations. He stayed there for many more years, learning the language of his adoptive people and integrating himself into what was left of the once-prosperous Indian nation. He left the plateau to head south, where he fully intended to war with the Spanish as they fought their way north. The guide had, by chance, found the comandante while wandering the rugged peaks and valleys of the Sierra Madre Occidental. It was there they first met under the banner of yet another peculiar archeo-astronomical site, known to Rodendros as "La Quemada." After surviving a societal collapse, suffering a harsh and lonely pilgrimage toward a new home, and protecting that home for the last decade, Aatuani was prepared to fight alone against the conquistador squad to the bitter and gruesome death, but instead, he was struck with a moment of clarity. The guide laid down his arms and kneeled at the comandante's feet, raising up his hands and pleading for his life. But when Rodendros heard the native speak his own Spanish tongue with fluency, he knew that destiny had brought the two of them together. He called on him to rise and prodded the native for further information. They had been looking for silver. From that moment on, Aatuani became "the guide," leaving behind the home he sought for years, to go journeying with his new friends. The guide knew he would never live a normal life, stuck in the domesticated confines of the complex. He'd return one day, but on one condition—that he had his revenge for the destruction of his people, the disregard of his gods, and the murder of a martyred Moctezuma.

So it was that the guide had worked out a plan of his own, and now, on this, the night of the winter solstice, the final fate of their great expedition would be revealed.

Aatuani rose from the ground where he sat cross legged and disappeared into the shadows, emerging a short while later. This time, a white spiral was painted over his narrow face. His braided black hair was shining once more from the Spanish oils the comandante gifted him for his good work and service. In those fox furs he stood, a figure from a storybook. This handsome and stoic Indian carried his walking stick in one hand and an obsidian blade in the other.

The chanting became different; it became a slower, deeper beat that thumped like a heartbeat. The people began to quiet down, taking their seats by the fires for the ceremony. Cristobal was nuzzling with Soyala as they sat together on the terrace. Dendrick Rodon was on edge, sitting by himself near one of the fires. All were silent, all eyes fixed on Aatuani as he approached the comandante, who was again trying to pick the brain of wise Oaxacaroa. Unfortunately, the old man was no longer speaking and instead fell mute with the rest of the people, of which there were many.

The place was crowded with peckish young girls and their tired mothers, the old ones, whom the young ones were too shy to hug, afraid of glimpsing at what their own mortal futures beheld. They too would grow up alone there, just them and their small tribe, continuing the story of their ancestors. They'd find mates and have children who would grow in the old ways of their people, there in the very heart of the mesa plateau. The young ones too would go gray if God so willed it.

Cristobal sensed the disturbance and looked over his shoulder to see what had caused the party to go quiet. The only thing heard was the sound of several roaring fires, casting the shadows of the people onto the walls of the complex, the rooms all vacant for the celebration, by Aatuani's orders.

The marvel of these ruins, and the mystery of these enigmatic people, had been sufficient enough to quell the long desire within the comandante's heart for great adventures and quests. After this, his days of expeditions were over. He'd soon be retired and on his own way home to a country he hadn't seen in forty years, yet everyone knew who he was. To know the conquistador was to know one who never stopped searching for glory. It was a vain endeavor that would consume their minds for the rest of their lives. Unable to shake off the chains of the institution, they'd look back as the shackles of old age gripped them, reminiscing, seeing their younger selves in the mirror, recalling that even though the years of this labor were the hardest and most challenging ones that they had known, they were still grateful for their opportunity and for their chance to grab hold of true immortality.

Cristobal held Soyala's hands, softly clutching them with a tender love that would never be more than dreams. Aatuani marched up to the comandante and addressed him sternly, sure of his voice.

"Rodendros, I'd like to offer you a farewell, you and all of your men," he said, motioning for the comandante to rise from his seat and join him. Raising his voice, he commanded the people to clear out, so that front and center were twenty-eight ragged conquistadors, the comandante included. Only two of them were missing—Dendrick Rodon, who was now on both feet, preparing himself for the worst, and Cristobal, who was still sitting with Soyala, the one who he'd briefly let himself love. It had been so long since he felt anything. He spoke to her without saying anything, but that was okay, because his eyes spoke for him.

Oaxacaroa stood too, and he placed on his head a great headdress, his turquoise jewelry catching the eye even in the darkness of night, the fires casting their light on the level, illuminating the ruins with an ominous orange glare. The drums began to quicken, the enchanting atmosphere surrounding the twenty-eight as they stood there before the swaths of Indigenous. Comandante Redondo proudly called for them to gather themselves into a clean-looking formation, right there in the clearing in front of the complex and their audience. Cristobal looked at Soyala one last time before he left, kissing her on the lips one more time. Disappearing from her life without a second look, it was a love he would remember for the rest of his life. Their short romance would be a happy memory of simpler times.

He hopped to his feet and ran over to join the formation. In his head, Cristobal was readying his own words for the men, the survivors, the men who had endured the harsh rigors at his side, and triumphed when so many others perished in the dangerous New World, becoming statistics in what would eventually become just another old legend.

They would be known to history as "*The Conquistadors of the Mesa Verde.*" Dendrick Rodon would see to that.

Aatuani called for their attention.

"My friends, you wish to leave us, and that makes us very sad. We grew to enjoy the different forms of company, and despite what you see, this place is a palace of solitude. Your presence here was welcome, and we hope the peace you found here will be waiting for you on the other side, to the place where all our souls must journey. To our home at the end of the line."

He raised a cup to toast them.

Everybody present lifted a cheer of some sort, and Aatuani grabbed hold of a torch that was burning brightly with a hot yellow glow. He walked over to the edge of the canyon lip, holding his torch out over the chasm, he looked down, then out into the dark plateau beyond. His red skin glowing from the flame, his black eyes blacker than ever.

Aatuani began to wave the torch with one arm from side to side over his head, looking out toward the vast plateau, and sending arcing flames left and right of him in big wide arc. The torch cut through the air, and after a brief minute of waving the flames, it appeared the fire dance had signaled the start of an unbelievable gesture. It could then be seen by all, that off in the distance, down in the valley, seemingly floating in space, was another flame that could barely be seen, insignificant at first, but growing in size and flailing around in the air in the same arced fashion.

Interpreting the rare event as being an omen, a month ago, the sky watchers hadn't the faintest idea what it could mean. They hoped that maybe the solstice would break the curse of the drought, but when Aatuani showed back up on their doorstep after all these years with his new friends, Oaxacaroa and the other elders knew things were now in motion that they could not control. Things outside the realm of human interference, things that belonged in the realm of spirits.

This event, taking place the night of a full moon on winter solstice, was not a coincidental occurrence but the timely fulfillment of a calculated prophecy.

"In times past, we charted a course through the heavens," He paused, dropping his torch down into the canyon. "We followed the star lines here, made this place our home; now the same star lines will guide you home as well."

"But you won't be sailing back to Spain."

Chapter 26

FARE THEE WELL

Dendrick Rodon had been watching the exchange from nearby, and his first thought was to flee, but the honor inside got the better of him, and he quickly took to arms, running roguishly into the shadows and disappearing from sight completely, stealth being his companion.

Aatuani pointed at the comandante, who was standing there with a look of confusion. "You may try to flee, but most of you will die here alone, to the last man," said the guide coldly, pointing his spear toward the conquistadors, who formed themselves into a tight phalanx. Comandante Redondo stood in the front, a look of gross disgust spread across his face.

"What are you saying? What demon has possessed you?" he shouted, unsheathing his blade. "Have you lost your sense?" he said, fury spreading to every corner of his being. He gave no second chances.

Quickly, Redondo ordered the men to arms, and more than a few of the sorry bastards found themselves without weapons. At that moment, Aatuani pulled from his person a black sculpture with a round base and narrow stem. He blew a powerful breath into the stem, and a horrifying whistle came from out of the bowl, piercing the ears of all with a high-pitched shriek that sounded like the mortified screams of the damned. It pierced the skies, scattering the birds and echoing throughout the canyons, striking absolute fear into the hearts of all who'd had the misfortune of hearing it. They hastily covered their ears, which seemed to do little against the long, shrill call to arms.

This death whistle was the signal for the Indian warriors who had been waiting in the canyon below to start climbing, and within seconds, Cristobal and the others watched as dozens of armed Indian warriors climbed up and over the canyon lip. This answered the question of the missing men. They had been lying in wait at the bottom of the canyon for weeks, waiting for that very call. Once they heard it, they climbed the rock, using vines or roots to pull themselves up, or trusting ladders that were either preexisting, or crudely fashioned more recently. The Indians not only climbed, but they descended. At first, only their silhouettes could be seen; two dozen more came down from above on what was left of the conquistador company. Their faces were visible against the fires and Cristobal saw the rage that burned in their eyes.

They kept coming, up and over the rim, down from up above, surrounding the conquistadors, who after forming their 360-degree protective posture saw that not only were the combatants approaching from up and over the canyon lip, but they were infiltrating from their flanks as well. In minutes, the conquistadors were surrounded by hundreds of indigenous warriors, painted for battle. They stood strong, united against the invaders, who had let their guard down and gotten too comfortable, falling into a hideous betrayal. The savage number surpassed the conquistadors' own three-to-one odds.

All hope was lost, and the men braced themselves for their last stand. Cristobal's mind was racing a million miles a second, as he was not yet prepared to be ripped from the world of the living. He was too young to die.

"You prepare for it, you traitor! You will rot next to Judas, Ephialtes, and Mephistopheles, in the lowest circle of hell for this! You will pay, and these people will pay the cost of your foolish malice! Be damned, coward!"

His gray eyes bloodshot and red, the tears of betrayal streaking his dirty cheeks, hatred for the guide, above all else, could be seen in Comandante Redondo's twisted expression.

Aatuani dropped his spear to the floor and pulled out his blade, pointing its tip toward Rodendros and Cristobal. With his remaining free hand, he held up a closed fist, to hold off his soldiers' attack.

"Remember those lessons, Rodendros? The Romans and the Greeks, do you remember those?" the guide asked him.

Of course, he remembered. They'd been friends for years.

"Remember Troy? The Trojan Horse?" he asked, leaning in toward the comandante. "Do you remember the story of the Trojan Horse, Rodendros?"

The comandante knew it inside and out. He had given the native a private education in the art of war, in exchange for the guide's translation and navigation services. They had their own understandings of the world around them, which they shared at length with one another, always having conversations on the different strategies and war tactics of powerful empires that came before. Having formed an almost brotherly companionship, Comandante Redondo considered the guide his closest friend out there in the wild, which made the pain of betrayal hurt even more.

The conquistadors were surrounded. The women, children, and elders were ushered into the complex, watching from the windows. The conquistadors could not back up, or they'd be in a corner, and they couldn't go forward, or they'd walk off the edge of a cliff. They were completely encircled by armed warriors, with heavy face and body paint, their athletic frames looking more battle-ready than the weakened conquistadors. The conquistadors did have the advantage of technology— their arquebuses, crossbows, and blades, which were far better than the natives' tools of stone, wood, and glass. Their weapons were primitive and old-fashioned, but highly lethal at close range in the hands of the skilled Indian melee fighters, which these mesa Indians appeared to be. There were also archers above, with arrows drawn and nocked, ready to loose at Aatuani's command.

The Trojan Horse? Comandante Redondo recalled the lesson, and young Cristobal was learned enough himself to recall the main idea. The Greeks had infiltrated Troy from the inside in a giant horse, spreading out once inside and opening the gates for the others to come and help them take the city.

The current circumstance appeared as though it were the conquistadors who had been caught in Aatuani's own version of a Trojan Horse, wherein the conquistadors were lured here on purpose, made comfortable, so they'd be disarmed, and when the timing was right, he would execute the plan he'd been scheming since he met the comandante that fateful day. It was revenge from the very start. To bring them here and swallow them from the outside in.

"A reverse Trojan Horse?" Cristobal quietly asked himself.

Aatuani pointed the blade his way. "Say that again, please, Captain, louder, for Rodendros to hear you."

"A reverse Trojan Horse!" Cristobal shouted, unsheathing his blades.

"Exactly." Aatuani dropped his arm down to his side.

The elders removed themselves hastily, retreating to the subterranean chambers for safety. When he lowered his arm, the native warriors started whooping and hollering, making so much noise that their sound was deafening to the tired conquistadors. Poised for the confrontation, they were ready to make their last stand, ready to do what they were meant to do.

The savage army imitated the wild calls of the animals of the plateau, screeching long and low, looking fearsome.

They're not going to make it easy, thought Cristobal.

He looked for Soyala, but he couldn't find her, and if he had, he'd have known her heart was crying out in fear for him. The man who was her very first love in life. She knew his name, and that was it.

The comandante made one last curse to the guide. "May the infant of your own strike you dead!"

Comandante Redondo sprang into action, lunging forward at the guide, who quickly deflected the conquistador's blow, his cursed obsidian blade flying down from above, penetrating deep into the side of the comandante's exposed neck. Cristobal watched in horror as Redondo went rigid, seized up and unable to move. Aatuani removed it quickly, and the blood sprayed out like a fountain from the wound. In his last breath, Comandante Redondo looked to Cristobal with one more thing to say, blood running down and out of his mouth, streaking red his gray beard. Cristobal ran over to Rodendros as Aatuani stood over the two, Javier's hot blood still dripping from his knife.

Rodendros whispered, his voice trembling as he struggled to find the strength for his last words. His gray eyes were now going hazy, as he lay there looking up at the night sky, with the Indians standing on all sides of him, looking down at him without pity.

"If there was no glory to be had of it," he paused, choking painfully, "then whatever was the point?"

And Rodendros was gone.

Aatuani blew the whistle once more, and the real assault began. Arquebus shots rang out into the air, followed by the immediate clashing of swords, spears, and flesh. The scene burst into full-blown chaos as the warriors rushed the conquistadors, circled together, fighting as one against the world coming down on top of them. Cristobal fought with his dual swords, striking down as many of the savages as he could. They fought with ferocity, swinging and chopping wildly, suffering themselves as he too was getting wounded. Arrows grazed him but never landed home. He suffered deep lacerations, a bad chop of an obsidian axe taking a piece of his shoulder. After receiving several stabs, Cristobal lashed out in a tremendous, uncontrollable fury. Looking for the guide amid the fog of war, the sheer volume of fighters meant he needed to furiously defend himself. He clearly saw everything happening around him as if he wasn't really there but merely was watching it happen. He didn't feel any more fear or worry about his own impending death. What was meant to happen was meant to happen. Now, he felt, he was in that moment.

His years of training showed, the countless hours of training were for something. They fell around him, a pile of bloody bodies next to the ground that he and his held courageously, despite being hopelessly outnumbered. The proud Spanish conquistadors fought and killed many of the Indian warriors, but there were not enough of them to hold off the inevitable, and stalling for time wasn't an option. Cristobal looked over at one point during the battle, watching in terror as the fires illuminated the forms of the combatants, climbing up to gain ground, raining down volleys of arrows on the helplessly exposed conquistadors. Cristobal knew in his heart that it was over. His hope began to fade, and he struggled to fight on, demoralized by the despondent odds.

It was then that Dendrick Rodon broke free of his attackers, who had cornered him on the canyon lip and were preparing to force him over its edge, sending the crow master plummeting hundreds of feet down the face to the rocks below. Dendrick did not plan on dying out there, however. He fought on, slashing at ankles, stabbing at black masses in the night. He used his eyes and remaining agility to find the path of least resistance, quickly getting himself the hell out of there and into the dark desert beyond. Call him a coward for not wishing to die alone in the desert for the good of some rich king, but he knew that for him, death would not be at the order of a spineless traitor.

When the fighting started, he broke the line, risking grave injury, but only suffering minor slashes and stabs. The crow master ran as quickly as he could to the cubby where he'd stashed his belongings, should this very event take place and the need to flee arise, and indeed it had. He'd been hit with an arrow in the back and suffered a terrible blow from a rock, which was slung so hard that it broke his arm. The crow master, too high on adrenaline and shock to notice, dodged from cover to cover, looking for his next hiding spot. With his sword in his good hand, he desperately searched with his tired eyes, but they too were weak, failing to accommodate the darkness, even under the full moon of the solstice.

They hunted for Dendrick, but he was carried on the winds by some unknown force that gave him the sight to find his cubby and the willpower to grab his hand-woven basket pack full of journals, artifacts, sketches, and maps, and through the delirium induced by massive blood loss, he staggered on wobbly legs, enduring horribly blurred vision and extreme pain. With no time to make a plan, the crow master started running. To where he did not know, but he kept going, heaving heavily, wheezing for air. He ran as far and as fast he could into the night. He didn't stop, and he didn't look back.

Cristobal fought on, searching for the heathen traitor, but he could not find him. He was being rushed by warriors from every direction, and finally, Cristobal was overwhelmed by them. Amid the scenes of raging fires, Cristobal looked out at the plateau, he saw the chaos in his periphery as they held him down. He heard the cries and shouts of his men as they were being executed, their bodies remorselessly thrown over the side of the canyon. There was nothing he could do, and looking out on that pale blue horizon, he recalled everything that his life had been up to that moment. Tears welled in his eyes as his last moments drew nearer, thinking of his beloved Fiorella, whom he'd be leaving behind. Never able to give her the love she deserved, and never fulfilling the promise he'd made with himself.

The savages held Cristobal down, and he closed his eyes, feeling so let down, just utterly destroyed, devastated, for his great glory was denied him, his chances of achieving it disappearing before his very eyes with every passing second. It was here that he would die, at the hands of one with no sense of integrity or honor. Cristobal ceased his futile struggling, stopped resisting, as two warriors held down each of his limbs. He was tired, and what was meant to be was always meant to be.

Aatuani stepped over young Cristobal, who in his last moments alive, had not even time to acknowledge he was no longer a virgin soldier; he was someone with kills. He did not have time to process it, but it wasn't what he'd built it up to be in his head. It was scary, and it happened quickly. The shouts and confusion, the blood, and agonized expressions of the maimed and dying was horrible to see, and Cristobal suffered too, losing much blood over his several deep lacerations. No one had been given as quick a death as Comandante Redondo, who had spent his whole life living this nightmarish hell. Cristobal felt that if for the last forty years, this was life the comandante knew so well, then the least God could do for him was a fast death. His death took only thirty seconds to a minute. Theirs would be drawn out.

Cristobal looked up at him, the fog of battle billowing past, blowing on the wind. Aatuani gripped tight the blade he'd used to slay the comandante, and he looked down at Cristobal, prostrate and helpless for himself.

Aatuani took that clear moment to help the captain understand why it was they could never exist together. He looked down on him with his buck eyes glowering.

"What Rodendros did years ago to our sister tribes in the south, the destruction of our people, the rape of our societies, our women, the sacking and pillages of our old sacred temples and holy sites, was a blasphemy that I could not allow to happen here, and I would personally see to it that we were not the victims of this saga," said the guide, twiddling the blade.

"You men were brave, the finest soldiers your world could offer up, but you made a mistake in coming here, to this place. It is for that reason, and for the crimes of your predecessors, that you must pay. Our people have endured far too much already." He looked solemn, but he continued.

"May the Lord bless and keep you always, young Cristobal." said the guide.

"Amen." said the captain as a single tear of quiet acceptance rolled past his temple, and into his bloodied hair as his voice broke.

Aatuani knelt down over a defenseless Cristobal, who would no longer struggle, too weak from his injuries, too exhausted from fighting his restraints—the several bloody, sweaty, painted warriors. They too had used almost every ounce of their strength in his detention. All were weary now, from the weeks of waiting for this exact moment, this brief blink in time that would define their future histories. Making his peace, he asked God to absolve him of his inadequacies, to forgive him of his sins, and to save his soul, for he only ever meant to do good in life, only wishing to pass the candle of Christ into the world and to conquer it in his name. Yet, as Cristobal lay there in that dark, lonesome dirt, in that emptiness, sadly he realized the futility of chasing glory and the waste of potential that his life was. Disappointment filled him.

Slowly, Aatuani drove the flaked obsidian edge deep into Cristobal's heart, and quietly, through gritted teeth, Cristobal suffered the pain, the blood coming down the sides of his cheeks, the tears coming down his face. He held his breath, and Aatuani freed one of his arms from the warriors' clutches. Taking a tight hold of Cristobal's hand, the guide bent down, whispering into his ears, "Forgive me God, for I am sorry." Holding his breath, and looking through scared, hazy eyes that were losing their focus, Cristobal struggled to make out the face of his double-crosser, but he looked hard at him anyway, and he found the savage's dark eyes, and he promised himself that he would have his vengeance. But Cristobal couldn't do anything from beyond the grave. No, he was content knowing what goes around comes around, and for this atrocious deed, karma would certainly come for Aatuani and his people. One day, these people would pay for these sins against humanity. Cristobal could've argued their massacre was a karmic payment for the decades-long destruction of the native peoples by the likes of Cortes and the comandante. Karma was a Hindu concept, which Cristobal was not aware of, but his religion had a similar euphemism: "You reap what you sow."

Cristobal would haunt this one's soul from the dead; he'd uttered a million curses at once over the Indian. His dying thoughts turned toward their grim misfortune. They were slain, each and every one, caught outnumbered and underprepared. The people watched with horror from inside the complex walls, and cried painful, agonized wails over the violence they were witnessing.

As Cristobal felt his life force beginning to flee his body, he remembered one more thing. He remembered the only thing that kept his cold heart warm on those long, lonely expedition nights. The only thing that kept him going through it all. He thought of his flower, and she was a marigold, Fiorella. She would go her whole life wondering what happened to him. But maybe that was his greatest memory of all.

His memory of her.

He dropped his head to the side, and with his last ounce of strength, kept his eyes open. As he looked out along the

plateau, a bloody sun was rising, Cristobal saw a powerful
light flying down from it, a light that glowed, as if it were
haloed. He fought to keep his eyes open, fought to make sense
of it. He felt so cold and weak, and he was ready to sleep, but
he felt the pull of that force as it approached him, and he
could not resist watching it glide along easily as it descended
from the dimming stars. The irony was applaudable, but its
energy gave him hope and eased his crying soul.

He struggled in his last breaths, but then the pain was
gone, and hit by a gust of warm wind, he felt at peace. The
light had now drawn close enough for him to make out the
figure standing before him, with his golden-blue hues bringing
the familiarity of family mosaics and the painted faces of
the carnival girls, whom he'd blushed over in youth. The sky
seemed low, like he could reach up and touch the stars if he
extended his hand. The face he could not fully see wore a
shimmering pearled masquerade mask, but when the figure
came up to him, it looked down, and Cristobal looked up,
and he felt he didn't need to speak, nor did the figure need
to express upon its face that it was sorry. They exchanged
these feelings without speaking. The figure was a male, with
a handsome jaw and skin that glowed like gold porcelain.
The radiant figure reached out a pale, anomalous hand to
Cristobal, who now could sense he was not in his own body
anymore. He knew this apparition here had come to take
him away. Where to, he did not know, and he did not ask. He
grabbed the angel's hand, and looking back at the gruesome
scene of his demise, felt the last human sensation he would
ever feel. It had begun to rain.

Watching the people cheer over their dead bodies didn't
upset Cristobal. His worrying was over now; it didn't matter
anymore. Walking with the angel along the star line road,
through the first heavy rains in years, made him feel for the
good people down there, the good women and children, and
Soyala. They shouldn't have to suffer because of spite. He
knew for the Indigenous, it further justified their belief in
sacrifice and ritual, but at the end of the day, they were alive,
and he no longer was. He was free of the inevitable mortal

suffering. He was going to the next world. His second new world in a year.

If this was death, then where was the Lord? He didn't know who this figure was; too many questions. The figure, on sensing Cristobal's nerves, squeezed his wrist firmly, confidently pulling him along softly by the hand, which was a ghostly nothing, just air, light as a feather.

The two of them walked on the air into the rainy night, toward the rare full moon of the winter solstice. The night of his death was written in the stars.

Drifting together on the wind, the pair passed over the mesas and buttes, the latter, were like great candlesticks out there in the empty plateau. At the complex, the grisly cleanup had already begun, with Aatuani being sure to scrub any evidence that proved conquistadors had ever arrived on the plateau. They would forget this part of the story, being uniform in their retelling of it, passing down their version of the history to their children, who would pass it down for generations to come, as they had done for a thousand years before.

The last scene of Cristobal's earthly life came to a close, and as the picture of the mesa plateau began to escape from his sight, the pair vanished into the clouds, now no longer present in the plane of the living. As the nighttime became dusk, they were walking closer to the stars, to the place where all our souls go in the end; back into the pupil of their Father's eyes.

Chapter 27

BEFORE YOU GO

In a different time and space, all he felt was a thought. It was the opposite of darkness, a soft white light; it felt like the plasmic form his energy had now assumed was being bathed in luxurious rolling silks. Being led by the hand of the figure, slowly they disintegrated back into the world without ego, into a world of learning and creation, to a place with a warm familiarity. It felt like home, and he knew then that all the worries of the human world were long behind him.

He followed the glowing figure through a long tunnel, not a dark tunnel, but a bright, crystalline wormhole. In the soft white light, the golden energy nudged him forward, and Cristobal, still getting a feel for whatever this was, did not know how he was moving or where he was going; he simply felt as though every fiber of energy in him was relaxed, being gently pulled on an easy current, devoid of any sensory stimuli, parallel only to the quantum vacuum energy of the cosmos.

They were pulled, both their light energies traveling through the divine passageway. Cristobal no longer remembered his Earthly appearance; he was now a golden glowing form as well. Beside him was what he recognized to be a friendly soul, who gave him telepathic encouragement when he felt like he needed it. When they came through to the other side, Cristobal waited for the figure, feeling antsy, ready to get moving, because with a clairvoyant foresight, he believed he already knew the way, and it was burning him that he had to wait for this guy who he knew but could not name.

He felt a tremendous and indescribable peace wash over him in the figure's presence. There were still emotions, and his understanding of those emotions was elevated. He did not get bothered by terrors of paranoia in this place, and the dilemmas that he used to wrestle with in his mortal mind for hours now seemed like pointless squandering of precious time. Cristobel went through the entire spectrum of complete emotion every second of every minute in this place, until a velvet cream came from the nebulous fabric beneath, climbing up his energized form, and cleansing him, releasing from Cristobal the anger and rage he had toward the guide, until against his own will, the burden of hate was gone.

His soul did not yet grasp how the spatial mechanics of this dimension worked. A place where time was not linear but cyclical. It had to be cyclical; only then could it repeat itself over and over again. Eternity never stops; it is straight, and definite, with no room for fluctuation. Eternity is forever; time is not. Eternity is an immeasurable unit, but time moved on, and if it moved in a loop, it meant now he was on the down loop, coming around again.

They entered the impossibly vast library of knowledge, which was not a great work of architecture but a shapeless space, and all of the wisdom of time immemorial was there to be plucked, if one knew how to gain admittance. It could've been described as a private lecture hall in the clouds, where one watched one's own life over again on the screen of the heavens, where under strict scrutiny, one rewatched those tests of character, those battles that were fought inside, all of which are meant for something. One had all eternity to spend in this realm, reconciling the comedies and tragedies of their stay in Earth's harsh mortal domain, but Cristobal was not here to stay, as he had already been here once before and reconciled with God the sins of this life, when he returned to the world of the dead in the middle 1540s, after Aatuani the savage cruelly punctured his heart with an obsidian blade cursed a million times over by Aztec death whispers. He and the figure went much deeper then, as that was his true dying, and his true entry into the spirit world.

Now, Cristobal was seeing the familiar shade again, but this time uninvited, in a visitation. The figure, with its superior intellect, knew already what magic Cristobal used to achieve the world of the unliving. The figure knew that it was Cristobal's successor soul, Clyde, who sought the answers to the secrets he was not yet ready to know. Clyde knew the figure knew about Ms. Claudia, and if his ego existed, he'd have shrunk down in his humble embarrassment.

It spoke again to him directly.

"You wish to see the resolution of your fate again?" the golden apparition asked in a bright, masculine voice that sounded more youthful, as Clyde heard it clearly ringing out in his mind. Clyde was scared then, in his dream state, that his private thoughts were floating away, being taken by the figure, drifting somewhere he was afraid to go but knew he had to. The figure told him not to be afraid, that it wasn't mad at him, and then his fears ceased. The being was taking possession of his psyche, to show him what he wanted to glimpse. With bravery, and without hesitation, Clyde told the voice he would be eager to see it.

"I was with you then, and I am with you now, Cristobal. We've traveled together a long time, but before you go, may you witness the reverberations of your sacrifice. Remember well the lessons of your life, for they are yours to live and yours alone to learn."

Cristobal let himself go, sucked into the mind of this higher form.

"Watch." it said, the speech evaporating into a breathy whisper. They ceased their unfamiliar buoyant wandering, as it could only be described, since it was not as if they were physically moving. They used no muscles, for there was no need for strength in this place. He had no outstretched limbs, no legs to stride forward or backward. They existed with all that was, residing in the very air of the world.

After suffering the painful trials of life's endless labors on Earth, they arrived in paradise. Cristobal saw then, the garden of the Lord, an endless land with towering waterfalls and glistening champagne cascades, the tallest mountains, and fields with every plant, tree, fungus, and herb known to the world. Species long extinct from Cristobal's world lived, and beyond the garden, Cristobal took in the sight of several crystalline kingdoms, with towering spires of the finest marble, which emitted a light cosmic frequency that went out and vibrated against every living thing, connecting the energy of all. The architecture of the otherworld is not one to be confined to the human conception of angles and geometrics. The spirit world was all-encompassing; it was the whole fabric of fillable space over volume and time. The quartz crystal Corinthian pillars lining the massive gate were ten times greater in diameter than Pompey's, the work of the Egyptians.

There was a shimmering silver-hued ambiance to this ethereal place.With the apparition leading him now up to God's front door, and with no sense of that cursed ego, that same glory-seeking ego that drove so many other brave young souls in time toward death instead of their dreams, he understood then, the immortal renown that came from being a hero was an earthly endeavor, an endeavor of vanity, and that vanity no longer existed.

The figure hovered its energy over Cristobal's phantom form, running amorphous fingers over him. Cristobal saw in his thought vision the crow master, Dendrick Rodon, blazing across the high plateau on the run for days, dodging capture from his pursuers. With the basketful of maps, journals, and sketches on his back, galloping full stride on Cristobal's own Simora, Rodon carried what was left of the expedition on his back. Cristobal felt love in his heart for the man, and for the beast, knowing Simora's loyalty to be so true. She waited for him, and Dendrick, the good friend that he was, would take good care of her.

Her golden blonde mane was unbrushed and wild, blowing ferociously in the wind as she carried on her back the only friendly face she knew out there in that dry, lonely land. He hunched down low over her, and she ran with a mighty swiftness that did not disturb her wounded rider. For days and days, she kept this pace, going without pause, weaving in and out of the low-lying valleys and canyons they'd crossed merely weeks ago. Dendrick, knocking on the very door of death itself, in and out of consciousness, still managed to get Cristobal's Simora to sleep or eat some dead grass every couple of days. He'd stop at any watering hole they could find, but there was no real food for either of them. Healing from his wounds, the crow master and Simora found their way back to the great river, where he was able to seek asylum within the thinly stretched forces of Captain Fernando de Malaga.

Simora stayed on the banks, following the reformed river posse for several months while the work continued. While Dendrick healed, fighting off fever and infection, the sailors finished their job. They floated down the river in crude rafts, which hardly appeared seaworthy. After several more weeks, they wrapped up their work on the river, having navigated and mapped many of its channels and tributaries completely. They had been busy since day one, with Fernando embracing the full force of his great responsibility. It was a damn near impossible mission. It became known to history as "The Great Pecos River Journey."

The next vision showed him his comrade, Fernando, promoted to the rank of comandante himself, surrounded by much military dog-and-pony theatrics and the all-important commanders in their costumes of medals and ribbons, showing off their impressive accolades. The masses of aristocrats and political demagogues cheered for him, applauding his accomplishments and his service. Cristobal was happy for his friend, to see he would live a long and prosperous life well after everything they had been through.

Cristobal felt immense gratitude for the family that Fernando would have. Deep within his heart, touching every corner of his emotions, he swelled with pride at Fernando's greatest achievement, which would happen many years later, as he embraced retirement from sea life and began to dive deep into the open ocean of his own uncontainable imagination.

Next, Clyde saw strange texts, in strange scripts, written over wide and colorful banners. Beautiful women of Spanish blood were dancing complicated steps with each other in colorfully frilled pastel gowns. Garishly dressed musicians were playing loud, languid melodies. He saw boys playing with girls, enjoying their toys, reading their books, and their parents, who kept a strict eye upon them. His people were always keen to watch over their own, and seeing familial harmony in a world farther in time from the one that Cristobal had known was an encouraging vision for his soul to see. Not only had he witnessed the flight of the crow master from the savage Indians, but he watched the evolution of his culture. Within the scene, written on the banners, were the words that marked the historic occasion. It was a small town, vibrant and alive, rich with lively celebration. Cristobal experienced in phantom the aromas of every ingredient, he clearly heard the music, and he saw the people for who they were. Over by the laguna, the banners read, "Welcome to Redondo Beach."

When Cristobal's spirit read those words, for the first time since arriving here in the realm of souls, he felt negative emotions. He felt the disappointment then, watching as his life and his dreams were prematurely snatched from him. He wanted to hate the guide, but a part of his former self gave him resistance, the good side of his heart. The part of him that did not wish to hate, but the principled soul, the true soul of Cristobal, that was troubled by morality always, only wished the world possessed a little more integrity and much more humanity.

Comandante Javier "Rodendros" Redondo, had a city named after him? It was in fact his own distant blood relatives who did their best to make sure it happened that way, to honor the sacrifice of their own martyred patriarch. Cristobal saw the glory and praises the people were singing of the comandante, and he asked the figure with thought and thought alone, how could it be?

Then he learned of the crow master's fate. After the expedition was over, Dendrick Rodon had gone into a deep state of reclusion, finding his only solace from the trauma of his experiences in the bottom of a glass or in some foreign drug that buzzed him just the same. He did not wish to speak on it; he did not wish to reminisce. He wished only to forget.

Dendrick and Fernando made a pact on the river together. While Dendrick was healing from his wounds, and Fernando was finishing his final drafts, the two of them agreed that when the time was right, they would tell their full, unabridged story to the world. But it wasn't shared until many years later, years after Comandante Fernando was laid to rest. And while it was fate that would allow Dendrick on his deathbed to produce an old, leatherbound tome, with old, coffee-colored pages, each page covered from top to bottom in the fine cursive script that had kept Dendrick's eyes so sharp all those years, and even now in his old age.

The oratory he gave the Crown in 1549 went like this. The conquistadors had come over on the beautiful *La Madre Rosa* galleon ship, with several other ships dutifully flying their motherland's flag. Dendrick Rodon recounted the long, arduous sea voyage for the Crown, recounting the frightening trek through the thick jungles, where they first joined up with Comandante Redondo, and the primary focus of their mission: to navigate and map the river, which they did as thoroughly and completely as they could. That was the story he gave to his superiors and to the inquiring minds of young boys dreaming of being conquistadors. He made no mention of the complex, or the Indians.

Even though this entirely contradicted the truth, since the truth was that the comandante was not a part of navigating or mapping the river, but was leading the ground party toward the ruins instead.

To spare their good names and protect them from living life as defeated outcasts in shame and exile, Dendrick changed the story to accommodate certain things. It was easier on everyone if he left out the part where the conquistadors were slain down to the last man and that they were slain because they were glory hunting.

Fernando and Dendrick both got their stories straight and kept them straight for the rest of their lives. Dendrick made sure he rehearsed what he was going to say before repeating his story in front of a panel of high-ranking Spanish officials, investigating him for obvious reasons. During his arraignment in military court, Dendrick Rodon told the story. They joined Comandante Redondo on the river, working with him to map the treacherous rapids, channels, and inlets of the great rushing waters, and when it was over, Rodendros got smallpox and died. Half of them stayed, and the other half came back home.

"I can only speak for myself," was his response when asked the question, "What did you see over there?"

Miraculously, the Spanish government bought it completely, and for Dendrick being the sole survivor of the ground party, he brought back enough of a surplus of incredible findings of his own, which, next to Fernando's impressive work on the river, was enough to keep the officials from asking many more questions. They ceased to examine it further, trusting that the military would smooth things out. They were terribly sorry to hear about the good Comandante Redondo, who succumbed to smallpox after living a life of such famous achievement. Rodendros accomplished much, and it was a tragedy he was taken the way that he was. Given that he was a national hero, they honored Comandante Javier "Rodendros" Redondo back home in Madrid, where he first found his bullfighting spirit, which was the trademark of the man.

However, the truth of their encounter within the Mesa Verde Plateau (as history would eventually call it), was not discovered until much later, and even then, no one knew for sure if it was the absolute truth, since the manuscript was the crow master's own brainchild. Dendrick Rodon had never been the sanest individual.

When a distant descendant of Dendrick's bloodline was fumbling through an old, beaten-up war footlocker in their farmhouse root cellar, nosily looking around, the young boy found a leather journal with coffee-colored pages, with that same beautiful handwriting.

After decades of silence, the long-lost account of their emboldened story, with the many different characters and conflicts, was written in the final months of Dendrick's old age and was a secret family heirloom that was passed down from patriarch to patriarch as the line descended through time, following the crow master's death.

When the boy read the book, he read the entirely true and grave recounting of that ill-fated expedition of conquistadors, who'd come to the New World in search of their great glories.

Who were being guided through a vast, untamable desert by their enigmatic Indigenous guide, a tall ranger of the land, who promised them great discovery in the form of ancient and mysterious ruins. They journeyed hard and relentlessly, eventually finding their way to the remarkable complex with its many chambers and passages. Once there, they were disarmed by the hospitality of their new hosts and made themselves too comfortable too soon. Their lack of situational awareness led to them being surrounded slowly from the outside, which they failed to notice.

In the end, their guide betrayed them, calling a surprise attack on the unsuspecting conquistadors. They found themselves trapped and cornered, with nowhere to go. They were then savagely cut down, every one. The narrator of this book claimed to be the sole survivor, recounting what the author himself prefaced in the beginning to be "A Fictitious Account of the Spanish/Indio Conflict in the New World." Not only was Dendrick's book meant to tell their story, but it was meant to explore strategy and war psychology from several different angles, restructuring the logic entirely. Constructing his book with intention, the texts explored the various themes of alliance, trauma, love, karma, and betrayal, without one ever knowing. Inside the cover was a stamp, which depicted an Ouroboros, a symbol he became familiar with later in life. "D.R. Rodon" was signed in fine red script by the crow master himself behind the front cover. The men of his family read the book, each one passing it down to the son after him, and so on, never sharing the story of their progenitor with anyone outside of the family. They too had questions about those who came before, where and whom they had come from. Reading the words of their distant father, his distant kin, only separated from Dendrick by the thin veil of death, were better able to understand the kind of man he was, by having undeniable proof of his imagination, his intelligence, and his personal philosophies. His words they used as a tool to better understand themselves, and from beyond the grave he watched, as they sat puzzled for hours deciphering his cryptic words, generation after generation.

Dendrick's emotional words made the reader feel the pain of that great betrayal on the Mesa Verde.

The crow master, a man who loved puzzles, left behind his masterwork in the form of a book that told a story that happened and never happened at the same time.

Dendrick Rodon would forever keep to himself the true identities of the men of their company. Claiming his work to be a work of fiction made it easier for everybody to accept the slayings of the poor conquistadors who, after such a hard road, were robbed of their reward.

Since there was no proof that the massacre had or had not happened, and there was never a spoken word about it after the pact Dendrick and Fernando made, as loyal brothers do, they kept their silence until they completed their mortal sentences.

Dendrick Rodon lay on his deathbed when he gave the world the conquistador's special tale, and when the crow master drew his last breath, the fact that their story was truth and not fiction became lost.

And so a work of fiction it remained.

And a fact of fiction it was.

The figure broke its silence to elaborate further the portents of that vision, the deeper knowledge within.

"He sought to protect the honor of your names, while doing your story an incredible justice. Yet you are hurt for not receiving that earthly glory you so wished for? Do you understand now why it was you could never attain this?"

"No," was the only thing Cristobal could muster.

The figure, radiant and omnipresent, strongly intimidated Cristobal, but it didn't mean to. "Do not be intimidated, Cristobal, I have been with you in lives past and will be with you for many more to come. You don't remember me, but the stories of your line, as it descends through time, are being written at this very moment, and have been my sole labor since the dawn of humanity."

Cristobal was both comforted and confused by those words; again he was moved across the wide expanse of the entire emotional spectrum. The figure said to Cristobal that it had one more thing to show him before it sent him away. For this, the figure focused its clean energy over Cristobal's shapeless glow.

The final vision from the figure was of Soyala, the native concubine he took for his love within the complex. Their late nights of innocent love led to her motherhood. Through intense contractions, she birthed a healthy boy. The first boy born with Spanish blood in the tribe. Cristobal made her a mother, and she felt deeply for him because of it, such as she had never known before. Attracted to his youth and his bravado, yet too, how very polite and gentle he could be. She remembered Cristobal as being a handsome man, and the heartbreak Soyala felt when Aatuani took the life of her lover pained her more than her words could say. Her own people had taken the life of her child's father and countless others, soon to be fatherless. A future generation of mixed-blood babies who would never know their fathers but would be raised by the whole village. Her last act of defiance was one of simple spite.

Soyala did not speak Spanish, nor did she need to know what his words really meant, for they communicated with their eyes more than their words, but she remembered his name. The only things about his identity, which Soyala carried in her imagination and dreams for the rest of her life, would be his full given name; Captain Cristobal Noriel Trujillo, and the memory of what he looked like as he was being executed.

Cristobal bore no grudge against those people who treated them well. They were unaware of what Aatuani was doing in the very shadows of broad daylight, orchestrating the deception, playing for both sides. From the moment he met Rodendros, he knew he was set on the path of revenge against the Spaniards, and it was his own evil aspirations that were to blame. It wasn't the will of the elders, although they too had colluded with the guide by not standing up to him, letting him run ungoverned, calling to arms his long-scattered people, bringing the warriors home once more from their diaspora, that they might dispel the invaders and avenge the toppled civilizations of Latin America. While living among the people, albeit a short, three-week retreat, Cristobal was able to observe the natives closely, coming to appreciate their

agrarian way of life. It gave them the freedom to practice
their crafts and be creative. They were hospitable, opening up
to the weary conquistadors their home and hearth, feeding
them, and sharing the stories of the legends of their people.
Cristobal was not mad at them one bit, and he respected
them tremendously, for carving a way of life for themselves in
that deadly madeira desert, where the odds of survival were
stacked against all living organisms.

Not wanting to choose between the path on the left or the
path on the right, common sense told her to go for the path
in the middle, and she gave her son the first Spanish name
the mesa would see, Cristobal's middle name, Noriel.

Since he was the very first son of Spanish-Indian blood,
Noriel too would have a strand of fate woven with the traitor,
Aatuani. The vision faded, and the image of Soyala nursing
their baby boy on her breast, the future of his blood, vanished,
but Cristobal knew his name would live on.

"That boy will attempt the unthinkable, when his mother
tells him who his father is. It is he who will carry forth the
fame of the name Cristobal. Your story was meant to be
something different, Cristobal. You are a dignified spirit,
highly sensitive to the energy fields around you, that is just
your heart. But without your history, none of your future
would have been possible." He paused, and Cristobal felt a
weird sensation pulsating around him.

"Wait, No, please! I have more questions! Please!" Cristobal
pleaded. "Fiorella? The Comandante!" Cristobal asked, his
energy desperately searching the figure for a hint of an answer.

"Yes, you'd do well to remember Fiorella. Remember them
all if you can," it said to him.

Cristobal did not know what that meant then, but he would
remember her because of the figure's hallowed words.

"I beg of you your name, please! Before I go!", he paused.
"Must I go?" he asked.

The figure then expressed its resounding love with a light
pulse glowing blue in the middle of its golden form. A warm
shroud surrounded Cristobal, blanketing him in a cream-
colored wash.

"I am Myrodoceus, your spirit guide," the figure said, releasing him from its psychic hold.

"Now rise again, Clyde! Be born again! Go! Rise! *Awake!*" Myrodoceus shouted, commanding with so much authority that Cristobal fell backward from fear, back into the crystalline wormhole from where the darkness had initially given way to the soft light of the afterlife. He opened his eyes to see that he was back in Ms. Claudia's basement. He was Clyde LeBouef once more, in the world of New Orleans, Louisiana.

No longer unconscious or unaware, no longer in the world of imagining distant memories of deserts or conquistadors or Indians, he was now back on the circle sofa with the hookah burning cherry tobacco and weed on the table. He was in a state of paralysis, still too weak. Ms. Claudia was watching the television in the corner of the bar, paying him no attention. The images of the world he'd just seen had been incredibly vivid while he was inside the recollection, but now those memories were fading, and the longer Clyde stayed there unmoving, the less clear the memories became. Clyde lay there motionless in a pool of cold sweat with terrible body aches, his heart beating incredibly fast. He was terribly anxious as he struggled to make sense of his surroundings. The textures and smells all seemed new and fresh to him. He had yet come to terms with his completely shattered sense of reality.

"Myrodoceus" was all he could remember at the current moment. He did not remember the details of the crystal palaces or the intricate carvings adorning the grand marble pillars, nor could he remember what the figure of Myrodoceus looked like or how many rooms were in the complex. All he had taken back with him was his name, and the vaguely foggy memories of an incredible story that was the work of its creator's great imagination. He couldn't move, still stuck, his faculties temporarily in a state of hibernation.

"Help," he called out in a quiet, raspy voice.

Ms. Claudia did not react. Unaware, consumed by the flickering color box.

He called out again. Louder this time. "Help?" He buckled weakly.

She paid no mind his way, listening to the voices on the television as she talked away on the corded bar phone.

"Excuse me!" Clyde shouted.

Claudia jumped up, startled at his awakening. She hopped up straight away and came right over to his side. He didn't even remember what she was supposed to look like.

"Oh my God," she said, looking at the ghostly pale face with sunken eyes and concave cheeks. It was the face of a man who's died.

Died, and come back.

Chapter 28

THE CATHARSIS OF

CLYDE LEBOUEF

Clyde felt incredibly drained as he managed to sit himself upright. Claudia was sitting next to him, befuddled because she had not snapped her subject out of his trance. Rather, unknown to her, it was Myrodoceus who had awakened him. She didn't know if that would cause any after-effects in the subject's psyche, but he was coming to, and that was all that mattered to her.

"What did you see?" she asked him, as he, with wild, wide eyes, looked at her as if she was asking him the obvious.

"Are you freakin' kidding me, lady! I gotta run!" Clyde exclaimed, as he struggled to his feet, staggering at first. She tried to help him gain his balance, but it was a struggle. His human body longed for that feeling of weightless bliss he'd experienced in the spirit world, but his time there was so short, he couldn't even begin to reimagine what it felt like.

Claudia shouted for him to get some rest as Clyde bolted up the stairs and out the door leading to the lobby, running out into the street, where there was no drizzle or breeze, just a calm evening. It was late, and he couldn't yet process the events of his experience. Rocked to the very foundations of his core, feeling moved with sacred information, having peeked behind the curtains of life and death, he now believed he held the answer to one of life's greatest questions: Was there life after death? Yes, there was, his burden of proof validated by reliving the very memories of a life he once lived.

He ran up the street, so excited he was fumbling around his pockets for his keys, trying to remember exactly where he had parked. Clyde looked like a ghost in the world of the living, stricken by a terrible pounding migraine, the mental circus taking its toll, searching with every one of his senses the components of life happening all around him—the changing streetlights, the still-wet pavement from a night of rain, the frog in the gutter, the concrete a gritty shade of mousse, the rhythmic thump of his feet hitting the ground as his breathing began to quicken with the sense of panic, as he could not find his truck anywhere.

Finally, he remembered it, tucked in a lot somewhere off the main drag. He approached the door and made ready his keys, rubbing the sleep out of his eyes. Clyde climbed inside and sat on the cool leather seats, his hot breath forming a cloud as he exhaled inside the frosted car. He started the engine and sat there for a second, letting it warm up.

His mind was racing as he recalled the vivid images of the mesa, the faces of his friend the comandante, not recalling in such detail the many hazards of the journey, but remembering well the great betrayal of Aatuani. Remembering any of it was a blessing, as a great deal of what had transpired within the window of observation would be lost now to the woken memory. However, Clyde could recall the situations that led to the downfall of his last life.

He remembered the visions of Myrodoceus, in which his native concubine, Soyala, bore him a son, who would fulfill the dream of the father. It was paradoxical; none of it made any actual sense, but to have lived a scene so extraordinary, the only feasible explanation would have been that the story of the conquistadors of the Mesa Verde was an autobiographical one, and for this, Clyde could not rationalize the many different facets of the story of his predecessor. The love of Fiorella lost with the expedition, it would be Soyala who would see that the legacy of Cristobal Trujillo was not lost, rather, in the twilight of his death, she decided it would be the catalyst that ushered in a new age for their people.

How he had these thoughts, he did not know. Why was he still so connected to the thoughts and feelings of Cristobal? Why did he feel so strongly for Cristobal, as if it were Clyde personally who stood there atop the canyons, watching the warriors climb over the canyon lip, or climb down from above, raining down their arrows and spears on the scared soldiers, who'd not expected an attack in the slightest. That lack of attention to detail, not listening to his gut, he would never again fall victim to evil, to suffer a betrayal such as that again; he would never be able to trust anyone. In his truck, which was finally warmed up enough, he decided that the sole determiner of his own story—of his past, his present, and his future—would be him. He'd control his own fate, lest others control it for him.

He pulled out of the lot with the tears running down his face as he felt the heavy burden of Cristobal come to surface in his soul, and he felt an angry type of sadness. Now understanding, it was never Voodoo, or brujeria that Ms. Claudia specialized in, but something else, something that had yet to have a name. Something that was actually, in a way, scarier than Voodoo, because it had shown long-hidden truths that required deep introspection and meditation to unlock its secrets.

He drove the speed limit, eyes glazed over as he turned the radio up to quiet his thoughts. Clyde drove and reflected and determined that he felt that he was screwed over twice, in not just one but two lives.

Cristobal, the youthful pride of the Spanish Crown, brave beyond comparison, was more than ready to take the world on with an admirable fervor, but he was unjustly slain, before he felt his time should have expired. Forever robbed of his opportunity for fame and glory. The soul of Cristobal, however, sought for himself another opportunity—to try to again achieve that which he could not, and for that, Cristobal had become Clyde, an admirable soldier and capable leader.

It was in South Vietnam, in those familiar horrifying jungles, that Cristobal sought out the enemy, commandeering the weaker parts of Clyde's soul to carry him through the fire of combat and the fog of war. He'd been there before.

Recklessly throwing himself into harm's way on more occasions than he should have. The courage of Clyde, with the gusto of Cristobal, earned him many accolades, medals, and decorations, but it was his own people in the end who denied him the hero's welcome he'd dreamed of for centuries. Thus, for the second time, denying his soul what he most deeply desired.

Clyde drove on into the night, unable to concentrate completely. Breaks in his thought let in thoughts that were not his own. Recalling the thoughts of his predecessor, he shook his head to knock loose the craziness. Gripping the steering wheel so hard his knuckles went white, Clyde further pieced together the different circumstances of his new debacle. He needed to make right the relationship that, in this life, was most important to him; he needed to fix his marriage with Santina.

The love of his previous life never came to be. The life he'd pictured at home with the beautiful Fiorella could never have come to be, and he knew it was not destined for him *then*, but—and he felt this in his heart—the woman he loved *now*, with every fiber of his being, his Santina, must actually be his lost love of old, Fiorella. He thought about the two, remembering long and hard the face that he had forgotten while he was trailblazing in the Americas. The spectacle of her was one to behold, and through the pained lenses which Clyde looked through life, he momentarily was free of all doubt and remorse. Remembering now the true purpose of his life, which was to guide and lead his wife and family, a role not offered to him in his incarnation as Cristobal. Cristobal was never a father, not while he was living, anyway. His unliving blood pulsed in unborn life, but he never got to experience fatherhood.

Clyde focused on the street signs, observing the different pictures and diagrams, simultaneously picturing the ancient petroglyphs and markings that served them in the plateaus, aiding the Indians' observation of passing time and their observation of the moving celestial bodies. These things Clyde did not understand seemed to present themselves in the front of his thoughts, as if they had been burned into his retinas, recollecting well the images of the towering buttes and the mystery of the star lines. Clyde struggled with his altered vision of reality; he felt as if he could talk to Cristobal if he wanted to, and of course he could. The spirit of Cristobal was the spirit of Clyde.

He could hardly concentrate behind the wheel as he drove home. He felt something deep inside of him that begged him to pull over, so he pulled over to the shoulder and shut off the truck, twisting the key and pulling it out. Clyde sat, with no breeze coming through his open windows. The cars passed by with the sound of the rubber whizzing past as it glided on the wet pavement. Shutting his eyes and grabbing at the sides of his head, Clyde was hearing and seeing things. The new fabric he'd been gifted to work with was too much to handle at once. He started to laugh, and the laughter gave way to hysterical sobs of deranged, lunatic laughs and bawling cries, a mixture of the two, as he fought the memories back. He heard Myrodoceus's voice in his head.

"Get home."

Clyde snapped himself together and pulled back onto the road, following the streetlights, reminiscing on his final moments with the Native, whom he had just as many questions about. The memory of the utter peace in the presence of the figure, the very vision of whom gave Clyde the hope that there was something more to all this, it gave him hope that it all meant something.

His humble home was waiting for him, just as it was when he left it several hours earlier. It was the strangest feeling, because Clyde felt he'd been awake for several years, living every memory of his old life in detail under Ms. Claudia's hypnotic spell. He really owed her an apology, and he said to himself he would make it right once he was thinking straight. Oddly, he noticed, he wasn't dying for a drink. In fact, he hadn't thought about booze once since waking up. He didn't desire the bottle anymore; it occluded his senses and denied him peace at home. The clouds parted, and the light began to come through, with the sun rising on a new day.

The curse of alcoholism was a weight lifted off of Clyde's shoulders on that day, and for that, he was always grateful, to whoever it was up above watching over him. That question, he found, was still yet unanswerable. But the angels must have been singing, because he heard the most beautiful birdsong.

His normally coffee-colored eyes glowed in wheat-colored gold under the majesty of a bayou sunrise. Clyde nodded his acceptance, because unlike his normal dreams, he now possessed a lifetime's worth of wisdom to unpack from the dreams of his past. Clyde's thoughts were very unorganized as his mind worked tirelessly to compartmentalize the memories and thoughts of both Clyde and Cristobal's separate personalities. Keeping separate the traits of the one that the other did not possess, or the vices of one compared to the other, they were indeed two different people, but they were also the very same soul. This Clyde knew. He didn't know how he knew, but he felt strongly the deja vu when he opened his truck door and stepped outside.

Clyde's head had been pounding, a terrible migraine that he assumed to be a Voodoo hangover. It was really just his brain working twice as hard as normal to take in the new information of Cristobal's life. It was a lot for the soft, mushy organ to process. He wasn't even close to being ready for Santina to burst out the screen door, at what must've been just before 6:00 a.m., because he'd yet to hear the morning rooster's crow. Then, on cue, he heard it as he thought it, which was strange. At 0600 hours, Santina burst through the screen door, stepping onto the porch to see her husband standing there blankly, with his keys in his hands and a very tired look on his face.

It took him less than three seconds to recognize her as she ran up to him, hugging him close, feeling the scrape of his five o'clock shadow against her face as she kissed him. She held him close, and he hugged her back.

"I'm sorry, baby. Really, I'm so sorry. I'll be better, I promise, I'm a reborn man today, I tell you. Reborn today, you watch." Clyde said, running his hands up to her cheeks and feeling her hair behind her nape. He looked her in her eyes and recognized the immortal eyes of his beautiful Lady Fiorella. It was her; they had ended up together after all. They were both crying while they stood there in the driveway, knowing that love would hold them together, and that when they found themselves slipping away from each other, love would bring them back.

Clyde kicked off his boots at the door, stepping inside. The place was tidy, very clean. It was a slow Sunday, so he was hoping to have a day of rest following his deep mental journey, but first he went to the bathroom, undressed, took a shower, and made himself ready for bed, emerging from the bathroom in his pajama robe, a fog of moisture sweeping out into the hallway as he opened the door. The sergeant cleaned up well, coming down the stairs with bounce in his step.

"Aren't you going to bed?" Santina asked as Clyde walked into the living room with his hair gelled, despite just showering.

"Santina, sweetie, I think it's time we start packing," he said flatly.

"Packing?" she said, rolling her eyes at him, as she always did.

"Yeah, packing really, let's move. Let's start over. Let's go somewhere neither one of us has been," he said. She looked over her shoulder.

"There ain't nothing for us here; there's nothing for me in Bossier. Life is out *there*, and we could use a good change," he said, coming over to grab hold of his woman's hands.

"As long as we're together, that's all I care about." said Clyde. Santina was struggling to halfway hear the television and Clyde's rambling.

"I'd consider it surely, but where are we going to go?" she asked, wondering what exactly was going through his mind. Her husband had crazy ideas in the past, back when they were young, before the war, back when life was simple.

"We could go live with my brother Dean."

That got Santina's attention, because Dean lived in San Francisco, next to the beach. He had started a window cleaning business after he left the war savagely maimed, but that aside, he was doing quite well, from what Clyde could tell given their limited correspondence. She thought of stretching out her short legs on the sandy beach, basking in the sun, working on her tan. These things always appealed to her, since she had been stuck in the bayous of Louisiana her whole life, never getting to leave the state where her family had chosen to lay down their roots.

"Don't joke around with me Clyde LeBouef because I'll move to San Francisco tomorrow, you just say the word!" she said squeezing his hands in hers with powerful force.

"Well, I could get a job working with him, I'm sure," he winced, "and once you finish school, we could move. Then we could both get good jobs; we'd really be making a fresh start. Maybe we should, change can be good."

Clyde felt like he needed some sunshine, and the more he thought about it, the more the idea appealed to him. He had always heard a lot about California, and it wasn't like he was a bum; he could handle himself out there on the streets, and he would always put Santina first, always. She was his number one.

She'd yet to ask him how his evening with Ms. Claudia went, but he wasn't going to divulge anything unless she asked, preferring to keep to himself the truth of their relationship and how they were destined for each other in a different place and time, centuries ago. Their love could never have come to be, though, because he had left her for the conquests and expeditions. He went off with the glory-seekers, and he paid the price for it once. He wasn't going to risk losing her again. He loved Fiorella, but he *really* loved Santina. He could caress her, make love to her. Santina was Fiorella, and they had found each other again, like needles in a haystack, but the needles were all the souls across time, and the haystack was time itself. Clyde inferred that as being fate, just another strange coincidence within the blueprints of divine planning.

Santina was holding his hands in hers and rubbing her red-painted thumbnail gently against the palm of his hand.

"I go where you go, Clyde. I'm yours; we're a team, and it's going to stay that way," she said, poking her head down to look up and into his eyes, which were fixed on the table.

"Okay, baby," he said, and the two of them shared a short, sweet moment together in silence at the kitchen table. They looked at each other once more, the connection between them like the great river's connection to the vast, blue sea, opening up before Clyde a lifetime of possibilities, wonders, pleasures and pains that he wanted to share with nobody but this woman right here.

"All right then, let's get packing!" Clyde said, retracting his hand back from Santina's grasp and clapping his hands together. He went around the house gathering empty boxes, empty bags, empty totes, tubs, crates, or buckets, and he started to pack them all up with personals. In the bags he tossed the junk he felt he no longer needed; it could go to the Salvation Army. He got rid of clothes, old toys, cards, trinkets, and other useless possessions. Objects with small personal value he chose to part with too. He was completely decluttering his new life.

Santina watched her husband, who, to her knowledge, must have been running on fumes from being up all night long, as he moved about the house, cleaning as he went along, tidying up, packing things, throwing things away. She helped him too, but she reminded him that they couldn't go anywhere until the summer, when she graduated.

"It's okay, baby, I know. We're just doing some spring cleaning," he said. She understood, and she knew he understood too, that in time, they could start their new lives together.

In the wet bayou night, the cicadas and crickets made a fantastic ensemble, suitable music for their intimate walk among the willows. It was the way they used to do it, swinging their arms as they clasped each other's hands.

Clyde cherished this woman; he'd loved her once before, and here he was, loving her again. They were meant to be together, in this life. This he knew in his heart. They enjoyed their rocking chairs, watching the twilight of dusky colors exploding across the sky. Blues faded into luminescent indigos, which faded into pale purples and Arabian oranges.

Something as simple as a sunset with the person you love can keep your heart full for many nights. He took her to bed, and he felt like he wanted to take her to bed from now until she was old and bent over from years of painful living. He'd carry her through the threshold then, as he did once, and the two of them would spend their days of old age together, enjoying the sunshine, until God called them home and they would once more be forced to wait before they could find each other again.

This Clyde felt and thought as he cuddled close to his wife, embracing her as she faced the wall, him smelling the strawberry shampoo, feeling her body heat. Soon, they were tucked away into a deep slumber, each seeing their own visions. Clyde wondered what Santina dreamed about. Clyde's dreams no longer seemed like nonsensical scenes of meaningless pictures, or nightmares from his past, but he now perceived dreams to be key pieces of knowledge, granted from the other side. Small tidbits of the future or past he thought, maybe even scenes the phantom Myrodoceus had sent to him specifically.

He was rudely woken up by a chiming alarm clock on his nightstand, jolting him from his dream-filled sleep, reminding him of the real beast of burden that awaited him—work.

Clyde felt like he hadn't been to work in months, but really, he saw them last week, and they were completely contented with going through the motions with, or without him. Doing the same monotonous work they've always done, with or without him. They too were just pawns, and Clyde felt a little sorry for them, watching them take the same abuse as he. He'd had his fill of that himself over the years, in the service. Those hard days also passed him by.

He didn't have much to say, doing more listening than speaking. Work actually could be fun sometimes, but he mostly kept to himself, and because he kept to himself, he had plenty of time to sit with his thoughts.

Clyde spent a lot of time at work thinking about the line connecting one's birth and death. The one liberating freedom of his job was that it was so simple, he didn't need to think about it. He went through the motions as everyone else did, and he let his mind wander the same as they did, everyone in their own worlds of thought, battling their own dilemmas of the head and heart, and dealing with themselves, the crushing blows that life delivers indiscriminately. They saw each other every day; they saw each other more than they saw their wives, so in a way, Clyde leaned on his work family. When there was cause for celebration, such as weddings, birthdays, or retirements, Clyde was the first with a congratulatory word of warm sincerity. He loved them too. And vice versa; when there was a loss to be grieved, they grieved it together.

Things were good at home, at least they were much better than before. He had newfound freedom to express his love and was no longer fearful to communicate his feelings to her, and although he preferred not to argue with Santina, she was funny when she was mad, he thought. Clyde and Santina would go spend time with Clyde's parents, on weekends or special occasions.

The months passed, and Santina finally finished her schooling. Although she was pushed into the profession by her family, she was still looking forward to helping people. Clyde thought it very admirable of her to take care of God's sick children; it was no small labor. He'd accepted that he'd have to work his life away, and that was fine, because it was not about the destination; it was about appreciating the road one took to get there. Every left or right turn you make leads somewhere different. The universe works in micromovements, meaning there are an infinite number of possibilities for the questions of what could've, what would've, and what should've happened during the course of our lives, which are much shorter than we think they are.

Holidays came and went, time moved on. All the while, Clyde was piecing together the fragmented memories of his counterpart, Cristobal. He could not pretend that none of that happened or that he wasn't experiencing odd side effects following his Voodoo trance. He was more aware but less paranoid. He thought more clearly, but his thoughts were still scattered. Here he was talking about starting a new life, when before, everything was strategic with him. He couldn't be any other way; he would never have acted like this before.

The story Cristobal lived, in the world of exploration, suffering the unfathomable betrayal of the guide, the scenes in between, what happened to Dendrick Rodon? What of Soyala, or the prophesied son Soyala would bear for him? These things were not clear to him yet, and he wasn't sure they ever would be. He had many questions to ask, but there was a trail to follow. He knew what he wanted for himself and what he wanted for their family, which they had hoped to grow.

He knew that life was calling him in a different direction, one that called on him to act with intention. He was being called west to the ocean, the adventurous spirit of Cristobal now standing center stage. Clyde planned to visit his brother Dean, staying in his home for a convenient couple of weeks, but ultimately, he wanted to lay down his roots somewhere near the water, because Bossier was nice, but it wasn't where he wanted his children's stories to start. Too narrow-minded, too slow, he needed a change of scenery, and a change of pace. Clyde was eager to hand in his two-week notice.

"Whaddya you mean you quit?" Mr. Blackrock said, spitting his chewing tobacco spit into a Styrofoam cup with a paper towel crumpled up inside, taken aback after Clyde handed in his formal resignation.

"Yes, sir, we're moving out west, the wife and I, so I'm going to be finding work elsewhere. It has been a pleasure working for you, sir. Thank you again for giving me a job when I came back. Thank you again for taking a chance on me." said Clyde, holding his hands at the small of his back.

Mr. Blackrock gave the bureaucratic, robotic smile he gave to everyone, but Clyde knew now, the secret of the eyes, and he could see the hard-shelled miser was touched by the words of the mild-mannered young man before him.

"You use me as a reference anytime, Mr. LeBouef," he said in his gruff, middle-aged monotone. "The pleasure was all mine. Good luck to you, son."

The two shook hands, and that was it.

There was no sendoff, no farewell cakes to bid him goodbye, just a couple of handshakes, well wishes, and he was out the door two weeks later.

They had finally felt comfortable enough to walk away from their jobs, and they had packed up most of their belongings. They sold the house as is, leaving everything that wasn't completely essential, as they were both committed to a simple, less cluttered lifestyle. They made sure they were square with the bank before beginning an expedition of their own, establishing the LeBouef family on the Golden Coast, and at the perfect time.

The new journey was starting. Together they would navigate the ocean of life, only to be separated by death until death united the two souls again.

Chapter 29

THE BAYOU OR THE BEACH

Clyde and Santina LeBouef left behind their precious memories, the adventures of youth, and young, untamable love, which had withered and waned under life's constant battery, but as they left, they knew they were both abandoning the same dream. Never going back to see Ms. Claudia Leblanc, Ma or Pa. The old days of monotonous living were something Clyde needed to escape, and Santina wanted to support him, as he wanted to give her everything she deserved, which was everything he could give her.

He'd yet to find his true life's work; his purpose, but Clyde knew that a fresh start would get him closer to being who the two of them needed him to be.

"I love you," they said, but they were beyond that now, for Clyde's love went beyond the superficial world of the living. Theirs had been a love story told across time. Clyde, now privy to certain events from his past, remembered when he looked into Santina's eyes, which were Fiorella's eyes, seeing that a person's eyes are doorways to their soul.

In his old Spanish days, Cristobal was never with Fiorella. He had left her in Spain while he went out exploring the far reaches of the world in search of glory. The two of them never had a child together in their old lives, but the love that connected them then connected them now. Clyde the thinker pondered the idea briefly that his destiny with Santina was already written, and if so, he feared the outcome of their story together. Because when last they walked this Earth together, they were robbed of their chances for a life together; the work of a heretic playing the role of God out there in the Mesa Plateau sent Cristobal to an untimely grave.

The realizations Clyde had in the months following his Spanish/American odyssey profoundly impacted his religious views, and he felt guilty. Clyde had long fallen away from the church, since before Nam at least. As a young sergeant, he prayed for his men before they went outside the wire. He prayed for the safety and the health of Santina, and of his parents, and of her parents. He prayed for others too, but that was during the private audiences, which he personally shared with God, just the two of them.

He just didn't feel the need to go to church; that didn't make him less of a believer. But he felt guilty for thinking that maybe everything he was taught about heaven and hell, or the afterlife and the images of great salvations, was not what he was raised to believe. There could be no denying the existence of an afterlife after seeing what he had seen. Ms. Claudia frightened Clyde, unleashing those memories on him, showing him the secrets of his life. It did a number on his psyche, and there were times in those months recovering from her spell when he battled severe depressive episodes due to his newfound and highly complex understanding of the world around him.

He was no stranger to death or dying people, but he was shaken up to gleam under the veil of shade. It was unlike anything he could have imagined. It was a place of no pain or heartache. He did not feel scared, but in the presence of Myrodoceus, he felt a childlike shame and timidity, something that humbled him greatly. Too busy trying to connect the dots that pieced together his Mesoamerican journey, he struggled to recollect the resolution of his fate. The fragmented memory breaks made it difficult to recreate exactly the chronological order of events. He knew it was in there somewhere, but he'd yet to figure out where to retrieve those lost memories, working harder and harder each day to remember faces, places, and names.

The evolution of his spirituality would be a long journey inward and would take Clyde many more years, but he eventually would find his path, as all of us do. He didn't know where they would eat next, or where they would be living in a week, but he knew they were heading for the Coast, he knew they were together, and for the reborn Clyde LeBouef, that was all he needed to know.

Clyde's experience with Ms. Claudia had made him a new man, and he did start treating Santina the way she was supposed to be treated. A new sense of chivalry overtook him, firm that alcohol no longer would consume the man. He was stone sober and sharp as a whistle for the first time in a long time.

He'd turned it around, bringing her flowers or leaving notes for her in her lunchbox. These simple gestures helped her love easier and stronger with every good week they put behind them. The flame grew stronger and stronger, until that rekindled flame of love that burned between the two of them was a fire again; which is the kind of love that one knows is eternal.

Leaving Louisiana granted them a certain optimism that things were looking up for the young couple. They had a long drive ahead of them, but what the heck, it would be a wide-open highway for most of it. They went west out of Baton Rouge, bringing with them everything they could fit in the truck. Santina had with her a little book of names with addresses and phone numbers. Clyde packed light, ditching many of his possessions before he left. He wanted to leave as much baggage behind as possible. There was nothing left for him in Louisiana anymore, but he was sincerely grateful he came from such humility. He was thankful for his life there and asked God to bless their journey as they left the only home they'd ever known.

Cruising into Houston, they made good time and were soon through San Antonio, driving up toward El Paso. After they'd left Texas and crossed over into Arizona, Clyde couldn't help but feel deja vu when he looked out at the desert plateaus, seeing the buttes and mesas as they approached the Mojave. It was still too soon for him, and he'd yet to let Santina know what truly transpired that night. The history of his former self was still a secret he aimed to keep. Santina drove them west through Phoenix, and after days of driving, they at last made it into the Golden State. Clyde drove them past Joshua Tree, toward Anaheim. He pulled them off the road for the night, checking them into some cheap hole-in-the-wall motel right before they hit LA. Neither got much sleep, and they were off at first light. Another day of driving saw them hit the infamous Los Angeles traffic before going through Bakersfield and Fresno, stopping for gas in Modesto before finishing the last leg of the journey.

They gasped as they laid their eyes on the Golden Gate Bridge. It was a marvel, a spectacular display of American architecture and engineering, a lasting symbol of the great power to be had in unity, hard work, and togetherness.

The American dream would be here, but Clyde's idea of the American dream was different now, also much different than the views of his parents, who, coming from an old-fashioned generation, knew better, and knew he was wasting his time going to California to begin with. They were content living life in a box, and he wouldn't do that anymore. He would live life now on his own terms, considering, of course, what was best for his wife and unborn children. It was the fall of 1971, and Clyde still had his youth, not even thirty years old yet.

Getting to San Francisco was like landing on familiar shores. Looking out at the great Pacific as they climbed up the coast, Clyde watched the waves roll in, the seafoam a welcome sight. Seeing the sailboats in the bay was even more a welcome sight, as it meant Clyde could go fishing. They rolled into Dean's driveway sometime after midnight, and the neighborhood dogs started to bark together, with porch lights coming on. Obviously they'd disturbed the slumber of the neighbors. The front door opened wide, and there Clyde saw the cheeky face of his older brother, Dean, who'd grown fatter since the last time they met. That, of course, was many years ago, before Clyde got on that bus out to the training depot, where Uncle Sam did the bare minimum to get him ready for life in the muck.

Dean had been there too, before Clyde, but he'd bought himself an early ticket home from the war, caught standing too close to a landmine his buddy stepped on. They heard the noise of the pressure plate falling, and the explosion messed up the left side of Dean's face, disfiguring him with third-degree burns. Clyde didn't say anything, but he noticed the scar tissue running up his brother's neck, deforming his ear as well. The concussion alone had nearly killed him, but his deep hatred for the enemy drove him onward. In the hospital, he begged them to quit wasting his time and hurry up getting him back out into the field. The damage was severe enough for them to discharge him and give him a disability pension, which was a lot more than he thought he'd get out of the deal. The money made the disfigurement easier to accept.

The two brothers stood together under the awning; the screen door open wide.

"Well, I don't believe it! Baby brother! How you doing, man? Come on, come in. Let's get you both inside," he said, offering up quick hugs to the two of them.

"Really sorry, man, for showing up so late. We don't want to keep you," Clyde said, but Dean assured him that it was no issue.

"No worries, man! We got the guest room set up already, and there's towels and soap in the bathroom for you. There's also leftovers in the fridge if you get hungry. Don't worry about waking us up; we're heavy sleepers. Make yourselves comfortable, really. We're happy to have you," Dean said, looking at his little brother and realizing that he was not so little anymore.

"Go get some sleep, man. We'll have time for visiting in the morning," "Goodnight, man. I love you too, we'll see you in the morning." said Clyde.

Their home was modest, but the extra bedroom served nicely as a temporary living arrangement for Clyde and Santina until they found a suitable place of their own. And employment, they needed work. Luckily, there was work to be had everywhere, an abundance of it. Clyde figured washing windows with his brother would be good work, and Dean was more than happy to add a member of the family to his crew.

Clyde and Santina brought in their suitcases with their clothes and toiletries inside and up the stairs. Flicking on the light, they looked at the twin mattress in the corner and gave each other a silly look, knowing somebody was going to be getting squished against the wall. Clyde's feet most likely would dangle off the edge of the bed too, but that didn't bother them, and they'd be laughing about it later as neither one of them got any quality rest. They set down their things, kicked off their shoes, and went to the bathroom for a quick rinse together.

It was a long road getting there, with many bends, turns and curves. They laughed with one another some nights, and on other nights, cried rivers of tears alone while enduring life's greatest losses. The two souls together had overcome so much adversity. Even in their passive days of old, the two of them had endured the pain of lost love. Love that was planted but never bloomed. They both were affected by the terrible tragedies of war, in both centuries. Despite the many twists in their road, they had seen it through together, through all the pain Clyde inflicted on her, still not in his right mind then, still haunted at the time by the demons of his karma. He could not rationalize inside himself his taking of a human life, his deep regret at having been so naive to be the same way as Cristobal, searching for prestige, that he too had dreamed of the parades of flowers and floats in the streets welcoming them home. Instead, Clyde was degraded immediately after getting off the plane.

Clyde could breathe easier, though, knowing he was *where* he was supposed to be, and closer to being *who* he was supposed to be, which was helping him to love Santina the way he always meant to. Ms. Claudia's trance had shown him the patterns his soul was comfortable with and showed him that in order to grow, he needed to change the patterns or be doomed to repeat his lessons again, until he finally learned what they were meant to teach. Standing naked with Santina under the shower as she washed herself, Clyde watched her, a new love alive in him, not just for his wife, but for life. No dreams came to him that night; his mind was settled down. He slept straight through, and slept well, well into the beginning of a new story.

Chapter 30

I WILL WALK YOU THERE

The people in San Francisco were very different, to say the least, and that took some adjustment. The first few days, Clyde and Santina stayed with Dean, who took the responsibility of his little brother personally, seeing to it that Clyde had a place to work right away. Both of them headed out the front door together at 6:30 a.m., brothers united again. Santina looked too, and it didn't take her long to find a hospital; she was working in a week.

They prayed with one another before he left for work. They put their faith in the Lord and asked him to guide them, to keep them safe so they might once again hug each other at the end of the day, by the heat of a hearth they built together. They were laughing more, and he was less absent now than he was before, for now when they spoke, he listened, and she felt heard. They felt close again like they were in days gone by.

They paid twenty-five dollars rent to Dean each month, saving up little by little for a place of their own. The places around the Bay Area were nice, and they had looked at a few houses but were still too poor to afford anything of their own, so Santina picked up extra shifts at work, and Clyde tried to get overtime with Dean, on top of taking a few extra odds-and-ends jobs here and there. Financially, they were on a shaky foundation at first, but after a few weeks, they'd begun carrying their own cash and checkbooks, able to get their way around the city and spending their own money at places like the grocery store or the mall.

Having yet to really explore downtown, they were both active in their goal of saving enough money to get out of Dean's place, as they didn't want to wear out their welcome. It's tough for anybody to start a new life in a new place, and this was a difficult but necessary move for soul development. It was in the name of progress that Clyde needed to get them out of Louisiana.

Santina dragged Clyde to the beach every chance she could. She loved the water, and she loved swimming. Clyde didn't mind, preferring to sit under the high sun, but when the heat became too much, he'd go get in the water with her, and they'd splash each other like kids without a care in the world, thinking about nothing other than how much fun they were having together. She was the order to his chaos and the calm in his storm.

Soulmates look for each other in every life they live.

About two months had gone by when Santina came home from work one day, opening the front door to Clyde, who was sitting on the loveseat, watching TV with Dean, his wife Dorothy, and their two children, his twelve-year-old son James, and their nine-year-old daughter Carmen. She walked in with her lunchbox and nurse's bag and went straight upstairs while Clyde was in the middle of welcoming her home. Clyde, seeing that she looked upset as she came in the door, walked upstairs and saw her sitting hunched over the toilet bowl. Something was not right.

"Babe, You okay?" Clyde asked, as he peeked his nose in the partially cracked doorway.

"I'm okay, honey, but would you come in here for a second?" she asked. "It's nothing bad, I swear."

Clyde opened the door and went over to the toilet. She was resting her chin on the toilet bowl, her arms propping her up. She looked white as a ghost when she turned to look at him.

"I'm pregnant," she said weakly, and she lifted up her hands.

Clyde's heart leaped into his throat, he couldn't speak, immediately at a loss for words. His heart raced with adrenaline, and his face showed the tremendous delight he took in hearing the good news, realizing that the ultimate experience of life was coming his way at last. He crouched down by the toilet to give her the biggest hug he could in their awkward position. Clyde, beyond restraining his joy, no longer cared for the late hour and started whooping and hollering like crazy, jumping for joy in the tiny bathroom. Santina squinted, grimacing from the bright lights, his loud noise, and the pounding pain of a headache she'd been suffering from, coupled with a side of nausea and a few tests free of charge at the hospital confirmed what she had suspected.

She quickly shushed him, holding her finger to her lips, reaching for his pant leg from where she sat.

"Shhhhh, no! You can't tell them yet, or they're going to kick us out! We need to save a little bit longer, Clyde. Please, don't say anything yet, please."

This did quell his excitement. Her reservation was understandable, but to hell with that. This was wonderful news! But still, he said he would respect his wife's wishes.

Seconds later, Dorothy came around the corner, asking Clyde if everything was all right.

"Oh yeah, everything's fine, Dorothy, thank you. We were just playing around."

She said, "Oh. Okay, just checking," and continued down the hall to the master bedroom. Clyde smiled again and looked back at Santina, who was now standing in front of the sink, brushing her teeth. His wife was pregnant, which meant he would be a dad, and that was to him one of the highest honors a man could have. To have a big family with lots of kids was something he always looked to do, to one day enrich his life and to fill his heart with joy, always sharing with them that unconditional love. They just weren't meant to raise their family there in Louisiana, and her being with child shortly after the move just validated Clyde's thinking that higher powers were at play. This was bigger than he knew, and he knew it.

Clyde felt tremendous love for his unborn baby, already thinking of names, writing them down when he was out working washing windows with Dean, even while being strapped into a harness fifty feet off the ground, he had a pen and paper nearby just in case. He and Santina would sit and think all day long, wracking their brains over it, just to come back home together and tell each other, "I don't like that one."

They had brought many different names to the table: boy names, girl names, middle names, unisex names, family names. Clyde said to her that he wanted to honor her Spanish heritage, because the baby would already have his French last name.

They were driving around one Sunday, looking at potential properties for sale in different areas. The state was huge, and in the summertime, it was a great place to live. The constantly circulating coastal air, mixed with year-round sunshine, made it a paradise. He knew they'd been meant to come here. Well, this particular Sunday, after Santina got them lost trying to read the map, Clyde decided to drive them to the nearest gas station in the nearest town and ask for directions to the city limits of another place he planned to visit, a place called *Redondo Beach*.

Cristobal's spirit guide, Myrodoceus, had shown him a vision, and Clyde recognized a waterfront town then, the same he saw now. As he drove further into it, they drove past palm trees and flying seagulls hungry for a bite. They were looking at the little beach houses, and Santina was over the moon.

Clyde just kept looking out at the beach, watching the waves wash up against the shore, seeing the seafoam roll along on top, disintegrating as the tide pulled it back in. It was a well-kept area, affluent, and low on crime. While stopped at a crosswalk, waiting for the light to change, a couple of shirtless young men with surfboards and their girlfriends crossed in front of Clyde's pickup with their beach bags, sunscreen, and towels.

Clyde looked over at Santina. "How about Cristobal for a boy?" he asked her.

"Cristobal?" she said, hearing the name roll off her tongue, and then thinking about the sound of it. "I like it a lot actually." She said, nodding with approval. "That might be the one!" she exclaimed, not knowing the true origins of the name.

"Baby, trust me, I'm telling you, it's the one," Clyde said, she nodded with him.

"All right then, Cristobal. Cristobal LeBouef. What about his middle name?" she asked, as Clyde stepped on the gas and pulled them forward. The lunch hour traffic was slow rolling.

"Middle name, huh?" He thought about it briefly before offering up, "Robert," which was another name on both their lists.

She said it all together, and she liked it. Very agreeable she was when her heart was healthy, and after hardly debating over it, they would go on to christen their baby Cristobal Robert LeBouef if it was a boy. If it was a girl, well, they hadn't quite nailed that one down yet.

They went to one of Santina's early doctor appointments, and they were more than intrigued when the doctor entered the room. He informed them of a new cutting-edge technology called ultrasound, which he could use, if they wanted him to, to determine the sex of the baby. It was a huge breakthrough in medical science and did a lot more than tell them the sex. It could detect abnormalities and early signs of birth complications. Many up-and-coming parents jumped at the opportunity to know if they were having a boy or a girl, but in the years past, one of the exciting parts of childbearing was the painstaking wait to know whether or not you were having a boy or a girl. That kind of surprise had been tradition forever, and Clyde would stay in keeping with the spirit of the old traditions.

"Nah, we're good, thanks, Doc," Clyde said, thanking the good doctor for his offer. Santina looked over at him from her hospital bed, a look of bewildered disappointment spread on her face because she was looking forward to knowing the sex early, so they could better prepare for his or her arrival.

"Clyde? You don't want to know?" she said.

"No. I'm pretty sure it's gonna be a boy," he said, turning to address the doctor.

"Does the baby look healthy, Doc?" he said, putting his hand on the doctor's shoulder while he sat next to Santina.

"Oh yes, Mr. LeBouef, everything looks fine so far as we can tell. You can expect her to carry the baby to full term, but don't be too confident you're going to have a boy. I don't want you to be disappointed.

"It's fifty-fifty, heads or tails," said the doctor, which Clyde knew was true, but he was listening to his intuition now, and his intuition told him he was having a son for sure.

"Believe me, you can expect a whole lot more discomfort once you enter your third trimester, but that's all quite normal. We'll run a few more tests, finish up some bloodwork, and you'll be free to go." He looked over to Santina and told her, "You come right in if you think something's not right, okay?" and the doctor patted his knees and wished the two of them the best of luck. He left the expectant parents in the room, free to go.

It was an exciting start to their new chapter, beginning their family, working their jobs. Soon they'd have a place they could call their own, and that was nice. Having gone through as much hardship as they had in their relatively short lives, Clyde had come to a point where he was content with going to work, making his money for the family, and doing his share. Through his journey, he had learned that things such as stability, safety, the love of family, and a good woman by your side could not be taken for granted. Those were blessings that did not happen to everybody every day. Those things were rare comforts to some.

The objective truth is that wars could not be won without men like Clyde LeBouef and Cristobal Trujillo, or without the Comandante Redondos and Dendrick Rodons of the world, fighting the same evil across the world as that which possessed their guide to lead them to a premeditated slaughter. They followed him, for he was their guide, and coldly he betrayed them, making them pay with their lives for their misplaced trust.

The conquistadors sought the glory, the adventure, and the challenge of the New World. Voyaging across ruthless seas, penetrating deep into foreign lands, and being forced to bear witness the horrors of the very life they glamorized. That was what was the same about Clyde and Cristobal. The call to service had been heard by the both in their lifetimes. Though Clyde never questioned the character of his service, he still wished he could have done more, achieved more, and that was saying something, considering he'd already taken it the furthest he could possibly take it.

It still haunted him in the broad daylight, and at work, in the grocery store, or at the mall, and he could always shift away back into his comfortable stare, where the quiet gave his mind a rest and he could settle his thoughts. Telling himself that he was just doing what any other scared twenty-year-old would've done, which was do his very best *not* to step over a tripwire or walk into an ambush. Clyde always looked at that as cowardly, fighting from the shadows, but afraid to face them on the level. Their opponents sought any strategic advantage they could find. It was the way of military men, who under the spell of blood, lost themselves to the darkness. Lost their sense of sympathy and empathy, walking around with empty thoughts, plotting against their fellow man, blind with disillusion.

They decided to make the next several months leading up to the birth of baby Cristobal count. That meant Santina pulled more shifts at the hospital, and Clyde was again asking his brother to give him his own crew at work. Clyde wanted a higher salary but also felt he could handle more responsibility. He'd done his due diligence, paying the proper attention to the family business, as Dean had called it, quickly picking up the tricks of the trade.

They quietly bought baby clothes, toys, and stocked up on diapers and formula, making sure their ducks were in a row. After a couple of months, there could be no denying Santina was pregnant. Her baby bump poked out from her skinny, short frame, and it was too obvious to hide any longer. Dorothy whispered into Santina's ear one night while they were chopping the vegetables for that night's supper, coaxing Santina into telling her how far along she was, to which Santina replied, "Twenty-six weeks."

Remembering that they were still guests in their home, she tried to be nonchalant about it, not wishing to burden the family any further.

Dorothy, however, was elated and set down her kitchen utensils to grab hold of her sister-in-law. She laughed and cheered as she shook her back and forth in excitement. This drew Dean and Clyde from the living room, and as Dean walked around the corner, he could see Dorothy pressing her head against Santina's little baby bump, listening for a sound or waiting for a kick.

"Santina's pregnant? Clyde! You didn't tell me, you son of a-! What the hell, man! Congratulations!" Dean said.

Clyde just smiled, laughing off the fact that it had been Santina's idea to withhold the truth from his brother. "We were waiting on the right time, man. We didn't know how you'd take it." Clyde said.

"How I would take it! How else would I take it? You've gotta call Ma and Pa soon! Birth of a grandchild? Oh yeah, you bet they'll be hitting the road." Dean said, hands resting on the back of one of his kitchen chairs. The rest of the family crowded into the tiny kitchen, celebrating the news. It was a weight off of Clyde's shoulders that his brother wasn't going to kick him to the curb. In fact, his brother had given him a place to stay, a job, and food. That was what brothers were for; each kept the other standing on his own two feet. They got to hang out all the time at work, and they had fun together, just like when they were kids. They'd splash each other with the buckets of soapy water solution or soak each other's cigarette packs in the suds buckets. Brotherly shenanigans always ensued when the two of them were on the job together. They had so much to catch up on; it was like getting to know each other all over again. Soon they both realized how unique and interesting the other was, and how common was the ground on which they both stood.

Santina worked up until she was thirty-six weeks. Her once-skinny frame struggled to carry the extra weight she had picked up in the short time she'd been expecting. Clyde didn't mind it; seeing her carry his child inside her for nine months gave him a new outlook on many things. He watched her glow, he watched the young girl he married turn into a woman before his very eyes, and he respected her for it. At the same time, he thanked her with every fiber of his soul for making him a father. It was the greatest gift anyone could have ever given him, for it was something he had dreamed of for a long, long time.

He was happy to settle down young because he'd had his share of the world already. Clyde fought battles every day that nobody would ever know about, biting his tongue to spare him of others' empty sympathies.

Thankfully, it was a Sunday night when her water broke. Clyde and Dean were watching the nightly news on the couch with the kids in the living room, and Santina was doing the dishes in the kitchen with Dorothy. It was a big chore, doing dishes in that house, but Santina was a true homemaker. She did it the same way every time, in every kitchen she was in, and she always left it sparkling clean for the next person. She got that strict discipline from stern Latino parents who gave her a tremendous work ethic.

Clyde floored the pedal all the way to hospital, a cigarette hanging out of his mouth as he drove down one-way streets and blew past stop signs and red lights. The only thing that mattered in this moment was getting his wife into the stirrups and his baby boy into the world. Dorothy sat in the back seat, grimacing as Santina held her hand with a crushingly strong grip. Dorothy tried to help her with her breathing, while Dean was giving Clyde the directions from the passenger seat, giving him all of the local shortcuts. They made it in eleven minutes flat. Clyde ran through the front doors shouting, "Help! Somebody help me! My wife's giving birth out here!"

The hospital staff stood up right away, running past Clyde and out the door to his truck as he grabbed the closest wheelchair he could find, dashing madly out to the car to retrieve the love of his life, who soon would embark on another of life's most beautiful journeys. The nurses helped her into the seat and swept her away to the delivery room.

Clyde's world was spinning a thousand miles an hour as Dean, Dorothy, and he followed the nurses to the labor and delivery wing. She got undressed and gowned up, showing tremendous courage getting into those stirrups. Shortly afterward, the nurses came into the room with the good doctor and the midwives, who quickly rushed to Santina's bedside. Clyde stood in the corner, giving them their space.

"Just breathe," he heard Dorothy say.

"You're doing great, honey. You're doing great," the midwife said. Clyde got the green light and rushed over to Santina. Grabbing hold of her hand, he was immediately stuck in the vise grip of his dearly beloved, who had converted all of her pain and agony into the last bit of grip strength she used on the man who did this to her. She used tremendous energy just to breathe, like Dorothy and the doctor were coaching her to. Clyde watched her fight through the excruciating pain as the contractions grew stronger and closer together, until finally her body said it was time to push. Seconds seemed like minutes, and minutes seemed like hours. Each time she pushed, she squeezed his hand more tightly, crushing the bones with her feminine power. Clyde thought he was about to have a heart attack, but he knew he was too young for that. He was so nervous, he could hardly stand it. He felt in his heart a bigger suspense than he had ever known, moments away from meeting the product of their centuries-long love, their own combined flesh and blood. This was the child they would've had in their last life if things had gone differently.

It was a blessing, and Clyde clutched his wife and prayed for her, asking God to bless their family and to bless their child. He asked for the strength to be the man Santina needed him to be and to be a fit father for the young soul. Overcome with love and the chaos happening around him, he shifted once more to his quiet, comfortable stare. He looked at Santina, her expression so twisted from pain that it would be burned into his memory. Clyde observed her from a different point of view now. She would be a mom, and he was proud of her.

In his quiet deliberation, Clyde heard a voice come through the fog, softly, barely a whisper, but clear as daylight. He heard it say to him, "He is born blessed."

Filling the whole room and down the hallway with her screams of pain, Santina pushed hard. Her breathing was labored, and she struggled through the searing pain of her insides being torn apart, fighting the pain through clenched fists that knotted up the bedsheets. "Keep going, you're almost there! I can see a head! Keep pushing, sweetie, you're almost there!" the doctor said, encouraging her, looking up and over at her from the end of her gown. Clyde was absorbed in his own feelings and thoughts, not paying any attention to what his brother or his sister-in-law were doing or saying. He knew they were equally excited; everybody was very excited. It was an overwhelming amount of external stimuli. She pushed and screamed, and he and Dorothy held her hands while the midwives did what they could to get her to control her breath-push cycle.

Clyde thought about what kind of dad he would be, and his mind raced at everything he would be responsible for. He had so much to impart on this child; it was his duty to usher him into this world and to take him by the hand, that he might lead him better on his own journey in life. He would always be there for him, he would always put him first, and he would work his ass off if that meant his son had what he needed. A change in him occurred in those moments leading up to the birth of his baby boy. All his hard work and effort in life would now be directed into something selfless and pure. And he'd ask for nothing but love in return.

Santina gasped for air as she writhed in her stirrups. Pushing with all her strength, she was ready to break. The pain was almost too much to bear, but she too sought the strength of God to get her through this crucible. She said in Spanish her holy Catholic verses, verses that Clyde remembered to be the same ones the padre had spoken centuries ago, the same holy blessings of the Father, the Son, and the Holy Spirit. The energy of the room was drawn to its great crescendo when at long last, the head was finally through, followed shortly by the rest of the tiny human. The doctor pulled the baby out and gave him to the mother.

"All right, Dad, it looks like you called it, it *is* a boy!" the doctor exclaimed, coming over to congratulate the new father. "Let's cut the cord!"

Clyde was more than honored to be addressed as *Dad* for the first time, and walking over to the other side of the bed, he took the hospital scissors from the doctor, cutting where he was told. He severed the physical connection, but not the maternal bond that Santina spent building for the last nine months. Baby Cristobal was crying, his little arms reaching out curiously into the world, and his baby hands were clenched into tiny fists, which he shook at the medical staff, as if to say he was mad they woke him up.

The rest of the family were coming down from their excitement, but Clyde knew the greatest miracle of his life had just taken place. The nurses swept the baby away to do their assessment, and quickly enough returned, with Baby Cristobal cleaned up and swaddled for Mama to hold.

Santina looked as though she had gone through battle. Sweat dripped off her brow, and tears of joy ran down her pale, clammy cheeks as she held their precious baby.

She looked down at him, her heart swept away by the new man in her life. Clyde could not compete with a newborn baby. Already with a crop of short, brown hair on the top of his head, Cristobal Robert LeBouef was born June 13, 1972, weighing six pounds, three ounces.

"You wanna hold him?" Santina asked as she held him to her chest. Clyde, who was still holding his hand over his mouth in awe, a river of joyful tears coming from his eyes, eagerly said, "I thought you'd never ask."

Reaching down to grab the swaddled newborn, Clyde pulled the baby to his chest, holding him in his arms, and looked down at his little face, with his little nose, lips, and eyes. Baby Cristobal waited to open his eyes until he felt his dad holding him for the first time. While waiting for his newborn son to look out into the world, Clyde gave thanks to God for allowing this miracle to happen. He would give all his glory to God from now on, because it was better to give glory away than to waste his own life searching for it in selfish vanity and illusions of grandiose personal legacy.

When baby Cristobal finally opened up his eyes to the world, Clyde was confused at first to see the Potomac gray orbs looking up at him, discerning with mirrorlike lenses the man who was to be his father. Paralyzed by his baby's open, omniscient eyes, in the middle of the delivery room, Clyde finally made sense of it all. Or so he thought.

"Hey, Rodendros," he said, with love.